Praise for *The Lagos Wife*

"A thrillingly suspenseful novel that reveals its riches, layers, and secrets through effortlessly elegant prose, while exposing the imprisoning dynamics inside transactional relationships of patriarchal power. I was hooked right through to the shocking end."

—Bernardine Evaristo, Booker Prize–winning author of *Girl, Woman, Other*

"The search for a missing woman, set against the backdrop of glamour and wealth, is utterly captivating. Lush, poignant, and gripping, with a killer ending to boot, *The Lagos Wife* shows that sometimes the perfect life and the perfect marriage aren't exactly what they seem. Vanessa Walters is one to watch!"

—Mary Kubica, *New York Times* bestselling author of *Local Woman Missing*

"Dark secrets seethe beneath the glamorous lives of Nigeria's über-rich. A propulsive and complex tale of passion and betrayal. Electrifying!"

—Liv Constantine, *New York Times* bestselling author of *The Last Mrs. Parrish*

"*The Lagos Wife* is a dazzling exploration of deceptions—both intimate and internet—that keep the everyday afloat, and the pages turning, despite the weight of our deepest secrets, regrets, and devotions. I raced through this sumptuous, suspenseful, and smartly layered book, and gasped at its fearless, soul-baring end."

—Nancy Jooyoun Kim, *New York Times* bestselling author of *The Last Story of Mina Lee*

"As wise as it is gripping, *The Lagos Wife* captures the glory of post-colonial literature in a masterfully paced thriller. Vanessa Walters's debut marks a major addition to the canon."

—Margaret Wilkerson Sexton, author of
Reese's Book Club pick *On the Rooftop*

"*The Lagos Wife* is a hypnotically lush and atmospheric novel about the lengths we go to for the ones we love most and all the ways we weave past traumas into strength for the future. A stellar debut!"

—Wanda M. Morris, award-winning author of
All Her Little Secrets and *Anywhere You Run*

"A murder mystery set in Nigerian high society, *The Lagos Wife* is an exceptional debut. Vanessa Walters has fashioned a fresh, edge-of-your-seat thriller that's pacy and unique. Her characters are so real, I felt complicit in their glamorous, stifling world, while cheering Claudine on as she searches for her missing niece. An absolute treat—it took all my expectations and threw them to the wind. I'm still in shock from those final chapters."

—Janice Hallett, internationally bestselling author of
The Appeal

"A brilliantly original novel about family, motherhood, identity, and diaspora, with a crime thriller twist."

—Afua Hirsch, author of *Brit(ish)*

"Evokes skillfully the atmosphere of a wealthy life by the Lagos Lagoon . . . A shimmering success."

—Diana Evans, author of *Ordinary People*

"*The Lagos Wife* solidifies Vanessa Walters as a literary force. Walters boldly and incisively examines race, class, and culture among a group of complicated women in a manner that will continue to resonate with me for years to come!"

—Catherine Adel West, author of *The Two Lives of Sara*

"*The Lagos Wife* explores the ways a set of expat women in Nigeria exchange autonomy for comfort. But it's a raw and potentially fatal deal. A murderously good read!"

—Sarah Langan, author of *Good Neighbors*

"A superb thriller with a devastating conclusion."

—Alex Wheatle, Guardian Children's Fiction Prize–winning author of *Cane Warriors*

"A surprising ending and well-done dialogue make this a perfectly good way to spend a night or two."

—*Kirkus Reviews*

"A remarkable book."

—*New York Journal of Books*

"*The Lagos Wife* is a gripping work of suspense, a psychological puzzle, a mystery, and a critique of marriage and high society. . . . In this riveting novel about a young woman's disappearance, Lagos high society hides personal struggles and larger cultural concerns."

—*Shelf Awareness*

"The snap-crackle-pop dialogue is a treat."

—NPR, 5 New Mysteries and Thrillers for the Start of Summer

"Cleverly keeps us guessing . . . *The Lagos Wife* is well worth reading, entrancing in its complex plotting and immersion in the Nigerian culture."

—*Mystery & Suspense Magazine*

THE
LAGOS WIFE

Previously titled *The Nigerwife*

A NOVEL

VANESSA WALTERS

ATRIA PAPERBACK

NEW YORK LONDON TORONTO SYDNEY NEW DELHI

ATRIA
PAPERBACK

An Imprint of Simon & Schuster, LLC
1230 Avenue of the Americas
New York, NY 10020

This book is a work of fiction. Any references to historical events, real people, or real places are used fictitiously. Other names, characters, places, and events are products of the author's imagination, and any resemblance to actual events or places or persons, living or dead, is entirely coincidental.

Copyright © 2023 by Vanessa Walters

All rights reserved, including the right to reproduce this book or portions thereof in any form whatsoever. For information, address Atria Books Subsidiary Rights Department, 1230 Avenue of the Americas, New York, NY 10020.

This Atria Paperback edition May 2024

ATRIA PAPERBACK and colophon are trademarks of Simon & Schuster, LLC

Simon & Schuster: Celebrating 100 Years of Publishing in 2024

For information about special discounts for bulk purchases, please contact Simon & Schuster Special Sales at 1-866-506-1949 or business@simonandschuster.com.

The Simon & Schuster Speakers Bureau can bring authors to your live event. For more information or to book an event, contact the Simon & Schuster Speakers Bureau at 1-866-248-3049 or visit our website at www.simonspeakers.com.

Interior design by Kyoko Watanabe

Manufactured in the United States of America

1 3 5 7 9 10 8 6 4 2

Library of Congress Cataloging-in-Publication Data is available.

ISBN 978-1-6680-1108-9
ISBN 978-1-6680-1109-6 (pbk)
ISBN 978-1-6680-1110-2 (ebook)

Originally published in 2023 as *The Nigerwife* in hardcover by Atria Books.

Lyrical excerpt of "Nigerwives-Nigeria Song" by Doris E. Fafunwa reprinted by permission of the author.

For the women who came before me,
especially Joyce Ivy Nelson (May 22, 1934–February 22, 2022)

Thank you for all the love

When a woman marries, she must know,
without being taught, how to be a wife.

—Euripides, *Medea*, translated by Vanessa Walters

NICOLE
Before

NICOLE OFTEN wondered what had happened to the body.

A few months after she arrived in Lagos, a body appeared in the lagoon close to the compound, bobbing along in a blanket of trash, a bloated starfish facedown in the water.

The barrel-shaped torso and splayed limbs, blackened where the skin was exposed, greenish-yellow where submerged, suggested it was a man.

She stared through the railings for a long time despite the stench. He was so close she could have reached him with a pole. From a distance, the lagoon's surface had appeared smooth, a mirror to the sky, but now, for the first time, she really saw the trash that came and went in this bottleneck between Tarkwa Bay and Victoria Island, the random shit the city spewed out: a minestrone of sweet wrappers, cardboard fragments, buckled coat hangers, paint pot lids, foils from biscuits, split Indomie noodle packets, buckets with holes in them, cut grasses, jagged shards of wood, polystyrene food trays, Spar plastic bags, pure water sachets, corroded poles, a flash mob of flip-flop parts, all of it turning over in the heat like a spit roast.

She was not alone in her interest. A white heron balanced on a cracked bucket, its long orange beak swiveling as it appraised the various articles nearby. Two men had moored their low-slung canoe a respectful distance from the house and cast small nets. Neither party seemed to notice the body or her or the West African sun climbing toward its fiery zenith. The waiting fishermen were more focused on the waterfront mansion with its swaying palm trees, sparkling swimming pool, and verdant garden, trying to imagine life on the other side of the electrified barbed-wire-topped fence.

Daydreaming as such, it was as if they were all seeing, but not *really*, the rotten fruit, soda bottles, the twisted inner sole of a shoe, and the body, bumping up and down in tandem with everything else. They were oblivious to just another piece of garbage. Perhaps to them, a body was just a body; she knew there were occasionally dead animals in the water—cows, pigs, dogs, rats; and the smell was just the smell.

"Close the windows, so the stink doesn't come in," Tonye said. Her husband refused to look outside. When she mentioned calling the police, he scoffed at the idea. "In this Nigeria?"

"And what happens to the body?" she asked.

"What happens to the trash?" Tonye shrugged. "Who knows?"

She remembered a strange feeling after he said that. Tension in her shoulders. At the time she didn't understand it, but now she knew it was fear. She was afraid. She'd never been afraid of him before.

CHAPTER ONE

CLAUDINE
After

THE LAST upload had been six months ago, in January. Nicole had posted only one photo of her, Tonye, and their two little sons next to a Batman-themed birthday cake outside in the garden. She looked very pretty posing in a white summer dress, Tonye's arm around her. Claudine traced their smiles with her finger.

"Phone off now, please!" The air hostess waited impatiently in the aisle until Claudine pressed the power button and the screen went dark.

Claudine settled back in her window seat and watched the Heathrow tarmac fall away. Slanted raindrops lashed the glass. *Rain, rain, go away.* She wouldn't miss the awful British summer. A thundering went through the aircraft, then a billowing sheet of cloud enveloped them, followed by a great calm and relief that it was too late to change her mind.

Through the intercom came the pilot's announcement that the flight would be six hours to Lagos, arriving around 6 p.m. local time. The weather would be 75 degrees Fahrenheit at their destination and sunny. She hoped she wouldn't get to the house too late to ask questions. She didn't want to have to wait until tomorrow. Another night with Nicole still missing, no word on whether she was alive or dead, was bad enough. But at least Claudine would be there. Waiting for news thousands of miles away back in London, powerless to help, unable to do anything but watch the flies creep from one end of the window to the other, had been unbearable.

Penny hadn't thought Claudine should go to Nigeria to find out what had happened. "This ain't on you, Claud," her sister had said. "You might've raised her, but you and Nicole haven't been close for years. Why go looking for someone who left and didn't look back?" Penny's question was fair. When Claudine didn't respond, she added, "It's not safe in Nigeria. Isn't there a war going on there with the Muslims? Boko—Boko something? They kidnapped all those girls. Hundreds of them. And I saw this program on BBC Two—*Welcome to Lagos*, it was called—where everyone lived on a rubbish dump. Everyone. They lived on it. The rubbish! How you supposed to find Nicole in a place like that? Bet Tonye forced her to move there."

Here we go again with the Nigeria-bashing convention, Claudine had thought. Never mind Nicole's husband and picture-perfect life. Being happy for someone was too much to ask in their family, so they had to peck it apart at every opportunity, going on about Nigeria as if Jamaica didn't have any poverty or corruption. What did they know about it? If you believed the pictures posted on social media, Nicole lived in a mansion by the water with a beautiful garden and a swimming pool. She had expensive clothes, even those shoes with red bottoms. She enjoyed parties and holidays, surrounded herself with rich friends.

But Claudine had learned not to get into it with Penny, whose hindsight was as bad as her foresight, always coming up with ridiculous revelations about things that happened years ago, like her insistence that her name was actually Pauletta, but Mummy had changed it to Penny on account of her being brown like a penny. That she knew there was something wrong with Len. And now, that Nicole had been forced to move to Nigeria. Honestly, you couldn't make up half of what came out of Penny's mouth.

Funny, Penny had been the first to cry when Claudine relayed the news about Nicole's disappearance, that she had gone on a boat trip in Lagos and hadn't come back. That there had been no sign of her since, that Tonye thought it was possible she had drowned in the lagoon. Claudine hadn't cried. She wasn't a crier. What good would crying do anyway? She had simply watched Mummy, Penny, and Michael—what was left of the Roberts family in the UK after almost fifty years—carrying on for Jesus as if she'd announced Nicole was dead. A Punch and Judy puppet show in the simple dining room of their nondescript semi with double-glazed windows in the middle of a street one wouldn't remember in deepest, darkest South London. That's how it went with them. Penny, crying for attention; Michael, overexcited, cursing at the moon; Mummy, striking her chest with her fist, calling on God with all his known aliases, meantime her eyes probably drier than concrete. None of it meant a damn thing. If Nicole was dead, all the howling in the world wouldn't bring her back.

Claudine's coworkers at Fashion Maxx were less fussed about her going to Nigeria. They helped her find some things she might need on the trip. A strong cross-body handbag with hidden inner pockets so she couldn't easily be pickpocketed. Some running shoes for all the walking she would have to do, and plenty of T-shirts. It was bound to be very hot.

"They say the sky's much bigger over in Africa," said one coworker, who had never left the UK due to a fear of flying and her dislike of the French. Everything she knew about the world came from the *Pick Me Up!* magazines she read on her lunch breaks. Claudine hadn't told them the full story, only that she urgently had to visit her niece, who had married a Nigerian man and was living out there. Another coworker's advice was more practical. She'd spent her childhood in Nigeria but had been wrestling with mystery immigration problems ever since her arrival in the UK and couldn't go back. "You'll be fine," she had said. "Just stick with the people you know."

That could be a problem.

"Complimentary champagne, madam?" the hostess asked.

Claudine took the glass, resting it on the mini tray table beside her. "Thank you. What movie are you showing today?"

"You choose the movie. Use your fingers and select whatever you want to watch." The hostess pressed the screen, flashing up the various options. "First time flying?"

"It's been a while," said Claudine. "And I've never sat in business class before."

"This is premium economy, but we'll take the compliment." The hostess laughed. Claudine was confused. The last time she had flown, thirty years ago, there'd been no such thing as premium economy. She'd sat in economy. So what was the point of business? What on earth was in first class? She couldn't imagine. Still, nice of Tonye to pay for it all. Tonye had also said someone would meet her when she got off the plane and escort her to a car that would take her to the compound. He didn't have to do all this. He hadn't wanted her to come at all.

The hostess demonstrated how to recline the chair, upending Claudine so her feet jerked into the air. "And here's your menu card," she said, tucking a fancy folded menu into the seat pocket. "We're likely to experience a little turbulence in this weather, so keep your seat belt on, and if you need anything at all, I'm right here." She tapped her name badge. "Annie."

Turbulence? Lord have mercy. The seat next to Claudine was vacant, but most of the nearby rows were filled. Many passengers seemed to be Nigerian, some already dressed for home in their brightly patterned fabrics. Just like Jamaicans heading home, they'd paid no mind to the baggage allowance and stuffed the overhead bins to bursting. She'd barely found room for her one carry-on. If they were to hit turbulence, the bins would fly open and the bric-a-brac would fly out, killing them all.

Claudine gulped her champagne quickly. Mind you, what were a few clouds compared to the storm she was likely flying into? She pictured the Oruwaris waiting for her to arrive, Tonye's father grim-faced as he had been throughout Tonye and Nicole's nuptials. "Like King

Jaffe Joffer in *Coming to America,*" Penny had hissed, watching them from across the aisle.

Two days ago, Claudine had called Tonye. "No word about the boat? Or the people Nicole was with? Have you checked all the hospitals?"

"My people are working through all that," he had said. "We can only wait."

"But it's been almost a week already. What are you waiting for?" Claudine thought of manhunts she had seen on the telly. Volunteers combing the forest with torches. Police out with their dogs to search for scents. TV appeals. It didn't sound like anything similar was happening in Lagos to find Nicole.

"Well, we've had to rule out other things. Kidnapping. Her not wanting to make contact. Various factors. But let's talk again in a few days. If I find out anything in the meantime, I'll be sure to let you know." He cleared his throat.

Claudine was quiet for a moment. *Let you know.* Something in his tone had sounded painfully familiar, reminded her of her youngest sister Jackie's death. That was what the family liaison officer had said while looking at his watch. And he never did come back to let them know exactly how Jackie had died. It had been a formality, just something said to end a conversation.

"What do you mean about her not wanting to make contact?" she finally asked.

"Sorry, what?"

"You said you had to rule out Nicole not wanting to make contact."

"It's . . . something the police said."

"But not wanting to make contact? Why wouldn't she want to?"

"It doesn't mean anything. Rest assured. Just procedure. They consider all possibilities."

Claudine breathed deeply. "I think I'd better come out there, Tonye."

"Out where?" he said, suddenly sounding much closer to the receiver. "To Lagos?"

"Yes, there are too many unanswered questions. I want to be there, talk to the police, help any way I can."

"But, auntie, why?" he said. "Everything is under control. *We* are talking to the police."

"So I shouldn't come?"

"I mean, come if you'd like. I really don't see what you're going to do here. You've not even been to Nigeria before. We have a certain way of doing things."

"I'd like to see the children," she said firmly. "And at least one relative should be representing our family. We have a certain way of doing things too."

Tonye had little to say after that, and the call soon ended. He'd even asked why. *Why?* As if she had no business going. Like a typical man, he'd assumed she'd go along with anything he had to say, and he seemed shocked that she, any of them, would care enough to travel there. Bloody cheek. It was difficult to shake off the feeling that Tonye was holding back a lot more. But at least it gave her hope that Nicole was still alive. She could be stranded somewhere, lying in a hospital, hurt but alive. Until Claudine laid eyes on Nicole's body herself, she wouldn't believe it.

Claudine fiddled with the entertainment screen and scrolled through the movie selection, deciding on *Unforgiven*. She didn't think she had seen it before, but the opening scene of a house, a tree, and someone digging underneath it seemed familiar. The house was plain. The tree was bare, but its network of branches fanned up and outward across the sunset, shading the person digging. Of course she thought of 49 Nedford Road and the pear tree by the living room window that grew thirsty and full of itself in summer, shrank shorn and sharp in winter.

Even if she had already watched *Unforgiven*, it would have been years ago, and so much from the past was hazy now, things done or said completely forgotten. Time didn't heal exactly, but crushed memories under its weight until they were no longer visible. Mercifully in most cases. At her age, you had to really want to remember, and in her shoes, who would want to? Looking back hurt too much. What if she'd done this differently, that differently? Never gone to the park that day? Life was hard enough without dragging all that shit along too.

Oh, Nicole, she fretted. *Where are you?*

She forced herself to pay attention to *Unforgiven*. It was the kind of movie she liked, with all the elements of a good Western, a tin-pot town in the middle of nowhere, pretty women in distress, everyone hell-bent on justice. Clint Eastwood. Good old Clint. It was no *Rawhide*, though. The memory of those Saturday mornings, curled up in front of the gas fire as a child, watching *Rawhide* with her siblings, flashed up, vivid, scalding, too painful to enjoy. It wasn't a childhood you would wish on anyone. It wasn't a childhood.

In her line of sight across the aisle were two little girls: one whose black shoes barely touched the floor and a slightly older one who held her hand protectively. Similarly dressed in pink cardigans with white blouses underneath, and sky-blue skirts with lacy knee-high socks. Sitting upright, so prim and proper on the wide seats, they looked just like dollies on the shelf in a toy store.

When food was served, Claudine nibbled at the chicken and jollof rice she had chosen. At least their food was nice and spicy. She'd never been one to jump to conclusions like Mummy and Penny did, that everything Nigerian was "bad" and "wicked." She'd liked Tonye the first time Nicole brought him to Nedford Road. "Too dark," Mummy had whispered loudly, squinting at him suspiciously. But even Mummy couldn't deny he was very handsome. Not a pretty face. No fine features and long lashes, not a light-skinned Harry Belafonte, whose songs Mummy would hum while kneading wet dough into dumplings, but a tall, broad-shouldered man with large eyes and a smile that made everyone feel happy. His beauty was in his solidness. His large, capable hands, his self-assurance. Everything about him looked stable. Regal. He looked you right in the eye when he spoke. And so polite, so charming, responding graciously as Mummy peppered him with ridiculous questions like, did they eat monkeys in Nigeria?

But since Tonye's call, she didn't know about him anymore. He'd sounded so cold, so emotionless. No tears. No urgency. Nothing you'd expect from someone whose wife had gone missing. Polite as ever, but no answers to any of her questions. Said he didn't know anything except that she went on a boat trip on Sunday, July 6, and didn't make it home. He couldn't tell Claudine who Nicole had gone on the trip with, where she went, what had happened to the boat, if she was dead or alive or was kidnapped or even had just run off somewhere. Claudine had barely slept for worrying about it.

The last photo of Tonye and Nicole showed a man in love with his wife, but pictures could lie. Men lied all the time. Men held you in their arms and lied and smiled and lied. Too lie! Even with their last breath. Tea arrived. An extra bag, milk and two sugars. She sipped, and felt better. A good cuppa always made things better.

Claudine glanced over at the girls again. The older one was helping the younger one with her snacks. Something about them reminded her of herself and Penny. They must have been about the same ages when they'd traveled to the UK from Jamaica for the first time. But these girls looked impossibly young. So vulnerable. Like babies. Even though she'd been practically the same age as Penny, she'd always mothered her like that little girl was doing now—taking the other girl's hand and telling her everything was going to be okay. Claudine knew what that felt like. The crushing weight of responsibility. To step up when no one else would.

CLAUDINE OPENED her eyes to lights on in the cabin and a flurry of activity as passengers threw off their blankets and made last dashes to the toilets. The seat belt sign came on, and the pilot announced they should prepare for landing.

Unforgiven had long since finished, but she couldn't remember how it ended. She noticed the two little girls were gone.

"I hope you had a nice rest," said Annie, appearing at her elbow. "Do you need help returning your seat to the upright position?"

Claudine nodded gratefully as Annie jerked her up.

"Annie, what happened to those two little girls sitting there?" She pointed to where they'd been.

"Two little girls?" asked Annie, looking around the cabin. "I didn't see them. Were they bothering you?"

"No, not at all. They were sitting right there for most of the flight, then they just disappeared. One bigger girl, one smaller. I think they were traveling alone."

Annie shook her head and stowed Claudine's tray. "Those seats have been empty the whole flight. I think I would have noticed two little nuggets sitting there. And we don't allow children under fourteen to fly alone anymore. Are you sure you didn't mean another row?"

Claudine frowned, then smiled quickly. "Must be my mistake. Thank you, Annie." She chastised herself for drinking the champagne and braced as the plane seemed to nose-dive toward land.

CHAPTER TWO

NICOLE

Before

Lagos

TIMI LOOPED through the garden and screamed in delight, a blue-and-red Spitfire, arms stretched out, cape fluttering behind him. Nicole smiled as he zigzagged toward the lagoon, then the house, followed by his friends and three-year-old brother in a synchronized display of childish joy.

"Hey, Mummy!" Timi passed the present table, where Nicole was rearranging the stack of gifts people had brought. She watched the children crash-land on the bouncy castle in a shrieking heap. Then they were off again, wheeling across the grass.

She was thankful he either hadn't noticed or wasn't bothered his dad wasn't there yet, but it bothered *her*. Other fathers were there. By now, most of the guests had arrived. The sun had settled down and the soothing lagoon breeze had lured the parents out from under the canopies onto the lawn where they mingled, watching their children enjoy the various attractions: a photo booth complete with a collection of oversized glasses, feather boas, and outrageous hats for guests to photograph themselves in; an entertainer dressed as Batman who knew all the moves to "Gangnam Style"; a "real" pizza parlor; a bouncy castle; a climbing frame; candy floss and ice cream stands. Tonye was all that was missing now. She hadn't seen him all day, and he hadn't responded to messages.

Nicole checked her phone again. Still nothing. She blinked, willing herself not to cry. If she started, she didn't know if she could stop, and people would think she was crying because her husband was late for their son's fifth birthday. It wasn't that. Not really. She had texted Tonye yesterday that they needed to talk and hadn't seen him since. She tried not to think about what she'd found in his suitcase. If he was avoiding her, she'd kill him, she really would.

By the time she woke that morning, Tonye had been gone. The sheets on his side of the bed were rumpled but cold to the touch, showing he had slept beside her at some point. She had lain listening to a distorted Muslim call to prayer carrying over from the warship moored farther up the lagoon, wondering what had been so pressing for Tonye to leave before sunrise.

There were places he sometimes went early on a Saturday: to the gym, riding while it was still cool, or running the Lekki Bridge with a friend. But he'd known she needed to speak to him that morning, before people arrived. Yesterday afternoon she had looked for him in his office on the compound, but he'd gone out riding. She'd tried again when he returned, but after showering he left immediately, declaring he was running late for General Ishaku's lavish eightieth birthday bash in LAD. "More of a networking event," he'd said as an explanation for not inviting her along. Before going to bed, she'd texted him to say they really needed to talk in the morning. His early disappearance was conspicuous.

Nicole faced away from the party, pretending to stack presents and tidy the goody bags on the end of the table. In Tonye's defense, men often came late to their children's parties. They left the women to it. No one else seemed to have noticed his absence. They were distracted by the views, the house. She watched guests strolling under the palm trees by the waterfront, craning to look at the gray warship on the horizon. Farther along the coastline, the first few finished skyscrapers of the LAD—Lagos Atlantic Dream project—were visible. Beyond, the ocean shimmered into golden sky. She saw a couple pointing up at the vastness of the tiered-wedding-cake mansion, the classical Roman columns, the decorative stucco on the balconies. She imagined their conversation. *Does it have to be Versailles every time? Why are we like this when we get money?* Naturally, they would change everything. *Get rid of the columns and all those pretentious swirls, put glass everywhere, like in Los Angeles.* And of course, the end result would be infinitely more tasteful. *It's not how much you can spend; it's a question of class.*

She allowed a laugh and told herself to relax. She was worrying about nothing.

Imani, a fellow Nigerwife, approached with a warm hello, her twin girls and nanny in tow. The girls, who looked like miniature versions of their mother in their summer dresses, hair in a twist-out, the same confidence and poise, presented Nicole with a gift, which she accepted with a smile and set on the table.

"This view is insane," Imani said in her amped American accent, hands on hips. The girls rushed off, their nanny running to keep up. "I would never expect this in the middle of Victoria Island."

Nicole had heard that a lot today. First-time visitors always seemed shocked to find this pocket of serenity and sky just off Ahmadu Bello Way, one of Victoria Island's most gridlocked streets. In the dusty, pockmarked back roads behind the shopping mall, there was no hint of the palatial waterfront compounds just meters away. It was only when you entered the house or walked around the side that you suddenly saw the silvery-blue lagoon and deserted islands, not a soul in sight. The view was the star attraction of this property, the thing that made people wonder how much money Chief was worth.

Imani seemed to make a big show of inhaling everything like a bouquet: the calm water, the agreeable sun, the graceful palms. Nicole wished she also could take a long, slow breath, but her chest was too tight. She straightened the row of goody bags, then began checking the contents of each, even though she'd filled them herself earlier.

"And look at you," Imani said. "Gorgeous. You really snapped back after number two."

Nicole laughed. *Too thin,* Chief had said recently, wagging his finger. *Our wife, people will say you are not happy.*

Imani looked around the party, shading her eyes from the sun that was now almost eye level across the water.

"Everything looks amazing. You've gone all out. Pizza parlor, candy floss, *and* an ice cream stall!"

Nicole smiled. "I know, it's a lot. Probably too much." But it still didn't feel like enough. She could imagine the Nigerwives saying on the way home that the party was nothing special—only one bouncy castle, no Ferris wheel, no railway train, no roller-skating rink, not even proper champagne. That they expected more from the Oruwaris.

"Where is everyone?" Imani asked, meaning the other Nigerwives. Nicole gestured to the huddle of women at the far end of the lawn, easily identifiable by their foreignness—not just their differing phenotypes but their short summer dresses, espadrilles, sun hats, and H&M tops. The open invite had been posted in their WhatsApp group, but she was surprised so many had come. She'd drifted away from meetings after her friend Christina abruptly left Nigeria, not being close to anyone else. But quite a few had shown up regardless and on time, even a few she hadn't met before. The Nigerwives were close, despite their frequent arguments. What was their saying again? "Sisters All"? They looked out for each other. Besides, who didn't like a party in Lagos?

"Come back to meetings," said Imani. "We miss you."

"I will," Nicole promised. "It's just been . . ." She faltered. "You know how it is."

"And where's Tonye?"

Nicole dropped the goody bag in her hand, its contents scattering on the ground. She scrambled after them. A pack of colored pencils, a ruler, a sticker pad, sweets, a stupid pocket arcade game that probably wouldn't even work. Imani bent down to help, passing items back to her. "Is everything okay?" she asked gently.

"Yes, yes." Nicole was quick to smile. She dared not go into how she really felt. She didn't want Imani running off to the other Niger-wives full of questions about her. Imani was head of the welfare committee. She'd heard Imani had "files" on all the Nigerwives, a running joke, maybe. She shoved everything back into the paper bag and clambered to her feet.

"Tonye had some last-minute business." She shrugged nonchalantly. "You know these men. They leave the parties to us." She laughed.

"I sure do know these men," said Imani dryly. Her tone and stare made Nicole acutely uncomfortable. Did Imani know something about Tonye? She was almost tempted to ask.

"I should go find him," Nicole said after a moment. "He's probably at his desk working. Work, work, work." She squeezed the brightness out of herself. "That's all they do, isn't it? I'll be back shortly."

Nicole walked toward the house, feeling Imani's eyes still on her. She looked back just as Imani reached the Nigerwives, saw how they absorbed her into their mass, and it pierced her heart, remembering how much she was a part of things until she wasn't.

It was a relief to finally enter the cool, dark central atrium, quiet as a church, away from the heat and noise of the party, all those eyes. And thank God there were no staff around. She leaned against a pillar. It had been a long day.

The house had looked so large when she'd first arrived in Lagos with Timi, not yet walking, in her arms. She had to bend her head back to look up at the roof. Three floors, a fifty-foot-high foyer, and a view straight down to the lagoon. Enormous chandeliers and super-sized sofas. Giant family portraits hung on the walls, like in an English great house. It was so large everyone had their "quarters," their own sitting room and bathroom. Chief and Mother-in-Law had obviously been inspired by their visits to Italy, since much of the original furniture was brightly colored, buttery Italian leather. The central ceiling had even been painted with a nod to the Sistine Chapel, the heavens opening up to reveal fat white cherubs blowing trumpets. And everywhere was bling, bling, bling: gold rosette medallions on the balustrades, gilded floral appliqué on the door casings and entrance tiles, countless expensive objets d'art like imitation Fabergé eggs, ornate candles, crystal vases, that sort of thing. But the luster had come off her life there. Perhaps the luster had come off her, and that was why Tonye was barely home. He hardly seemed to notice her these days.

Nicole approached Chief's office, where Tonye's and his father's voices floated through the dark corridor. "Now is a great time to invest," Tonye was saying with what sounded like veiled frustration. She paused outside. "An apartment for just over a million dollars now will hold its value, even if they never finish the city."

"After the subsidence from their constant dredging, ruining this coastline, this is how you want to reward them—with *my* money?" Chief said, sounding testy. Nicole suppressed a laugh, knowing how much the random rumbling from the ground beneath them had unsettled him. It bothered her too, the strangest sensation, like the house was levitating. Though it lasted only seconds at a time, it was long enough to make her dizzy and stay up until 3 a.m. googling earthquakes in Lagos.

"LAD is here now, Dad. They're clearing out the squatters from Bar Beach. The Dubai of Africa is happening."

"What is here? What is happening? Property speculation will ruin everyone."

"The oil price is up. We have a new president. It's a good time. We are the sleeping giant of Africa, soon to awake like Sleeping Beauty."

Chief's laugh became a groan. "Sleeping Beauty. What prince will kiss us and wake us from this coma?" Another bellow of laughter, then the sound of Tonye joining in halfheartedly.

"Can I just look into it? There's a lot of optimism. I was talking with the Khourys last night, and—"

"Stay away from those boys." Chief's tone shifted. "Their father is in bed with that Northerner, that crooked former general Ishaku. If your dealings with such people go bad, I can't protect you. A lot can still go wrong with that project, and they are beyond ordinary justice."

"But, Dad—" Nicole heard the high note of frustration in Tonye's voice and felt briefly sorry for him. He had such great ideas, but Chief didn't want to loosen the reins.

"Be patient, Tonye. You're handling things well. The farm in Epe is yielding strong catfish. The hotel in Bayelsa is doing as well as can be expected. Focus on your house now. Your boys. Give me more grandchildren. Have I not provided? The time to strike out on your own will come one day. Keep up the good work."

Nicole took a moment to straighten her dress, wicking away the sweat beads that had sprung up on her face, then entered the office to see Tonye seated on a chair opposite his father's gold and mahogany desk. Tonye's defeated expression turned into a smile when he saw her. He looked guilty too, slapping his forehead as if only now remembering the party. At least he was dressed for it, in the white trad she'd picked out to match her dress.

Chief wore his usual Ijaw attire, a collarless knee-length white tunic shirt buttoned up to the neck, a decorative diamantée fob chain looping down his chest and across his breast pocket, and black trousers underneath. A black felt gambler hat lay on the desk beside a ceremonial gold-topped cane that leaned against his chair. He smiled at Nicole, sharp eyes assessing her.

"Our wife," he said, waving her in. "How is the party going?"

Nicole smiled. "It is going well, Dad. How are you?" She approached him and leaned over the desk to kiss his cheek.

Chief nodded.

"Tonye, our guests are asking for you," she said. "I asked Bilal to fetch you."

"Yes, yes, of course. Give me a minute. I was just telling Dad about an urgent business opportunity. This LAD project, you know. Gotta get in there quick." He turned back to his father, who looked at his gold watch.

"Don't worry, we can resume later."

"But what do you—"

"Tonye, let us focus on your first son today. I'll join you outside later."

Cut off, Tonye hesitated before closing his laptop. At least he didn't seem suspicious or worried about anything she might say. As he made some parting comments to his father, she looked around at the family portraits on the wall. There was a framed group photo of Tonye and his sisters with their parents. They all looked so young. It must have been taken about twenty years ago. Chief was slimmer with more hair, seated in the middle on an ornate chair. His children stood directly behind him in traditional gold fabrics. One sister was on either side of Tonye, both wearing geles on their heads. On one side, Mother-in-Law leaned over Chief as if cradling him fondly. It might have been for his sixtieth, years before Nicole started dating Tonye. Directly opposite Chief's desk was the painting of Tonye's older brother, who'd died young in a swimming accident, standing amid the heavens with an enigmatic smile and a halo of light shining around him. The portrait imagined the tall and handsome young man he might have become, not unlike Tonye. This family. There were photos of her and Tonye and the grandchildren in the hallway, near the front door. But this wall she always felt was more for Chief's memories. His idea of who the Oruwaris were. The way he liked to think of them, of himself.

"Okay, let's go." Tonye ushered Nicole out of the room. As they walked through the corridor, he said, "What's the hurry anyway that you needed Bilal to 'fetch' me, like a small boy?"

"We started at three."

"I thought it was four." He sounded genuinely surprised, and she was about to list all the reminders she'd given him until he chuckled and patted her shoulder. "You mustn't get so stressed about these things. It's mostly your Nigerwives anyway, isn't it? More time for you all to complain about how terrible Nigeria is." She heard a rattle of laughter in his throat and ignored him. They reached the door and paused, taking each other in. "Nice dress," he said. "My pretty wife." He leaned over and kissed her on the forehead. "You wanted to speak to me?"

He was acting so normal now, as if nothing was amiss, and perhaps nothing was, she thought. There could be a reasonable explanation for what she had found, and she could forgive anything if he just explained.

"Later," she said. He shrugged and headed out onto the patio. When they arrived at the lawn, the adults under the canopy applauded him without irony. It put him in a good mood; she could tell by the way he posed laughing, as if it were his birthday. The emcee hailed him, and Tonye gamely hoisted Timi onto his back and galloped up and down the lawn while the photographer snapped away. Then there was the dads' gele-tying competition: the fathers sitting on a row of plastic chairs, haplessly trying to fasten the shiny women's head wraps around their own heads in sixty seconds, something that could take twenty minutes. It had everyone laughing and clapping for Tonye once more.

He joined the men sitting together by the tables under the white canopies. Most wore starched trad, like him, and were dark-skinned, the thicker side of athletic now with square shoulders and similar expansive laughs. The sons of big men, traditional providers. The laughter was part of this world, an identifier that said, *I'm here.*

He sat with his back to the water. He always sat facing away. But the men wouldn't know that. They went to the same schools and were forever telling stories about their adventures. They seemed to know so much about each other. But not the important things.

The other family members showed up in time for the cake cutting. Chief and Mother-in-Law undertook a regal tour of the attractions. Mother-in-Law congratulated Nicole on the setup. Tonye's sisters, Abi and Tamara, fussed over Timi and Tari. They all posed together for the photographer. As the birthday boy plunged the long knife into the fondant icing, Tonye put an arm around Nicole and grinned. It felt real. But as the shuttering stopped, he spotted someone on the lawn he wanted to speak to and walked off, leaving Nicole alone.

THAT EVENING, after the last stragglers followed the sunlight home, leaving scattered juice boxes and popped balloons all over the grass,

Nicole found Tonye in their dressing room. He had showered and changed into another trad, a black tunic this time, with velvet trim at the collar and along the waistband of the pants. "You're going out?" Nicole asked. She was exhausted herself. Standing in the sun for hours had drained her.

A lot of thought had gone into the room's design, which had wall-to-wall lacquered white closet shelving and a matching central round table. They had imported everything from South Africa. It was no mean feat for their steward, Samuel, to keep all the clothes folded, shoes polished, and surfaces spotless to Tonye's exacting standards. A white leather sofa and matching sectional footstools formed a semi-circle on one side of the room. Her glittering party shoes were neatly arranged on display in one glass cabinet, her rainbow of designer bags in another. Tonye's feet sank into the deep pile rug as he lightly sprayed cologne over himself, humming "Gangnam Style," focusing on his reflection in the full-length mirror.

"Polo club." Tonye went to the metal safe at the bottom of the closet, entered the combination, and retrieved one of his watches and a money clip of notes.

Her heart sank. Even if he had said the Silver Fox, she would have felt better about it. Strip clubs had rules. The only rule for the after-hours polo club was that you couldn't bring your wife.

"I've been trying to speak to you all day. Is that why you were avoiding me?" she asked.

He shrugged and contemplated a row of sandals. Gucci, Hermès, Prada. "So, what is it?"

Nicole produced a plastic package from behind her back. She held it up so they both could see. The image on the packaging showed a woman in lacy underwear and silver leather hooker heels lying on her tummy with her wrists and feet tied taut behind her, making a bow out of her body. She faced the camera awkwardly, her mouth open in a sort of cry, but her eyes knowing, consenting, after a fashion.

He had the grace to look startled.

"Hog-ties?" she asked. He reassumed his unfazed demeanor.

"Digging in my suitcase?" He shook his head dismissively, picked up Louis Vuitton flip-flops, and sat down on a footstool to put them on. "I brought them in for a friend," he said casually. She'd expected him to say this. It was a possibility. People often asked friends to bring in something small they couldn't get in Lagos. But this wasn't one of the usual things.

"What kind of *friend* wants hog-ties? Why would anyone want something like that?"

He rolled his eyes. "It doesn't concern you."

"And this hotel receipt? From your blazer pocket?" She showed it to him. A Google search had revealed the hotel was a tucked-away boutique place on Victoria Island not far from the compound. "Why did you need a room?"

He just glanced at it. "This is all very childish," he said with a sigh. "It was a conference room for a business meeting. Sometimes I prefer to do business outside the house."

"But it says a king-sized room."

"They mislabeled it. It's nothing. Don't be so dramatic."

"Dramatic?"

"You're losing it." He patted his pockets and looked around.

She was the one losing it? She wasn't the one with hog-ties in her carry-on. *Hog-ties!* She wanted to scream it. She snatched his wallet off the central table and held on to it for just a second. He still didn't care. He knew there was nothing she could do. Where could she go? Who could she tell about something like this? It would spread like wildfire. The shame.

She handed the wallet to him. With a grunt, he slipped it into his pocket.

"We still need to talk about it, though," she said. "And that isn't the only thing."

"You need help. Sitting around the house in your pajamas all day, going through my things, making up stories. Too much time on your hands is driving you crazy."

There was some truth to this. The days went quickly and then not quickly enough. She didn't know why all of a sudden the children were home and she was still not showered or dressed. The hours passed in a haze. It didn't seem to matter whether she stayed in bed or not. The tiles were still mopped clean, smelling of Pine-Sol. The nanny, Blessing, bathed and fed the boys, took them to school, picked them up. Nicole hadn't thought anyone noticed what she did all day or what she wore.

"I'm not saying I don't believe you," she explained. And the truth was that she desperately *wanted* to believe him, to feel his desire for her, to receive any plausible explanation for the hog-ties, the nightly disappearances, to know there weren't other women, something Imani or the Nigerwives might know about, or even if there had been, that it was over. "Perhaps we both need help. Some kind of couples therapy. Things haven't been great for a while, but you never want to talk about it."

He let out a short laugh. "Therapy." He paused as if there was something else he was forgetting. Nicole passed him his house keys, and his eyes flickered to hers. "You look tired," he said. "Rest."

Prickly tears began forcing their way out. As soon as he saw them, he groaned and stood up.

"Save your tears, abeg. There are no victims in this house," he snapped, then let out a short, bemused laugh.

Without thinking, she swung her right arm and hit him in the face with the package. He yelled as it connected and left a small gash just above his right eye.

They were both mesmerized by the warm, thick red drops that sprouted. He touched the wound, and the blood dripped down his fingers and onto the floor. She was holding her breath.

"You cut me." Tonye staggered as if she'd hit him with a brick. Calculating his unsteadiness, Nicole thought he might faint in a dramatic six-foot-two-inch heap.

"You should sit down," she said. He obeyed, dropping onto the sofa. She yanked a handful of tissues out of the enameled box beside his perfumes and thrust them at him. With a baleful look in his free eye, he pressed them to his injured one and dabbed dolefully, checking the amount of blood spotting the white tissue each time. "Keep it there," she said. "It's just a nick."

Nicole had never been a violent person, rarely, if ever, hitting the boys. That was more Tonye's thing, what he called "necessary discipline." She had certainly never attacked Tonye before, not once in their seven years together. She was surprised it gave her so much pleasure—the moment the sharp edge of the packaging connected with his face, the resulting yelp that came from him. It felt briefly satisfying to pierce his smugness, to see him suddenly at a loss, no smart comments, no laughing at her. Of course, the feeling passed as quickly as it arrived, and she was filled with remorse. Overwhelmed once more by a feeling of powerlessness and futility, she sank into the sofa next to him. She wanted to put a hand on his arm but didn't dare. Already he was shifting, gathering his things. The blood had dried. And she was discarded along with the bloodstained tissues. Now he moved with increasing urgency. Out of the dressing room. He didn't even look at her. She heard his steps across the tiled hallway. And then the door to their apartment closed. They would never talk about this again. There was so much about him that he didn't want her to know. He would come home later, get into bed, and the next day their picture-perfect life would resume.

After he left, Nicole picked up the package of hog-ties and went outside. She couldn't put it in the rubbish bins, where Samuel might see it, or Blessing, or someone else. Staff talked. The sensor lights came on hard and bright, illuminating her way through the dark garden. She walked gingerly across the lawn, hearing all sorts of noises. The night was for darting lizards, bats spinning through the sky, crabs scuttling around; she rarely came out here after dark. Arriving at the waterfront, she slipped the hog-ties through the railings, and they dropped—*plop!*—into the lagoon, which smelled like car exhaust in the humid night. But better diesel than dead things. The package slowly filled with murky water, sinking until it disappeared.

CHAPTER THREE

CLAUDINE
After

DEEP BLUE and starry, the Lagos twilight reminded Claudine of that song "Blue Velvet." Looking around at the other passengers hurrying to their cars, the waiting taxis, and the patrolling soldiers, she was almost surprised at herself. She really was in Nigeria. She hadn't known what to expect, but everything had gone smoothly so far, contrary to Penny's predictions of chaos. Tonye had arranged for an official to escort her through immigration and for a driver and an armed police officer to pick her up. Soon she was en route to the Oruwari house.

As they headed along the highway, she peered out of the car window half-hoping, however wild the possibility, to suddenly spot Nicole in the gloom, at a bus stop or in a crowd, to recognize a flash of her light skin or the afro hair Nicole had always refused to straighten. But through the tinted windows, everything looked much darker. Only a sickly yellow glow from occasional roadside kiosks revealed the shadowy figures of pedestrians. It was like looking for someone underwater.

After a while, they were on a bridge high above an inky void and the world on either side of the car fell away completely. Was it the lagoon? She wanted to ask the men in front, but they didn't seem conversational, although they had been very polite. Overly so. They had bowed at first meeting her.

The lagoon seemed very wide. You'd have to be a strong swimmer to cross it. Nicole had had swimming lessons at school but wasn't that kind of swimmer. If Nicole had fallen into the middle, could she have swum over to one of the banks? Claudine toyed with the possibilities. Tiredness tugged at her, pulling her eyelids down after so many days hardly sleeping. She sat up straighter. She couldn't sleep now. She had to keep looking. It especially wouldn't make sense to fall asleep with the two men she'd refused to trust with her carry-on, which lay beside her on the backseat where she could see it. After the bridge, the road got busier again. There was more lighting. Office buildings, fast-food restaurants, furniture shops, supermarkets, billboards flashed past. Even though it was late, people were still out shopping, dining, exiting cars. They passed a group of men praying on carpets by the side of the road, kneeling, their heads to the ground. Here and there, the streets looked rough. Derelict buildings, unfinished or in disrepair, stood out in ghostly contrast to an otherwise bustling city, and holes in the pavement gaped like missing teeth.

Penny was right about one thing. The photos Nicole posted on Instagram, fabulous parties, her wonderful home, and her rich friends, didn't show the whole truth about Lagos.

They soon juddered into a dusty side street next to a busy shopping mall, passing makeshift street-food stalls around which men sat on benches eating. Now the buildings started to get more residential, to look fancier, big houses and white-painted apartment blocks with balconies and palm trees peeking over high walls. At last they arrived at a set of tall gates and entered a brightly lit courtyard containing several expensive cars, then drove around a fountain with a statue of a praying white Jesus in the middle. *Mummy would love that*, thought Claudine. Pink bougainvillea skirted the walls. Lush plants sprang from ornate flowerpots as big as barrels. And the house itself loomed white and intimidating like something out of *Miami Vice*, mirrored windows reflecting the now-black sky.

The driver stopped. "Ma, we are here."

As he opened Claudine's car door, a man in a white buttoned jacket exited the house. He bowed and greeted her on the threshold before retrieving her suitcase from the car. Claudine followed him through a doorway twice the height of the doors on Nedford Road, inwardly cursing her carry-on for squeaking loudly over the marble floor.

He gestured to a chair by a pillar, and she sat down gingerly, taking in the gold-framed mirrors and chandeliers, the *Gone with the Wind* twin staircases, and the high ceiling painted with a mural of white angels in a blue sky like that one in Italy. An impressive home, to be sure. She'd felt the weight of it as soon as she'd walked in.

Claudine looked around at all the gleaming, shiny things, recognizing some of them from Nicole's Instagram posts. Personally, she'd pick Nedford Road over this place in a heartbeat. Home might not be glamorous—the sofa sagged, and the only treasures in their cabinets were out-of-date coins and old remote controls they were keeping for Armageddon—but it was more comfortable than this house for all its frills, and people who needed so much to be happy generally weren't.

Tonye appeared in the hallway, followed by another uniformed servant. Tonye, in a well-ironed tunic and matching trousers, struck her as minuscule against the ridiculous proportions of the house, not the imposing man who made their living room at Nedford Road seem so small. As he drew closer, she saw the tiredness, his furrowed brow, hair thinner on top with early speckles of gray around the sides, and the faint hope he'd have some good news died. He seemed so changed. The excitement of youth and its possibilities was gone. It goes for everyone in the end, she supposed. Even those who have it all.

"Auntie, good to see you." He smiled and hugged her. His warmth surprised her, and the hug made her a little emotional. They didn't do those in her family. As Claudine had left for the airport, Mummy just said, "Tek care ah yourself, Claud," and Claudine replied, "You too." Both women held themselves tightly, in case something fell out. But what? What were they afraid of?

"Was there any more news?" she said, even though she had asked just before boarding the plane. "Have you checked all the hospitals?"

"Please, auntie. It's not a day's work."

"I just thought—you said your people were on it."

He looked pained. "There are thousands of health facilities of all kinds in Lagos. Even narrowing it down by area, still hundreds, so it will take more time. It's frustrating. We're doing all we can."

She was disappointed, even though she suspected she was being unfair. Why, she wondered, were his people not on the phone now, working around the clock? She watched him go to the front door and fold a wad of notes into the hands of the driver and the guard. They bowed to him as they had done to her.

After they left, he asked, "How was your flight? No trouble at the airport?"

"Everything went all right, thank you."

"Samuel will take your bags upstairs to your room," Tonye said. "You should eat, though. We have some food ready for you."

She let Samuel take the suitcase but held on to her carry-on for a second too long. Feeling them watching her, she stiffened. "I just don't want to lose track of my things," she explained. "This is a big house."

"No problem." Tonye smiled, seeming to understand how anxious she was, and ushered her through a door to another reception area and into what seemed like a separate apartment. Nicole had said they had their own part of the house, and this looked more like a place Nicole would live in. A shoe rack by the door held flip-flops. There was a coffee table with books. Still very fancy, but not as over-the-top as the rest. Nicole wasn't a showy person, even if she liked nice things.

Claudine followed him into a living room with a dining table at one end, bright with lamps. At the other end was a cozy sitting area with a large television unit and sectional sofas set around it. Floor-to-ceiling blinds covered the windows. On a side table, Claudine noticed a collection of framed photos of the boys. She stopped and picked one up briefly. She'd last seen them in person just after Nicole had given birth to Tari in London. Timi had been only two at the time. They wouldn't know her.

The dining table was laid with a covered bowl of chicken in tomato sauce and another of plain white rice. Samuel arrived to remove the covers and pour juice into tall glasses. She sat down at the table and spooned some food onto her plate. She was hungry by now, and again, the food was delicious. She didn't usually cook with tomato unless making Bolognese, but this sauce was interestingly peppery with a curry undertone she wasn't expecting and a satisfying sweetness. Tonye joined her at the table but didn't eat. He sipped some sort of liquor from a crystal glass and enquired about Mummy and the rest of her family. He was still handsome in his way. The silver flecks in his hair suited him. He remembered Penny, had to be reminded about Michael, who ran a Caribbean restaurant, and Yvonne, who lived in Florida. He only dimly remembered Papason, her father, whom he'd met the one time at his wedding. She explained how Papason was still living in Jamaica, happily watching the world go by from his veranda.

"I can see why your father would prefer Jamaica to the UK," said Tonye, nodding. "Maybe it's something about us men. Eventually we want to go home."

Men and their wants, Claudine thought. *They want what they want and blow the consequences.*

"Do you think Nicole will come home?" she asked.

Tonye looked down at his glass.

"I kept looking for her through the car window on the drive from the airport," said Claudine.

"On the road from the airport? Why?"

"Silly of me, I know, but I couldn't help it. I think she's still alive, waiting to be found. What about you?"

"What about me?" He sounded defensive.

"Do you think she's still alive?"

"It's hard to know."

"You still think she drowned?"

"It's easy to drown around here." She raised her eyebrows at the matter-of-fact way he spoke. "The water is deceptive. People underestimate it. They think because they can swim or feel the ground under their feet that they're safe. That a life vest will save them or one of their friends will pull them out. They don't understand the threat is not where they can see or feel it but where they can't. By the time you realize you're in trouble, it's too late."

Claudine frowned. Did he care about his wife at all? She opened her mouth to question him further, but Tonye looked at his watch. It glittered under the light.

"I'm sure you're tired. Let me show you to your room, auntie." He called for Samuel. "My family wishes to have breakfast with you in the morning." He patted her arm. "They're really happy you've come."

She doubted that. She wanted to ask more questions, but it *was* late. She felt the tiredness pressing on her from all sides. "So we'll talk tomorrow?"

"Yes, it would be better."

They left the living room and took a more ordinary stairway leading up to the second floor. She allowed Tonye to lift her carry-on case up the stairs and asked after the boys.

"You'll see them at breakfast," he said. "They'll be looking forward to seeing you. They need the distraction. They think Mummy has just traveled. We still haven't told them what's happened." He winced at the thought. "I keep hoping we won't have to."

They arrived at a bedroom decorated with feminine colors, pinks, a rug on the tiled floor, a walk-in closet, an en suite bathroom, and a dressing table. Claudine was relieved to see her suitcase in the middle of the room.

"Whose room is this?"

"Just an overflow room for Nicole's things. A woman can never have too many shoes," he said, wheeling her carry-on over to the bed. "There's water on your nightstand." He pointed to the two small bottles of Nestlé water. "Blessing, the children's nanny, will be here early if you need anything. Just call out for her." He paused in the doorway, his tall frame filling it. "You know, seeing you here, you look like her. You could be her mother." Then, looking embarrassed, he said, "I mean—"

"Well, I'm the closest thing she's got," said Claudine.

He nodded. He stood awkwardly for a moment, as if at a loss. "Good night." He shut the door behind him quietly.

The water is deceptive. What on earth was Tonye going on about? She still didn't know what to make of him, whether she could trust him or not. Not that she had any choice. She'd noticed that he'd not wanted to get into the details, hurried her off to bed as soon as she'd started asking questions. But it was late and she was so tired, her thoughts swam in her head.

She walked around the room and entered the closet, looking at the many fabrics, the dresses, the shoes on the shelves. Some of them were unworn, tags hanging from various items. A faint smell of perfume hung in the air, heavy and sweet like the smell of tobacco plants at night. She inhaled it and went to the dressing table, opening drawers and feeling around. You never knew what you might find. But it was only the usual: makeup brushes, lipsticks, hair bonnets, combs. She checked out Nicole's pots and potions. She picked one up—Crème de la Mer—and uncapped it. Looked like the Pond's cold cream she and Penny had rubbed on their faces in their twenties, hoping never to look old. They took it for granted that they would grow old. She scooped out a dollop and rubbed her hands together, then closed the jar and returned it to its original spot.

Eventually she decided to get dressed for sleep. A white mosquito net was suspended from the ceiling over the bed. She laid her case flat on the floor with a slight bang and unlocked the combination. She took out a new nightdress, midcalf-length with cap sleeves, sprinkled with tiny blue and green flowers. Thin material. She'd thought the nights here would be hot, but the room was cold. High on the wall, the AC quietly pooled dry, chilled air into the room. From some- where outside the house she could hear *chug ah chug ah chug ah* like an old man's chesty breathing. She went to the window and pulled the curtain aside, but there was nothing to see except her own reflection against the night.

She turned the key in the door and got undressed, then took one of the water bottles and used it to brush her teeth in the bathroom. She'd read up on the things not to do in Nigeria, and not trusting the water was high on the list. She wasn't taking any chances, despite the water coming out of the tap crystal clear. Though there didn't seem to be any mosquitos in the room, she sprayed a little repellent over herself, turned off the light, and folded herself inside the crisp, cool sheets. As an afterthought, she decided it was best to tuck the bottom edge of the mosquito net under the mattress. The mosquitos had all night to find their way under the edge of the net; she didn't want to take a chance they'd get in. It only took one to catch malaria in the brain and die. Besides, there could be snakes, spiders, or worse. She didn't know what could be worse, but better to be safe than sorry. She lifted the edge of the mattress by the headboard and used her hand to slide the netting underneath. As she did so, her hand hit cold metal, something sharp. She pulled it out to see a small knife.

What on earth? She got up and switched the light on again to get a better look. She sat on the bed turning the knife over and over. It was the length of her hand, something you might peel an apple with. Strange to find a knife under a mattress; stranger still in a room no one slept in. *An overflow room*, Tonye had said. She would ask him about it tomorrow. Not knowing what to do with it, she put it in her handbag. The police might find it interesting. Sleep suddenly seemed far away. Cold fingertips traveled her body as she lay down with the light on, listening to the *chug ah chug ah chug ah*, wondering why this knife would be under the bed. Someone was sleeping in here. Was it Nicole? Why would she be so scared, she needed a knife? Who or what was she afraid of? If Nicole slept in this room, which Claudine now suspected she did, what kind of marriage did they have? What was the point of all the security and locks if she still felt she needed to protect herself? Tonye didn't know about the knife. She was sure he would have removed it. He seemed keen to make her think the room was not being used. It worried her. She double-checked that the door was locked, then lay back down, unable to sleep.

CHAPTER FOUR

NICOLE
Before

O N THE first Saturday in February, Nicole hurried into the school hall for the monthly Nigerwives Association meeting and looked around for a seat. About fifty women were seated on plastic chairs, nattering away as Shelly Nnodim, the Nigerwives Lagos president, got ready to address them onstage. The music of their multilingual chatter, an orchestra warming up, stirred Nicole after her months-long absence. On the compound, her London accent stood out like a false note no matter how much she tried to soften it. But here, mixed in with the accents of other foreign wives, it made sense. She made sense.

Among the women, she spotted some familiar faces—Soo-yin, a Chinese Nigerwife who ran a flip-flop factory off the Lekki Express-way, and Mary from India, her distinctive ropelike braid hanging over the back of her chair. On the right of the hall were the older Caribbean women who had been in Nigeria a long time. They always sat together. Seeing them made her feel somewhat guilty for staying away so many months. They had been nothing but kind to her, often asking to see baby pictures of her boys or slipping her hard-boiled butter mints, and she had deserted them without explanation. She hoped they hadn't noticed.

The Nigerwives were so different, a pick 'n' mix of skin tones, hair textures, body shapes, and facial features, but their stories were one and the same. They had all defied the pride and prejudices of their families, sacrificed friendships and careers and independence, and followed heart and husband to Nigeria for what they believed would be an epic adventure. The Nigerwives' meetings were important, not only for the butter mints and baby photos, but also to remind them what it was all for. In spite of everything, they were all still here. Everyone except Christina.

Nicole could see Imani with the other younger Nigerwives in the front rows to the left, but no empty chairs near them, so she slipped into a seat at the back. She had meant to come earlier to catch up with Imani beforehand, but on her way out, Mother-in-Law wanted to introduce her to the wedding planner for Tamara's forthcoming nuptials to the Governor's Son. It had taken Nicole several minutes to excuse herself. Mother-in-Law was stressed about her first big fat Lagos wedding and wanted everyone involved.

"This wedding cannot be like other weddings o," she had emphasized to the planner, explaining with upturned palms, "It's the Governor's Son. I want it to be . . ." She took a while to find the word and enunciated it with slow deliberation: "*Extra*vagant."

Nicole was looking forward to discussing it all with Kemi later. She checked her phone messages to see if their meetup was still on. Her friend had also said she had some news but hadn't elaborated, and Nicole suspected a new playboy was in town. Kemi had a thing for red Ferraris and red flags.

The air was hot and tugging in the hall. The ACs above them were lifeless. No power. Nicole could feel wet patches under her armpits. As she rummaged in her bag for a fan, she could hear the distinctive cackle of Mildred Obosi, one of the founding members of the Nigerwives. Good old Auntie Mildred, always cheerful and encouraging. Nicole had often admired her charity work with the Nigerwives'

Braille Centre and enjoyed listening to her hair-raising stories of using her Scottish accent to charm the machete-wielding mobs that stormed her compound during the Biafran War. The aunties who had lived in Nigeria since before the war, before the internet and mobile phones, lectured the younger women about the Nigeria of yore, when fifty-five kobos got you a whole US dollar. How they'd survived because they had each other. They loved to mother the younger ones with unsolicited advice about child-rearing—"You've gotta wean your babies on the pap!"—and urged them to come to meetings more regularly.

Three years ago, Nicole had met a Nigerwife at the British High Commission playgroup who invited her to the meetings. At her first one, she'd thrown herself into the events and activities. There were Christmas parties for the children, fundraisers, committees, and seminars for everything you could think of: how to navigate family law, perform first aid, make perfect jollof rice or your own soap.

She joined the social committee and met Christina, a Canadian-Ghanaian woman who was married to a property developer. They hit it off right away and organized a fundraising garden party, a monumental undertaking with months spent ringing various businesses looking for sponsorship, making use of Chief Oruwari's impressive list of corporate contacts. The event had sold out. Most importantly, this was the first friend she'd made in Nigeria.

Before Christina left Nigeria last summer, she had been in a phase similar to Nicole's—champagne playdates, school applications, and toddler tantrums. Her husband was rapidly transforming Lekki's bushland into fancy gated estates that mimicked America's smooth tarmacked driveways and identikit town houses. She had moved to Nigeria a couple of years before Nicole and lived in the prestigious Parkview Estate with her husband and four children. The two women dubbed themselves the Desperate Housewives of Hibiscus Lane, unsure about this life they had found themselves living, and used to laugh at how useless they both were compared to most of the Nigerian women they knew, who tended to be very entrepreneurial—up at dawn, with multiple income streams and looking like glamour models every time you bumped into them. Nicole and Christina spent their time commiserating over their lost reasons to exist and discussing the other Nigerwives and what might really be happening behind closed doors. It seemed ironic now, but what else was there to do when the sun's pink fingers found you by a pool with a cold vodka and Sprite, and the kids were away with the nannies?

They wondered at those Nigerwives who, elevated by their husbands' statuses and lifestyles they wouldn't get back home, had done very well in Nigeria and started businesses and cultivated social networks. How they'd benefited from their exotic foreignness, the privilege of lighter skin in some cases, a Western education in others. Even believing themselves culturally superior, they were often encouraged and validated by people they met to a sad degree. Both Nicole and Christina had benefited. Their husbands were popular and well-connected, from wealthy families. They both moved in elite circles and enjoyed a standard of living they'd never experienced in their home countries. Christina, like Nicole, had met her husband at university. Christina had only worked briefly as an administrative assistant before getting married and quickly starting her family. They talked about how their children benefited too, growing up in Africa, where they were largely protected from the frequent microaggressions the women themselves had experienced growing up. Being told you had the wrong sort of hair, or nose. Assumed to be delinquent or poor. It would be many years before they understood why they were Black, not brown. Nicole felt this especially with two boys. Black boys were often marginalized in the UK, but in Nigeria they were on a pedestal. Timi and Tari were of this place, already strutting about like roosters, their loud voices gobbling up space until the day mothers would stress over their proposals, plan big fat weddings, and demand the most "*extra*vagant" decorations money could buy.

Christina and Nicole also discussed those Nigerwives who struggled to be good Nigerian wives. Nicole remembered clearly one who ran away from her husband's jealous fists. Another vanished when the money ran out. This one was hysterical about the pollution. Apparently, that one—it leaked out during an infamously boozy playdate—

had confessed she "couldn't get used to all the Black people." And there were horror stories: A young Italian woman had followed her husband to Nigeria after his deportation from Italy, only to be chased from his village because she wasn't Igbo. Another Nigerwife was devastated when her husband married a second wife against her will. "We don't start counting unless we see boys," one mother-in-law from hell reportedly told a Nigerwife who didn't want any more children after having three daughters. Nigerwives didn't like to talk openly about their troubles, of course. In Lagos, large extended families meant you had to be careful what you said to whom. It didn't take much to cause a scandal. So Nicole and Christina drew their own conclusions from what little they knew.

Last year, Christina had been griping about how awful everything was, from the theft of jewelry by her maid to the mold taking over her house. The dehumidifiers kept breaking down, unable to cope with the Lagos humidity. She moaned for hours about the obscenely skimpy trunks worn by her children's swimming instructor. Nicole had suspected Christina's husband was the real problem, but Christina was careful not to complain about him and Nicole didn't take it seriously until Christina disappeared.

The members stood for the Nigerwives song they sang at the start of every meeting.

> *Nigerwives across the nation*
> *Sing our song of celebration*
> *Born to serve, born to serve,*
> *Nigerwives across the land*
> *Singing songs and joining hands*
> *We are one—we are one*

Shelly—a stout Indonesian woman who had lived in Nigeria for at least twenty years but still greeted everyone with a friendly *"Selamat Datang!"*—began reading the day's agenda aloud. The Small World Festival that had taken place last week at the Federal Palace Hotel had been a success. The Nigerwives' food stand had done particularly well, and the event had sold out, resulting in two million naira for their Braille Centre.

A cheer went up from the women as Mildred stood to talk. She was sturdy for her ninety-one years, with short tapered white hair and skin yellowed from a lifetime in the sun. "We at the Braille Centre thank you for your participation," she said in an accent that was Scottish one second and startlingly Nigerian the next. "This two million naira will cover our costs for the next six months."

"And special thanks to Condola for organizing the vodka sponsorship," added the president. "The pink lemonade was very popular."

"Too popular for some," someone shouted. There was laughter.

Before Christina disappeared, Nicole had thrown herself into organizing events like these during her time on the social committee. But had they really been fun, or just necessary distractions from the major questions about their lives?

Earlier that morning, Nicole had sat in the shade of her balcony and watched the Saturday catamaran crews crisscrossing the lagoon, the crazy white expats fighting with their sails. She enjoyed snacking on fresh pineapple while guessing which of them would capsize next.

"Mummy, why are you here?"

Focused on the lagoon, she hadn't noticed Timi watching her from the open doorway, his little head cocked to one side.

"Getting some air," she had said with a sigh.

Then he said, "No, not here. Why are you here in Nigeria?"

The effort of articulating himself had caused his forehead to pucker, and the question bothered her. It didn't feel like something her older son would say.

"Why do you ask that?" she said. He shrank back and said nothing, making her suspicious that he'd overheard a conversation about her in the compound. Maybe something an in-law said. They probably knew that things between her and Tonye were rocky. Heard the fights.

But Nicole smiled. "I'm here for the family—so we can all live here together." His face brightened. They hugged, and he climbed onto her lap to enjoy the Day-Glo-colored catamarans that twirled like pinwheels in the Atlantic gusts.

But why *was* she there? Nicole remembered the day Tonye had asked her to move to Nigeria. It was Easter Sunday. Chief and Mother-in-Law were visiting. Having recently had Timi, Nicole had been a bit out of things. The breastfeeding had drained her energy. She remembered Chief putting a hand on her shoulder, saying they should move to Lagos. There would be a better environment for Timi, opportunities for Tonye, and plenty of help for her. Glassy-eyed with exhaustion, she had nodded along, something to consider. But a month later, Tonye flew to Lagos to prepare for the move. "It'll just be a few years," he had said. "We'll just see how it goes." But a few years became four years, then five, and Tonye wouldn't hear of leaving now. "Who cares about the UK?" he had said. "They can keep it."

After finding the hog-ties, Nicole had moved into the spare room. She didn't know what else to do. Tonye refused to discuss it. He continued to get dressed and go wherever he wanted. He pretended not to notice that she slept in the other room. There didn't seem to be any way to make him feel anything. If she didn't sleep with him, he got it elsewhere. If she stayed in bed all day, the meals were still made, the flat still cleaned, the children taken care of, the lawn watered and trimmed. The message was clear. She was irrelevant. Free to go—without the children, of course.

A bang on the table from the VP brought the rising chatter to a close. They moved on to discussing the welfare committee's forthcoming trip to the Regina Mundi Home for the Elderly being organized by Imani, who came to the front. She wore a blouse and tapered pants. She wasn't so into the ankara looks.

"Good afternoon, ladies. Please remember our trip to the Regina Mundi home next week, Monday tenth February at eleven a.m., to visit our Nigerwife and see what she needs and support the home. I'd really appreciate your attendance for this trip."

"Is she a paid-up member?" called out one auntie, setting off an argument as to whether she was or not and, if not, whether they should support her. The aunties often quarreled like fruit bats over relatively minor issues. This or that charity, the time an event should be held.

Imani calmly answered everyone's questions and went over the reason for the trip and the plan for the visit. Nicole admired how capable Imani was, confident in dealing with the most difficult aunties. She proudly talked about being a Spelman graduate and Alpha Kappa Alpha member and made it sound like being a certain kind of person: responsible, a leader, an activist type. Imani was very vocal in expressing her frustration at the sexism, police corruption, and obsession with religion she had witnessed in Lagos. She often spoke about the African American civil rights struggles and how dismayed she was to encounter "tribalism" in Nigeria and see how terribly poor people and women were treated. Nicole could see Imani as a future Mildred, a local hero known for her good works, not frittering away the hours sipping mummy juice, gossiping with her friends, and feeling sorry for herself.

Initially, when Christina wouldn't reply to messages and her calls didn't go through, Nicole wasn't overly worried. Christina had mentioned that she might travel, and SIM cards could be removed or lost. Different time zones made it difficult to keep track of a conversation, and Christina wasn't on social media. But Nicole could tell the messages had been read from the blue tick beside them, and eventually, when weeks became months, she became concerned Christina wasn't coming back at all. Imani confirmed it. Christina had gone. But she wouldn't say anything else, just shrugged and said she didn't know, which Nicole didn't believe, because Christina had told her Imani knew everything about everyone. But she was too embarrassed to press further, wondering if she had done or said something for Christina to distrust her. She didn't think so. But who knew? Lagos was a strange place where friends and even family members lied about travel plans in case it led to them being kidnapped. Sometimes people concealed pregnancies or other exciting news for fear of spiritual sabotage. Also, keeping up appearances was paramount. People performed fake happiness on social media with loving photos and captions, showing off their holidays and material possessions. Didn't she do the same thing? And wouldn't it make sense then that friendships could also be just for show? Perhaps Christina had used her as a cover, even to her husband, while she was plotting to run away. Perhaps they were never real friends despite the committees, meetings, and playdates. It bothered Nicole so much she stopped going to meetings. But that didn't help either. She'd just gotten lonelier and more in her own head.

After a fruitless discussion about the latest immigration issues—Nigerwives were supposed to be exempt from visa charges, but each new minister of immigration kept forgetting—the president brought the meeting to an official close, and they all bought raffle tickets for prizes that were obvious Christmas regifts, like a box of tumblers with green spots and a few bottles of wine, plus food items like a donation of a dozen eggs from someone's farm and an unopened box of dates. The women got up to stretch their legs and snack. Nicole gathered her things and saw Imani chatting with a blond woman who looked like Grace Kelly. Nicole remembered watching *Dial M for Murder* with her aunts and their hilarious Jamaican ad-libbing throughout. "Lick dat man!" when Grace Kelly got hold of the scissors, and, "Yes! Lick 'im good!" as she plunged them into the killer's back.

"Hey, Imani," Nicole said. "Do you have a minute?"

"Nicole!" said Imani, seeming pleased to see her. "You should've said you were coming. I would've saved you a seat." Imani gestured to her blond friend. "Meet Astrid. She's new to Nigeria. I've just been explaining to her that it's Nigerwife, not the slang Naijawife, for a Nigerian wife. They sound the same but they're different." She laughed. "We are our own thing."

"It's confusing," said Astrid. "But perhaps I will soon be a"—she tried out the word—"Nigerwife. My boyfriend is trying to persuade me to live here. We met in London, but he's based here."

"You'll love Nigeria," gushed Imani. "It's such an exciting place to live. So much to do. And anytime you need advice or support, we're here for you, like family." She turned to Nicole. "A few of us are heading to the American Club now. Do you wanna join?"

"I can't," said Nicole. "I'm meeting a friend and heading back into VI now. But I wanted to ask you—"

"Wait, can I put you down for that Regina Mundi visit?" Imani interrupted.

"I don't know," said Nicole quickly. "It's quite far into the mainland. I don't think my husband would allow it."

"Your husband?" Imani sounded cross. "You can't live your life according to your husband! And you know the Nigerwife I spoke about is actually Caribbean. All the Caribbean aunties are coming so I'd think you'd want to support, no?"

Nicole hesitated, racking her brain for a different excuse.

"Come on, Nicole," urged Imani. "You used to do so much with us Nigerwives. Now we never see you."

Nicole thought about it. Perhaps she could ask Imani during the trip what had really happened to Christina. A sort of quid pro quo.

"Okay, sure. I'll come."

"Great!" Imani beamed. "And what did you want to ask me?"

"Never mind," Nicole said. "I'll save it for the trip."

Nicole and Astrid exchanged numbers and promised to meet for coffee. But Nicole knew she wouldn't. Why make another friend when the pain of losing one was like a bereavement? She was fresh out of cheerful Lagos anecdotes anyway. If Astrid moved to Lagos, she hoped it would all work out for her, but she couldn't advise blindly following your heart. Not when hers was broken. Love burned brightly, but it cast such dark shadows.

CHAPTER FIVE

LATER THAT day, Nicole was reminded that Saturdays were for weddings, as her car inched along Falomo Bridge toward Victoria Island. Lagos traffic was a thing of wonder most days, a python coiled around the city, tightening its grip during the morning and evening rush. Even on Saturdays, the islands could be brought to a juddering halt due to the numerous weddings taking place. Mile-long tailbacks of cars lined up to be checked for explosives, and inadequate parking resulted in stymied streets and sun-stoked rage.

Rubbing salt into the frustrations of the trapped motorists were the personal police escorts who would jump down from shiny black SUVs and try to clear a path for their impatient bosses by threatening to break windows with the butts of their AK-47s.

In her early days she would have railed against such entitled behavior, but now it barely registered. She wasn't Dorothy anymore, clicking her heels saying, "There's no place like home." Where was home anyway? Was it still 49 Nedford Road in spite of everything?

The memory of Claudine triggered by Astrid was a surprisingly happy one, but it had been so long since Nicole had been in touch. She felt bad for not calling or visiting, but something always seemed to get in the way of it. They hadn't called either. Claudine had looked after her. Almost like a mother. Always there—to tuck her into bed, iron her school uniform, make her bush tea when she was sick. Remembering Nicole didn't like too much pepper in her food, bringing her books from the library when she noticed what an eager reader she was, cornrowing her hair in crazy styles, telling her about Jamaica and all the strange fruits you could find there: starchy breadfruit, the funny-named ugli, heart-shaped custard apples. Helping her apply for university even though, like the others, she thought Nicole should go straight to work. Claudine even gave her blessing for Nicole to move to Nigeria with Tonye. Perhaps if she had stayed in London, they could have repaired their relationship. But being so far away, it was easier to forget and be forgotten. Hard to explain, to put into words, how she felt about things that had happened. Things that had seemed settled at the time but as the years had gone on caused her pain whenever she thought about them. Things she couldn't forgive.

Immobilized now on Ozumba, Nicole's driver, Bilal, lambasted the political negligence and corruption that had led to such a state of affairs. "Ah! Nigerians! We are ruled by godless people!" he exclaimed, a favorite expression for times like this, throwing up his hands as if he couldn't quite believe things were the same as they had been yesterday.

Nicole had learned a lot about Bilal's Nigeria during go-slows like this. The long hours in Lagos traffic had turned them into prison cellmates, trading stories like cigarettes, sharing worlds the other would never visit. His was a superstitious country where grudges were made into spells, cats were vectors of witchcraft, and demons posed as beggars to whisk you off to the underworld. "Madam, it happens," he would insist, offended when she dismissed theories as nonsense. He clung to his village ways, even after many years in Lagos, relying on his religious devotion to protect him from its many terrors.

Tonye had not responded to Nicole's text letting him know she was meeting Kemi at the West, a wedding-free hotel on Ozumba. It wasn't entirely surprising. He had never liked Kemi, calling her "the mosquito," forever whining in his wife's ear. He loved to mimic her voice:

"Let's go to BodyLine, Nicole! Lots of eye candy working out there tonight!"

"Let's run the Lekki Bridge together. Senator Martins runs the bridge, we might see him!"

"Look how many followers I have on Instagram! Hashtag Boss Chick!"

He complained about the way Kemi walked through his house "like a man," off to find Chief and whichever politician or tycoon he was sitting with, drawing out the greeting as long as she could and presenting her business cards as if they were gold-plated. Nicole often had to hide a smile at how nettled he was by Kemi's ability to parry his jabs and return them with a point twice as sharp.

THE DOORS of the West slid open to a world of high ceilings and cool, scented air. A few smartly dressed people were milling around the lobby, making reservations, chatting on the pink sofas, and coming and going from the restaurant. Nicole crossed through the reception to the outdoor café, where, from this side of Victoria Island, you could watch Jet Skis, speedboats, and the occasional yacht pass along the slender ribbon of lagoon separating the financial center from Ikoyi's old money.

Kemi was immediately visible, propping up the bar in her six-inch heels and an eye-catching yellow blazer. The sun glinted off her black braids, which poured down to her waist. Nicole could hear her almost shouting as she stepped outside.

"This is the small wineglass," Kemi said, then, flipping to local vernacular, "Do you get?"

She gestured toward a row of different-sized glasses lined up on the counter, and the bartender returned an embattled smile in an attempt to appease his self-appointed madam.

Kemi lifted each glass and then put it down again heavily. "This larger wineglass is for the red wine. You see?" she said, and he nodded, each time rescuing the glass from her unsteady hands. "The flute for the sparkling wine, to keep the bubbles, and this one the martini. Can you remember now?"

"Yes, ma," he said, seeming to hope she would leave.

"So now let's say I ask for a Bellini. Which glass will you choose?"

He hesitated. Diners at a nearby table looked on expectantly, enjoying the show. He picked up the champagne flute to some applause mixed in with cheers and laughter.

"Hmm." Kemi looked disappointed that he'd graduated so quickly.

"Please release him, Kemi," said Nicole, arriving at her elbow. "Or will you cause him to jump into the lagoon over a small wineglass?"

"Oh, you." Kemi instantly forgot the bartender, who looked relieved. "I thought I would grow old and die waiting here."

"It's carnage out there," said Nicole. "Nothing's moving. I've just bought two jars of groundnuts I don't eat and five handkerchief packs I don't need to pass the time."

They crashed on rattan sofas closest to the water so they could enjoy the lagoon's breeze. A server quickly appeared with a standing fan and adjusted their umbrella for better coverage, even though the sun was no longer cracking its surly whip and gave off a heat that soaked rather than seared. The server passed them menus and smiled warily at Kemi, but Kemi had switched out of her hectoring persona into something more friendly. Both women kicked off their shoes and stretched their limbs.

Nicole ordered a Chapman spiked with vodka. Kemi opted for a glass of white wine. She wasn't slurring, at least.

"You were giving that guy a hard time."

"Ugh, I can't with this country. The West is a top international hotel chain, so I don't expect sparkling wine to be served in a glass for red wine. It's a shame."

"This isn't New York."

"It's not Mississippi either. I'm tired of people saying, 'It's Africa, lower your standards.' Why, when I'm in a city worth over a hundred billion dollars? Nigerian art sells for millions. Ten years ago, Dubai was like Lagos Atlantic Dream. See Dubai now? It's only our low expectations holding us back."

"I missed you at Timi's birthday," said Nicole.

"Oh, sorry. I meant to come. I had to ship some artwork. It took a long time. You know how it is. You have to be there shouting at everyone. They don't listen. I was exhausted afterward."

"Mm-hmm."

Kemi laughed. "Okay, honestly, I love you but I can't do the boring married women and talking about nannies and wooden toys. These Lagos babes, once they get married, jeez." She made a face. "Overnight, they're above you—even sorry for you, because you're single. Meanwhile half of them, their husbands are coming on to me. So, ugh, I can*not*."

"Maybe an overgeneralization."

"It's a shame to see such fun, independent women reduced to Stepford Wives. I mean, what is this shapeless auntie bubu you're wearing? You're taking this whole Nigerwives thing too far."

"What? This?" Nicole looked down at the olive-colored ankara with a turquoise-and-orange teardrop print and bronze beading, material she had gushed over in an Accra market but that suddenly looked frumpy after Kemi's critique.

"Shift, bubu—one is square, the other is shapeless," said Kemi, rolling her eyes. "You really must stop using that tailor of yours. It's like he doesn't even measure you." Then, ignoring Nicole's discomfort, she closed her eyes and faced the whirring fan. "How was it, anyway? The party, I mean."

"It was really nice. Everything went as planned." Nicole looked out across the water. She couldn't bring herself to tell Kemi about the hogties and the argument. "So tell me more about this new guy."

Kemi showed Nicole a slightly blurry image of a man on her phone. Nothing stood out except for the uncle-looking jacket he was wearing, double-breasted and heavy on the shoulder pads.

"Stylish, I see," Nicole said. "Who is he then?"

"Yohanna Ishaku," said Kemi gleefully. "His family owns the Kuramo Waters Hotel. You know them."

"I know them but have never seen him before."

"He's been abroad for a long time. He's back in Lagos. Cute, huh?"

"Can't see much from this photo. He looks all right, I guess."

"He's invited us to his beach house tomorrow," Kemi said, putting her phone down.

"Tomorrow as in Sunday? That's very short notice. I'll have to run it past Tonye."

"Please! I need my besto! This could be it, you know. He could be the one. Say you'll come."

Nicole took her drink from the returning server and settled back onto the gray-and-black geometric print cushions, hoping this romance would have a happier ending than the last. Wale Coker Williams had lured Kemi to Lagos from London a few years ago with the promise of a serious relationship. Only perhaps he didn't expect her to take him at his word, because when Kemi arrived in Lagos, he was reluctant to offer any form of commitment. In a year of tortured dating, she'd never met his family, and he'd avoided acknowledging the relationship publicly.

Wale had promised she could move into his Banana Island apartment, but first there was the excuse of a bad leak, and then he was hosting cousins. The following month he was unwell, then his ex-wife started causing legal trouble indefinitely. He wasn't exactly unkind, just unreliable. He was well-liked and well-connected—extremely pretty, slim, and immaculately groomed with carefully landscaped facial hair, but off-puttingly aware of himself, a total show pony. Yes, he ticked Kemi's boxes—English boarding school, polo player, flat in London's fancy Kensington area—but Nicole thought him a self-absorbed snob, an immature sort of person who stormed Ferraris over Lagos's cratered streets and fell out of Quilox high on coke at 6 a.m. He reminded Nicole of the orange-and-green dragonflies Timi and Tari chased around the lawn. They hovered tantalizingly in front of you, taunted you with their iridescent wings, but darted out of reach the minute you tried to catch them.

Nicole had been surprised when her old friend had gotten in touch to say she was visiting Lagos. They had met working retail one summer, midway through their degrees. Kemi, born and raised in the UK like her, was as British as they came and had never expressed any desire to visit Nigeria, her parents' country of origin. She was even more surprised when Kemi opted to stay, dusting off her humiliation and falling in love with Lagos on the rebound. The city seemed to stimulate her in a way London no longer could and gave her a new sense of self. Thanks to a conveniently located aunt she could stay with, Kemi found that the extroversion that sometimes intimidated people in reserved London was an advantage in boisterous Lagos. She had arrived at the right time for the growing art market. Her international experience and English accent, which she enjoyed mashing up with the local cadence, helped establish her as a key consultant to the influential and wealthy in less than a year. She'd ridden the Goodluck Jonathan wave of ambitious returnees, enthusiastically writing Nigeria's new afropolitan narrative as the Giant of Africa, taking its fashion, art, and entertainment global. Where better to find a husband, too? Kemi had long complained about London's low-energy beta men who griped about paying the whole bill and took pride in a scruffy, unwashed appearance. Lagos's alpha males led with their wallets and their designer shades.

"So the Wura Gallery in VI is one of my clients," Kemi continued. "I was there earlier to help them set up for an event tonight when *this guy*, Yohanna, walks in, looking hot."

"If you say so." Nicole tried not to laugh.

"He collects art for investment. Not exactly knowledgeable, but very enthusiastic. Of course, art is my department, so we ended up talking and hit it off."

"He buy anything?"

"Oh, stop!" She playfully slapped Nicole's hand. "Don't worry, he will. We went to Kuramo Waters for lunch. The Japanese restaurant there. Just business."

"Sure."

"So I still didn't know who he was then. He gave me his card, but it didn't register until lunch, when all the staff kept bowing to him, that the whole hotel is his." Kemi couldn't stop smiling.

"What—the hotel is now his?" said Nicole with a raised eyebrow, stabbing at the slice of cucumber at the bottom of her glass. "You said 'family' before."

"Well, he's A. J.'s only son." But the more pleased Kemi looked, the more skeptical Nicole felt. That General A. J. Ishaku was one of Nigeria's richest and most legendary figures just made the whole thing sound even more pie-in-the-sky.

"So you only met him today, and tomorrow you're riding on his boat to his beach house? Kemi, no."

"It's a group trip. There's a few of us. Plus, do you think Ishaku's son can just throw me overboard and disappear?"

"Can the son of a former military general even be arrested?" Nicole wondered aloud. Tonye had quipped once about throwing her into the lagoon. He was just joking, but it had struck her at the time that he could do exactly that and continue with his life.

"Come with me to Wura tonight if you want to meet him first. He's a nice guy. I'm good at reading people."

"Party tonight, beach tomorrow morning? Do I sleep on the boat?"

"Ah-ah." Kemi entreated her with open palms. "When did you become old?"

"When I got married and had two kids," Nicole retorted.

"Nic, you're thirty-four. Are you just going to spend the next fifty years getting fat underneath your square-shaped ankara? Tonye jumps and you say how high. Look, you know I can get you a job in the gallery, right? I'm restructuring there."

"What do I know about art?"

"You'll learn. For now, you can just be a liaison, showing clients the artworks. I'll tell you what to say. To be honest, a lot of it is the accent and the look. The clients would be flattered to be shown around by an Oruwari foreign babe. You know, part of the experience."

"It's not just him. I have two children to look after," Nicole said, wanting to change the subject.

"Your children? Are you being serious right now?" said Kemi. "You know you have the rest of your life to spend with them. What about you?"

Nicole considered silently. She understood that Kemi was literally trying to give her money. She'd hardly have to do anything except stand there and look pretty. And it was bound to annoy Tonye, which was a plus.

"We need to detach this umbilical cord," Kemi insisted. "You were a person before you were an Oruwari. The Nicole I met in London paid her bills herself and lived life on her own terms."

"The small print of those terms wasn't great, if you want to know the truth."

"I remember you had just finished law school. You were so ambitious, wanting to be this international lawyer, earning tons of money and traveling the world. Will you now bury your identity under someone else's altar?"

"I don't know how much I really wanted all that," said Nicole with a shrug. "I just wanted a different life." And it was true. She had just wanted to leave Nedford Road. Yes, she'd studied hard and gotten to university, out of the house, and then a training contract. She'd qualified as a solicitor. But beyond that, there had been nothing, no real plan or purpose, until she'd bumped into Tonye, just a guy from her university, on Kensington High Street.

Kemi rolled her eyes. "This is why I can't with married women. You pump out a couple of children, then wander around like overfed cows complaining."

Nicole laughed and shook her head. "But you still want to get married. Make it make sense!"

"Marriage shouldn't mean being some kind of doormat. It depends on *who* you marry. I won't marry some traditionalist or religious stick-in-the-mud. Yohanna's very laid-back, very modern. He was living in LA for years. He won't have those old-fashioned expectations of women like Tonye does."

"You've just met the guy. You don't know anything about him. I'm just saying, you talk about Tonye, but when I met him, he was laid-back and modern too."

Nicole recalled when they'd first met at University College London.

Tonye was halfway through a second degree, one of the wealthy African students who turned up the collars of their polo shirts and hid their hangovers behind designer shades at the student union bar—the G-Spot—on Gordon Street. She had seen him every Tuesday and Thursday evening when she worked as a delivery girl for the pizzeria on the same floor. It had been difficult, being a first-year law student financing her tuition and accommodation with loans and part-time jobs. Of course, she'd noticed him from a safe distance, not fancying her chances. He was that cool, popular guy the others looked up to, who always seemed to pay the bill. She never caught him looking in her direction. There'd been no conversation apart from "A large pepperoni with extra cheese, please." But once, when she was delivering the pizzas to his crowd, she'd tripped over someone's Gucci trainer, and the pizza had fallen splat onto the floor. Some of them had groaned rudely about it, but he'd rushed to help her pick it up. He'd put her at ease with his smile. And she noticed the attitudes of the others changed when he did that. That's how she'd thought of him, as kind, polite, and nonjudgmental. She'd heard him arguing about social justice and decrying his friends' chauvinistic views. Strange to compare that Tonye with Lagos Tonye, whose sense of entitlement had grown to be a thing of wonder, a towering pyramid, its peak hidden amid the clouds.

"Lagos changes men," she said finally.

"So if he's such an asshole now, get out there and live your life. Get a job. Don't ask his permission, just do it."

"That's not fair."

"You know, my father was a wonderful man," said Kemi. "He was the best father, the most amazing husband, a great provider. We had everything. But it was all a lie. He was in a lot of debt and couldn't bear it. He killed himself." Nicole knew Kemi's father had passed away, but not that he'd died by suicide. Kemi said it matter-of-factly. "I had to leave my nice school and go to the one down the road where they mangled my name and your people called me Monkey." She stuck her tongue out at Nicole and laughed. "Just to say, you can't rely on anyone but yourself in this life, Nic. Even if you think you're set up. If it's not yours, then you can't be sure."

"I'm sorry about your father. I didn't know that."

"Yes," said Kemi. "It was a shock. Especially to me. I was his perfect Oluwafeyikemi. I never imagined he would abandon us like that." Nicole wondered at Kemi saying all this without shedding a tear.

"So then why do you care so much about finding some rich man to marry?" said Nicole. "You're independent and successful. You earn lots of money. Why ring-chase at all? You clearly don't think much of us married people."

Kemi thought about it, then shrugged. "It doesn't matter what I've achieved. Being unmarried at my age carries a shame that overshadows everything else. Not being a wife, a mother, is seen as kind of a death. You wouldn't understand anyway, you're not Nigerian." She broke off with a dismissive wave and called the server over. "Hey, get rid of this umbrella, would you? The sun isn't hot anymore. It's blocking our view for nothing."

Nicole was hurt and confused by Kemi's hostility. No, she would never fully understand the pressures of being an unmarried woman in Nigeria, but did that make her the enemy? She'd never seen this side of Kemi before, so sharp and cold. She wondered if Lagos had changed her too, into someone the sun could no longer warm.

CHAPTER SIX

CLAUDINE
After

THE MORNING after her arrival in Lagos, Claudine leaned over the balcony, taking in the manicured lawn, the children's brightly colored climbing frame, the swimming pool catching the sun in its glistening ripples, and the serenity of the lagoon beyond, calm and blue. Birds called to each other as they swooped through the sky. If only she could make a postcard out of it and send it to Penny. She hadn't spoken to her yet.

She found her mind wandering to the milkman's daughter. Claudine and Penny had often wondered what she looked like.

"You look like the milkman's daughter," their father would say to Jackie, whirling her through the air to encourage her infant giggles.

Their milkman at the time had striking ginger hair, pale-blue eyes, and ruddy cheeks sprinkled with freckles. Naturally Claudine assumed his daughter would look quite similar, perhaps less ruddy and with longer hair, but certainly not like a Black child. Jackie had dark frizzy hair. She was light-skinned but not white, and her storm-cloud eyes were far from blue, so back then they didn't understand what Papason meant or why Mummy would cackle and look pleased with herself when he said it.

Claudine and Penny speculated that maybe the milkman's wife was Black—unlikely in those days—and from the window they would watch his cart trundle along Nedford Road to see if his wife came with him, which she never did. But how then could Papason know what their daughter looked like? they wondered.

Papason said it so often, it became Jackie's nickname. The Milkman's Daughter. It was even mentioned in her eulogy. Jackie Roberts, the Milkman's Daughter, known for her good looks, dreamed of being a model and an air hostess.

Of course, long before Jackie's passing, Claudine realized Papason was referring to Jackie's whiteness. She was so red-skin, if you pinched her the skin went pink, and when she got upset her cheeks flushed. The rest of them were somewhere on the spectrum between Papason's very dark skin and Mummy's much lighter tone. But Jackie was noticeably whiter and that meant prettier, more special. That was why Papason favored her.

The two siblings born in the UK were favored over the Jamaican ones. They weren't treated like servants and spoken to with fists, a belt, a slipper, and the like. When Claudine arrived in the UK from Jamaica aged nine, meeting her parents and siblings for the first time, no one commented on her appearance. It wasn't deemed important, and neither was she.

Yvonne and Jackie laughed at their Jamaican siblings—Claudine, Penny, and Michael—even though they were senior, at their "jungle" accents and their backward ways, even calling them monkeys. The English children were spoiled, not expected to do the cooking or heavy cleaning. Claudine was charged with most of that, as well as the bathing and cainrowing. If her younger siblings were found to be dirty or they complained about her, she got punished. Especially where Jackie was concerned. Papason gave all his love to the Milkman's Daughter and never understood how she could throw it all away on the drugs and the horrible crowd she ran with. His spoiling hadn't prepared her for life as an adult in the UK. Becoming a mother too young was a big shock to her. She went off the rails. The drugs did the rest. Nicole was different.

Jackie hadn't spoiled her. Far from. She'd been neglected, had come to them malnourished with rotten teeth. But she'd been observant and happy to do as she was told. They'd gotten on very well. It was mostly Claudine looking after Nicole since Penny had moved out with her own children, and Papason had moved back to Jamaica, brokenhearted after Jackie's death. Perhaps Claudine wasn't the best mother, but they enjoyed each other. They needed each other. Until it had all gone so wrong.

BOYS AND girls come out to play, the moon doth shine as bright as day. Leave your supper and leave your sleep, come join your playfellows in the street.

Hardly had the jingle of the ice cream van started when Claudine heard footsteps thudding down the stairs and turned from the sink to see Nicole already in the doorway, jumping up and down with excitement.

"Okay," said Claudine, "let's get ice cream and go to the park," and Nicole shrieked. She ran to get her inflatable ball. Claudine brought a towel and they stopped by the ice cream truck. Then walked down the winding lane to Lewisham Park, Nicole eating her ice cream, skipping, and tugging on her hand.

"Come on, Claudine. Let's go faster."

As soon as they were on the same side of the road as the park, she would let go of Claudine's hand and race ahead. Claudine would arrive at the paddling pool to the dress and sandals Nicole had thrown off and Nicole would already be in the water, splashing around with the other children.

"The ball, the ball, Claudine!" Claudine would throw her the ball and pick up her things. She'd had to get over the dirty water. She'd given up warning Nicole not to put her face or hair anywhere near it; with all that splashing she'd still be shaking water out of her plaits.

The paddling pool was in the shadow of the tower blocks where Nicole had lived with her mother briefly. While Nicole played, Claudine always thought about Jackie, how sad it was she would never know her daughter. They looked so alike. The same gray eyes and light coloring. Nicole was too young to remember the blocks or her mother. Claudine was her mother.

She wasn't a mother but she gave as a mother, raised as a mother, loved as a mother. Is it just birth that makes you a mother? Jackie had neglected Nicole, and if she hadn't taken herself out of the picture with a drug overdose, the council was getting ready to remove Nicole from her care anyway. Mummy became Nicole's legal guardian, but it was Claudine who did all the mothering.

Worrying about the dirt, Claudine hadn't realized someone was watching her and probably had been for a while.

KNOCKING AT the door disturbed her thoughts.

"Good morning, ma!" A young woman's voice. It must be the nanny. "Breakfast is ready."

"I'll be out shortly."

"Okay, ma," the voice trilled back.

Claudine quickly made her bed. Her pillow was damp, as if she'd been crying. If she had, it must've been in her sleep, but she'd hardly slept for worrying about Nicole, the discovery of the knife, and that chugging beast outside. Dreaming last night, she had searched for Nicole among her grandmother Miss Hortense's orange trees, in the three-room board house, in the outside kitchen, but Nicole wasn't there. Claudine saw her sister Jackie hiding in the waist-high sorrel, the flash of her white dress among the red stalks, and then Jackie wandering the rutted lane, looking for something in the dirt, but no sign of her daughter. Finally Claudine gave up. She joined Miss Hortense on the veranda, climbed onto her lap, and forgot about Nicole.

Until Claudine was sent to the UK, it was Miss Hortense who Claudine curled up against at night, who washed and cainrowed her hair while telling stories about people in their family who were long gone. Sometimes Miss Hortense spoke of her great-grandmother, who had been born into slavery and lived long enough for Miss Hortense to remember her. She didn't keep names, but she remembered the sea of candles people brought to her great-grandmother's wake, like hundreds of flickering peenie wallies lighting up the hillside. Other times, Miss Hortense talked about Fred, their grandfather, the whitish-looking man she'd married, who came and went, came and went, and left gray eyes behind.

They had a name for children like Claudine, Michael, and Penny now: barrel children. She'd seen it in the *Gleaner*. All these children messed up and abused because their parents left the country for work and only sent a barrel home once a year. In her day, it was a parcel they sent. Maybe she got one a year, with some pretty clothes inside. She hadn't minded being a barrel child. Rather, it was the lack of love and affection from her parents when she did live with them that hurt most, especially Mummy.

Sometimes she questioned moving back in to take care of Mummy. It had made sense—Mummy approaching eighty and needing someone to help her manage, and Claudine, without a partner or children, worried about her own future. Mummy wouldn't drive alone ever since a carjacking several years ago, but she required a lot more visits to the GP and things done around the house. So Claudine's help was definitely needed, she told herself. Needed, but not appreciated.

Since arriving in the UK at age nine, Claudine had been trying in vain to build a bond with Mummy. Her life might have been different if Mummy had cared. Even now, it was hard to stop looking for something that wasn't there. They had all been left with different relatives. Claudine had been left with Miss Hortense. Penny lived with one of Papason's sisters, a domestic worker who went wherever the job was around the island. She'd raised Penny as her own until she suddenly got sick and died. Afterward, Penny had stayed with her employer as part of the help, performing light duties around the house and gardens. They expected even young children to work hard in those days, anything from collecting firewood to picking fruit to sweeping floors. Claudine had done it herself. They didn't really talk to each other about their lives before coming to London. Something stopped them talking about it, and to this day, no one knew where Michael had been all those years or what happened to him there. But he had a long, thin scar traveling horizontally on his back that looked like someone had drawn chalk across his brown skin.

As she got ready in the bathroom, Claudine examined herself in the mirror. The age spots creeping across her cheekbones. She tugged at the crepe-like skin under her chin, which, twenty years ago, had been smooth and tight. A few wiry gray hairs sprouted underneath. Not enough to call it a beard yet, but if Mummy's ferocious bristle was anything to go by, more would soon come. She was graying, fraying, but somehow she was still here when so many others weren't. Every other week now, there was a nine night. But she felt fine. The doctor had recommended watching her cholesterol more closely, and some days she could feel every joint in her body turning like a screw, but otherwise everything was still in good working order. And she didn't mind growing old. She was ready. It was a relief, in some ways, to have people stop asking what she planned to do with her life, to offer useless advice.

She didn't miss her clear skin, nor the rainforest of black hair that Mummy complained was too "tough" to comb. The girlish softness in her face, the honey in her voice back then had just attracted insects. Who had pretty ever helped? Jackie had been pretty. Very pretty. The boys chased her and when they had caught her, snuffed her light out. Beauty was a kind of curse, wasn't it? It had been freeing to cut off all her hair. Now she had stopped dyeing it too. They'd thought she was going mad, but she only wished she'd done it sooner.

She brushed her teeth and soaped her face on autopilot, as she had taught Nicole to do. She had raised Nicole right. She must have, for Nicole to have earned that fancy degree, become a lawyer, gotten married. Despite everything that had happened, she had turned out okay. Claudine had made sure of it.

BREAKFAST WAS in a dome-shaped dining room downstairs. The family was seated around a long, ornate rectangular table. They had already started eating but all stood up to welcome her, hugging her one by one. Tonye formally reintroduced his parents. Chief—a little fatter and balder, who must be approaching eighty now—and Chief's Wife, a high-maintenance-looking woman who Claudine knew must be at least as old as her, but was suspiciously wrinkle-free with very white teeth that made Claudine not want to smile and reveal her yellowed ones. Her wig was pinned into a French roll and her makeup was already done for the day. She sparkled with several jeweled rings, drop earrings, a necklace of beads and gold, and an expensive-looking watch. It seemed a lot of jewelry for a family breakfast at home. Claudine wondered if Chief's Wife was wearing all her jewelry at once for security reasons. She thought again of the knife, whether all these servants running around the place were the reason for weapons under mattresses.

The two women looked at each other like curiosities. No doubt, Chief's Wife thought Claudine's blouse and jeans too simple. But they were simple folk. There was no point trying to be otherwise.

Tonye's sisters, Abi and Tamara, were dressed up too in their "African clothes." And there were the boys, finally, in white outfits that matched Tonye's. How little they were. How precious. They seemed used to strangers hugging them, because they went to hug her without being asked and smiled, giving no sign that they understood the gravity of their situation.

"We welcome you to Nigeria," said Chief warmly. "We only wish the circumstances were better."

They ushered her to a seat at the long dining table beside Chief's Wife. The children sat opposite, with the sisters on either side of them and Tonye closest to his father, who was at the head of the table. Claudine had noticed a big engagement ring on the finger of the younger sister, who was her mother's mini-me—not in looks, exactly, but in the similar floor-length kaftan and Rapunzel-like wig that she wore, her flashy nails, bracelets, and fake lashes. Preening birds of a feather. The older sister, by contrast, had a more muted style. Claudine had a good feeling about her; she seemed genuine. Tonye, on the other hand, looked vacant. He was very well put together in a white tunic-and-trouser set, and said all the right things, but he seemed nothing like the gregarious guy in London who'd occupied most of the attention. He picked at his food and only spoke to the boys to correct their behavior.

Claudine asked Timi and Tari if they recognized her, knowing they couldn't possibly. But they quickly chimed, "Yes, auntie," after a look from Tonye, making everyone laugh. It broke the ice. The boys resumed pointing to what they wanted to eat on the table, which their aunts would get them. She watched the boys for signs of Nicole. They seemed well-behaved like she was, but perhaps it was the occasion. There was an array of food. The scrambled eggs and sausages, omelets with peppers, and fried plantain were familiar, but there were some other dishes Claudine didn't know, a platter of some sort of scrambled egg in a sauce, and chips that were bigger, fluffier, whiter than regular chips. "Yam chips and egg sauce," Chief's Wife explained. Standing behind the boys, Blessing, the one who had called her to breakfast, reached now and then to serve them more food, rearrange their napkins, or wipe them clean. She seemed pleasant enough. Claudine wondered what she might know about Nicole's sleeping arrangements and why. It didn't seem like you could keep much secret when everyone lived on the same compound.

Claudine enjoyed the food. She'd never had yam chips and egg sauce before, but she liked the taste so much she thought about adding the yam chips to ackee and saltfish when she got back to London.

"How was your flight, dear?" asked Chief's Wife. The *dear* sounded condescending.

"It all went very well," said Claudine. "Tonye got me a very nice seat."

Chief nodded approvingly. "Well, you *are* family," he said. So far, so cordial.

They all ate. The boys finished their food, and Chief's Wife— Claudine wasn't sure if Tonye had mentioned her name—nodded to Blessing, who whisked them out of the dining room. She watched the boys disappear. It had meant so much to see them again. Her mind went back to the day Nicole told her she was moving to Nigeria with Tonye and their oldest child, still a baby in her arms. They had been sitting around the dining table, as they were doing now. Nicole had been fussing over the child. She said he was teething and wouldn't go to anyone else. He seemed fine to her. Nicole and Tonye passed the child back and forth like pass the parcel. She'd said it as if she were moving to Coventry: "Yeah, we're moving to Nigeria." As if it were just a train journey away. And even that would've been a shock. Claudine had thought they'd come round for Sunday dinner, the family all together. She had been hoping to see more of Nicole once she had the baby. It might bring them closer. They could forget the past—all those misunderstandings—and start again. She had been looking forward to being a sort of grandmother. She'd even picked out a name for Nicole's children to call her, Didi. Embarrassing thinking about it now. Nicole had delivered the news with a smile that she expected to be reciprocated, as if Claudine should be happy for her. She would have help, she said. They would have a better lifestyle, better weather. She wouldn't have to work. Tonye would be working on the family business, whatever that meant. Nicole had never said what he did. The whole while she was speaking, Claudine was horrified. It felt like a very deliberate gut punch. But all she said was, "Nigeria? That will be nice." What else could she say with Tonye sitting right next to her? A few weeks later, sooner than she'd anticipated, they were gone—their flat emptied, the car sold. She'd put on a brave face about it afterward for so long she believed it herself, that it was for the best for everyone. She'd stopped thinking about it, really. You have to get on with things, or things will get on without you.

The lighthearted mood seemed to leave with the boys. It was almost as if the sun outside had dipped, and even the chair Claudine was sitting on felt a little harder.

Chief cleared his throat, and everyone quieted. "We want you to know how anxious we all are," he said.

"It's a lot to take in," Chief's Wife added. "She was a daughter to us. We have a saying, 'Iyàwó, our wife.' She was *our* wife, and our hearts are very broken." As she said this, she rolled her big rings over and over.

"So you think she's dead and not just missing?" Claudine asked.

"Oh, did I say 'was'?" said Chief's Wife, looking mortified. "I didn't mean that."

"We are looking for answers," said Chief with a cross glance at his wife. "I'm sure Tonye's explained—the police have been making enquiries."

"But are they doing enough?" Claudine asked.

Chief looked at Tonye, who sat up and said, "Remember, auntie, I said it takes time."

"You should know in advance," Chief interjected, "the police here are not as they are in the UK. But we have prayer on our side. We are a nation of prayer warriors. We do it well."

"I'd like to know what exactly is going on with their investigation," said Claudine, ignoring his attempt at humor.

"But give them a chance to do their work." Chief looked around the table, and everyone nodded dutifully. The engaged sister looked at her phone, and the older one looked at her plate. It surprised Claudine that Chief's Wife had fingers left from all the ring-twisting she was doing.

"But what have they discovered? How many hospitals have been checked? How many are left? Who has been interviewed? Has the boat driver been arrested?"

"They're taking cautious steps," said Chief.

"Isn't there anything we can do ourselves? We could talk to people, surely."

Chief glanced at Tonye, but Tonye said nothing. "What do you have in mind?" he asked Claudine.

"Talk to people, get out there—you know, raise the alarm."

Chief's Wife shifted in her seat, which irked Claudine.

"It's not that simple," said Chief. "We don't want a media feeding frenzy. We are trying to keep a sense of normality for the children."

"Isn't it better to keep matters to ourselves?" added Chief's Wife.

"That's strange. Usually, if someone goes missing, the first thing you do is raise the alarm, go public, stick photos to trees. Get people out to help look for the person."

Chief was incredulous. "Stick photos to trees?" he echoed.

"Why not?" asked Claudine. She cautioned herself to simmer down. She could feel herself getting hot.

Tonye and his father looked at each other.

"Auntie, let's talk about things properly a bit later," Tonye said. "I can tell you where we are on things." He stood. "I have a meeting now, but you can find me in my office. Anyone can show you where it is."

He kissed his father and mother and then left the room.

Chief leaned forward. "We have taken every care of Nicole since she moved here. She has wanted for nothing. She is the mother of our grandsons. If she did nothing else, just for that, we are eternally grateful to her. There would always be a place in our hearts for her."

"But don't you see what you've done?" argued Claudine. "You've just assumed she's dead when not one person saw her drown. And there's no body."

"But—" began Chief's Wife. Chief interrupted her with a loud harrumph.

"No, no, you're right. We *don't* know, and it's good that you're here. You can see for yourself, ask questions. Now"—Chief also stood up, his chair shuddering back—"I also have a meeting. We can talk again later," he said unconvincingly, then hurried out of the dining room.

"Anyone else have a meeting?" Claudine asked. Only Chief's Wife and Tonye's two sisters remained at the table. There was an uncomfortable silence.

"Can I show you around the compound while Tonye has his meeting?" asked Chief's Wife. "Just so you will know where everything is. It's a big place."

"But, Mum," the younger daughter said, looking up in dismay. "What about the tailor's for my—" Chief's Wife gave Tamara a silencing look. Tamara sulked and folded her arms. "You agreed!"

"I'll come with you to the tailor's, Tamara," said the older sister with a sigh.

"Fine," snapped Tamara.

Chief's Wife's silk kaftan flounced as she walked Claudine to the window and slid it across, stepping out onto the patio that extended from the house out to the lawn.

———

IT WAS already hot outside even though it was still early and the sun was hidden on the other side of the house.

As they crossed onto the lawn, something buzzed past Claudine. A dragonfly. Shimmering green.

"You have a wonderful house," Claudine said to break the silence.

"Thank you," said Chief's Wife. She smiled and took in a breath of fresh air.

The swimming pool was to their right, a pool boy dragging a net on a large pole through the water. When he saw them he shouted a loud greeting and dropped to one knee. Chief's Wife gave a little wave the way royalty might do.

"How long have you lived here?" asked Claudine.

"We built the house when the children were younger. They grew up here. The house was constructed by Italian builders. And you see, around the side, the new extension." She pointed to the part of the house where Claudine was staying. "We couldn't get it quite the same. Local builders don't have the same finish."

She seemed to be leading Claudine toward the water, presumably the draw of this property. From the balcony, the lagoon had looked peaceful, idyllic, a steely-blue color that made you think about going for a swim; but close up, the water was rather muddy with a reddish sheen on the edge of the waves and all manner of trash bobbing around in it.

"This is the Lagos Lagoon," said Chief's Wife. "Where we are here is the Commodore's Channel."

"Are those beaches inhabited?" asked Claudine, pointing across the water.

"Some of them," Chief's Wife said. "Villagers, fishermen, local tribes only."

A foghorn boomed as a cargo ship promenaded by, heading out to sea.

"Is it around here that Nicole disappeared?"

"Ah, no. That was closer to Ikoyi," she said, gesturing along the lagoon to the right. "Victoria Island, Ikoyi, and Lekki together are the islands. Then you have the mainland. The lagoon goes far, all the way to Ogun State."

Claudine looked at the trash floating in the water. "What do you think could have happened?"

Chief's Wife merely shook her head.

"Was she having any problems before this?" Claudine persisted.

"Problems like what?" asked Chief's Wife impatiently.

"Was she happy?"

"Of course she was happy." Chief's Wife seemed personally offended by the question. "Why would she not be happy? Who would not be happy?" *With all this* was unsaid. The house, the husband, the money, the children, the view. All the boxes ticked. *Defensive,* thought Claudine.

Chief's Wife turned back toward the house. Claudine wondered what Chief's Wife might say if she knew about the knife. Her reaction could be interesting. But no, she decided against it. Better to speak to the police first. Claudine didn't trust her. She couldn't trust anyone for now.

They were interrupted by a loud sob. They turned. From underneath a large tree—Claudine recognized it immediately from her childhood days in Jamaica as a mango tree, a strong and mature one with trademark dense spearhead leaves—a man rushed out. It was the driver who had picked her up from the airport. His shirt was too big; she saw such things immediately after years helping people try on clothes. It hung off his shoulders, drowning him, poor man. It sounded like he was drowning in life too. He didn't seem to see them, hurrying away around the side of the house.

Chief's Wife laughed in surprise as he disappeared around the house, her drawn-on eyebrows raised. "Funny little man. That's Bilal. He drives the children."

"He looked upset."

Chief's Wife again said nothing and kept moving across the lawn.

"Here are the Boys' Quarters," Chief's Wife explained as they passed a modest two-story building like a small apartment complex. "If you're looking for the staff, they might be in there."

"Boys' Quarters?"

Chief's Wife laughed. "Servants' quarters. We still follow the British way there." It seemed disrespectful to Claudine even if it was "the British way." How were you calling grown men and women "boys" like that? But it wasn't her business.

Outside, women bobbed as they passed by. "Good morning, madam," they chorused, to which Chief's Wife waved benevolently. Women were hanging their washing. One carried a bucket on her head. A child peeped from behind a wall. He looked about Timi's age, wearing flip-flops and briefs. They turned around at the front of the house. The security guards bowed and they exchanged waves. Claudine wondered if she was supposed to have bowed too. They reached the front door, which was much more impressive in the daytime. On either side of the pillars stood outsize terra-cotta clay pots that three men would struggle to lift. There were even orchids in the corners. Not wild, but they were pretty. It was all very pretty.

Chief's Wife paused in front of the heavy entrance door. "I trust in God," she said, making the sign of a cross on her bosom. "What He wants us to know, He shall reveal it to us."

"Everybody waiting on God," said Claudine, a little more pointedly than she'd intended.

Chief's Wife looked startled, as if she wasn't used to being spoken to like that. The door magically opened, and a servant stood at attention. She directed him—Emmanuel—to take Claudine to Tonye, and Claudine thanked her for the tour.

Tonye was in a suite with four suited staff at desks with computers and a separate office at the end for him. They didn't pay her much attention. Tonye rose from behind the computer at his desk when she entered his office.

"Oh, auntie," he said, ushering her in. She sat in the chair opposite his desk. "Do you have everything you need?"

"There was something I wanted to ask you about," she said. "Something happened last night."

"Yes, let's talk," he said, shuffling papers away into the cabinet behind him and closing it. "I also wanted to go over some things with you for your stay. Samuel, my houseboy, is the one who will prepare any meals for you or run errands."

*House*boy? Claudine thought. "I'm pretty self-sufficient. Just point me to a stove and a pot."

He opened a drawer and took out an old phone and a large wad of Nigerian cash. "This phone needs charging, but you can use this for now. It has a SIM card in it already. You'll need it for the internet and to call locally. This money should be enough for anything you need, but if you want to change pounds, the closest place to change your money is the Eko Hotel car park. Bilal can take you there or anywhere else you need to go. He will make sure you get the right rate, but those mallams are okay. They shouldn't cheat you."

She thanked him but politely refused the cash. "I'll change my own. And I can walk and catch buses."

"This isn't a walk-around city," he insisted.

"It looked like a lot of people were walking, driving in from the airport."

"Those people—" He looked like he was going to explain but then changed his mind. "It's safer this way. Especially if you're new to this. Best not to go walking or jumping on buses and talking to people."

"But I—"

"Please, auntie. Just use Bilal for all your needs." He softened the plea with a smile.

"Fine, but this afternoon or tomorrow, I want to go to where she was supposed to have gotten off the boat. Your mother said it's in Ikoyi? Did I say that right?"

He nodded.

"I want to go and see the police too," she continued. "Find out what investigations they've done."

Tonye blinked rapidly. "Wow—look, we need to think about this. We can't have you talking, us talking, the police talking. It doesn't make sense. It's just going to confuse people. We are handling everything."

"Well, I am a little confused about what's happening. You have no new information. You haven't even told me anything about these friends Nicole was with."

"It's more complicated than you think." Tonye took a deep breath. "Those friends Nicole was involved with were bad news. Dangerous people."

That was a shock. She wasn't expecting to hear something like that. But it didn't explain the knife.

"It doesn't matter to me anymore," he said, taking her silence for agreement. "We can't dwell on that now. I just want to find her so we can move on." He looked for her assent. "Tomorrow I will arrange for you to speak to the police, but in the meantime, please do not go around asking questions." She nodded, and he relaxed. "So, what happened last night? I hope there weren't any mosquitos in the room."

"No mosquitos." She decided then and there not to tell him about the knife yet. She would speak to the police first. "But I kept hearing this strange chugging noise all night."

"Oh, that's the generator," he explained. "When the power goes out, the generator comes on. I hope it didn't disturb you too much."

"No. I slept well," Claudine lied.

"That's good to hear," he said, smiling like they were back on the same page. Claudine smiled back, but she felt light-headed, as if she didn't know quite what was real anymore.

"I'm going to the room to rest," she said, getting to her feet. She needed a moment to herself, to regroup.

"Yes, you've come a long way," Tonye said soothingly.

Outside in the passage, Claudine clasped her arms, rubbed them vigorously. Dread washed over her. She hoped the meeting with the police would happen as promised. She wanted to trust Tonye, to believe in this marriage, because if she didn't, she wasn't sure what she might do next.

CHAPTER SEVEN

NICOLE
Before

CROSSING BONNY Camp Bridge so early on a Sunday, Nicole found Lagos deliciously quiet except for the solitary caw of a bird passing overhead. No honking of cars, no bus drivers quarreling with passengers at bus stops, no okadas zinging by, not even a sputtering keke maruwa. They passed the stadium and the police headquarters, seeing only a man crumpled in a huddle of rags on the Awolowo Road sidewalk.

The gates of the Ikoyi Boat Club groaned open, the security checked them off the guest list, and Bilal drove into the car park where Nicole dismounted, taking her huge tote bag from him.

When Tonye was a child, the family had had a boat and were members of the club. It had been one of the first things Nicole asked about after seeing the jetty at the rear of the compound—whether they had a boat. "Boats are a waste of money," Mother-in-Law had said airily. "You never use them as much as you think you will." But Nicole didn't buy that, having seen old videos that Tonye had shown her of them all waving gaily from a motorboat manned by a much-younger Chief. Nicole had visited the boat club a few times. It was also an event center for fairs, parties, and so on. Some of the Nigerwives were members and invited the boys for playdates. It had a decent playground. It was a nice place to enjoy a drink on the boardwalk, with the boats coming and going, to see and be seen and then, of course, gist about it all.

She signed in at the wood-paneled reception, seeing the names of venerable members engraved on a huge plaque behind the desk. The men at reception smiled approvingly and indicated the café, beyond which she could get to the jetty. She followed the smell of baked bread and coffee into the café, which was empty except for the waitress and Wale Coker Williams, Kemi's ex, lounging in the archway that led outside to the boats, keeping his body inside but craning his neck to spy on whoever was out there. He straightened up when he saw her. He was beautifully dressed as usual, in a crisp, mint-green trad with a silver, mint, and bronze fila perched atop his closely shaven head. He greeted her with an air hug.

"Nice day for a boat ride," he said, with some sourness, it seemed to Nicole. She guessed he must have already seen Kemi.

"How are you, Wale?" said Nicole. "Are you going on a boat too?"

"Me? No. I just like the breakfast here." He pulled out a chair from one of the tables and sat down as if to make the point, then preened himself in the stainless-steel napkin box on the table. "I went to church earlier—I like to get it out of the way." He caught himself glancing toward the archway leading to the boardwalk again and turned back to Nicole awkwardly. "So whose boat is that?" he asked with a frown.

Nicole almost laughed. "Yohanna Ishaku's. Do you know him?"

"No. I'm assuming that's a son of A. J. Ishaku?" Before he could ask another question, the phone in his pocket beeped. He took it out to look at it. Then he jerked his thumb toward the boardwalk. "I think your guys are ready to leave," he said. "They were already loading when you walked in."

"Oh, really?" As she went to look, there was an exclamation in a Scandinavian accent, and Nicole turned to see Astrid enter the café in a froufrou summer dress. She threw herself on Wale with an unnecessary amount of PDA before noticing Nicole.

"Oh, wow. Nicole, isn't it?"

They hugged lightly.

"You two know each other?" Wale looked so horrified Nicole laughed out loud.

"Yes, we're both Nigerwives. Right, Astrid?"

"Almost," Astrid said with a wink at Wale, who looked several shades paler. "Can you believe it? We just met yesterday at the Nigerwives meeting I told you about," she gushed. Nicole understood now why he was trying to rush her along. Probably he thought there wouldn't be anyone he knew at the boat club on a Sunday morning. It wasn't a typical brunch spot. But he should have known better. As much as Lagos was a megacity, living on the islands was like living in a village. There was always someone watching.

Nicole promised again to meet with Astrid, although now even less convincingly. Things were getting weird. She said good-bye and headed out onto the boardwalk, wondering how Kemi would feel about Wale's new girlfriend.

A small group clustered around a white motorboat with pink trim that sparkled on the bank, ready to be pushed into the water. It looked brand-new, fitted with cream leather board seats running along either side plus a love seat at the front. Kemi was in jean shorts and a Middle Eastern–style tunic top. She waved Nicole over excitedly and introduced her to everyone: Yohanna, whom she recognized from the blurry photo, and another man both looked like Northerners, tall with slimmer noses. There were also two girls Nicole had never met. Everyone was friendly but muted, as if they were nursing hangovers, which they probably were if they'd been out on the town all night with Kemi.

WITH THE boat finally bobbing in the water, they walked along the wooden pier and were helped in. Life jackets were passed around—snazzy new ones, not the useless foam pallets you got on the Tarkwa Bay Ferry. Yohanna was at the helm. He was a large man, more so than the photo conveyed. Better-looking in person, preppy in a polo shirt and boating shorts, perhaps even a little *hot*, as Kemi said. His huge hands straddled the wheel. The motor churned to life, and they cut into the flip-flapping water through the part of the lagoon called Five Cowries Creek, which separated Lagos Island and Ikoyi from Victoria Island, then passed under the Falomo Bridge, where waves echoed with the hollow, tinny rumblings of a steel band.

Once on the water, the group spread about the boat like butter melting under the sky's pearlescence. The sun might not be out, a good thing, but it still hurt to look up, and Nicole could feel her skin getting hot. She put on a wide-brimmed hat.

They passed the yachts of Dangote, Africa's richest man, and Otedola, an ordinary billionaire, moored along Walter Carrington Crescent where the embassies were, both sleek and monochrome like a Bond villain's, and then the Federal Palace Hotel and the remaining waterfront properties. The Victoria Island shoreline receded along with Nicole's anxieties, and a deep breath worked its way up and out of her.

She forgot sometimes how much she liked the water. It made her a child again. Water, like a spray of glitter. Laughter cascading around her. Screaming along with the other children as the cold splashes hit their bare legs and arms. Claudine anxiously standing on the edge of the paddling pool at Lewisham Park with a towel, vainly reminding her not to get her hair wet each time she came close. Wading through the water in her knickers and vest. Feeling like she was in an ocean, although she was barely knee-deep. She always made friends with other kids there. Sometimes her cousins came too. They would end up chasing each other around the pool. Maybe someone had brought a ball and they tossed it to and fro. Or water pistols. They enjoyed wetting each other up, their shrieks audible from outer space.

And afterward, Claudine would wrap her in the fluffy towel and they would walk home up the hill. Talking about life. Their favorite biscuits. She liked the chocolate fingers and iced rings; Claudine preferred the bourbon and custard creams. Why they couldn't get a dog—the idea of it being inside the house made Claudine shudder. What a tooth fairy was. Claudine didn't understand the concept. "That is a white people thing," she said. "It's not real. Just like Santa." "Santa my back foot!" she'd say whenever Nicole brought him up. They both liked the soft-serve spiral with a Flake in the cone and strawberry or chocolate sauce twirled around. The bliss of eating the ice cream quickly before the cone got too soft and ice cream started leaking out the bottom. Getting home a sticky mess of syrup and chocolate and straight into the bath.

As the boat passed through a graveyard of rusted old ship carcasses by Tin Can Island, dredgers and such lying on their sides like beached whales, the conversation waned in a natural moment of silence for these forgotten wrecks. On the island itself, stacked-up red and blue containers and cylindrical oil tanks towered above them tall as skyscrapers. Nicole pondered whether to tell Kemi about her encounter with Wale and his belle du jour. She decided against it. Kemi got jealous easily. Such news could ruin her day, and then everyone else's.

They turned into the brown-green waters of the Badagry Creeks, fringed by overhanging trees and shallow mangroves. Here and there, bushes gave way to village areas where they could see women with babies tied onto their backs, hanging washing on lines strung between wooden cabins on stilts over the water. The smoky smell of fish carried on the breeze. There were also a few resorts visible from the lagoon, cleared land with hotels and swimming pools. Nicole had once met a Nigerwife who had fallen in love with a musician from one of these island villages and had a child with him. Quite a romantic story. She lived in London but often came to stay there, preferring the rural experience to the city existence of the other Nigerwives, whom she appeared to find odd. These creeks led all the way to the Benin Republic, past the old slave port of Badagry, where, during the time of the transatlantic slave trade, people were kept prisoner, to be sold to the Portuguese, then later to other Europeans, then to Americans, and occasionally even to Africans who had survived enslavement abroad and returned to buy their own people. Some original Brazilian barracoons were still standing. She had visited them a few times, finding them and the nearby museums fascinating. They were not visually imposing, quite the opposite: single-story buildings housing the grisly souvenirs of slavery; a courtyard of cells where enslaved people were kept—perhaps forty at a time until the slave ships arrived to transport them to the labor camps across the Atlantic. "Thirty percent died before the ships came," a guide had told her once. For the price of a Starbucks coffee, you could peer into the tiny pens, standing room only. You could try to lift the chains used to restrain people, even children. There were some of the expected but still shocking prints of the torture implements—metal guards across the mouth to stop prisoners from talking or eating; people hanging from trees disemboweled; diagrams of the Middle Passage, showing how the Africans were packed onto the slave ships, head to toe like sardines. She had seen a lot of those pictures before, online or in books. A stunning lack of protocol meant you could actually finger the now-faded ceremonial umbrellas and other items that were traded for human currency. In glass cabinets were glass bottles, ornate vases, cowrie shells, and the guide would tell you how much. Forty slaves for the umbrella. Twenty-five for an imported wooden table, six for a bottle of rum. Fifteen for a rifle, and so on, with children thrown in as a bonus. Nicole had taken the rickety canoe across the channel of water between the mainland and the islet of Gberefu, which translated as "take them and go," a two-mile-long stretch of sandy scrub and wild bush down to the Atlantic. This was their point of no return, the end of life as they had known it, the people that they were, but the beginning of a new identity and heritage. This was where her story as a British Afro-Caribbean began.

Each time she went, she noticed something different, she changed her mind, she felt a rush of emotions that lingered long after she had left. Now when she saw the big cargo ships pass through the lagoon, Nicole always wondered if Mummy's great-great-grandmother or -grandfather might have been cargo on a ship heading out to the Atlantic.

"But it was just money," Tonye loved to remind her. "It wasn't personal. *We* sold the slaves to them. We had slaves too, in Africa. Before and after." He said it matter-of-factly because he had never been to Badagry, had learned nothing about chattel slavery or even prior local practices of enslavement. It wasn't personal because none of his ancestors had been trafficked as slaves, so gray eyes and light skin were simply an advantage in his mind, not a reminder that many ancestors were raped or bred like animals. Tonye was a pragmatist and a realist, not a historian or psychologist; actually, it made things easier that he lived in the here and now and didn't care too much for the past. The father she had no knowledge of, her late mother, the childhood she didn't like to talk about were her business, not his. He didn't like to be asked questions either, so it worked for them both. And really, what use was knowing?

Yohanna, at the wheel of the boat, made a funny face at Nicole. He stuck out his tongue and rolled it around his lips. Wait, was he . . . flirting?

Nicole looked for Kemi to rescue her, but Kemi was chatting up a storm with the two girls, one of them a successful Instagram influencer with a hundred thousand followers who also owned a hairdressing salon in Lagos and distributed wigs. She looked very different from her heavily filtered Instagram posts, but she was fun and down-to-earth and talked shop with Kemi while holding on to her Chaka Khan wig, as though the tugging wind might snatch it off at any moment and fling it across the waves. The other girl, who sported a grade-one platinum afro, worked for a drinks conglomerate and did not stop talking about all the Afrobeat stars she knew personally. Nicole felt a little out of her depth with such hard-nosed career girls. Instagram was where she occasionally posted selfies and photos of parties and holidays. She didn't get many followers, unsurprisingly. Her last post was from Timi's fifth birthday party back in January. If it had gotten over ten likes, she would be surprised. Anyway, the din of the motor and the rushing wind drowned out their conversation too much to join in. Nicole's own hair whipped savagely around her face in thick strands damp with sea spray.

The other man was at the front of the boat, sitting back against the seat with his polished limbs extended, sunglasses warding off the spray, head still as though he was sleeping.

Her stomach grouched. She hoped there was going to be food. She hadn't had time to make anything because she kept putting off asking Tonye about the beach until it got late, just after the children had gone to bed—and they always went to bed late on Saturday nights because there was no Blessing to deal with them, so they ran the hallways like street urchins, shooting each other across marble floors with Nerf guns, indifferent to Mother-in-Law's antique glass beads or the hallowed portrait of Chief's mother, who'd died in the war.

She'd put it off until she couldn't anymore, and just told him in a mangled rush that she was going to the beach with Kemi's friends. She'd emphasized that it was Yohanna Ishaku's beach house, expecting a long interrogation: *Ishaku who? Beach house where? Who else is going? Why is Kemi dragging you, a married woman?* But although Tonye had looked alarmed and a little hurt, he'd said nothing. Strangely, it had pleased her momentarily, like striking him with the hog-tie packaging all over again, and seeing the bright-red bulb of blood suddenly bloom above his eye. Before Tonye spun on his heel and stomped out, crushing foam Nerf bullets underfoot, his face was the bright-red bulb, and the tongue in her licked its saltiness and wanted more.

THE MOTOR suddenly cut off, causing the boat to rock from side to side like a cradle. Then the engine was eased on again gently as they approached a simple wooden jetty. People were already waiting for them: men, women, and a few children of varying ages all staring at them as if waiting for celebrities to get out of a limo. As they drew closer, men came to rope the boat to the posts and carry out the bags. The passengers were helped up onto dry land and the children mingled among them, competing to carry anything they could.

The group trudged up a raggedy sandy path lined with stones, tall grasses, and rough bushes on either side. They wound their way up the shore until they reached a white house. The villagers carried their bags inside.

The beach house was minimalist in style, its simple white stucco exterior reminiscent of a Mediterranean villa. From within, a two-hundred-meter view opened out over the Atlantic as far as the eye could see. A patio of white poured concrete flowed from the house toward a rippling blue swimming pool, beyond which sand like milky coffee descended to the shore. She spotted a barbecue grill by the fence, and, thankfully, it looked like the locals were already firing it up. So there *must* be food. Farther down the property was a wooden cabana, slightly to the side so as not to break the view. The fence ran along both sides of the rectangular lot, separating the property from a dark-wood beach house to the left that towered above them, and a more modest one to the right, both of which seemed empty today.

Folded white towels were already set out for their convenience on the edge of the pool and a large stand-alone speaker was wheeled out. Yohanna connected his Bluetooth to the speaker while the women sat down at the long teak dining table and the other guy directed the staff where to set up the cooler and which food to place on the table and which to take to the grill just to the right of the house. Yohanna took a few bottles of champagne from the cooler, then grabbed some plastic cups. He indicated the Nectar Rosé should be opened. Fruit, potato chips, boxes of small chops, and tubs of rice and other snacks were laid out. American pop music soon blared out over the patio. Kemi filled some glasses and passed them around.

Looking out to the dark-blue sea and then up at the seamless sky, listening to American music and sipping on champagne at a teak table surrounded by white stucco walls, Nicole felt she could be anywhere in the world right then. Miami, Portugal, Bali, South Africa, St. Tropez, the Amalfi coast. Relaxed and happy, she took off her cover-up and headed to the pool.

As she climbed down the ladder, the chilly water licked at her thighs, making her shiver, and entered her crevices like icy fingers until it reached her chest, where she acclimatized. Nicole eased herself fully into the water, where Kemi was already splashing about in a tiny leopard-print bikini. Tari was now three, and without too much trouble, Nicole had pretty much regained her slim waist, but now she felt slightly self-conscious about the tiger stretch marks running down her thighs and conversely embarrassed about the prudish black swimming shorts and full-length vest she was wearing.

"His father owns that beach house there," whispered Kemi, pointing to the tall dark-wood house on the left as Nicole shuddered next to her. "The right I think is owned by his sister and her husband."

"And where does the money come from?" Nicole asked. "I guess generals always get rich one way or another."

"Oh, he wasn't an ordinary general," said Kemi. "He had a big role in the civil war and got several oil blocks."

"Hold that pose, ladies." The man who'd been at the front of the boat waded toward them, snapping away with his phone in a waterproof case. He'd taken off his T-shirt and his dark torso glowed against the water.

"I'm not ready, Elias," whined Kemi. He waited. Kemi and Nicole did a few different poses for fun.

"Gorgeous," he said, and showed them a photo.

The candid aspect of the picture surprised Nicole. She'd gotten used to more formal snaps in Lagos, with overdone hair and lots of makeup. But this one caught her off guard.

"Are you a photographer?" she asked.

He laughed. "Sort of. I just enjoy taking photos of interesting people and things. I have a whole Instagram account dedicated to it."

"Ooh," Nicole said. "Let's see it."

As he showed her some photos on his phone, Kemi caught sight of Yohanna sitting at the table, talking animatedly to the other two women, and quickly got out of the water, slipping on her flip-flops and hurrying over, not even bothering to towel away the glistening drops all over her body. Elias's pictures were of landscapes and intimate moments. Friends, animals at close quarters, pictures of himself and Yohanna, and candid shots of unsuspecting strangers. The silhouette of a man leaning over his oar on the water, the sun caught in a small boy's eyes as he danced at a street party.

"Let's do some more photos?" he said.

"Gosh, no—I'm not that interesting," Nicole said.

"You're joking. I could shoot you all day." He stared at her for a brief moment, then continued, "But let's take a break. I smell grilled chicken."

They sat around a rectangular wooden table on the veranda of the beach house. The pool was now still but for the filter's ripples. Yohanna's village staff had brought the grilled meats from the barbecue to the table. They all happily dug into the food and drinks. Then it was the usual "men are from Mars, women are from Venus" discussion, with Kemi dominating.

At times, Nicole caught Yohanna's eyes on her in a way she found intrusive. They seemed to be measuring, appraising her the way Tonye did a prospective polo pony. But she couldn't help imagining his large hands circling her waist, grabbing her thighs. She rose from her chair. "I think I'll take a walk down to the ocean before I forget."

"Well, why don't we get the quads out?" suggested Elias. He said a few words in Hausa to Yohanna, who nodded. They both walked around to the front of the house; a few minutes later, they roared around the back on gleaming quad bikes.

Kemi and the other girls clambered on behind Yohanna, and they sped off across the beach, the girls shrieking.

"Hop on," Elias called out to Nicole. She climbed on behind him. He revved up, and they bumped along the beach, clearing the two-hundred-meter walk down to the ocean in seconds. Instead of following Yohanna, he turned right, and they were alone.

The sun never really came out to play. A golden skein stretched across the sky like a pair of nylon tights. The sun was dimly visible behind it, a blurred disk. They sped along the shoreline, past the other beach houses. Some were recently built glass-and-concrete structures, like Yohanna's, while others were brick and wood. Some were falling into disrepair. Most were empty but for a lazy dog or a caretaker stretched out behind the fence. Nicole would have loved to have a beach house like these to go to during the weekends. Of course, that was never going to happen with Tonye's dislike of the sea.

It was fairly quiet until they reached Pop Beach, a beach club Nicole had visited before. A yoga workshop was under way. Elias stopped outside to greet some of the participants. Nicole was suddenly nervous, recognizing a few there and realizing how sitting behind Elias—holding on to his waist—might look.

They moved off again toward a crop of thoughtfully planted umbrella trees close to the water, their dark-green leaves making bowl-shaped shadows on the sand.

"These trees are stunning, eh," said Elias. "I should do some pictures here." He started rapidly taking pictures of the ocean and the vista of the beach houses behind them.

Nicole sat on the sand under the shade of a tree, watching his athletic silhouette. Although the beach was deserted now in both directions, she felt safe with him.

"You know, your eyes are the strangest color." Elias was back and focusing his phone on her. He wielded it as if it were a Nikon and clicked away. "Are they gray?"

Nicole just smiled. If she had a pound for every time someone asked her that . . .

"Sorry, you probably get that a lot. I just don't think I've ever seen gray eyes before," he said, pausing his shoot. "And definitely not in a Black person. Are you mixed-race?"

Nicole shook her head. "Just a mixed-up family from slavery."

"Your eyes look just like the ocean behind you right now." Elias leaned toward her, eyes locked onto hers. His were soft dark pools fringed with long lashes. He had a tiny scar on the bridge of his nose. Nicole reached out and touched it.

"Childhood battle wound," he said, eyes still on her. "I was a little wild."

"Let me see my pictures," she said, reaching for the phone. But he held it out of reach.

"Not now. I have a lot of pictures. Let me play with them and I'll send them to you. What's your number?" He sank onto the sand beside her.

Nicole's voice shook very slightly with nervousness as she told him. The other girls had been exchanging numbers nonstop, but she had not given her number to anyone in this way since she had started dating Tonye. Still, it was just for the photos, nothing more.

Elias propped himself up on one elbow and started to sing in Hausa. He had a dramatic voice, baritone-deep, not ambitious in its vocal gymnastics but confident and rich with emotion. She understood not a word.

He read her mind. "His mother rejected the lady he loves and harasses her, but over time the girl still respects the mother, so the mother finally accepts her as a daughter-in-law."

"Oh, how kind," said Nicole sarcastically.

Elias laughed. "That's how it is here."

"I know. I'm always being harassed by my mother-in-law," said Nicole.

"She wanted her son to marry a Nigerian girl she could manage?" Elias smiled. "Well, they all do."

"She can have him back," said Nicole.

Elias looked at her curiously, a little intensely, then said, "You are not enjoying being the big madam gracing society magazines and telling others what to do?"

Nicole stirred, noticing that the sky was darkening.

"What time is it?" she asked.

"Oh, Jesu," said Elias. He reached out an arm and pulled her up. "We'd better go."

Back at the beach house, it was safe to say that Yohanna was in a fury at their prolonged disappearance. The food and drinks had been packed up. How much time had passed? It seemed like only minutes on the beach with Elias. Yohanna barked in Hausa at Elias, who replied with what sounded like a yelp and went into hyperdrive, shouting at staff to get their things back to the boat.

Yohanna was left standing near Nicole. "I was about to leave you two here," he said, glaring at Nicole until Kemi came over and put her arms around his waist. "Yo-Yo, let's just leave it and go." Then he grabbed his things and they all hurried to the boat.

Even as they loaded up, the sky was bluing, shadowing. By the time they were back at the boat club, the water was black as squid ink.

CHAPTER EIGHT

CLAUDINE
After

WHERE'VE YOU been these past three days, Claud?" Penny demanded. "I thought Boko Haram had gotten you too. I've been watching the news thinking any minute now, they'll show your face. Claudine Roberts from Lewisham, kidnapped in Nigeria! Mummy said she's not paying your ransom, by the way."

Trust a Roberts to make a joke out of a crisis, thought Claudine. They never were funnier than when the sky was falling in. "I texted you to say I'd arrived safely," she said.

"Yes, but it don't beat a call."

It was good to hear Penny's voice. She'd rather have called with the news that, surprise, Nicole had been found, but it wasn't turning out to be so easy. Three days in and there was no sign of her, no updates. The police contact had been dodging her, and the family claimed not to know anything.

Claudine was speaking to Penny from the lawn. The mango tree seemed a good place from which to call. It was cool and dark within its branches, and the old plastic chair with a missing slat was still functional. The blushing mangoes were heavy around her. Some were wrapped in newspaper to protect them until they were ready to be picked. A few gnarled rejects lay on the grass. It almost felt like home. Miss Hortense's home in Jamaica. Claudine's pear tree back in London. She wondered if Nicole ever stood here. It seemed to be the only place in the garden where you could get complete shade and privacy. Claudine had been dying to talk to Penny for a while but didn't trust calling from inside the house, and it had rained on and off yesterday afternoon. Now she was far enough away not to be heard. No doors for someone to lurk behind. No rooms within rooms, or wondering who might be inside.

Penny filled her in on the family comings and goings. Mummy was behaving herself. Penny was giving Mummy her meds as she said she would. Two pills daily. One in the morning and one with her evening meal and she was fine. The London weather hadn't improved. It might as well be December as July, how cold and wet it was.

"My pear tree still there?" Claudine half-joked.

"Still here blocking all the light. When are you gonna call the people to chop it down?"

Claudine pictured the leaves pressed up against the window, the rust staining the leaves with bloodlike spatters. "No one's chopping down my pear tree," she said. "I mean it."

Claudine described Lagos as best she could. It had all gone smoothly so far, the flight, the stay at the house, meeting the Oruwaris again. The house was impressive, just like the photos. There was no sign of Nicole, and the family was very cagey about the whole thing, not wanting to make a fuss. She'd tried calling the police investigator repeatedly, but it had rung out each time. Her text messages had gone unacknowledged too. It was only once she'd gone to find Tonye working in his office and complained about being ignored that Tonye sent a text message to Mr. Ogunsanya, receiving a reply within seconds.

"He'll answer now," Tonye said, and returned to his laptop.

"How come he responded to you, just like that?" she asked.

"I mean, I called him not ten minutes ago. Most likely he didn't know your number." Tonye looked down again, squinting hard at whatever was on the screen.

"But I texted him too," she insisted. "I explained who I was and everything."

Tonye shrugged, started typing on his keyboard. "He's a busy man. Don't worry, he knows who you are now."

Claudine got up from the chair. Nothing about this felt right. "But—"

"Look," Tonye began crossly before catching himself. He stood up. "Auntie," he said in a gentler tone, "didn't I tell you it was better to let me handle things?" He ushered Claudine to the door of his office and made the prayer sign with his hands for her to leave. "He *will* answer your call now, auntie," he said, then shut the door.

She looked at the closed door for a second, wanting to fling it open again and give him a piece of her mind. But what good would that have done? As frustrated as she felt, he'd helped her thus far. He'd welcomed her into his home, and he seemed to be grieving, after a fashion.

"Ooh, I would've cussed him!" said Penny now. "What, is he Tony's personal detective?" Penny was speaking in heated whispers because she was at her NHS call center job. British accents could be heard in the background, and Claudine suddenly missed London with a pang.

"It's *Ton-YAY*, and that's what I'm wondering."

"Whatever, but yeah, you better talk to him."

"Well, of course I'm going to talk to him. I just wanted to see what you thought first."

"I don't think you should be there at all, Claud. God knows what they've done to Nicole—and now they've got you. Buy one, get one free."

"I'm here now," Claudine said firmly, "and I'm not leaving without answers."

"Just hurry up. I can't deal with *your* mother anymore. Today she accused me of hiding her false teeth."

They both laughed, and their laughter became long sighs. They didn't have words for the heaviness, but they could hear it in each other.

"I gotta go," Penny whispered, and abruptly hung up.

As Claudine walked back across the grass, raindrops started falling, big and heavy, though warm.

At least in between fruitless calls to Mr. Ogunsanya, Claudine had gotten to spend a few hours with the boys, enough to finally feel confident in saying each of their names out loud without mistakes. Now she was really getting to know Timi and Tari. Timi was the elder at five. Thoughtful and observant but with a lordly swagger, he was the dead stamp of his father. Tari was three, loud and lovable with cheeks that were still pudgy and big lashy eyes like Nicole's. They showed her their books and favorite toys. She'd helped Blessing tidy the big playroom they shared and sat with them to watch their cartoons. Claudine's arrival confused them initially because "Mummy isn't here, she's traveled." They understood Nicole had gone for a vacation, nothing more serious. "Are you going to wait for her?" asked Tari, which broke her heart. And Timi said little about it, she noticed. He was old enough to sense something was wrong. It seemed like she was the only one who'd noticed how intently he listened when grown-ups were talking.

Both boys had taken to Blessing like a mother. She could see that from the way they trusted her. Blessing did most things that a mother would. She was there when they woke up, brushed their teeth, dressed them, fed them, bathed them, and put them to bed. She organized their clothes into neat, color-coded folds on their closet shelves and cleaned their rooms thoroughly. The previous day, she'd helped Timi with his homework, and after Claudine had read them a bedtime story, Blessing tucked them in and kissed them good night. She was very sweet, never rough. Chatty, but careful. She told Claudine she was from a rural area far from Lagos and dreamed of having a clothes boutique in London. She was impressed upon hearing that Claudine worked in a big clothing store. When Claudine asked her about life in the compound, she was vague and positive. Everything was "fine." Her room in the Boys' Quarters, the other staff, Chief and his wife, Tonye, the school. Everything was "fine," "fine," "fine."

Tonye was not a particularly engaged dad, Claudine noticed. She got that it must be hard for him now, but she suspected he'd never been hands-on. It was the way Blessing didn't even wait for instructions from him and the boys never asked where Daddy was. Yesterday, he'd seemed to be in his office all day and then out all evening. He was probably avoiding Claudine too. Oh, sure, he'd been polite and all that, a perfect gentleman, as when she had originally met him. But there was something closed and off-putting about him. Who wanted to be stuck in a strange country with someone like that all the time? That would be a very lonely life.

Of course, her duties back in London had not gone away just because she had. Penny would still need daily counsel and reminders about Mummy's blood pressure medication, to put the rubbish out in time for collection day, to make sure Michael had passed through the house and at least laid eyes on Mummy.

Since the initial breakfast gathering, she had not seen the other family members again. She understood that her part of the house was Tonye's and Nicole's, that they had their own staff and operated like a separate household. The children went to "visit" next door, but no one came over. When she had gone to the main part of the house to speak to the butler, Emmanuel, and the cook, David, she'd felt like an intruder. Their chatter had ground to a halt as soon as she'd entered the kitchen. She could see they'd been warned not to tell her anything, not even what time of day it was, though they were very respectful clams.

Still, there were things she didn't need to be told. Something was going on in the compound. A lot of coming and going at the main house. From the upstairs hallway, she could hear the chatter back and forth, laughs, shouts, harried voices, the huge front door slamming, then opening. Cars beeping loudly to be let in at the gate. There had been men coming in with garments and boxes. She'd heard Chief's Wife quickly ushering this or that visitor into her private sitting room, and then shouting upstairs about this or that—often in a fast patois Samuel said was pidgin.

Samuel had prepared her food since she'd arrived. He was an interesting guy. From Benin, a migrant worker whose family was back home in the village. He talked nonstop. Not about the family—oh, then he knew nothing, of course—but he was happy to chat breeze about his customs and relatives, his superstitious beliefs, the things happening in Lagos. He had three girls and was hoping for a boy. He had a bit on the side in Lagos who sold cloth and gave him money, which made no sense to Claudine because he was short, fat, and balding and smelled of onions, in a city full of tall, handsome young men. She didn't think much of his cooking either. He had a vast repertoire of Western foods, or so he claimed: lasagna, potatoes gratin, shepherd's pie, cauliflower cheese. Obviously, Nicole still liked to eat a lot of Western food, but Claudine preferred the food Blessing made the children: jollof rice, local stews, soups. Yesterday Samuel had cooked her spaghetti Bolognese, and there was something funny-tasting in there that didn't seem to belong. The same with breakfast, something in the scrambled egg, like five-spice. She couldn't finish the spaghetti. She wouldn't ask him to cook again.

She missed the comfort of yellow ackee, saltfish, and peppers piled over boiled green banana; potato melting in spiced butter; the security of a thick slice of toasted hard-dough bread and a cup of ginger tea. The calming sensations of stirring, kneading, rubbing, grinding.

Eventually Claudine found a quiet moment to call Mr. Ogunsanya again. Now he answered immediately.

"Good evening, Mrs. Roberts. I've been expecting your call." His voice was polite and surprisingly friendly, given that he hadn't answered her calls or returned messages.

"Good evening. It's *Miss*. Is this Mr. Ogunsanya?"

"Yes, ma. Mr. Oruwari said you were trying to get hold of me."

"I've called and texted," she reproached. "You didn't answer."

"Sorry, ma, it's been very busy, and I did not know your number then."

"I explained who I was in the messages. Didn't you read them?"

"So sorry, I was not aware Mrs. Oruwari had family in Lagos." His voice had cooled slightly. He sounded more serious, like he was sitting up straight. Good.

"She does now."

After an awkward pause, he said, "My condolences for your loss. We are doing all we can to find out what has happened to your relative."

"Good, so what have you found out so far?"

She could hear Mr. Ogunsanya moistening his lips.

"We have reported her as a missing person for now. We have distributed the report with our various security agencies and are still gathering essential details."

"It's been over a week. What new details have you found?"

Mr. Ogunsanya cleared his throat. "On July sixth, a Sunday"—he sounded like he was reading from a script—"Mrs. Oruwari attended a beach trip with friends. She went late in the morning. She was de-livered back to the Ikoyi Boat Club that evening, and that seems to be the last sighting of her."

"But I knew all this already. Is there anything new?"

"So far, no, but it's an open investigation. We are still gathering information."

"Have you finished checking the hospitals?"

"We searched the main ones, but found nothing."

"How many have you checked? Tonye said there were a lot to contact!"

"Please, ma," he said. "This no be small work."

"Why? Don't you have proper resources?"

"Ah-ah," he exclaimed, sounding affronted. "It is not a question of resources. We follow the same procedures as in the UK, I assure you. Such things take time. Until we have checked the hospitals thor-oughly, we cannot make further investigations. You understand?"

"Why don't you just drag the lagoon?" asked Claudine.

"Impossible," Mr. Ogunsanya said, as if she'd asked him to go to Mars. "It is too large to drag. These riverine areas stretch from the

Atlantic to Ogun State and even Benin Republic. We are talking fifty kilometers. In any case, since we know she came down at the boat club, there's no need."

"But did anyone actually see her at the boat club?"

He hesitated as if on the verge of saying something but then fell quiet.

"So how can you say—" Claudine broke off. She took a breath. She didn't want to lose it.

"We have word that is what took place."

"Whose word?"

"Ma, I cannot reveal, but I can assure you—"

"So what could have happened when she got to the boat club?" interrupted Claudine, finding him maddening.

"Criminal elements roam the water: smugglers, vandals, bandits. They look for soft targets, people on the water, after dark especially—" He sounded back on script again, rehearsed, too smooth.

"Do you think she's still alive?" Claudine interrupted, her throat clamped again around those words.

"So far, we have no body, no suspicious sightings. We have notified LASWA to make enquiries with fishermen in the creeks. We have checked the water around the boat club where she should have disembarked. There is nothing."

"LASWA?"

"The Lagos State Waterways Authority."

Claudine was quiet.

"Be encouraged, ma." He sounded kinder now at least. "She may have gone somewhere to rest and will soon be back."

"Rest? What on earth do you mean?"

Mr. Ogunsanya paused, then said, "This is a delicate matter. Probably you are not aware. Mrs. Oruwari was, erm, involved with some people." From the way he let it hang in the air, Claudine sensed what was coming next.

"Yes, I heard this."

"We do not know to what extent."

"What do you mean, to what extent?"

Mr. Ogunsanya was silent.

"Well?"

"She was having an extramarital affair."

Finally. It was said. Claudine almost felt relieved. She'd known Tonye was hiding something. So much made sense now: his strange mood on the call from London, his not wanting her to come to Lagos, the thing about him not wanting her to make contact. But it raised more questions.

"I worry that she was afraid of Tonye," Claudine said. "Perhaps he or someone had threatened her."

"What makes you think that?" Mr. Ogunsanya sounded genuinely surprised. Clearly he hadn't suspected Tonye at all.

"She was sleeping in the spare room. She moved all her things in there. I even found a knife under the mattress!"

"A knife? What kind of knife?"

"A small one, sharp, like a peeler."

"Okay, but she may have been cutting something," he said.

"But under the mattress? Why hide it? Have you investigated whether Tonye might have"—she hesitated—"been hiding anything?"

"Consider her husband's feelings before making such allegations," he said. His tone was cold, reprimanding. "Mr. Oruwari is of exemplary character, and he was not even with her that day."

Exemplary character? So what was Nicole? A kettle was starting to sing inside Claudine.

"Mr. Ogunsanya, I'm really not happy about how your investigation is going. Should I go to the papers, start handing out flyers with Nicole's name and photo on them? I will if I have to. And she's still a British citizen. What would the High Commission make of all this?"

"Please, Mrs. Roberts." He suddenly sounded rocked. "It will cause a scandal."

"It's *Miss* Roberts, and I *want* a scandal." Her voice was rising, but she didn't care. "A mother is missing! It's a scandal that you call yourself police and you can't tell me anything, not even who these friends are."

"We know who they are," he said hurriedly. "We have the names."

"Great. Tell me who they are."

"As I said, I can't release the names to you, but we are communicating with them through lawyers. I can assure you that after the wedding we will escalate the investigation if she has still not appeared." She heard him stop abruptly as if he'd said something he wasn't supposed to.

"What wedding?"

"Erm, Mr. Oruwari and the family asked us to delay," he said, suddenly sounding anxious. "In our culture, such news would cast a shadow over the union. It would bring terrible shame to the family."

"What *wedding*? Who is getting married?"

"I see you are not aware," said Mr. Ogunsanya miserably, as if he had failed in his duty. "Miss Roberts, understand that in our culture—"

Click.

She let the phone drop onto the bed next to her and walked out of the bedroom, calling for Tonye. Samuel met her in the hallway.

"Ma, Oga is not here. Is anything wrong?"

"Where is Tonye?"

"He is in the big house," said Samuel. Claudine went downstairs and he followed. When he saw her looking for her shoes in the reception area, he said, "But please, ma, they are having ceremony now." He positioned himself between Claudine and the door.

She paused. "What ceremony?" She could actually hear noise now, just beyond the door. People's voices. Drums playing. "Is something happening?"

"Today is the Door Knocking," he explained, tense. "The introduction for Miss Tamara and her future in-laws, when they pay bride price and exchange gifts. It's taking place now."

"Out of my way," ordered Claudine, and barged past Samuel through the door into the main part of the house.

She was shocked that she hadn't heard the commotion she now witnessed. There must have been about fifty people in the reception area dressed traditionally, all the men in the black top hats that Chief wore and brightly colored shirts, the women in head wraps and long patterned dresses. There was a cloying smell of too many bodies and an air of excitement, the attention of the guests held by something happening in the middle. Most people were gathered around a long cloth-covered table. The Oruwaris sat together on one side: Tonye, his father, Chief's Wife—fanning herself frantically—and the older sister, all dressed in their finery. Their backs were to her, but she could make them out without being noticed herself. And she supposed the people sitting in the opposite rows were the in-laws, also very dressed-up in traditional clothes. Looking important. Admiring the house. Making small talk. Gift hampers rested on the table, wrapped in decorative cellophane: fruit, other groceries. There was a collective hush. Everyone looked up to the double staircase where Tamara was carefully being helped down by two friends, clad in a beaded skirt made of tied cloth and a short-sleeved corseted top gleaming with crystals, her head and face covered by an ornate shawl. Her arrival was heralded by a master of ceremonies in the middle of the room, who loudly praised her beauty and accomplishments as she descended. He then asked her if she knew a man named Efe Igho. Everyone looked over at the young man in a white long-sleeved tunic and trousers who stood patiently by the table. Claudine guessed that must be the groom. Tamara said no, and everyone seemed to find that hilarious, laughing and clapping. Claudine saw the joke when the groom brought more gift boxes to the table, drinks in metallic gift wrap. The emcee asked her again. Tamara replied no once more. And again there was laughter, and the groom brought gifts to the table, this time several cases of monogrammed luggage, each of which he unzipped to reveal fabric, shoes, perfumes, and jewelry.

Now Tamara replied that, yes, she knew Efe Igho, and the shawl was removed. Everyone cheered as Efe Igho approached Tamara and began to shower her with money, walking around her, dropping the notes, which floated down her elaborately beaded top and wrapped skirt to the floor and piled up like fallen leaves, onto her head. Someone shouted, "More!" from the hallway near where Claudine stood, to further laughter. Someone played a drum. There was singing in a native language, and then the emcee started praising again.

Claudine stepped back into the shadows. It all fell into place now—the boxes, the tailor, the comings and goings. There had been a wedding magazine on the side table by the sofas in the main reception, she recalled. It hit her that not only were they not even trying to find Nicole—they simply didn't care. Mr. Ogunsanya's job was to protect the Oruwaris at all costs, even if the cost was Nicole. But Claudine was going to find out the truth, even if it took them all down with it, including herself.

CHAPTER NINE

NICOLE
Before

MUSHIN WAS deeper into the mainland than Nicole usually went alone. For the first few years, Tonye had asked her not to leave the "safe" environs of Victoria Island, Ikoyi, and Lekki Phase 1. Then Yaba, just over the bridge, became doable. The market there was an excellent place to find fabric for curtains. Ikeja Mall opened with a cinema, and that also became an acceptable destination. As a result, she'd gradually ventured farther. Badagry's barracoons were a special trip, and she took an armed police escort. More recently, she had visited a friend in the Palmgrove Estate, a Nigerwife from Maryland, and made trips to the Ikeja Saddle Club for Tari and Timi to feed the horses. But when Nicole mentioned the welfare trip to Mushin, Tonye thought it too close to Oshodi, a rough neighborhood known for area-boy clashes. Nevertheless, he considered the idea for a while before deciding that since it was daytime and the boys were not going, it wasn't such a big deal. "Just plan to be back by four," he'd warned.

For all his concerns, the journey to Mushin to join the other Niger-wives was unremarkable. It was after the morning rush, so any traffic was heading into the center, and Mushin seemed quiet compared to the frenetic commercial activity on Victoria Island. Apart from the insistent street hawkers and beggars banging on the SUV for attention, it was fine.

The high-walled Regina Mundi compound was on the main road, lined with street traders sitting under large umbrellas, their goods laid out in piles on the ground. Keke maruwas rattled past precariously on their three wheels. Inside was an orderly and peaceful courtyard, surrounded on all sides by peach-colored buildings, what looked like a hospital, offices, and modest apartments. Nuns walked through the square in their pale-blue habits, and Nicole could see Imani with a group of women clustered underneath a sign that read HOME FOR THE ELDERLY.

As Bilal parked the car, Imani waved eagerly at her. Nicole recognized most of the West Indian Nigerwives, as they called themselves. They loved to tell Nicole how they had met their Nigerian husbands—many of whom were sent to the University of the West Indies in the fifties and sixties to study civil administration in preparation for Nigeria's independence. They often spoke about the close-knit group they had formed to keep each other sane in a culture they didn't understand. Their closeness was evident in how they finished one another's sentences and referenced one another's children as if they were their own. On the whole, Nicole found them to be a quaint, old-fashioned type of Caribbean. They still grew their food in their gardens and obsessed over Queen Elizabeth, displaying a prissy Englishness that was fading away in the UK's Caribbean community. They were kind, always asking after her boys. But she didn't really feel like one of them. Their world had been created out of a need that no longer existed. She was a visitor in that too.

Several elderly residents sat outside the home, dressed in matching ankara clothes as if there were an event. A guide greeted the Nigerians in the parking lot and rattled off a quick history of the residence. She led them inside, through large communal rooms, the dormitories, and a sitting room with scattered sofas and armchairs and a wooden dining table that could seat twenty. She showed them the kitchen, where staff cooked. Donated foodstuffs were stacked up like a woodpile. Saucepan-sized cans of powdered Peak milk, boxes of Indomie noodles. Cooking oil. Poundo yam flour. Barrels of rice. It was well-stocked. The home was clearly a popular cause for the community.

The guide made a big show of their chief attraction, an old woman in an armchair who squinted as if the world hurt her eyes. She had scraps of frosted hair and the frailty of someone in her nineties, maybe even a hundred. Her skin crinkled like a plastic bag, and her head drooped to one side as if it were too heavy. When the representative touched her shoulder and said, "Good morning, Mummy," the woman frowned slightly, as if she'd heard a floorboard creak or a whistling draft, but nothing more.

"Ethel can't see or hear much now," the guide explained. "She's our precious mystery. About twenty years ago, locals found her destitute and brought her here. They said she was from Barbados. But she doesn't speak, so that's all we can say." Nicole couldn't look at her anymore. Instead, she focused on a man shuffling across the room while the Caribbean women consulted each other as if they were internet search engines:

"Did you know about an Ethel?"

"Who is Bajan here?"

"Yuh think she really Bajan?"

"She look St. Lucian from dat forehead?"

"Mavis might remember her."

"Mavis is ninety-plus."

"But her memory is sharp."

"Who has Mavis's phone number?"

NICOLE'S PHONE beeped and lit up with an incoming message. It was Elias. He had sent her all the images from the day at the pool. She wandered out of the home onto the veranda in the courtyard and flipped through the candid photos. They all looked slightly drunk and crazy, herself included, but happy and carefree. In each one, she looked like a person she had forgotten. Her hair wet and shrinking into afro wisps. Her limbs stretched out. Lying under an umbrella tree on the biscuit-colored sand. She could still feel the sea's heaving breaths as she looked at them.

"What's down there?" she'd asked, pointing farther along the beach.

"I'm not sure," he said. "Let's see."

"Might be dangerous."

"You can't think like that, or else you won't live."

She recalled the feel of his body on the quad bike—its reassuring protection against the whip of the wind. His camera lens traveling over her like curious fingers. To be seen is to be felt, to be held, to be real, not just a figment of someone's imagination, their idea of a woman, a wife, a mother.

I enjoyed talking with you, his next text read. I'd like to talk more, maybe take more photos of you. You shouldn't ever feel you are less than beautiful. And then a smiley emoji.

"Hard to imagine ending up in a place like this, isn't it?"

Nicole jumped and put her phone away. Imani had joined her on the veranda.

"It happens to us more than you think," she continued. "Our husbands pass away, and our children, if we have any, are gone. Eventually the local community discovers us, rotting away in some old house, and gets in touch with the Nigerwives or a place like this. It could happen to any of us. It doesn't matter how popular you were or how rich. Once you're old and there's no one around to protect you, you're at the mercy of whoever is left. Sometimes it's only when they see the rats that neighbors intervene." Imani sighed. "I love Nigeria, but as soon as my kids go to college I'm leaving. I'm not ending up like Ethel, bless her. What about you?"

"What about me?"

Imani's intense stare was back. "How long will you be here, do you think?"

"I don't know. Tonye doesn't want to leave."

"But what do you want?"

"Does what I want matter?"

Imani regarded her coolly. "You know, Nicole, I've often envied you. You're so pretty. What my grandmama would have called 'high yellow' back in the day. And you live in that amazing house. You're wealthier than a lot of us. You've had boys—let me tell you, that's a thing." She grimaced. At previous cocktail confessionals, some Nigerwives had complained about in-laws pestering them for boy children.

"We once had a Nigerwife—before you came—from Italy. She was young, about twenty, with a toddler. Her husband had been deported from there, I think, and she'd come with him. He was Igbo and took her to his village, but his people wouldn't accept her."

"I heard about that," said Nicole. "The death threats."

Imani nodded. "They were in hiding in Lagos, destitute, when people came to us and asked us to help them. We tried our best. Found him a job. Even found them somewhere to stay for a while till they got back on their feet. But it wasn't enough. The woman was struggling. She couldn't cope, and we worried she was out of her depth with this guy. He was twice her age and didn't seem to have told her the truth about his situation. We ended up sending her home. We can do that, you know, if Nigerwives are unhappy or in danger."

"So, what, you just buy them a ticket?" asked Nicole.

Imani laughed. "You know it's not that simple. We can't be accused of aiding and abetting child abduction. It's a serious crime. Also, some Nigerwives don't have anywhere to go—family or their own resources in the country they came from. We usually work with the Nigerwife's particular consulate in Lagos. They are the ones who ultimately decide if there is a case to help one of their citizens leave."

"Is that what happened with Christina?"

Imani said nothing.

"It's just that she left so abruptly and didn't reply."

"I can't comment on Christina," Imani said firmly but gently. "I know she was a friend of yours."

"She didn't say anything to me! She just complained about the usual things, the swimming instructor, the maid who steals, the AC that doesn't work. The things we all whine about."

"Sometimes those things are a cover for something else."

Nicole thought back to the playdates and the coffees. But wasn't everyone going through it? Wasn't it just marriage?

The other Nigerwives streamed out chattering, thanking the guide for the visit. Imani was swept up with them. Their conversation was over. Nicole said her good-byes and wandered over to meet Bilal.

On the drive back, Bilal turned down the radio. "Madam, what happens in that place?"

"The old people's home? They live there until they die."

"Why are they there? Why not with their families?"

"They don't have any family."

He digested this poorly. "Ah, no, madam, everyone has family. Where are their children?"

"Who knows? They're alone in the world."

"Does this happen in the white man's country? I can't understand who would abandon senior relatives to this place. This is not African at all!" Bilal seemed entirely worked up. Angry, even.

"It happens a lot in the UK. Elderly people there often end up in homes, whether or not they have children. It's not only white people, either. It's just how it is."

Her response seemed to agitate him even more. "Ah-ah, this is an abomination, madam," he said. It didn't take much to make Bilal's list of abominations, the things he couldn't fathom. So far, unmarried mothers, married women who still partied in nightclubs—as she did—the country's corrupt leaders, and, now, putting elders in homes. Having never left Nigeria and rarely been exposed to non-Black people, he was mystified by the strangeness of the West—the weird and wonderful Obodo Oyinbo. Some of his questions or comments made her laugh, but others were sad, like when he'd asked her once if white people never got sick since "they invented medicine, madam." For the most part, Africa—at least the countries she'd visited, Ghana and Benin, along with Nigeria—felt like an escape from racism, but she still frequently encountered Black people who viewed white people through rose-tinted white-savior lenses.

The journey home was straightforward. All the congestion was on the opposite side of the road. The evening rush from the islands had begun. Already a never-ending train of cars shuddered along with a lot of honking and hollering. Eventually the radio volume went back up and Bilal lapsed into silence. But Nicole was left with thoughts of Ethel, Christina, and the Italian woman, women who had given up their lives and moved here to Nigeria for a man. Their wants and needs were secondary. They had made themselves expendable to some man's dream to "go home," to pursue his raison d'être at the expense of theirs. And once you were there, you were taken for granted. A seen unseen. You were part of their storyline. And it was worth it when they loved you, when things were good; but when you were forgotten, discarded, you had to find your own reasons to be in a place. You had to go back to living for you.

Her phone buzzed with a text from Elias. What are you doing now?

NICOLE REDIRECTED Bilal to Idikan Close, as per Elias's instructions and her Maps app, passing the bubblegum-pink Blowfish Hotel, where Indians congregated for happy hour drinks, and the 9 to 7 supermarket, which was painted an equally lurid turquoise—the only place Nicole could find tiramisu and ready-rolled pastry sheets from France. After missing the building twice before noticing its wooden gates, they arrived at a compound and were let in by a lone gateman who looked like he had hastily dressed at their beep.

It was a simply constructed concrete apartment complex—clean, quiet, with only one or two cars in the empty parking lot. There was a drained swimming pool at the end with uncollected dust-covered toys stacked beside it, adding to a sense of desertion. Nicole hesitated. She would just go up and say hello to Elias. Thank him for the photos. It was just like going for a coffee. Nothing inappropriate. Why couldn't they be friends?

"Is it here, madam?" asked Bilal, peering around.

"This is the right place. Just wait. I won't be long." She didn't see the need to send Bilal away. That would be like saying something was going to happen, which it wasn't.

She exited the car and walked up the concrete block stairs two flights. After the second flight, she turned to the apartment on her left. The front door was slightly ajar.

"Hello?" She pushed open the door.

"I'm inside," Elias called from a back room. She could hear running water.

Nicole shut the door behind her and stood on the threshold, half-minded to back out of the apartment and flee before anyone could say she was there. Her earlier reasoning abandoned her. No one would think she was just there for coffee. Elias appeared from a side room in a T-shirt and cargo shorts, smiling.

She took a step into the small open-plan kitchen and living area. The air was cool. She immediately noticed the walls covered with artwork, the tidiness of the room. At least it seemed comfortable and clean.

"I didn't know if you would really come," he said.

"Why wouldn't I?" Nicole put her bag down on the counter that separated the kitchen from the living room. "I was in the area. I thought we could have coffee quickly. I can't stay long."

"You could have changed your mind."

Nicole laughed. "Why would I change my mind? I just wanted to say hi."

Elias didn't answer, just smiled.

"Your hair is dripping," she said. "Or are you sweating?"

He put a hand to his forehead sheepishly. "I took a second shower, just to be sure." He used the hem of his T-shirt to wipe the drops away. Nicole tried not to stare at his defined muscles.

"This is a nice place." She surveyed the room, going deeper into it, taking in the soft L-shaped sofa, the flat-screen with CDs and DVDs neatly stacked underneath by the DStv box. The artworks were grand paintings by famous artists—not what she'd expected. She could see a bedroom through the side door Elias had come out of.

"Let me give you the tour. There's a lot to see," he joked. He held out his hand and Nicole took it. "My kitchen"—he gave an airy wave toward the pristine surfaces—"living room"—he led her the few steps through the living area—"and bedroom."

Nicole popped her head in and saw a double bed, night table, wardrobes, windows looking down onto lower rooftops. There was an en suite bathroom to her left.

"I should wash my hands," she said.

"Go ahead." He backed out of the bedroom with his hands up.

She shut the door. It was slightly steamy and smelled of lemongrass and pine and man. She stared at herself in the mirror, pulling her neckline down as far as it would go. A shame she was wearing her boxy ankara.

"Did you really want coffee?" said Elias when she came out. "I don't have any. But I can get some."

"No."

Elias looked confused for a moment. He went to his fridge, which was set behind the door next to Nicole, and opened it, revealing clean, mostly empty shelves. He obviously wasn't one for cooking. "I've got Coke, Fanta, water, cranberry. Do you want wine? I have red and white."

"White wine would be nice," said Nicole. He unscrewed the cap and poured it into a wineglass. He handed it to her and watched her sip it.

"But what are you drinking?" she asked.

"Water. I just bought the wine for you. Women like wine, don't they?"

"Drink with me," she said. "Since you didn't think I was coming, we should celebrate that I'm actually here."

He grabbed a second glass and poured some wine for himself. "You're right. In case we never have this moment again." He drank it, watching her.

She gulped at hers. It felt strange to be the focus of someone's attention like this.

"Joseph Eze," she said eventually, unable to bear his intensity any longer. She pointed to one of the paintings on the wall. "I recognize his work." She set her glass down, then walked over and examined it. The profile of a dark-skinned woman, almost in the shadows, looking out. Wearing a heavy turban of newspapers. Bright-green vines snaking through the turban and behind the woman. She stood against the painting and imitated the side glance of the woman. "What do you think? Resemblance?"

Elias walked over to her. Straightened her shoulders. Turned her chin slightly. Tidied a coil of hair behind one ear. Then he stood back and pretended to take photos with his camera.

"I know just how she feels," said Nicole, taking in the painting once more. She turned this way and that, aligning her eyes with those of the woman in the frame so that they seemed to be looking at each other out of the corners of their eyes.

"What do you think about the one next to it?" he asked.

Nicole considered the ankara-covered canvas that was also molded into a face. "No idea," she confessed.

"Peju Alatise," he said.

She nodded. "I only know the Joseph Eze because of Kemi. She's your girl for all things art."

"Yes, Kemi," he replied neutrally. "She's quite a character, isn't she?" He walked back to the counter.

"She's totally into your boy."

Elias shrugged. "Everyone is. He's an Ishaku." He poured another glass of wine for Nicole and handed it to her. She hadn't eaten all day, but she drank anyway.

"Aren't you too? You're not related? But there's a similarity in your look."

"We're all from the same area. Sort of cousins, I guess. We all tend to have this long, straight nose."

She shifted closer to him. "So you're from the North?"

"That is where I grew up. I've lived in different places. Jos, Minna, Taraba. My father's a pastor and we moved with his church."

"You look Northern."

"Really? What does a person from the North look like?"

Nicole had been thinking dark-skinned, slim build, tall—but her thoughts suddenly seemed so silly that she decided not to voice them. Instead, she asked, "Isn't it dangerous to be a Christian in the North? I mean, there's always something in the news about Christians in the North being attacked."

"Christians have always been in the North. We are Fulani and Hausa too. Yes, there is trouble there, but don't believe everything you read about the North. It's not all Boko Haram like Southerners think." He sat on a barstool by the counter. "I go there all the time with no problems." When Nicole sat on the stool next to him, he asked, "You said you feel like the woman in the painting?"

"She looks tired. I'm tired too."

"Tell me about it."

Nicole hesitated. "If I start talking, I won't stop."

"So just start," he said. "You have my time."

CHAPTER TEN

CLAUDINE
After

THE CALL to Mr. Ogunsanya had left Claudine too troubled for sleep. She had been awake for hours when at 7 a.m. she heard Blessing waking the boys. The nanny's flip-flops slapped across the tiles as she walked to the kitchen. The creak of the fridge door. The clatter of cutlery. The whir and ping of the microwave. She was quietly singing a popular song Claudine was now familiar with. *Slap, slap* back across the hallway to the boys' bedroom. Sleepy whining that traveled from the bedroom to the living room. The jingle of cartoon shows. The sizzle of something in the frying pan. Claudine lay there, listening to the house getting louder as the household grew more awake.

When she heard the heavy *harrumph* of Tonye clearing his throat, she wanted to leap out of bed to confront him, but stopped herself for the children. After some time, she could hear Blessing rushing the boys to their bathroom. Tonye shouted good-bye to the children and told Blessing to make sure Samuel shined his shoes properly. The front door clanged shut.

Claudine got out of bed and walked over to the boys' bedroom, where she found Blessing trying to get their clothes on as they ran around the bedroom defiantly.

"Oh, good morning, ma," said Blessing with a little bob. "How was your night?"

"Don't bother with that bowing and scraping," Claudine said quickly. "I can't bear it. I didn't sleep much, but I'm okay. How are you?"

"Am fine, ma."

"What a beautiful morning after all that rain yesterday."

"Yes, ma," said Blessing. The boys calmed down seeing Claudine in the room and went to stand behind Blessing. Blessing and Claudine both laughed.

"Greet your aunt," Blessing urged.

"I don't bite," said Claudine. "Let me help you with your shirt, Timi."

Timi shyly approached her, and Claudine fastened his buttons. The boys were nice and clean. Blessing was doing a great job taking care of them.

"The view over the lagoon is so peaceful," said Claudine to Blessing. "The water and the sun rising and those little islands in the background. And this is such a lovely house. Nicole must have been very happy to live here."

Blessing smiled politely.

"Did she seem happy to you?"

Blessing looked stricken at being put on the spot. "Ma?"

"Mummy wasn't happy," said Timi solemnly.

"Timi, quiet," said Blessing.

"It's okay," said Claudine. "Let him talk." Timi looked from Blessing to Claudine enquiringly. "Why not?" prompted Claudine.

"Mummy was sad. That's why she traveled," he continued. "Daddy always shouting. Mummy crying. So she left."

"Please, ma," said Blessing nervously.

"She slept in that room, didn't she?" Claudine pointed. "The one I'm in."

"Ma, I don't know."

The front door swung open. There was the loud blather of Samuel chattering on his mobile phone in his language. Blessing froze as Samuel climbed the stairs, still yapping. His phone call ended.

"Blessing? Mr. Bilal is waiting in the car!"

Blessing called out, "Yes, Mr. Samuel! Boys, go put on your shoes." The boys rushed out of the room into the hallway, greeting the housekeeper enthusiastically before thudding downstairs to get their shoes. Blessing moved to follow them, but Claudine blocked the door.

"Please, ma," Blessing whispered frantically. "I can't lose my job."

"Just nod then. If she stayed in the room, nod."

Blessing nodded quickly, not looking at her, and rushed out of the room. Claudine followed her to the doorway. Samuel was standing just outside, in the passage, frowning as Blessing hurried past him.

"Good morning, ma," he called. "What for your breakfast? Sausage and egg again? And tea?" he said, addressing Claudine with a worried smile.

"Yes, thank you, Samuel. That's fine."

"Blessing, come," said Samuel. When Samuel went downstairs again, Claudine heard him scold Blessing with a barrage of unintelligible pidgin, and Blessing sounded fearful and apologetic in response. Claudine went into the living room. Moments later, a sniffling Blessing slipped out of the apartment.

AFTER BREAKFAST, Claudine went to find Tonye in his office. His face fell as she entered. *Yes, it's me again,* thought Claudine with a grim smile. *And it will be me again until I find out the truth.*

"Good morning, auntie," he said weakly, standing and ushering her to the seat. "Mr. Ogunsanya said he spoke with you. I hope the conversation answered at least some of your questions."

Tonye didn't mention the knife. As Claudine sat down, she wondered what Mr. Ogunsanya had told him about it. "I wanted to talk to you about the investigation yesterday, but you were having your family introduction," she said pointedly.

He cleared his throat and looked embarrassed. "It was a traditional family event for my sister. I didn't want to bother you."

"Tonye, you haven't been truthful with me. Mr. Ogunsanya told me Nicole was having an affair and that's why the investigation was on hold until after your family wedding. You didn't mention the wedding either. What's going on?"

He sighed. "I wasn't hiding it. I just wanted you to get settled first. I hope you can see now why it's complicated."

It was all Claudine could do not to curse. She leaned forward. "Tonye. Your wife is *missing*. You even think she's dead, and in the same breath, you're having a family wedding? What the living hell?" She wanted to grab the laptop and smash it over the ginnal's head.

He breathed like he was limbering up for a boxing match. "I wanted to tell you, but—"

"Nah. You didn't. You've been avoiding me like the plague. You haven't tried to tell me shit." *Rein it in, Claud*, she thought.

"It's not my wish. It's not my decision."

"No, Tonye—I can't believe that. This is the most wicked thing I've ever heard."

"Can you let me explain?"

"What kind of person has a wedding at a time like this?"

"If you—"

"And you're not even *looking* for Nicole. You've done nothing. Less than nothing. A blind person can see that none of you could care less."

He waited for her to finish, but she was not done.

"I would've expected you to pull out all the stops looking for her. Turn over every stone! But you told that detective whatever-his-name-was not to do his job? And what kind of detective was that? Doesn't sound like any police I know. He's supposed to be looking out for the victim. He should investigate *you*! Just ridiculous."

Finally she stopped, worn out by her rush of words.

"Let me try to explain things better, auntie," said Tonye quietly.

"I don't believe a word you've said," said Claudine. "I bet this

Ogunsanya's not even a real police officer. I'm going to the British High Commission. Nicole's still a British citizen."

He closed his laptop hurriedly. "Please, listen to me first, and then go ahead and raise hell if you'd like. I assure you, Mr. Ogunsanya *is* a police officer. He's the deputy commissioner of police. You can go online and check for yourself."

"But you've paid for him."

"It's not that I've paid for him. I mean, obviously, I've paid for him. But that's just how things work here. You get what you pay for."

"But I—"

"No, listen. This isn't the UK. We all know how fair the justice system is there. I'm sure if Nicole had gone missing in London, they would have pulled out all the stops."

Claudine thought about Jackie and how the family liaison officer had done nothing. Nothing! Didn't even remember her name.

"Lagos is just money," Tonye continued. "I won't pretend. That's it. No one is above the economic forces around them here. This family is no different. The people we are dealing with are worth a hundred times what my father is worth. So when you say I've paid for Mr. Ogunsanya, yes, I've paid, but others can pay more."

"So?"

"So this is the thing. Nicole got involved with very powerful people. The kind of people who are never arrested, never stand trial, and certainly are never convicted. They've denied any knowledge of what happened to Nicole. They are adamant they dropped her off."

"You knew who they were all this time and you said nothing! Can't we get at them ourselves if you know where they are? Raise hell? Shame them through the media into giving answers?"

Tonye gave a short laugh. "Raise hell? Sure, let's splash the lurid details all over the newspapers and social media. Get everyone talking. Is that justice? I promise you, it won't get the answers you want. In the meantime, Nicole's name will be ruined, this family will be ruined. Tamara's engagement will be canceled."

Claudine didn't feel a shred of sympathy.

"This is a conservative society," Tonye continued. "It doesn't digest scandal well. For the sake of your nephews, please."

She looked dully into Tonye's face. "But why can't you tell me who the affair was with?"

"Because I'm not sure what you'll do with the information. This was for your own protection—and ours, auntie." Tonye sighed and rubbed his eyes. "Nicole rarely spoke of you. I know you helped raise her after her mother died, but the two of you have not really spoken in years. Suddenly you turn up wanting answers? I am Nicole's next of kin, not you. I have taken care of her for the last five years we have been here. Where were you? She hardly even spoke of her relatives, and when she did, it sounded like things were not so great for her growing up." Claudine felt Tonye looked at her with pity. "So you may not like it, but I'll decide what's best for her and my family. I've welcomed you as a courtesy, but I owe you *nothing*. When the time is right, I'll tell you more. Be patient."

Claudine got up to go. She could hardly speak. "You're right. I let her down. We all did. Her childhood was awful. I'm sorry about that, but I can't change the past. This has hit me hard, and I need to understand it." A thought occurred to her. "You know, it might be enough just to know more about Nicole's life here." She tried her best to smile. Seem agreeable. Wasn't it Penny who always said you catch more flies with honey? She wanted to tear his eyes out. "Where she went, the people around her—it would help me so much to know that. I could go back to London knowing that she had had a good life."

Tonye looked relieved at her turnaround. His shoulders relaxed. He even smiled. "Well, sure. The Nigerwives can tell you some of that."

"Nigerwives?"

"Nigerwives is an association of foreign wives she was—*is*—a part of. She would go to their meetings every now and then—like a social club. Go to the beach together, go for coffee, that sort of thing. Bilal knows the address and when the meetings are held. He can take you. You'll get a great sense of her life from them. But just say that Nicole has traveled unexpectedly. Don't stir things up. Can we agree?"

It was something. "All right. Thank you." She walked to the door, then paused and turned around. "Do you think she's still alive?"

Tonye opened his laptop without looking at her. "It's still possible. I'm praying."

You better pray, Claudine thought. She didn't know what she'd do if she found out Tonye had hurt Nicole, but she knew what she was capable of.

CHAPTER ELEVEN

NICOLE
Before

R EMEMBER NOT to suck in too much smoke," said Elias, passing his vape to Nicole in the rooftop lounge of the Kuramo Waters Hotel. She drew the breath in through her mouth slowly, as he had pain-stakingly taught her, avoiding the burning sensation in the back of her throat that would cause a coughing fit. The high felt like the milk coming down in her breasts. A warmth, a sigh going through her, and her tension broke into pieces that scattered across the diesel-scented sky.

Down below, cars were still back-to-back along Adetokunbo Ademola's double carriageway to the Zenith Bank Roundabout. The jangle of horns clashed with the smooth Afrobeat coming from the speakers of the hotel patio behind them. Vendors still hugged the side-walk with their wares. Pedestrians were caught like mime artists in the zigzagging headlights, trying to maneuver from one side of the road to the other in the absence of safe crossings.

To the left, the frustrated LAD project—a few almost-finished, uninhabited luxury towers stark against an inky sky—was an as-yet-undeveloped nothingness that became one with the ocean. To the right, by the roundabout, was the multi-pillared First Bank building.

The wind whined around the patchwork of rooftops spread over the island. The spire decorating the Civic Tower on the Ozumba Mbadiwe highway shone as the highest and most brightly lit point on the skyline. Far away in the distance, the horizon's ebbing halo bled into the purple sky.

Nicole looked over at Elias, a dark silhouette in front of the column lamp behind him. She wondered what he was thinking. Kemi's words rang in her ears. "It's fine as long as you know nothing can happen with him," she'd warned Nicole recently over neon margaritas that glowed under the lightbulbs of Bottles restaurant. "Couldn't care less about Tonye, but don't let it be more than light fun. I'm sorry." Kemi sometimes added this *I'm sorry* when she wanted to sound even more judgmental than usual. "A guy like Elias can never." She didn't need to say what he could never do. Yohanna owned the apartment complex Elias lived in, all the artwork in his living room, even his car—it was all Yohanna's, and the Ishaku Foundation paid a significant part of Elias's salary, without which the reality would be a flat share somewhere past Lekki's third roundabout. None of it seemed to bother Elias. He wasn't the worrying type.

Perhaps that was why Tonye was not threatened by her late nights, beyond people's perceptions. And nothing had happened yet. Not physically. They were still just friends.

A few feet away, Kemi, Yohanna, and a visiting friend shot the breeze together on plush sofas around a coffee table. The visiting friend was a lanky Kenyan man with a posh English accent, a boarding school friend of Yohanna's visiting from Abidjan in Côte d'Ivoire, where he worked for the African Development Bank. Screens separated their party from the rest of the rooftop patio. Regardless, it was a quiet night up there. The real entertainment was downstairs in the hotel's popular Mexican restaurant, which converted to a nightclub after dark. The friend was regaling Yohanna and Kemi with stories of Abidjan. They laughed a lot in strangely harmonious symphony with the tooting cars and the Afrobeat and the city's whistling breath.

Elias took Nicole's hand and pulled her over toward the sofas.

"Come to Abidjan, man," the Kenyan friend was saying in between sips of champagne. "It's a great city, lots to do and see—beaches, art galleries, beautiful buildings, good nightlife."

None of the rest of them had ever been. "Isn't it crazy?" said Kemi. "I'm sure between us, we've covered most of Europe. But our own continent—our own part of the continent, even—we haven't thoroughly visited. Why not?"

"Paris versus Abidjan?" Yohanna weighed it up with his hands. "Hmm, a thousand years of history versus a beach and a local market? Chanel versus ankara? But what do I know?"

"The British destroyed our history," said Kemi. Nicole could tell she was trying to keep her voice light. "The Ashanti Kingdom in Kumasi. The Benin Empire. The colonizers took all the gold, the ivory."

"And the people," Nicole interjected.

Yohanna looked bemused. "So what am I supposed to do if they've stolen everything or burned it all down—imagine it's there?"

"There are the . . ." Kemi faltered because she didn't know.

"The libraries in Timbuktu," said the Kenyan helpfully.

"Didn't the Islamists destroy all of that?" retorted Yohanna.

"What about the seventh-century churches in Ethiopia?" said Kemi. "I've always wanted to visit them."

Yohanna rolled his eyes. "Who wants to scrabble around in the dust looking for Africa's lost treasure when you can enjoy the best luxury in West Africa right here at the Kuramo Waters?" He laughed and plumped the cushions. "Naija no dey carry last."

Platters of fried seafood and sides of fries and mozzarella sticks arrived, and they tucked in. After a few minutes, Elias lured Kemi and Nicole away to pose against pillars as he played the role of animated photographer. Yohanna initially found it entertaining, but after several minutes of this, shouted, "Hey, how is it I'm the one paying for everything and getting the least attention?" The visiting friend laughed heartily, and Nicole and Kemi hurried back to the table, anxious not to upset their host.

Still on the subject of travel, Kemi jumped into her favorite Dubai story: the time she fell afoul of the secret police, who'd thought she was a prostitute and had arrested her. She was on a camel ride with a guy she was dating, who'd fallen off the camel and hit his head badly, knocked unconscious. And the police had arrested her for sharing a hotel room with the guy. A powerful client had to get her hastily released with personal apologies from the local sheikh.

"No lashes?" Yohanna asked mischievously, and everyone duly laughed again. "Surely your insolence deserved some lashes. At least thirty, no, fifty. Extra for you."

"Do you know how easy it is for women to get arrested in Dubai?" Kemi asked.

"I'm sure they know plenty of runs girls from Nigeria there," said Yohanna.

"What the hell are runs girls?" asked the visiting friend, highly amused.

"Girls who date rich men, usually politicians, and have to 'run' to Abuja or wherever to meet them. Hence 'runs,'" said Kemi.

"Tell me the truth," said Yohanna. "You're not really an art consultant, are you? If I check the private jet flight manifests at Lagos Airport, will I see you on the list for Dangote's jet?"

Kemi slapped him playfully when she could have eviscerated him, Nicole noted.

Elias, on the periphery of the conversation, soon wandered off to the railings to take photos of the night.

"And you, Miss Jamaica," Yohanna said to Nicole. He'd started calling her that after the beach. He knew it irked her. "How do you find our country?" he asked with the false interest of a taxi driver. He had been downing champagne like medication, swiftly and with a grimace after every glass.

"I don't know the country," she said with a smile. "I've only really been here in Lagos, but I like it, I guess. I'm still here after seven years."

"And you, Kemi—how do you find our country?" Yohanna asked playfully.

"How do *you* find it?" retorted Kemi. "I've been here longer than you. You're the JGB here." The visiting friend held out his hands. "It means Just Got Back," she explained. "So how does it compare to LA, Yo-Yo?"

"LA was great. Beautiful." He closed his eyes briefly and smiled. "But, oh well, I'm Nigerian for better or worse." He shrugged. "It's my country and my cross to bear."

"Hardly a cross being the son of a powerful man," said Nicole.

"A toast to the sons of powerful men, then," said Yohanna, his eyes steady on her. "Refill your glasses. Go on."

They all raised their glasses a little uncertainly. "The luckiest of men." Down the champagne went. Yohanna's smile was sour. Now he grabbed at his vape like it was an asthma inhaler.

"Well, perhaps we will come to Abidjan to look at the art there," said Kemi, indicating herself and Nicole. "Nicole is going to start working for me at the Wura Gallery."

"What do you know about Nigerian art?" Yohanna asked rudely.

"She's just a pretty face," said Kemi. Nicole rolled her eyes. "But I will teach her."

"Do you even know Peju Alatise from Ben Enwonwu?" Yohanna asked skeptically.

"I know Peju Alatise," Nicole said. "There's one on Elias's wall."

"Oh, yes. You two are spending a lot of time together." He looked over at Elias, who shrugged.

"She will know her art soon enough," said Kemi, patting his knee. "She won't be a South London heathen forever." She laughed.

"Maybe I should go into art too then," said Elias playfully.

"Me, I can't buy everyone's art," joked Yohanna.

A little later, Kemi and Nicole found themselves alone by the balcony.

"Don't mind Yohanna's jokes," said Kemi.

"I don't care. He can say what he likes. And I don't know anything about art. I'm only doing this job for you."

"Well, it works out for you too. You get more time outside of the compound. You've got an excuse now to mess around with Elias. Sow your oats."

"Ugh. That's gross."

"Yes, sorry, only men get to do that. We're ladies. We have to act chaste and virginal. Fuck that. I'm liking this new Nicole. We even got you out of that awful ankara."

Nicole said nothing.

"You know, you're just starting out, but who knows, the art market is growing. You could make a career out of it if you want to. You could make a lot of money. Enough to support yourself."

"I doubt that's gonna happen." It cost a lot more money to live in Lagos than it did in London. The cost of generators and diesel had to be factored in on top of the unreliable electricity. That didn't include the investment in the generators themselves. Water came from a borehole in the compound, filtered and pumped up to all parts of the house, maintained by a full-time plumber. To rent a decent two-bed flat on Victoria Island would set you back about $50,000 per year, not including a 20 percent service charge. Tonye had laid it out for her when she had suggested they move to their own apartment away from the Oruwari compound. Then there were private school fees for the children, much cheaper than the UK, but still several million naira per year. The cost of imported SUVs, staff, medical insurance, flights. Food if you wanted to eat anything other than pounded yam and local croaker fish. You also had to grease many bureaucratic palms just to exist.

"I mean, Tonye would still have to support you. He couldn't let you starve."

"Big assumptions."

"Maybe. Look, girl, when I marry Yohanna, you'll have nothing to worry about. I'll make sure you're good." She pumped Nicole's shoulder theatrically, then went back to Yohanna, settling next to him on the sofa. He draped his arm across her shoulders and she intertwined her fingers with his, but then he looked over at Nicole and stuck his tongue out in that horrid way he had on the boat. No one else seemed to notice. Nicole quickly went to stand beside Elias. He hadn't registered anything.

"They say Los Angeles is the city of dreams," he said, looking down to the never-ending traffic scene below. "But I more think Lagos is." He leaned over the glass railing. "We are a city of dreamers." He pointed down to a man hailing a taxi, then a girl kissing her boyfriend good-bye. "Many of us came here, or our parents did, full of dreams. But sometimes I think we are drowning, dreaming we are swimming. And it's just our dreams keeping us afloat."

"What do you dream about?"

"I dream about you," he said. "You are my dream. You're the most beautiful, amazing person I've ever met."

"Be serious."

"I am. I dream that we are in a relationship. That I wake up and you're already there. That whatever happens, we are together."

"Kemi doesn't think we can have any kind of relationship."

"Oh yeah?"

"She said you can't do anything for me."

A bitter little smile played about Elias's lips. "Look, don't let Kemi get in your head. I know she's your friend, and she thinks she's got it all worked out, but she doesn't know anything."

"What do you mean by that?"

He drew himself up. "Kemi is definitely someone drowning, thinking she is swimming. She inhales the fumes and thinks she will soon be driving the car. None of it means anything. Yo-Yo won't marry her."

"How can you know that?" asked Nicole, shocked. She wished she hadn't said anything.

A bark from Yohanna broke their moment. They looked over to see him waving a hand at them impatiently. Elias looked at Nicole. "Because we all have our masters. Even him."

CHAPTER TWELVE

NICOLE NAVIGATED the crush of people spilling out of the white-walled gallery onto the waterfront, where the younger set, mostly Kemi's crowd, congregated, enjoying the lower evening temperatures. Their champagne-tipped voices and the buzzy house music carried over the lagoon into the lavender-tinted sunset. The real money mingled inside, where paintings adorned every spare wall and were strategically displayed on easels. Suited businessmen—in groups of white or Middle Eastern faces—and heavily perfumed madams in flowing kaftans and Hermès sandals moved quickly past the artworks with sold stickers to pause in front of one that was available. Nicole recognized several society people: Prince Balogun, chair of the polo club; Auntie Em, the film producer and broadcaster; billionaire Kolo Sekoni; and others. More sold signs started to appear above the paintings. The glamorously dressed female ushers, an essential feature of any Lagos event, adorned the doorways, greeting guests or moving through the crowd with mini sliders and spicy breaded shrimp on sticks.

Nicole's first evening had gone well so far. She had made a sale, even if it was one of the cheaper paintings that had gone fast. When Kemi had mentioned her doing this a few weeks ago, she'd been skeptical, but was thankful now for her friend's urging. Kemi was right. People seemed to seek her out in the gallery as if the black, asymmetrical

Issey Miyake dress Kemi had lent her suggested something about her knowledge—which was still next to nothing, despite Kemi's coaching.

"I'm looking for something for my reception area," Mrs. Faremi had said. "Something very wow." She had been easy to sell to, being as clueless as Nicole herself. Nicole had ushered her to a Peju Alatise, the same artist who hung in Elias's living room. This was a mixed-media piece of beaten gold leaf against a black background, with an upper estimate of 4.5 million naira, betting that if Mrs. Faremi was anything like Mother-in-Law, she would want something gold and eye-catching.

Mrs. Faremi had peered at the card on the wall. "*Every night they sleep, they sleep they dream of nothing.* What does that mean? I hope it's nothing ritual." Once assured the wording was meaningless, just a clever title, Mrs. Faremi had been quick to buy. "Make sure it's delivered tomorrow morning because I'm traveling soon and I want to know it is with me," she had huffed, the gold on her wrists jingling as she gestured for emphasis.

Kemi patted Nicole on the back as she passed by with her own client. "Doing well," she whispered encouragingly.

Wrapping up with Mrs. Faremi, Nicole was pleased at Kemi's praise. She'd felt she had something to prove ever since Kemi's overfed cow comment. But she also enjoyed feeling a little like the old Nic again. The one who stood on her own two feet and worked hard.

It was a much busier event than she had expected. Quite nerve-racking. Usually when she attended such things, she drank a lot of wine and chatted with friends. Kemi, of course, was in her professional element, moving confidently between the VIPs in her white pantsuit and heels, negotiating in a hard-nosed way, but still very relaxed about the whole thing, smiling all the way.

"Kilode? Or should I say wagwan, Miss Jamaica?"

She turned. It was Yohanna, wearing an ugly double-breasted jacket in houndstooth. He smiled mischievously, pointing to a nearby artwork. She hadn't seen him since that night at the Kuramo Waters almost a month ago.

"Could I get some assistance with this piece?" he enquired with mock earnestness.

Nicole looked around for Kemi, but she was ensconced with a group of foreign clients, so Nicole walked across to the painting. It was a very large piece, two meters across and a meter high, with images made out of panels of carved and etched wood and an overall cosmic effect.

"Is Elias with you?" she asked.

"No, we're not conjoined twins." Grinning and looking her up and down, Yohanna seemed to find the fact of her working there hilarious. "Nice dress. Now for your sales pitch."

"So this is the, erm—" Nicole flipped through the booklet in her hands with summary information on each of the artworks.

"El Anatsui," Yohanna said smugly before she could find it.

"Yes, thank you. *Duve* by El Anatsui, mixed media on wood panels."

"Well read," he said, slow-clapping with those big hands of his. "But I can see that for myself. Can you tell me something that's not written on the card next to the painting?"

"You want to know about the painting itself, or . . . ?"

He rolled his eyes. "About El Anatsui. Why is this an artist I should invest in?"

Nicole looked around for Kemi in desperation. "Kemi probably knows more about his career path than I do."

"But she's busy sucking up to the Italian ambassador." He jabbed over his shoulder to Kemi's group. Nicole wondered if he was jealous. He leaned forward. "Maybe we should go to Abidjan and talk about it there."

"Stop being a knob," said Nicole. She tried to move off, but he put a hand on her arm.

"Now, now, this isn't good business." His voice was brimming with laughter. "You wouldn't want me to complain to the gallery owners about your poor customer service, would you?"

He sounded like he was joking, but Nicole wasn't sure. You never knew with Yohanna. Tonight was her first big test and she didn't want to let Kemi down, so she decided to humor him and looked at the pamphlet.

"El Anatsui is a Ghanaian sculptor who has spent much of his career here in Nigeria. He's known for his bottle-top installations, recycled from aluminum. His work has been shown all over the world."

"Good. I'm liking the sound of this."

"He had a showing at the Biennale in Venice some years ago."

"I know. I attended."

"Oh, so you know all about him," said Nicole. "You're just torturing me."

"Of course I know. I'm an art investor. I'm testing you. If you want to get yourself out of trouble next time, don't worry about what you know or don't know. It's not rocket science to win at this game. The market is still so new, if you can afford to invest in artwork at this level, you're pretty much guaranteed to make money no matter what you buy. Six years ago Ben Enwonwu was selling for less than ten thousand dollars. Now he's over a hundred thousand."

Nicole nodded.

Yohanna shook his head. "You do at least know who Ben Enwonwu is now, right?"

"How did you get so interested in art anyway?" she deflected. "Do you paint yourself?"

He looked surprised. "Me? Paint?" He shrugged. "Once upon a time, yes. When I lived in LA. Just for myself. Funny, you're the first person to ask me."

"What sort of painting did you do?"

"Self-portraits mostly, but distorted—so you wouldn't know it was me. Like perhaps I would take a photo of myself and cut it into random pieces, then reassemble them wrongly, or paint myself but changing some of my features, my nose or my hair or my clothes." She saw that Yohanna enjoyed talking about his art. His face opened up, and he spoke of LA as if it was somewhere he'd much rather be. She imagined him in a Hawaiian shirt that fluttered open at a beach party, sipping on a lurid cocktail, surrounded by Kardashian types. Happy and carefree, not so in his own head. She guessed Nigeria was tough for him in some ways. Unlike Kemi and Elias, who were excited to be in Nigeria, trading on their strengths, he'd been dragged back under family duress that seemed to bring out the worst in him.

"Kemi and Elias didn't mention you painted," she said.

His face closed up at the mention of them, and the sarcastic look was back. "What would me painting have to do with either of them? They're not interested in my artistic inclinations."

"Then they're stupid."

He laughed. "You don't know how things work, do you? How long did you say you've lived here? Do you think they also like you for you? Nothing to do with wanting anything you have?"

Nicole crossed her arms. "So, buying anything then?"

Yohanna seemed to find her about-turn amusing enough to play along. "Let's see how generous I'm feeling. How much is it?"

"Eighteen million naira."

Yohanna shrugged. "That's a little steep. How about a discount?"

"No discounts for sons of billionaires," she quipped.

"Well, then, how about something extra?"

"Something extra?" Nicole frowned.

He leaned in again. "Come back to my beach house. Just you and me this time."

"What?" She took a step back.

"I feel like perhaps we got off on the wrong foot that day we met. Things could have gone differently. I didn't expect you to hit it off with my boy so quickly."

"What do you mean? I don't understand. Hit it off with Elias? We're just friends."

"Just friends?"

A smile played about his lips as he waited for Nicole's response. She crossed her arms, waiting for him to clarify what he meant.

"Anyway, I'm just joking," he breezed finally, looking around the room as though suddenly bored. "And I do like the artwork. Let me see what else is here and I'll come back to you."

He turned abruptly and walked away, leaving Nicole shaking her head. He poked fun at her, yet sought her validation. He was a jerk, but they had these surprising moments of deeper connection. And then there was Elias. Were they really just friends as she'd claimed? It felt like they were becoming something more, but she couldn't visualize the finished piece.

CHAPTER THIRTEEN

CLAUDINE
After

Penny was laughing as she answered the phone. A high-pitched cackle signaled to Claudine that Mummy was in the room with her. So much for all their initial bawling. Life had gone on without Nicole, without her. She remembered that was how they had been after Jackie died too. Moved on swiftly, hardly mentioning her again. When you are already broken, what is one more crack?

"Oh, hey, Claud. Mummy, it's Claud. Any news?"

"What's going on there?" asked Claudine. Her heart suddenly ached for the comfort of the old sofa and the sharp scent of jerk chicken.

"Watching *Desmond's*. Remember *Desmond's*? I forgot how funny that show was. I'm crying real tears."

"You're always crying about something."

"God, that show brings back memories. And we used to joke about how our Michael was exactly like Michael Ambrose from the show. Always taking everything too seriously."

Claudine tried to think back, but the memories seemed so far away. "No, I—" Another peal from Mummy interrupted her. She could imagine Mummy's pendulous breasts jiggling like jelly on a plate. She hadn't heard her laugh like that since—well, a long time. "Turn it down, I can hardly hear you."

The television went off abruptly.

Penny sighed. "So, what's up?"

"Has Mummy been attending her doctor's appointments?"

"Yes."

"What about the medication? Two tablets a day, one in the—"

"Claud, it's getting done, tek it easy nuh. You don't have to sound so suspicious. I can tek care of my own mother."

"I'm just checking, because I know how you stay."

"What do you mean, 'how I stay'?"

"No need to bristle up. I'm just saying."

There was a brief silence—a mini standoff.

Finally Penny said, "So how are you doing, Claud?"

"I wanted to ask you something." Claudine hesitated. "Was I a bad parent to Nicole—you know, overall?"

"A bad parent? How you mean?"

"I was talking with Tonye, and he implied Nicole didn't want anything to do with us because of me."

"You and Tonye had an argument?"

"He turned on me. I found out they've told the police to keep things hush-hush and I said that's not good enough. Then he said, why am I here, Nicole wasn't that close to us, she never spoke about us."

"What a cheek. I hope you set him straight."

"It kind of upset me—you know?"

"I would've hit him in his bloodclart mouth. Who the hell does he think he is?"

Claudine instantly felt a little better. "I dunno. Can't help wondering about it. Do you think it's true?"

"Think what was true?"

"That she left the UK because of us. Because of me."

"As you said, she was happy—she had this amazing life. *You* said that. *That's* why she left."

"I did my best. I fed her, dressed her, took her to school, church."

"Claud. Don't work yourself up."

"I'm not. It just didn't make sense to me why he would say that."

"Do you think Nicole could have told him about Len?"

"But that was years ago. She was a child then."

"Yeah, it was a long time ago, but—"

"So why bring it up?" Claudine said harshly, then continued, "That's not what he meant. He was talking generally, that she never talked about us as a family, not about one specific incident. I mean, if you really want to go there, we could talk about her real mother not taking care of her properly and ending up dead, or her father denying her."

"Okay, Claud."

Neither of them said anything. Claudine took a breath. It wasn't right to bite Penny's hand off like that. "They said she was having an affair."

"You what?"

"Nicole. Tonye and the police officer said she was involved with whoever she went on the boat trip with."

"Well, if they know who it is, why hasn't he been arrested?"

"They won't tell me. They don't want to cause a scandal. There's a family wedding, and honestly it's too much to take in. I can't get my head around it."

"So Nicole was having an affair, and that person might be hiding her or know something, and they won't even say the person's name? What are you going to do? You need to go to the British embassy! The papers! Anything at this point!"

"It's not an embassy. It's called the High Commission here."

"Whatever it's called, just go there!"

"I'm trying to act like I'm on Tonye's side for now. He's directed me to an association Nicole was part of called the Nigerwives. The foreign wives of Nigerian men."

"God, why do they need their own association? Things must be bad out there."

"They might know something."

"I never trusted Tony. You waiting on him is a waste of time." She paused. "Be careful."

Claudine said she would and hung up the phone.

BILAL HAD acted like he didn't know a darn thing about the Niger-wives until Tonye had gone to talk to him. Now, as they drove into the school compound, Claudine noticed the gateman hailed him like he knew him. She wondered what else Bilal was hiding. As Nicole's driver, he probably knew something about the affair or who Nicole was involved with, but he was so tight-lipped and serious—all *Yes, ma, no, ma, three bags full, ma*, and not a word more. All the staff were wary of her, clams snapping shut whenever she asked about Nicole. Seeing as how her questioning had almost cost Blessing her job, she understood their reluctance to talk, but she was getting desperate. Possibilities were feeling like dead ends. She was running out of time.

She entered the hall from the back. It was hot and airless, full of women—young, old, all complexions. Claudine hadn't seen so many white people in one place since leaving the UK. An Asian-looking woman was speaking at the front of the hall. She had a strong Nigerian accent.

Claudine sat down in the first available seat in the back. She still had Penny's words in her head. So far, she'd done everything Tonye's way. And where had it gotten her? Nowhere. She felt disappointed in herself. She'd let him get to her, bringing up things from the past. None of that mattered now. Even if Nicole didn't want to see her again, Claudine was still the only person who loved her enough to do what needed to be done.

It took a while to get up to speed about what the women were discussing. Something to do with ID cards. She wondered if she should make her way to the front and get someone's attention or just wait until the end. But what was she going to say? Tonye had said she shouldn't divulge the whole truth—but why not? At this point, did it even matter? Wherever Nicole was, Claudine doubted she was coming back to play happy families.

Eventually the woman at the front said, "Before we do the raffle, do we have any visitors or notices?"

There was a silence. Claudine's chair scraped the floor loudly as she stood. The woman smiled at her and waved her up to the front. She realized she was going to have to take a risk and deal with Tonye later.

"Ladies, we have a visitor. Please come and introduce yourself."

Facing everyone, Claudine felt besieged by eyes. The women cocked their heads to one side, squinting, trying to place her, whispering to each other. *Pull it together, Claud.*

"Good afternoon," she said. "My name is Claudine Roberts. I've come from the UK because—I don't know if you've heard, but my niece, Nicole Oruwari, is missing."

Waves of "Oh no! What did she say? Nicole who?" traveled across the room in little ripples. The hard-of-hearing wanted everything repeated. Others seemed confused. Some seemed to just want to talk. The Asian woman hushed them.

"Nicole has been missing since July sixth—when she went for a boat ride," said Claudine. "She left from the boat club in Ikoyi with friends and never returned."

Another wave of whispers.

"She hasn't been seen since," Claudine said, and took a breath. This was more reaction than what she'd seen from Tonye and his family so far. "I need help. The family wants to keep things discreet, but I'm getting desperate for information now. Unfortunately, we have to consider that Nicole might have drowned somehow."

The women had to be hushed again.

"Obviously, I hope that's not the case, and so far there's been no evidence that she drowned. No actual body has been sighted. If you have any information—if you saw her that day, if you know anything about her life that can be useful, anything at all—please approach me after the meeting, take my phone number, or, in case you think of something later, the president will have my contact details. Please reach me through her."

It struck Claudine how alone she felt right now. Why was she alone? Why was she the only one looking for information about Nicole when that so-called family was sitting on their asses doing nothing? Even Bilal, watching from the doorway, seemed more invested than they were.

She went to sit down, tingling with adrenaline, feeling everyone's eyes on her and hearing the shock in their voices. The rest of the proceedings floated over her head, the raffle, the other notices. Finally the meeting formally closed. She sat there numbly, wondering what to do next as the women circulated in little swirls and eddies through the hall, saying their good-byes to each other.

A line of them formed to offer their—what? Condolences, support, the usual thoughts and prayers, probably empty promises to find information. It was mostly a blur to her. Some hugged her. It was comforting to see that some people cared about what had happened to Nicole, even though it was obvious most didn't really know her. Some asked Claudine to remind them what her family name was, to show her a photo from her phone, and enquired after her children. Others offered opinions about how dangerous Lagos was—pirates on the lagoon, the threat of kidnapping, the rotten boats that sank, and the useless sponge "life jackets" they gave out on the ferries. They reassured Claudine that Nicole was one of them and it was their duty to help in any way they could and rally round her. She was part of their family. A sister, as one of the women put it.

Eventually the line petered out, and there were only two women left.

"Good afternoon, auntie," said the first, stepping forward. She spoke with an American accent. "My name is Imani, and this is Astrid. We should talk in private." She said they had information about Nicole that could be useful.

Imani directed Claudine to meet her and Astrid at a café called Orchid Bistro in Ikoyi. She spoke to Bilal, who said he knew the place well, and they all left in their own cars. It wasn't far from the meeting place, a small restaurant with, as the name suggested, a lot of potted orchids on the grounds.

The café was quiet inside. A few customers on laptops. No one paid them any mind. Imani had already secured a table when Claudine arrived. Astrid ordered a coffee for herself and Claudine a tea. Imani launched straight into the discussion.

"It's always great to meet another Nigerwife's relative," Imani said with a smile. "I'm sorry about the circumstances, but it's almost like our own family visiting. The next best thing."

"It's very good you are here," added Astrid. She sounded Scandinavian. Claudine noticed she seemed quite nervous and reluctant to talk. "If anything happened to me, I would hope that someone would come looking for me too."

"And thank God you ladies have each other—for support," said Claudine.

Imani gave Claudine a brief history of the Nigerwives Association and her own story of meeting her husband at university and moving with him to Lagos in the mid-2000s, "when there were hardly any of the restaurants there are now, and no WhatsApp!" Astrid also talked about herself, being new to Lagos, having only arrived in January and only being engaged, not a proper Nigerwife yet. She showed off a sparkly diamond.

You marry someone and move four thousand miles away to a country you've never lived in, with a completely different culture, and where you don't know anyone except the man who brought you there. What could possibly go wrong? But Claudine said only, "Lovely ring. I wish you all the best."

"It's not forever," said Astrid. "I think just a few years, then we'll probably move to the UK."

Nicole had said much the same. *It's not forever. We'll move back soon.* Something in Claudine wanted to tell this young woman not to move here. She didn't know why she thought that. Nothing to do with the country. It was the part about leaving family. Nothing compensated for having family around to look out for you. But then, what kind of family? She looked at Astrid and Imani, feeling slightly choked. She could see they thought she was about to cry. She cleared her throat.

The tea arrived. Didn't anyone do a proper tea? Claudine wondered, seeing the yellowed water in the cup.

"I'm sorry Nicole has disappeared like this. She seemed like a sweet person," said Astrid.

"Are you friends?"

"Not really. It's complicated. But we—my fiancé—move in the same circles. And I've seen her out and about, you know, not just at the association meetings. But I didn't say something in the hall because . . ."

Imani jumped in. "We wanted to talk to you because Nicole was going through some things. We thought you should know."

"It seems so," said Claudine. "She didn't tell me about it."

"Didn't Nicole ever visit or call you?" Imani asked.

Claudine shook her head. "We were estranged. It's a long story."

"I remember when she came to Lagos," said Imani. "She was very chatty the first few years, but things changed for her over the past year. She withdrew, stopped coming to meetings until a few months ago. She had a birthday party for her son in January. She started coming again after that."

"Yes, Timi's birthday. I saw the photos," Claudine said. "They all looked happy."

"She actually seemed quite down at the party," said Imani, and Astrid nodded. "And soon after that . . ." The women looked at each other. Claudine knew what was coming.

"She was having an affair, wasn't she?" she said. The women looked relieved that Claudine had said it first.

"How do you know?" asked Imani. "Did Tonye know?"

"He said so. He wouldn't tell me anything else, though. He said I should leave it to the police, but they haven't done anything."

"We know who," said Imani.

"No, we can't be sure," countered Astrid.

"That's true. We both saw her with different people."

Claudine blinked. Multiple affairs? "Which people?"

The women looked at each other.

"Astrid, just tell her," said Imani. Astrid looked uncomfortable.

"I don't know!" she said.

"Astrid!" said Imani.

"I think I know who she went on the boat trip with," continued Astrid finally.

Imani nodded encouragingly.

"His name is Yohanna. Yohanna Ishaku."

CHAPTER FOURTEEN

NICOLE
Before

CHIEF SET his glass down on the varnished wood table inlaid with delicate gold scrolls around the edges. He burped and scooted back a little in his chair. He had just returned from his farm out in Epe, his pet project, and seemed irritable, a frown on his face. Perhaps it wasn't going so well, Nicole guessed, or he'd gotten stuck in traffic on the expressway. He usually loved to hold court over family dinner, and be teased by his women, and speculate about the volatile political and economic situation. But today he was a pissed-off bear not to be messed with. The dinner tonight was a lavish serving of pepper soup—his favorite—jumbo prawns, jollof rice, plain rice, plantain, chicken, vegetables, salad, and snails. Chief looked at it all with dissatisfaction, and no one dared to help themselves while he was speaking.

"Tell me, Tonye. We've not seen so much of our wife these days. I hear she has a job." He spoke as if Nicole weren't there.

Tonye cleared his throat. "Erm, yes, Dad."

"Tell me, what is it?" Chief asked.

"She's working in an art gallery, hosting exhibitions, liaising with clients, that sort of thing." Tonye's tone was carefully devoid of emotion one way or the other, for which Nicole was grateful.

Chief was quiet. They all waited for his next utterance: Tonye, on his father's right, looking like his father's younger self in his similar trad, just slimmer. Both tall, strong-backed men with dark skin, except Tonye had the slightly squarer jaw of Mother-in-Law, to his left. Abi and Tamara sat next to each other. Both had features similar to their mother's, but they had very different personalities, evidenced by the fact that Abi was self-contained and slim while Tamara tended to be indulged in every way as the youngest, evident in her ample curves. Timi and Tari sat beside Nicole. Blessing was just inside the kitchen door, awaiting their call. Emmanuel and David were standing to attention in their white uniforms, ready to serve or clear. Everyone seemed tense. Even the AC seemed to hold its breath.

"I don't understand. Is it necessary?" Chief said to Tonye. "How much can this kind of thing possibly pay?"

"Ahn, every woman needs her own," said Mother-in-Law. "You know, you want something for yourself." She opened her palms outward in entreaty. As she spoke, the sisters were careful to maintain neutral expressions and not draw attention to themselves. Tonye didn't look up at first, and when he did, it was just to read his father's expression and look down again.

"It's not really about the money," said Nicole in as natural a tone as she could muster. Tonye kicked her foot.

Chief ignored her as he at last reached for his fiery pepper soup, studded with huge chunks of croaker fish. Tonye cracked his knuckles nervously. Mother-in-Law took the opportunity to push snails toward him, then jumbo shrimp, but Tonye declined. She looked at him anxiously. He smiled back to reassure her. At least Chief eating gave everyone else a chance to fill their plates.

"Something for yourself," pondered Chief aloud when he'd emptied his bowl. He motioned for a refill. Emmanuel moved forward and brought the bowl, but it was Mother-in-Law who ladled the soup into Chief's bowl. Chief asked her, "Aren't the home and children enough?"

"Of course, but life is not just about children," said Mother-in-Law with a hopeless smile. "We all need something for ourselves, that we've made ourselves."

"What is this nonsense you're saying?" asked Chief angrily. Abi studied her phone. Tamara's fork froze between the plate and her mouth. "Something for yourself?" He snorted. "So all this—your fabric, all your jewelry, your homes—still not enough, but you must also have something for yourself?"

Everyone knew better than to speak.

"Tell me, Abi." She jerked to attention as her father continued: "If I have paid for your restaurant, bought the land, hired the interior designer, ordered the materials, paid the salaries for months, the initial orders of food—is this something you have done yourself?" Abi shook her head slightly. Chief turned to Tamara. "If I gift your husband with a house on Banana Island, a new Prado, a seat on the board of my oil company, is that not of yourself? Is it not coming through you? Or when I have also spent one hundred fifty million naira on your wedding, will you come to me and say, 'Daddy, I also need something for myself?' Tamara!" he shouted when she did not answer. She jumped in her seat.

"No, Daddy," she said quickly.

"Tonye, are you seeing this feminism rubbish?"

Tonye pretended to act nonchalant. He shrugged. "I hadn't looked at it that way, Dad," he said.

Chief looked at Mother-in-Law. "Please look around this house, my wife, and tell me what is of yourself." He hurled a word at her that Nicole couldn't decipher, and Mother-in-Law cringed. She looked over at her daughters for support. Abi's eyes were furious, Tamara seemed fearful, but both were now pressed into their phones.

"Tonye, since you are just moving food around your plate, please follow me to my study. I have some other things to discuss with you. Boys!"

Tonye rose to follow his father. He called for Blessing. Meanwhile, the boys unfurled themselves from the too-big dining chairs and lolloped after the men Nicole feared they would one day become. Blessing exited the kitchen into the dining room and followed the boys.

Mother-in-Law brushed imaginary dust off the rings on her fingers. Her nails today were enviously long, a gleaming metallic peach.

With Chief out of the room, they could breathe freely again. The girls looked at each other, still a little shocked, as if creeping out of a storm shelter after the tornado had passed. Mother-in-Law gave the palms again. "What did I say?" she lamented.

"Oh, Mummy," said Abi, "never mind all those times you were telling us how to be submissive wives. You *are* a feminist. Who knew?"

Mother-in-Law laughed a little sheepishly along with them. She smiled at Nicole. "Don't mind him. He's just stressed with this Knocking of the Doors. This family, the Governor's Son, you know, they have been so fussy. A lot of meetings, questions. Bride price. They want baptism certificates and medical tests." She shook her head in a bewildered fashion. "They're asking about her university days, if she has past boyfriends, her religious commitment, looking for any hint of scandal. All silly nonsense. Just forgive him. He is tired. Did you find something to wear yet—for the Knocking?"

Nicole hadn't given it any thought. She shook her head.

"What about the aso ebi from the Oyelowo wedding?" Mother-in-Law suggested. "That is pretty and simple, the blouse and the wrapper. We can't risk any modern styles. You would think Tamara was marrying into the British royal family." But she smiled as if this were indeed the case.

Nicole nodded.

"It's not a big deal for you anyway," she told Nicole reassuringly. "Just look nice so everyone is happy."

"Big deal for you, though, Mummy," said Tamara fondly.

"Yes." Mother-in-Law took a deep breath. "It will make me very happy." She looked as if she was getting emotional. "Come, Tam-tam, let's go over details in my room. I just want everything to go smoothly." They rose from the table, and she allowed Tamara to tuck her arm through hers, then led her out of the dining room.

It was just Abi left at the table with Nicole. Emmanuel and David were gathering up the dinner items and cleaning. Abi generally wasn't around that much. Her workdays were mostly spent hiding upstairs in the upmarket, casual dining spot she owned, going over figures and recipes. Now Abi walked around the table and sat next to Nicole in Tonye's empty chair. "We survived," she said. They both laughed. Abi placed a hand on Nicole's arm. "Don't worry about them. I think it's just taken everyone by surprise. You know what a traditionalist Dad is." She smiled, and Nicole started to relax.

Nicole agreed. Chief loved to talk about his growing up in the village, living a fairly simple life before his schooling began. She remembered the time Chief had told her that, as an incoming wife, her status was lower than that of the rest of the family and she should consider herself a servant to them. "Oh, he's just traditional, ignore him," Tonye had said too, finding that funny.

"And good for you," Abi added now. "I've watched you all these years and I know it hasn't been easy for you, moving here. It's good to see you finally getting out there."

Nicole could see Abi was making an effort. She'd previously found Abi to be haughty, but now she was being nice. "Thank you," she said. "It hasn't. I didn't think anyone noticed, though."

"Ah, no," Abi agreed. "They are not looking for that, only their son's happiness. You know how it is with sons." She glanced away briefly.

Chief had also told her she should feel sorry for Abi because Abi was unmarried and without children, but Nicole didn't tell Abi that.

Abi watched her intently. "He's all about the family. He's worked so hard for us." She tapped her watch. "Right now, he'll be boring Tonye to death about a real estate opportunity in Ghana or South Africa."

They laughed a little. It was true that Tonye was often randomly summoned from the sofa late in the evening to receive Chief's latest brain wave. It was a disadvantage of living within easy reach of parents. Nicole thought how pretty Abi was when she smiled. She wasn't one to go overboard like Tamara. She kept her hair in natural-style twists, neat and corporate, and preferred a shirt and pants over eye-catching clothes. She certainly didn't go in for the long, wavy "Brazilian" hair and layers of makeup that many Lagos women aspired to. She was also on the slim side, another of Chief's dislikes. "No one will marry an unhappy woman," he would sometimes say to Abi crossly. But she wasn't single because of her looks. It was clearly a choice.

"It's funny. Tonye tries too hard to please him and falls short," Abi continued. "I think I'm the one naturally most like my father. I have more of the skills he respects. Tonye was not a hard worker growing up. He has . . . ideas." Her lip curled momentarily. "But he gets side-tracked by his friends. He made it to university, I suppose, but come on, first degree was geography and he nearly failed that. I was the mathematician of the family. I got the MBA. But, oh well, none of that matters. You know how fathers are about their daughters."

Nicole shifted uncomfortably in her chair. She didn't know anything about fathers. She'd never had one who gave her the time of day. She wondered if Abi was expecting sympathy. She could only imagine how loudly Chief must complain about Abi's unmarried status when Nicole wasn't around.

"But you've done so well with the restaurant," said Nicole.

Abi sighed. "You think so?"

"Yes!" said Nicole, surprised that Abi was seeking her validation. "You have a beautiful restaurant that's the hip place to go in VI. I always hear such good reviews from people I know."

"You should come to Hibiscus and try our new agbalumo sorbet. I promise you, it's the perfect combo of sweet and sour. I'm obsessed with it."

Suddenly the lights in the compound went out. Everything stopped: the whir of the AC, the sound of the tap running in the kitchen, the music Nicole hadn't realized was playing somewhere in the house. It was so quiet she could hear rustling in the mango tree outside, the bats getting ready to lift from the tree en masse and sweep across the sky in a screeching black wave as they often did at twilight. "Ugh, NEPA," said Abi in disgust. "It's been on, off, on, off all week.

We've had to buy extra diesel for the restaurant, but still they chase you for their money as if you've been enjoying twenty-four-hour power the whole time." There was a shout from outside the house, somewhere near the security office. A response of tired voices.

"So this job," said Abi, flipping to a different topic. "Is it serious or just something for fun? I think it's great, by the way. This house will swallow you if you don't leave it sometimes."

"It could be something serious," said Nicole. "My friend Kemi is helping me get to know the artists and buyers."

"I know Kemi. She's a nice girl, and I can see you being good at something like that, especially with your looks—but in that sense, you must be careful. You know how Lagos men can be. So entitled. The fact that you're married is only a partial deterrent."

Abi's face was shrouded in darkness, impossible to read her expression. Nicole felt a sense of dread, wondering where this was going, if Abi suspected anything.

"Dad, as you can see, is a bushman at heart. Tonye doesn't say much, but . . ." She paused. "Did he ever tell you what happened with our brother, Ebipade?"

"The swimming accident?" said Nicole. "He's told me about it, how Ebipade drowned in front of him. He's still quite traumatized about it."

"Ebipade really was the best of us. So handsome and clever. Very even-tempered too. A perfect son in many ways, but more than that, he seemed to fill my father's cup in a way nothing else could. They were so close, it almost hurt to see it, to feel so outside of their bond. Tonye and I were almost invisible.

"Tonye was always jealous of Ebipade, who could do no wrong. In fact, he never did anything wrong. He was always jealous of that perfection. You think Tonye doesn't care, but he does. That day they argued relentlessly."

"Are you saying it wasn't an accident?" Nicole was shocked. This was the first time she was hearing anything like this.

"It was an accident. Just that accidents are rarely completely accidental with hindsight. If someone was in a rage and saw you struggling in the water—instead of helping you in that moment, they waited just a second. A second that was the difference between life and death." Abi's tears glistened in the dark. They could hear the repeated labored cranking of the generator. "I think it weighs on him. But these men, they will never look inside, do any internal work. It is always left to us women to manage it as best we can."

There was a brief electrical whine as the power surged from the generator and the dining room was flooded with yellow light. They could hear the click of the AC flap closing, then opening, and the purr of cold air coming out of it. Abi wiped her eyes hastily and stood up to go. Nicole didn't know what to say. They hugged, then both left the room, disappearing off to opposite ends of the house.

CHAPTER FIFTEEN

CLAUDINE
After

CLAUDINE'S PHONE rang just as Bilal drove up to the boat club's gate. She kissed her teeth. This was the second time Penny had called that morning. She couldn't deal with Penny's dramas right now.

"Ma," barked Bilal, just as she put the phone to her ear. He nodded toward the security detail, one of whom approached her window. She lowered it, and the man smiled apologetically.

"Can you name what member invited you?"

"Yes, it's Astrid." As she said it, Claudine realized she didn't have Astrid's surname, and Astrid probably wasn't the member. Her fiancé was. "I don't remember anything else."

"Please, we need you to call them for the name. It's very strict." He waved his pad. Whatever was on there?

Claudine dialed Astrid, who gave her full name to the gateman, and after a long while of searching his pad, he allowed them to roll into the car park.

"So Nicole came here a lot?" she asked Bilal as he stopped by the entrance to the club.

"I don't know, ma."

"Why don't you know? You were driving her, weren't you?"

"Madam took taxis, ma."

She hesitated to ask if it was because of the affair, whether he knew about the affair, and the car behind them beeped. She saw that other cars were waiting to drop off too, and let it go.

The boat club was busy with people as Claudine entered through the double doors. They milled about the passageways, sitting on sofas chatting, walking out onto the boardwalk—and, to the left, there was a café full of families. Children ran about. There was a general air of merriment.

She paused by the entrance, unable to spot Astrid in the crowd.

"Hello, are you looking for the servants' entrance?" said the doorman, seeing her looking lost and analyzing Claudine's short afro, her jelly shoes, T-shirt, and jeans.

"I'm a visitor!" Claudine snapped, giving him a dirty look. "I'm right where I need to be, as are you."

The man seemed a bit startled by her British accent. He gestured for her to go through to the front desk. Claudine gave her name to one of the receptionists; as he took forever to write her details into his logbook, she heard a familiar voice behind her and was thankful to see Astrid rushing toward her.

"There you are, auntie," she said. Astrid smiled warmly and kissed her on the cheek, which made Claudine suddenly emotional. Disarmed of her adrenaline, she felt tired and exposed and in need of a friendly face. She thanked Astrid for agreeing to ask her boyfriend to sign her in to the boat club so she could see this Yohanna guy for herself. Astrid had been reluctant until Imani nudged her.

Claudine followed Astrid out to the decked patio, which had a long bar and was dotted with tables and chairs.

"The weather is better than I thought," burbled Astrid.

"Is it always busy like this?" asked Claudine.

"It's more of a social place to catch up with people. We're over here."

Penny called again as Claudine followed Astrid along the boardwalk beside the lagoon. Pretty much guaranteed to be a man-crisis. The moored yachts and other boats swayed on the water before them. Uniformed staff moved between tables and chairs. Claudine tried to answer Penny's call, but it was too late. Perhaps it was for the best. She was still annoyed at Penny for bringing up the whole Len business, and she wasn't keen on talking to her nor losing her temper again in front of all these people. She put her phone on silent. Most of the people seemed overdressed just for sitting down and watching the world go by. Women wore heels and designer labels. This must be what all of Nicole's shoes and handbags were for, thought Claudine.

"This is Wale," Astrid said. A tall man with smooth skin and neatly shaved hair stood up to greet her. *He's a beauty,* thought Claudine. One of Mummy's Belafonte types. His nails, when he offered his hand, were pink and neatly trimmed, and his white tunic was starched to within an inch of its life. Bit of a dandy, though. He must forever be looking in the mirror for nostril hairs out of place. But he was friendly enough. He pulled out a chair for her and waved someone over to take her drink order.

"Terrible, just terrible," Wale said once the server had moved away. "Have you found out any more about what's happened to Nicole?"

"No more than what I've told Astrid," said Claudine. "She went on a boat ride with friends. Astrid told me it was on Yohanna Ishaku's boat, and that's all anyone knows. Trying to get to the friends has been hard. The police have been rubbish, and the family is taking their sweet time. I'm at a dead end."

He sighed. "I wish the police could have been of more help, but you know, this is Nigeria."

"That's what everyone says," said Claudine. " 'This is Nigeria, this is Nigeria.' I could understand if it was a small village with one sheriff in town, but it's the capital!"

"Abuja's the capital," said Wale. Astrid turned to him. "But I know what you mean," he quickly added. "It should be better here. Although even in the UK, you might have a problem with this guy." Lowering his voice, Wale continued, "His father—you know such people are above the law, really. I can understand the police not wanting to get involved or them being influenced."

"That's why I'm here. I'm not going to the police anymore. I'm gonna talk to Yohanna myself today. If he wants to kill me or arrest me, then . . ." She threw up her hands.

"No, auntie," said Astrid, reaching over and rubbing Claudine's arm. "It won't come to that."

The drinks arrived. Claudine took a sip of the brandy and Coke she had ordered. Her first stiff drink of the trip, and boy, did it feel good going down.

"I told her about Yohanna Ishaku," said Astrid, "that he's a member here, the one whose boat Nicole went on, many times, to his beach house in Ilashe."

"We haven't been to his beach house," Wale clarified. "Ilashe is an island strip not far away. There are a lot of beach houses there. She went a lot more recently. I think she went on the day she disappeared. We saw her that day."

"You remember?"

"It was a Sunday. We were sitting inside the club's café. It wasn't raining, but the sky was dark, like it would rain at any moment. And I remember seeing her go out toward the boat, and we said to each other, 'Who would go to the beach in this weather?'"

Astrid nodded, adding: "Someone else said, 'Well, they're not going to sit on the sand.' Then everyone laughed." Her tone faltered.

Claudine digested this. Even though she didn't particularly like Tonye, she could accept that the idea of people talking about them and laughing was horrible.

"I wouldn't say everyone laughed," Wale corrected Astrid with a look. "But it seemed odd."

"So this Yohanna Ishaku? Why is everyone so afraid of him? Do you know him personally?"

"No, but everyone knows who he is. His father is very powerful, a famous Nigerian figure, a billionaire. Such people—everyone knows who they are, their wives, their children. I understood that he moved back to Lagos perhaps a year ago. He doesn't have a lot of friends, but he's well-known."

"So how would I get to speak to him?"

Astrid pondered. "Sorry, I don't know."

"I don't know what Astrid's been telling you," said Wale, patting Astrid's hand, "but we can't get involved."

"I was hoping to see him here."

"The thing is," he said, "we saw her going on the boat, but honestly, it wasn't just with—that person." He looked around nervously. "There were often others. Friends, you know?"

Claudine nodded.

"What I mean is, we can't be sure what, if anything, was going on, enough to make any kind of statement. Does the family know you're here?"

Claudine hadn't told Tonye where she was going. She'd made an excuse about going to the Wheatbaker Hotel spa. He had recommended it as a place to unwind. Of course, he might check with Bilal, but she doubted he had been paying much attention to her movements over the last few days. The whole house seemed preoccupied with the imminent wedding. Every day people arrived to spruce up the lawn, wipe down exterior walls, prune the bougainvillea, paint the gates. There was a cow tethered to one of the palm trees in the garden that Blessing had said would be fattened, then carved up on the day of the wedding as a gift to all the staff. The cow seemed to sense its dim future because it paced the lawn nervously, snorting and pulling at the rope around its neck. She made sure to give it a wide berth when she went outside to walk around. Inside the house, mirrors and stairs were cleaned, new cushions brought in. Tailors came and went with fabric, dresses, suits. She could hear Chief's Wife shouting a lot, although for the most part it sounded like happy, excited shouting, the way Mummy shouted when she won at bingo. When Claudine bumped into Chief's Wife around the house or garden, she would swiftly change her demeanor, dim her eyes, as if suddenly remembering she had a daughter-in-law who was missing.

It made Claudine grimly pleased to imagine how horrified they would all be if they knew of her plans, that she had been talking to people. *But that's their business,* she concluded matter-of-factly.

"I'm done talking to them about it," she said.

Wale seemed uneasy. "You really need them for something like this."

"I need to speak to Yohanna Ishaku," said Claudine, surprised it wasn't obvious. "If he's here somewhere, can you introduce me?" She saw Wale's smile fade.

"Me?" he said, glancing around as if there were someone else. "No, I can't. Did Astrid say that? No. I don't know him at all. I could lose my membership." He actually blanched. She watched his hand creep to Astrid's shoulder and gently squeeze. Astrid kept quiet. Claudine suspected Astrid was going to catch some flak later if her fiancé was anything like Tonye—and he seemed cut from the same cloth. Nicole was missing, and all he could think about was his membership. *Don't stir things up.* Wasn't that what Tonye had said? She could understand to a certain extent, but she felt hot and frustrated. A stranger again, out here with all these people.

She looked from table to table. The men with their expensive watches and Gucci flip-flops. The women on their phones, taking selfies or just swiping. They all seemed like the same person. Full of themselves and just worried about their images. They could spare her the puppet show. It didn't impress her. It shouldn't matter whether you wore expensive clothes or cheap ones. Servants' entrance, indeed. You shouldn't need a long weave and one bag ah makeup just to go out in public.

Claudine swallowed the sharp words she had for Wale. Instead, she said, "So if you don't know him at all, how did you know it was his boat she went on?"

Wale looked embarrassed.

"Wale dated one of Nicole's friends," explained Astrid. "Kemi?"

"I don't know a Kemi, who is that?" asked Claudine. "Another Nigerwife?"

"No, Kemi is Nigerian. One of Nicole's best friends." Claudine couldn't remember Tonye mentioning a Kemi.

"Kemi was often on the boat too," Astrid said. "Yohanna knew them both pretty well."

Pretty well. A story within a story.

"*Astrid,*" said Wale. He put a hand to his head. "This wahala will finish us."

"There's not going to be any wahala," said Claudine. She'd learned that word already. "I just want to ask him some questions. I'm not gonna make a scene. Point me in his direction and I'll do the rest."

Wale looked down at the table. Astrid said nothing, but she turned and looked pointedly over to the far end of the boardwalk. Claudine, following Astrid's eyes, could see boats stacked in some sort of garage; a tall, broad-shouldered man in a lime-green polo shirt and cargo shorts was directing a group of men who were pushing a white boat toward the sandy shoreline.

"Looks like he's leaving," said Astrid. "It's a bit gloomy for sailing, but these diehards."

"Is that him?" asked Claudine, rising to her feet. "Thank you, dear."

"You can't just go over there!" said Wale, jumping up as well. But Claudine was off, walking fast toward the white boat.

As she approached, the man looked briefly in Claudine's direction, then away, not registering her intention to speak to him.

Suddenly a pair of large white dogs charged at her, barking savagely. Terrified, she shrank back from their attack, barely prevented by leashes tied around a bollard, and screamed to get the men's attention.

"Calm," the man in the polo shirt ordered the dogs, which made them stop barking. But they stood tensed, ears pricked up, ready to charge again.

He looked her up and down briefly. "Yes?" he said rudely, although there was a flicker of something like recognition. She remembered the doorman had taken her for a servant and drew herself up as much as she could.

"Yohanna Ishaku?" she said, mustering confidence despite still feeling very shaken. "I'm Nicole's relative from London. Claudine Roberts. Can I talk to you for a minute?"

He froze for a moment. Then he nodded. She stepped forward warily. "Continue," he ordered the men, who resumed launching the boat into the water. She noticed the boat now: pretty, with cream leather seats and pink trim around the side.

"You know Nicole's been missing for over a week now," she said over the din of the men. He looked at her fully now and then past her, perhaps to see if anyone was with her.

"I'm here alone," she lied. "I've come to Nigeria to find out what's going on with Nicole. Nicole Oruwari?"

He glanced back at the boat, now bobbing ready on the water, and gave the men a thumbs-up. "I'm about to sail out. I've nothing to say."

"But you do know who I'm talking about," pressed Claudine.

He bent down and gathered a heavy braided rope that trailed on the sand.

"She went with you on the boat sometimes."

He started walking away. Claudine followed until the dogs started growling and pulling again. "I'm trying to trace her last movements," she said loudly. "She was on your boat, wasn't she?"

"I've nothing to say," he repeated. "Go through my lawyers."

"I'm not with the family," she said. "This is just for me and for Nicole."

He walked to the water's edge and handed the men the rope. Exchanged a few words. Claudine waited. After a moment, he returned, but only to untie his dogs and crouch to pet them.

"It's all right, my babies, there you go." They nestled against him, jumping up and trying to lick him. He looked at Claudine. "Argentine Dogos are very protective," he explained. Claudine didn't doubt it. Satan and Lucifer looked ready to rip her to shreds if she made a sudden move.

"So am I," she said. "I'm the closest thing to a mother she has. I'm just trying to find out what happened."

He seemed to be listening.

"Do you think she's dead?" Claudine asked.

"Dead?" he said. "I thought she'd traveled. That she might be in London."

"But the police contacted you, didn't they? They told you she was missing."

He shrugged. "Police can say what they like. People go missing and show up days later as if nothing happened."

"Let's please talk," she said. "And whatever you have to say, I promise that will be it."

He thought about it. Eventually he stood up. "Fine," he said. "Let's talk. What do I care, really? I'm sailing out, though." He looked around again, as if expecting a SWAT team to rush out onto the decking. She didn't dare to look back at Astrid and Wale.

She trailed him onto the wooden jetty, his dogs circling her with what seemed like suspicion. The boat was now waiting below. One of the men was in the boat, arranging containers. The dogs clambered down into the boat at Yohanna's command, then Yohanna followed. The other man helped Claudine down. She said the first line of the Lord's Prayer as she took a seat. The dogs sniffed her, sizing her up. They were nearly as tall as she was seated, with powerful chests, and could easily hold her head in their long jaws. One jumped onto the seat next to her, snarling until Yohanna pulled it away and smacked it harshly, sending it whimpering to the other end of the boat. The dogs slumped down, but their watch continued.

The other man passed her a life jacket, which she hurriedly put on as the boat slid smoothly away from the bank. Apart from dogs, her other fear was water. She had never learned to swim. *Claudine, what are you doing?* She didn't know. But it was too late to change her mind. The shoreline was receding. Astrid was waving frantically from the deck, but she didn't dare to wave back.

It was noisy with the motor. Yohanna was driving. The other man sat in the front of the boat, giving them privacy. She wondered where they were going. The boat club long vanished behind them, they churned past fancy hotels and developments lining the shore, went under a bridge, and emerged in a more open part of the lagoon, a no-man's-land with unkempt bushes on the closest bank. Ahead was an area of islands that looked familiar.

She realized they might be close to the Oruwari compound. She looked around but couldn't place it.

Yohanna headed for an overgrown stretch of the shore that had a disused jetty with rotten wooden boards. The area smelled of sewage. He stopped the boat, turned off the motor. Why had he brought her to such a deserted place? She remembered Nicole's knife was still in her bag, could feel it through the soft material. Would she need it? Should she try to slip it into her sleeve while he wasn't looking, just in case?

He turned. He had disappeared behind oversized sunglasses, mirrored squares reflecting the cloudy sky. Satan and Lucifer jumped up and ran forward again. Claudine braced herself.

"Calm!" he shouted, and they simmered down. "They won't attack," he said. "As long as you don't run. They can sense when someone means ill to me. You're not a threat."

Claudine looked at them doubtfully.

"It's better if you don't stare."

She went against her instincts, turning her back on the dogs. "Why are we here?"

"Just a stop on the way to my beach house," he said. "You wanted to talk."

"Yes." She put a hand to her chest, trying to stop her heart from pounding.

Yohanna opened a cooler, retrieved a bottle of water, and passed it to her. She accepted it gratefully. "You look like her," he said. She nodded, quenching her thirst. She could tell he had thought of Nicole as soon as he saw her.

"Tonye called me in London, I think it was July eighth, to say Nicole was missing and there had been no sign of her," said Claudine. "A few days earlier, she left the boat club in this boat. I came to Lagos to find out what is going on. She's still missing. It's not looking good."

He said nothing, and it was impossible to know what he was think-ing when she could only see her own face distorted in his mirrored shades.

"So she's really missing." He seemed to consider it a theory.

"You don't think so?"

"Oh, I don't think anything. Obviously, I confirmed to the police that she had been on my boat, but I wasn't on the boat and didn't see her on the day in question."

"So who was?"

He clammed up.

"Weren't you having an affair with her?"

His face jerked up. "Me?" So he was surprised. "Is that what people are saying?"

"Well, they've seen her on your boat, going to your beach house with you? Tonye said she was having an affair. If not you, then who?"

He shook his head. "Wow. I assure you, I was not having an affair with your—your—"

"Niece," said Claudine.

"Niece. *She* had an affair with my friend."

"Who?"

"A family friend."

"What's his name?"

"It's not important. He wasn't involved in her disappearance. He just dropped her off. He saw her go."

"Of course it's important. Where is your friend now?"

"He's left town."

"How do you know they're not together?" asked Claudine, feeling a sliver of hope. But then it was dashed.

"Because *I* sent him away."

"Why run if—"

"He didn't *run*. I *sent* him. When it was obvious her in-laws knew about the affair, I sent him away to lie low. I thought she was hiding from them too!" As if anticipating her questions, he added: "He's in-nocent. He saw her go."

He sounded sure, but how could she trust that? Claudine thought it best not to challenge him out here.

"So people are saying *I* had the affair with Nicole?" Yohanna leaned back against the driver's seat, looking up at the sky. His tone was incredulous. "What else? Am I holding her against her will too? Have I killed her? Or perhaps she's at my beach house now enjoying a margarita by the pool. She likes those. Shall we go and see?"

"It's a joke to you," said Claudine. "But we are at our wits' end. She's a wife and a mother. Think of her children."

"A wife and a mother." He sneered. "I'm sure her in-laws are crying for this wonderful wife and mother who was fucking my friend for months." Claudine wished she could refute this, but she hadn't seen any tears from the Oruwaris.

"No, actually, you're right," she said. "They don't want to know what happened. They're pretending she's traveled too. Only I seem to want answers."

"Or perhaps they knew Nicole better than you."

Claudine didn't know what to say. She wondered herself.

"The Nicole I knew didn't care about her children or being a wife. She seemed crazy, if you want the truth. For all you know, there was another man and she ran off with him. She broke up with my friend before this disappearance. He's still shattered. Being with a married woman is not a small thing. Can you understand the risk to his reputation, his safety? In this country, it's hardly a crime to kill a man for defiling your wife. She told him she was going back to her husband and family. So he dropped her back."

Claudine sat up. "Where?"

Yohanna shrugged. "A jetty somewhere. I don't know. There are many."

"The police said she had been dropped at the boat club."

"I might have said boat club at the time to protect their secrets."

"Can you ask him where?" Claudine said. "It could be life or death."

"Everything is life or death in this country," he said. If he was moved, there was no sign of it. "Anyway, he's not reachable, and my lawyers have advised me not to comment further."

He turned away from her, to pet his blasted dogs again.

Claudine clenched her fists and told herself to calm down, knowing they were alone on his boat and she had no power to force him to help her. She scanned the shoreline and spotted a jetty that looked dilapidated and unstable. She tried to imagine Nicole getting off a boat there in the middle of the night and waiting for a stranger to pick her up. "I don't believe Nicole would get off at some random jetty in the dark. It seems too dangerous."

"Let me know when we can go back to talking about the things you don't know about Saint Nicole," he said.

"But why wouldn't she just go to the boat club, where it was safe?"

"Why do you think? To avoid those who would report her." Seeing her stricken face, he said, "Ah, you see the games now. Who was waiting for her at the jetty? She took a *lot* of taxis. Any of those taxi people could have abducted her. Perhaps there was even another guy. Perhaps her husband killed her in anger when she got home and everyone is lying about it. There's also her running away, faking her disappearance, even killing herself. I don't like to say that, but you can't rule anything out."

Claudine didn't say anything. Nothing made sense to her right now. She had thought talking to Yohanna would bring answers, but she felt more lost than ever.

"And what about Kemi? Nicole's friend. She was often on the boat, right?"

"Ah, Kemi." Yohanna smiled bitterly. "Kemi is easy to find. She works at the Wura Gallery."

"What should I know? Tonye didn't mention her to me. Is she involved?"

"All I'll say is people in Lagos are not what you think. Everyone is hiding behind a façade that matters more than the truth. We play our roles too well." He started up the motor and turned the boat around. There was no way to speak above the din. After some minutes, she could see the Ikoyi Boat Club coming back into view. He pulled into the dock.

As she got up to disembark, Yohanna put a hand on her arm. "I'm sorry if something has happened to Nicole. I only spoke to you because I hope she's found safe. But we have a phrase: 'Shine your eyes.' Nothing here is what it seems."

CHAPTER SIXTEEN

NICOLE
Before

S HE COULDN'T remember the first time Elias kissed her—what led to it or the day it happened. Not that first day because she'd been so nervous and careful to leave before Bilal started a fuss about closing for the day. He sometimes complained to Tonye if she kept him out late. Even over the next few days she would drop by in the mornings when the boys were at school but left before the evening rush. They'd order takeout for lunch. She learned so much about Elias, the Christian Hausa man. His parents were still in Kaduna, where his dad ran a church. Surprisingly, he was an only child, something he didn't elaborate on, but with many cousins, including Yohanna, who was almost like family but not blood-related. And it was obvious they'd had very different lives. General Ishaku had shipped Yohanna off to fancy boarding schools in the UK, then to an American university. On the other hand, Elias had attended a religious college, graduating with a degree in theology but no desire to preach. He'd moved to Lagos and found a job in advertising. It wasn't easy surviving on those wages in the city, but his fortunes changed when Yohanna returned to Nigeria after living it up in Los Angeles for several years, giving in to his father's insistence that he take on more familial responsibility. Nicole pictured Yohanna in LA, spending his days on lounge chairs and waking up in hotel suites with women he didn't know, and a stern father, like Chief, running out of patience and finally ordering him home. The two bonded as Northerners in Yorubaland. Elias ended up on the Ishaku payroll, working on their philanthropic initiatives. As with any Lagosian, there were other hustles—freelance jobs, projects with other friends—but to Nicole, it seemed as if Yohanna was the main gig. Elias helped him navigate life. Accompanied him everywhere. Acted as a buffer between him and opportunists. A kind of fixer-cum-therapist. As it turned out, even an Ishaku needed friends in a city of sharks.

No, their romance began soon after Nicole's strange encounter with Yohanna at the Wura Gallery in March. As the weather alternated between red-hot days and flash thunderstorms, they sheltered in place at his apartment, sitting on barstools at the kitchen counter, plotting how to have more time together. The gallery was a perfect cover for late meetings, and now a new Northern dairy company Elias had worked for as a graphic designer and photographer was launching a range of yogurts. They wanted Nicole to come on board as a consultant, advising them on how best to speak to middle-class mothers, and to be the face of the brand, which would provide excuses for more days, even weeknights out of town. Elias outlined his vision for a new life waiting for them, in which they would both be self-sufficient, free to live as they chose, together. Over sushi from Izanagi and biryanis from Spice Route, he made it sound like they would take over the world.

To prepare Nicole for her gallery work, Kemi had taken her shopping to the various boutiques in Lagos, finding figure-hugging outfits the old Nicole would have worn, with shorter hemlines and more cleavage. The ankara dresses disappeared. Tonye grumbled that her new occupation and the many events she said she had to attend were disruptive to the household. She wasn't there to manage Samuel. The children pestered him for attention when Blessing wasn't around. But he was making a good show of not caring that she had been sleeping in a separate bedroom since hog-tie-gate, and also acted unbothered by her changing looks. She had begun straightening her hair, which she had never done before.

But Elias noticed. He looked at her and *saw* her.

He asked about and listened without judgment to the story of her mother dying of a drug overdose in their council flat when she was seven. The rest of her childhood growing up with her aunts and grandmother. Her marriage to Tonye, how they'd become estranged but never been right because, as she explained, they were both closed-off people, unable to reach each other. Elias hated Tonye on principle, even though, for him, the issues with her in-laws, her closeted life, were normal. That's how families were. Even, his silence sometimes implied, how they *should* be.

He talked about his past relationships too. Lagos had broken his heart a few times already. There had been girls on their way up the social ladder who left him as soon as they found more eligible options. His mother had been beautiful and intellectual and could have married anyone but fell in love with a pastor who would never be rich. The women in Lagos were not like his mother, he said. They fell in love with money.

Nicole's favorite thing was for him to lie on her. His muscles were taut and rounded. Chest on chest, his weight pushing her farther into the bed, arms on either side of her like walls. She had never asked Tonye to do this. She had asked nothing of him. Nor he of her, nicknaming her Prudence.

When pregnant with Timi, she'd met a woman in one of her prenatal classes who told the group she could never get enough sex, stunning them into silence. Nicole had blanched at that. Pregnancy and a new baby had been a saving grace from her "wifely duties."

Now, she could also never get enough.

Elias would trace her collarbone and tell her he had been waiting forever for someone to unlock his innermost thoughts. He said Nicole reminded him of his mother. It fascinated him—Nicole's ability to look beyond riches in a world where money was everything.

They lay together on the bed afterward, their calming bodies glistening as they talked, staring up at the ceiling or at each other, trying to calculate how much time they had left by the length of the shadows on the wall.

"You are so beautiful," he would say. Tonye had said the same countless times, but it sounded like he was congratulating himself. When Elias said it, it didn't feel related to her looks at all.

She found herself telling him how strange her life was. "Sometimes I wake up, and the house is so quiet. Everyone has gone. The children are at school. Tonye has left for his office. The staff clean and cook, so no one cares what I do, how I spend my day. If I don't change out of my pajamas, they won't notice. Nobody asks how I am, what I want, almost as if I'm not there. Not real. Not in my life, just watching it from above. A ghost, a piece of furniture, a chair. Once Tonye called me a chair with three legs, useless. But at the beach, you saw me."

After she told him that, he began to take more photos of her, some candid shots, some posed with perfect lighting. Sometimes they planned shoots, with dramatic dresses from past parties, or even cloth styled around her.

He often returned to discussing his mother, who had walked away from everything for love, and the women who'd left him for men with more money. He remembered their names, their faces, the things they'd said. How they'd all betrayed him in the end, that he would die for them, but they didn't care. He showed her their accounts on Instagram, updated her on their lives since, speculated whether they were happier than if they had remained with him.

She didn't mind him talking about them. Finally, someone wanted to share himself with her, and he wanted to know all about her too in a way no one ever had. He asked her to explain her life in the UK and strove to understand her Jamaican-ness. How cold was it there? Were the Jamaican people like the ones he saw on YouTube? He'd noticed a funny but disturbing trend of Jamaican women setting fire to their pussies in dancehall parties in videos. What was that about? Was it difficult to satisfy Jamaican women? How would life in the UK suit him? Where would they live?

But when she asked if he wanted to leave Nigeria, Elias seemed certain that he didn't. Things were finally happening for him now, and through the Ishakus, there would be limitless opportunities. "But when I'm with you," he would say, tracing a finger in circles on her back, "I feel like I've traveled."

If his exes could see him today, rolling with an Ishaku, and lying there with Nicole, their mouths would drop open in shock, he assured her. His place in the world made him angry. Anger made him hard. He would turn her over and handle her as if she had rejected him for a wealthy man.

The bed was a deserted beach they visited often. The daylight was the only witness and even it lost interest in them. They were not remarkable except to each other. In a short time, she'd come to know Elias better than she knew Tonye, who seemed even more of a stranger since Abi's revelation.

Sometimes she still wondered who Tonye's hog-ties were for, what that woman was like, and then she'd imagine herself with them on, trussed up like a turkey, and push Elias to try new things with her. "Use my ass," she told him one day. He frowned. Another day: "Choke me." He would laugh, asking, "You like that?" He was still a pastor's son. She would shrug; then, despite his initial reluctance, he would harden and comply.

Together they created a reality that existed only within Elias's small apartment. She knew her way around blind. The fridge freezer behind the door that held only drinks, rarely food. The number of steps to the sofa. Where the light was strong enough for selfies and where he kept the strawberry gummies for his sweet tooth. They made love, played house, danced to Trace TV music videos in the living room. In their world, she was just Nicole, and he was Elias. The rest was circumstantial until finally, when the April rain began, an insistent drizzle, a whisper of the storms to come that would drench them all, Nicole watched Elias sleeping like a sated child, the moon on his shoulder, and doubted this Lagos that would be theirs. It was all fantasy. As tires crept across the gravel downstairs, she stooped to pick her dress up off the floor, where it had ended up in a hasty heap. She struggled with her zip—her tailor always made them so flimsy. The weight in the bed shifted and then Elias's fingers were easing the zip up past her shoulder blades, brushing away her hair as it reached her neck. The moon threw shapes at the wall as he kissed her, gently at first, but then with increasing desire until she pulled away.

This was the second taxi. The first had driven off in exasperation.

"When can I see you next?" Elias asked, as he always did before she left, as though afraid each time was the last. Trying to maintain some kind of continuity between their impromptu interactions.

Nicole wondered too. Since the beginning, he'd always wanted more, but it was getting dangerous. No one noticed a few hours in the day, but when it grew late, it caused whispers.

"Can you come tomorrow?" he asked.

In the twilight, she couldn't make out his expression, but felt the intensity of his stare and smelled herself on his breath. Did her breath carry his scent too? He got out of bed, leading her by the hand out the bedroom through the living room to the front door, where they heard the car's Afrobeats floating up, saw the gleam of its lights from the balcony. He held her tight. His embrace was fortifying. His lips found hers, but there was loss now in every kiss, like water leaking from a bucket as quickly as you tried to fill it. She left filled with his optimism, but knowing she would be empty by the time her compound gates clattered open.

IT RESUMED soon after she moved into the spare room, the prickles from the sheets that became crawlers, thoughts like nails on a blackboard, ears sharp for the sound of heavy footsteps on the carpet, the unavoidable creaks from worn floorboards underneath. The doorknob turning quietly with a click. Sometimes a sliver of light under the door disturbed her sleep; sometimes the faint smell of days-old grease triggered the memory of a wifebeater vest not changed for days, armpit, brandy, aftershave, and Nicole's nine-year-old self would brace under the covers and pretend she was asleep as long as she could. She took to wedging a knife under the mattress again.

It had been a relief not to face the nights alone anymore when she had moved in with Tonye. His bulk, reassuringly close in the bed, permitted her to accept sounds for what they were. A door opening or closing somewhere, the patchy banter floating up from the gatemen trying to keep themselves awake with tall tales, the generator's growl, the beep as the AC clicked back on after a power changeover, the whining compound gates that squealed and shuddered in the wind, the rain that fell like a drumroll on a snare were just those things, nothing more.

When she'd lived alone, and even during her marriage whenever Tonye traveled, she had discovered that a knife under the mattress helped her sleep better. Given media representation of Nigeria as a desperate and lawless country, she hadn't trusted anyone at first, especially not people who earned so little. And even after arriving, people regularly shared stories of terrifying home invasions. She read a story in the newspaper about someone who'd kidnapped his neighbor's child for just 5,000 naira. He didn't get the money, and he killed the child. Samuel earned 70,000 naira per month, less than £400, but some of the gatemen earned less than 20,000. And she'd heard of a nanny who, for that same amount, delivered the child of her Canadian employer to kidnappers who then demanded $250,000 in ransom. Meanwhile stories of servants getting their revenge were rife: a hated madam chopped up with a machete in her fancy Ikoyi home by her cook, a whole family poisoned, a house set on fire in the middle of the night. For years, she'd slept with the knife when she was alone, traveled everywhere with the children, and insisted on GPS tracking for the car. Eventually, though, she'd started to relax, to trust her staff. The gatemen were just boys. People were mostly good. She stopped worrying so much. She let Blessing and Bilal take the children to playdates or to school. She and Tonye could track them from their phones. She started to feel safe.

Tonye knew she had issues sleeping at night, but not why. He'd never asked, just as she'd never asked why he didn't like water. He teased her for scaring herself with sensational news stories. "This is the safest place in Lagos," he reminded her often, pointing out that, apart from having their own security staff, they lived less than a mile from the Bonny Camp army barracks and the Victoria Island police barracks. They were a stone's throw from the highly guarded Nigerian Security Printing and Minting Company, from which the naira rolled out in convoys of armored tanks periodically, and that was opposite a naval yard. There was also a warship permanently moored on the lagoon, and constant security tugboats powering up and down the shipping lane. It wasn't a place where a score of armed robbers could confidently slip off the boat or march up the street marauding house to house.

ONE NIGHT in early April, a few weeks into her relationship with Elias, she hurried into her room late and was shocked to find Tonye sitting at her dressing table, his long legs sticking out awkwardly from the pink leather stool. He was looking into the mirror, a hand in her Créme de la Mer pot, scooping out the cream with his fingers.

"What are you doing? Are you drunk?" she said, trying to seem unconcerned as she put down her handbag but kept a safe distance, conscious of where she had been and what she had been doing.

He daubed cream on his face and rubbed it in. He looked like he had just come home himself, fully dressed in his going-out trad with the velvet trim, stinking of the nightclub—cigarettes and Hennessy.

"Stop it," she said, and rushed to rescue her face cream. "That stuff's expensive."

"Good morning," he said. He wasn't slurring but didn't seem completely there. His eyes rested on her, seeing her as if for the first time in ages, her messy hair, her smudged makeup. "It's late. Where have you been?"

It *was* late. She had fallen asleep at Elias's place, woken in a panic in his arms. He hadn't seemed bothered by her situation. Sleepily told her to stay and not worry about it. It made her wonder if he'd watched her sleeping, deliberately not woken her. She'd rushed to call a cab despite his protests. Their gateman, shining the flashlight into the car, had been shocked to see her.

She went into the bathroom and shut the door. How ironic that Tonye finally cared, finally saw her, and it was like this. She wiped her face as quietly as she could and brushed her teeth, hoping that when she came out of the bathroom he would be gone—but he was standing in the middle of the room, looking more awake. His eyes followed her as she slipped out of her dress and into pajamas, then sat down to begin securing her hair with bobby pins.

The first few years of marriage, she'd felt so lucky. She would lie in bed next to Tonye, wriggling her toes with excitement for the life they had together. Her gorgeous husband, their two boys, a luxurious life in Africa. No need to look back or dwell on the past.

When things changed, or rather when she first noticed all was not well, was during her second pregnancy. Tonye had been detached about the whole thing. Indifferent when she showed him the positive test result. Disappointed on hearing it was another boy. She didn't know why. He was grateful for Tari's safe delivery in London, and Tari, bless him, had always been a sweet baby, but Tonye rarely engaged with him. When he played with the children, Timi got most of whatever affection Tonye had. When she raised the issue, loud, nasty rows were the result. The insults they hurled at each other came from the pit of hell. Bore no correlation to reality. Both said the other ruined their life. Both said the other wanted them dead.

They used to lie in bed chatting happily. Tonye had hoped to open a chain of hotels across West Africa, a shopping mall in Port Harcourt, an office block in Accra. He even dreamed about starting a helicopter company, and they would never need to drive to Murtala Muhammed Airport again. They would move out of the compound in perhaps a year, build their own forever home on Banana Island. He would be his own boss, a tycoon of sorts, and she would be—well, she would be there, cheering from the sidelines, enjoying the ride, the first lady of everything.

Except five years later, he was still his father's employee, managing his father's companies, with not a single business of his own.

Chief and Tonye didn't seem to see eye to eye on anything. Tonye wanted to take risks. Chief wanted slow and steady. When things went wrong—the catfish got sick on the farm, the hotel manager stole $100,000 right under their noses and gambled it away before he was caught, the political environment became less favorable to oil and gas exploration—Chief found fault in Tonye. The leash got shorter every year, and so did Tonye's laugh. He slept facing away from her, stopped talking to her, stopped seeing her. The lies began. Apparently it was easier to see other people. And one day the hog-ties showed up in his carry-on.

"Why are you using taxis when you have a driver?" Tonye said now.

Nicole secured a section of hair with pins. "I'm doing a lot more now with the gallery work. I wouldn't want to overwork Bilal."

Tonye rolled his eyes. "Be sensible. You have a driver for a reason."

"But I need to go out seven days a week."

"Yesterday I went outside to see Bilal praying next to the car, while you had already left in a minicab. It was the middle of the afternoon."

"He needed to rest."

"Then, tonight, you come back in a cab while he sleeps in the BQ. I'm paying him to drive, not pray or sleep."

"Well, I don't know what it is anymore," she said as airily as she could. "Am I to respect Bilal's working hours or not? He starts at eight a.m., and by five p.m., he wants to close. Am I to keep driving him until the early hours of the morning?"

Tonye shook his head. "So suddenly you're more concerned about Bilal's working hours than your own safety coming home in a taxi driven by God knows who in the middle of the night? You—who're always going on about how dangerous Lagos is?"

"It's like you always say—there's a risk to everything, and Victoria Island is very safe." She looked into the mirror and kept doing her hair.

"I was out late, and even so came in before you," continued Tonye. She could feel his eyes boring into her back. "Where were you for so long?"

"Errands. Friends. Do you want an itinerary?"

"Now you have friends who want to hang out till three a.m.?"

She shrugged. "Afternoon cocktails at the West, then RSVP for dinner, and after that, Zen Lounge, Maroccaine, wherever. It's all part of my job now to be out and about, networking. I have to catch up after not working for so long."

She stood up from her stool and walked toward him. He stood aside as she went to her dresser and removed a bonnet from the top drawer, then trailed her to the bathroom, where she put her dirty clothes in the wash basket. "Where were you, anyway?" she asked, coming out of the bathroom. "Silver Fox again? Rubbing oil on some stripper's ass?" She felt his eyes following her as she went back into the bedroom and tidied the dressing table.

"It might seem like everyone's partying on Instagram, but Lagos is conservative, and small. The people who matter—they will soon talk," he said.

"Do they also talk about you and where you go every night?"

"It's not about me. I'm a man. You will see what happens if you embarrass us."

Nicole suddenly threw the pot of cream at him. He took a step back.

"So, I can't be embarrassed?" she said. "Or does my embarrassment at the things you do not count?"

"I'm just saying."

Nicole pushed past him, snatching her cream from where it had landed on the floor. Luckily it hadn't burst open.

"Now, don't play the victim and cry about how terrible your life is," he said.

She put the cream on the dresser, her hand shaking. "Yeah, a husband who can't talk about anything. A liar always off with different women. Whose main job is groveling to his father all the time."

She watched his face start to change. His jaw hardened. Then there it was—the short laugh.

"What would *you* know? Where is your father? Your people have no culture to worry about, but here in Nigeria, we all have our role to play so we don't end up completely dysfunctional like you guys."

"I don't want to play a role and live a fake life."

"My father warned me not to marry you. I didn't listen."

"Because you wanted your British passport."

"I didn't need you for that."

"Saved you some time, though. I should go back to London and leave you to it now."

"Go and live wherever you want, do what you like, but don't even think about involving my children in your stupid plans." His tone was controlled.

"They go where I go!"

He leapt through the air balletically and slammed her back against the vanity, scattering the various pots on top of it. She cried out as she fell to the floor. He straddled her, his hands on her neck. He looked directly at her, searchingly, as she choked and pulled vainly at his grip. "I will *never* let you take my children away from this house." Before he could say more, they both heard cries from the doorway and turned to see Timi sobbing in alarm. Tonye released her and she scrambled up from the floor, coughing, but Tonye stood and grabbed her arm to keep her from going to Timi.

"Blessing!" he shouted. "Blessing. Come here!"

Nicole struggled to get past him, but he blocked her with his body until Blessing arrived, pulling her nightclothes around her.

"Take him!" he ordered. Blessing picked Timi up, comforting him as she did so. She threw Nicole a worried look, then left the room, closing the door behind her.

CHAPTER SEVENTEEN

CLAUDINE
After

CLAUDINE WAS exhausted after her confrontation with Yohanna, but she called Mr. Ogunsanya from the car on the way back to the house from the boat club anyway.

"Yes, Mrs. Roberts?" he said. She didn't have the energy to correct him.

"Did you check the jetties around the boat club? The other ones? Perhaps the ones that aren't used much? She might have used those, because of—well, because of the affair."

"Did you find some more information?"

"It's just a hunch, talking to her friends, seeing where they all went." She couldn't let him know she had been speaking to Yohanna. Not that he seemed particularly interested.

"Thank you," he said. "I have noted it down for my team. We will let you know if we find anything."

She said good-bye, doubting he would tell her if he found anything anyway. She needed time to think things through. What it all meant. What her next steps should be.

Emmanuel opened the front door for her before she could ring the bell and bowed as per usual as she entered. Claudine thanked him. What a strange, self-contained man he seemed to be, buttoned up in his starched white uniform and speaking as little as possible, like Bilal. It might be the best way to survive on this compound, she supposed—keep your head down and speak little. But what did it do to you over time?

"Good afternoon, ma," he said. "Chief would like to see you in his boardroom."

"Oh, really? What is it about?"

Emmanuel just smiled, said nothing.

"Well? He wants to see me now—this minute?"

"Yes, ma."

"But suppose I've got things to do. What then?"

His smile faltered as she glared at him. He looked worried, poor man. She imagined the tongue-lashing he received anytime he put a foot wrong.

"Well, I'm going to the toilet first. He'll have to wait."

Claudine started toward Tonye's apartment, but noticed Emmanuel following a few steps behind. It was almost like being summoned to the headmaster. Well, she wouldn't let him intimidate her.

"For God's sake, am I under arrest?" Claudine snapped, and halted.

Emmanuel abruptly stopped, almost tipping into her. "No, ma. Sorry, ma." He bowed and backed away, but continued to wait.

"I'll come when I'm good and ready, and you're not gonna stand against the door. Go about your business."

"I will tell him you will be with him now."

"Just go away."

He bowed again, then turned on his heels and off he went, his tail between his legs.

It was a relief to go into Tonye's apartment and shut the door behind her, her hands sweaty, still bristling. Why was her heart pounding? She washed her hands in her bathroom and splashed water on her face. It could be anything. He might just be asking how she was doing—he did that sometimes if he saw her in the reception area.

Chief was a large man like Tonye, with a sterner face, but it wasn't like he was going to get out the bamboo cane. Claudine laughed at herself in the mirror. But how rude to summon her like one of his lackeys. Why didn't he get off his overfed ass and waddle over himself if he wanted to talk to her? What a cheek! She had a good mind not to go. What was so urgent? Had he heard about her trip to the boat club? Surely not—she'd just gotten back. Perhaps Bilal had said something about it to Tonye while she was there, but surely Tonye himself would've called her if he had an issue. Could Yohanna have complained to them, made threats? Not likely; he wanted nothing to do with it. Gosh, this family. This house. They knew how to put the frighteners on you. Nicole was a meek little thing. These big personalities must have crushed her. "Duppy know who fi frighten and who fi tell good night," as Mummy liked to say if someone bullied her out there in the world. Many tried, but few succeeded. Mummy was the one everyone was afraid of. Claudine straightened up. If Chief wanted words, she had words for him, all right.

She didn't really know where the boardroom was, but headed toward a shadowy corridor where it might be, and soon enough, raised voices met her. She paused. It sounded like the whole family was in there, talking at once. The door was open enough for her to see Chief's Wife and the sisters, Abi and Tamara. The young one who was getting married was sobbing at the top of her lungs, hardly making sense. Tonye and Chief were invisible behind the door. She looked up and down the corridor—no one was coming—and listened.

"Why mention the wedding?" Chief's Wife was saying. "What does that have to do with Nicole? Does this gist woman think *we* killed her?"

"The story even names the Governor's Son. Jesu." That was Chief, sounding a lot less sure of himself for once. This was something he couldn't control. "She's offering us a chance to add comments to the story or pay to keep it off her blog. Shall we just pay?"

"How much?" Tonye asked.

"Fifteen million naira," said Chief. Claudine's eyes widened. Ten thousand naira was forty quid, so anything in the millions was serious money.

"Na wao," Claudine heard Abi exclaim, but with a certain sarcasm, as if it was all a bit of a joke. Though Claudine was too tense to laugh, it reaffirmed her sense of kinship with Abi, whom she'd always liked—they both seemed to be the only ones with sense in their families. "With all these secrets this woman keeps, no wonder she lives in Banana Island," Abi added.

Had Claudine's announcement about Nicole's disappearance at the Nigerwives meeting the other day anything to do with this? Word must've traveled fast if they were already being blackmailed by some kind of journalist. And the family was having a crisis meeting about it. Feeling some dread about how angry they might be toward her, but also strangely exhilarated, she wondered what they would do now. *Finally*, it was out in the open. Their dirty secret. Wouldn't this force them to do something?

"Banana Island?" asked Chief's Wife.

"So they say," said Abi.

"All that from blogging?" asked Tonye.

"It's one of the most visited websites in Nigeria." That was Abi again. "Gossip sells. And keeping secrets is even more lucrative."

"It's not as simple as writing a check." Tonye again.

"Why not?" Chief said. "Isn't it just about the money? Fifteen million. We can negotiate, nau."

Claudine's heart sank. Would they just pay off the blogger to sweep everything underneath the carpet?

"Fifteen million is just one Hermès bag," added Abi.

"Will you be serious?" snapped Tonye.

"They want to ruin us," cried Chief's Wife, and it gratified Claudine that at least it had shaken up this family. Now that their reputation was at stake—they cared. She had never heard them like this.

"The word is out," said Tonye. "It will soon be on the front pages of *Vanguard, Punch, This Day*, all the papers. Even if we pay her off, some other blog will publish. Word is spreading. What do we do now?"

That self-absorbed girl cried harder, making it impossible for Claudine to hear what the others were saying. Ooh, she wanted to grab her and shake her quiet.

"This woman has brought ruin on us." Chief's Wife meant Claudine, of course.

"Mummy, please don't stress yourself." Tonye sounded genuinely worried. The woman appeared to be hyperventilating. Good.

"How can I not stress myself? Two thousand people, Tonye. Caterer, venue paid. Planner all paid. What is fifteen million naira anymore if we have to postpone?" *Blah, blah, blah, blah, blah.* Claudine raised her eyebrows. More fool them. They should have canceled the wedding straightaway.

"Postpone?" The girl's voice was so high-pitched she squeaked.

"Postpone." A short laugh. Tonye again, but she wasn't sure—Chief had a similar laugh. "Why should we postpone? Haven't they already paid the bride price?"

"Oh yes, bride price." It could only be Abi. "They've bought her like a chicken at market. I hope we specified no return to sender on the receipt."

"Why, will they ask for it back?" Tamara's horrified wails started up again. Couldn't someone put her out of her misery?

"They can," said Chief.

"Maybe they will say we have done juju on Nicole and made her disappear." Claudine could imagine Chief's Wife twisting her rings frantically until they flew off.

"I warned you not to marry her." Chief's words fell on Claudine like stones. She didn't know why that hurt so much. She would have been surprised if they'd never said this. Even so, it stung and made her furious. She was about to throw the door open, but Tonye spoke first.

"Dad, no."

"You had your pick. You chose this Akata woman over a Nigerian. Yoruba, Igbo, even Osu would have been better."

"Ah, no." Claudine couldn't tell which of those "others" Chief's Wife objected to.

"Their wahala is too much," Chief went on. "Someone who understands our ways would have been a better choice."

"Ehen." Chief's Wife now seemed to agree.

"You didn't listen."

"You didn't approve of my wife, but you approve of the former governor's son?" said Tonye. "The son of a man who stole his state's money and spent it on cocaine and whores? During his tenure, he didn't even lay one road."

"Tonye, calm down."

"Igho cannot even visit his home state again. I hear that whenever the townspeople get word he is coming, they collect rocks to throw. He cannot even get out of the car. They promise that if they ever find him in the street, they will throw a tire over him. And the son is not far from his papa."

"Calm yourself!"

"I should never have listened to you and moved back here." Claudine clicked her fingers. *Thank you. Tell him.* "She would still be here." Before Chief could reply, there was the sound of something clattering onto the tiled floor. A chair? Footsteps. Claudine shrank back against the wall as the door flew open, but it was too late to hide. Tonye looked startled to see her in the shadows, but if he suspected she had been standing outside the room listening, he said nothing. Perhaps he didn't even really notice her as he strode away. He seemed to tremble with anger. She had never seen him like that. Seconds later, the front door of the house slammed. She could hear him shouting for his driver. Then the screech of the compound gates. Tires. He was gone.

It was quiet in the room now. Exposed in the doorway, Claudine had no choice but to enter the room. The family was all seated around a long oval wooden table. Paintings hung on the wall—horses; Tonye and other men on a field, holding a trophy. The room smelled of despair and frustration. No one met her eyes except for Chief, who looked as though he wanted to smash something. Probably over her head.

"Claudine, how are you?"

"Good afternoon, Chief. You called? Family meeting?"

"Yes, except Tonye—he had to go," said Chief. "Please join us. He's coming back."

Claudine sat down in an empty chair. "I don't think so," she said. "He just left the compound. What is this about?"

Chief closed his eyes. He pressed a hand to his head. "Let's talk privately," he said, waving his wife and daughters out of the room. Abi and Tamara looked at each other. They stood up and headed to the door, but Chief's Wife hesitated.

"It's all right, go," he said.

Still she didn't move. "But shouldn't I—"

"Go!"

She rose, and the three left the room, shutting the door behind them. Claudine took it as a sign that he was about to let fly at her and clenched her fists on her lap under the table, steeling herself.

"This rubbish," Chief muttered, wiping his brow. "I am *tired*." For a while, he drummed his fingers on the table, which only made her anxiety worse.

"Did Tonye tell you about Ebipade?" he asked eventually. "My first son. Did he tell you what happened?"

Claudine shook her head.

"Tonye is not much of a talker when it comes to the things that really matter to him," said Chief. "We are similar in that way. I wasn't raised to show my face. You know what I mean?"

"I think so."

"My first son was Ebipade. He drowned some years ago. It was an accident. He and Tonye were roughhousing in the water at the beach. A riptide came and pulled Ebipade under. There was nothing anyone could do."

"I'm sorry," said Claudine. It made sense now, what Tonye had said about the water being *deceptive*.

Chief cleared something in his throat. "My father was a hard man. A good man, but very strict. He died young, during Biafra." Claudine didn't know what that was. "The civil war we had in the seventies.

Millions died, including my father, who resisted the occupiers. He never got to see the man I would become. I tried not to be so harsh with Ebipade, but it didn't make any difference. I also didn't get to see the man he would become. It's hard losing a child. Even the thought . . . I kept hoping that he had washed up somewhere farther along the beach, dazed and confused. I searched for him. But he was never recovered. I even bought this house so I could look for him daily in the water. As if he might swim past."

Claudine nodded, sensing what he was trying to say but couldn't speak aloud, afraid of what might come gushing out. She sat up straighter, stiffer.

"We are not so different, you and I," he said slowly. "We both have our traditions. Some of ours you may think are good, some no longer right. Our people have a saying: 'What is God in one town is meat in another.' But as with yours, our traditions serve a purpose. They keep our families together. I think we can find somewhere in the middle. We have the wedding on Saturday. I should have canceled it, but I have this anxiety about time running out. Time is always against us. I should have done more to investigate. I'm sorry."

He *seemed* sorry. It was hard to know. In spite of herself, she felt sorry for him.

"I didn't approve of Tonye's marriage. I still don't. Culture is very important, and the woman is the heart of the culture. It was important to me that as head of our house, Tonye married a woman who understood. Nicole did not. But I still embraced her as a daughter. She has given me two grandsons, and we thank God for them." He seemed somewhat genuine. "I hope you will find her."

Claudine wanted to ask him what he would do about the blogger but didn't want to admit to eavesdropping.

"I asked the Nigerwives for help," she said.

"Yes, I know," he replied. He didn't volunteer any further information. "Ah, well, what's done is done. We will deal with the consequences. Hopefully, the wedding will still go ahead." Before she could object, he added, "Try to understand. The traditional engagement isn't just a party—although it often looks that way. It's difficult to explain. Please, allow us this. Our rituals are heavy with superstition and significance. If it doesn't happen, under these circumstances—Tamara's dignity will suffer. I worry a stigma will attach to her forever. I already have one spinster."

"There are worse things than being a spinster," Claudine said. Tamara's fiancé didn't sound so great anymore. But she knew Chief wouldn't listen. And why should he? This was his world. The rules were different here, and although she herself had chosen to be alone—many men had looked at her, some still did—there wasn't any magic about it. She still depended on others, was still spoken to as if she were a child. There hadn't been anyone she'd liked before Len, but afterward she saw his face in every man who desired her, like a ghost.

Mercifully, her phone rang. It was Penny again.

"Okay, take your call," he said cheerily, as if they had just been chatting about how awful the weather was in London. "It was good to talk."

They rose to their feet, and he patted her on the arm as he escorted her out of the room.

Claudine knew what she needed to do next. She had another message from Penny, but put her phone on silent. She would call her later. This wasn't the time to get distracted.

She needed to find Kemi.

CHAPTER EIGHTEEN

NICOLE
Before

S HE'S HERE," Abi called up when Nicole arrived at the main house. Mother-in-Law soon came down the stairs with Tamara clattering after her in stilettos and—today—long blond hair.

Mother-in-Law's Mercedes was ready outside, and the three younger women squeezed into the back with Mother-in-Law in front next to her driver, whom Nicole liked very much. Nicole had worn a Masai choker necklace from a safari trip to hide the bruising at her neck. Abi gave her a sharp look but said nothing.

Mother-in-Law fretted and dabbed at her face with a handkerchief as the gates were unlocked and dragged back. "I hope there isn't much traffic," she said anxiously. "We are already so late. Mrs. Sanomi is always busy. If we miss our appointment—" She clucked at the thought.

"What are we getting from the fabric shop?" asked Nicole.

"We are so behind," said Mother-in-Law. "We have the Knocking of the Doors and the traditional ceremony in just a few months. Now that things are agreed, Daddy wants to move quickly." She crunched into some nuts she had brought with her.

"Mrs. Sanomi?" Nicole stared blankly.

"Oh, you'll recognize her from various weddings," said Mother-in-Law. "She can be a little—familiar. But unless you want to fly to China yourself, her cloths are the best."

They were over Carter Bridge and on the mainland quickly. Traffic wasn't as bad as Mother-in-Law had feared. Tamara and Abi spent most of the journey glued to their phones, washed by Mother-in-Law's constant chatter.

I will never let you take my children. Recalling Tonye's words from last night made Nicole shiver, though she was not cold. She wondered if she should carry the knife on her instead of leaving it under the mattress. They hadn't spoken since. This morning, they'd stayed out of each other's way, but who knew what the next argument might bring? *Your people have no culture.* As if she was inferior and should feel grateful to be putting up with all his chauvinistic rules and restrictions just because of his family name.

". . . at Tamara's wedding," Mother-in-Law was saying. "Nicole, you will see a real Oruwari wedding now. Your own was small," she added regretfully. Nicole remembered her wedding dimly as a glamorous, frothy blur with over two hundred people—most of whom she didn't know. The Park Lane Hotel was the venue, with the best suites booked for VIP guests. There were three cakes, half a dozen photographers, and fancy gifts for the guests.

A satisfied laugh escaped Mother-in-Law. "After this, Abi, it's only you, my eldest daughter. Don't worry. We still have enough saved for your wedding also."

"Give it up, Mum," Abi said, rolling her eyes. "That ship sailed a long time ago."

"Ah-ah, God forbid," Mother-in-Law said, still in good humor. "Just leave a space for God. He has his plans. And who can question His timing? When you see the house Tamara's husband has built for her in Parkview Estate, you will change your mind, nau." She tried to catch Abi's eyes through the makeup mirror, but Abi looked pointedly out of the window. "When she's a big madam with her own house, her own driver, her own staff, hey—I promise you will want to marry and also be called madam."

"I have staff now, and they call me madam already," said Abi a little crossly.

"Is it the same? Are you sure it's not because you are paying them? But if you are a *married woman*, then every person has to respect you. Staff or not."

"So I should marry for a house and a car? Why don't I just do runs like ashawo?"

Mother-in-Law sputtered. "And what is it called when you are running around with men you don't want to marry for free?" Tamara gulped her laughter down until Abi dug her in the ribs. "You are lucky because your father is rich, but think of the future," Mother-in-Law continued. "Will you be begging your younger brother for the rest of your life?"

Abi didn't reply, but Mother-in-Law kept going, a meanness entering her tone. "I'm sure all your friends are saying you are bad luck. You have collected all the bad luck in this family." She waited for a response, and when it didn't come, added, "Your father is being considered for kingship in his village. This is how they will blame your stubborn spirit for not giving it to him. Oh, well. Daddy is very kind. He has forgiven me for spoiling you."

Fortunately for Abi, they soon pulled into a leafy compound with the main house at the end of a drive and parked outside a smaller building to the side. Nicole knew Abi was livid from the way she slammed the car door and then sullenly greeted Mrs. Sanomi.

Nicole did recognize Mrs. Sanomi from the weddings she had attended, a slim, ebony woman with a head wrap and understated bubu, who was a little younger than Mother-in-Law. Mrs. Sanomi ushered them into a carpeted reception room with a long table and some velvet-padded chairs. There was a display cabinet for jewelry sets, hanging gold earrings and necklaces set with matching stones, and another cabinet for handbag and shoe arrangements in a rainbow of colors. And then wall-to-wall, floor-to-ceiling shelving full of brightly colored folded fabrics in every shade and pattern you could imagine. A corridor led to what looked like a rabbit warren of similar rooms.

Abi sat abruptly on the nearest chair and buried herself in her phone. Nicole and Tamara settled on chairs beside her. A young assistant offered them a tray with bottled drinks. They were clearly going to be there for a while. Nicole's thoughts drifted toward Elias. Rushing to get dressed and upset by the argument with Tonye, she'd not been able to text him that morning. She knew she would already have several unread messages from him. He would message her throughout the day and send photos he had taken of her, often candid shots when she wasn't aware. She dared not open her phone with Tamara sitting so close to her that their dresses overlapped.

"And who is the groom?" asked Mrs. Sanomi as her assistants laid out an array of stiff taffeta, a cocktail of pinks, aquamarines, and citrus colors. "Is he from Lagos?"

"Igho," said Mother-in-Law. "Delta State."

"Is that the former governor Igho?"

"His son," said Mother-in-Law, trying to hide her triumphant grin behind a roll of emerald silk she had in front of her.

"Is it the *first* son?" asked Mrs. Sanomi. "I know he has three."

"Second," said Mother-in-Law, then quickly added, "Who wants the weight of a first son these days? They end up being so—so—" She searched for the word.

"Boring," said Mrs. Sanomi helpfully. "They carry all the cares, and it makes them so serious."

"Ehen," said Mother-in-Law, emphasizing with her open palms. "Do you have this fabric in onion pink?"

"Of course." Mrs. Sanomi pointed one of her girls to a roll of cloth higher up. The girl stood on a footstool to retrieve it. "First sons generally do inherit the most, though," she said, turning back to Mother-in-Law, who simply smiled.

"He has enough money, nau. He is building a marital home in Banana Island."

Mrs. Sanomi murmured how wonderful it was.

Mother-in-Law received the onion pink and handed it to Tamara. "And what about Abi, your oldest daughter? When is her day?"

Mother-in-Law's neck snapped straight, and her daughters glanced at each other. Nicole threw Abi a sympathetic look.

"Abi will marry soon enough," Mother-in-Law said with narrowed eyes. She turned away from Mrs. Sanomi. "Tamara, what do you think of this pink? Shall we order it and go?"

Tamara raised the cloth to the light. "Ah, no, too drab. We'll look dark in the pictures." She passed it back to Mrs. Sanomi. "What about salmon for the traditional ceremony?"

"Abi, dear, still looking for Mr. Right?" said Mrs. Sanomi, carefully rerolling the pink silk while an assistant hurried to get the salmon-colored fabric.

"She is busy working," interjected Mother-in-Law. "But this year, God willing, she will focus."

"How old are you now, Abi?" said Mrs. Sanomi, giving Abi a sharp look. "I might know someone suitable to match you with."

"She's almost forty," lied Mother-in-Law, twisting her rings. "God has his time."

Abi looked away. Nicole reached out and squeezed her hand. Abi squeezed back. "It won't get better," she whispered. "Don't bother hiding the bruises. They won't care. Leave if you can. Take your boys and go someplace where you can be happy."

It took all Nicole's energy not to cry at the thought of happiness. She was so tired of the fighting. She tried to focus on what Mrs. Sanomi was saying instead.

"Hmm, but God forbid, it's not nice to see such a fine girl left by the roadside. People have been saying, 'Ah-ah, why is this girl still single, without children, unless something is very wrong?' You know me, I don't gossip. I'm even happy that you are standing up for her, knowing how some mothers would be tearing their bubu from stress because, at forty, to still be unmarried . . . When people talk about spinsters in this community, how misfortunate they are, it so irritates me. I'm telling you. Anyway, I'm just happy to see she is looking well, not malnourished or anything. She will soon marry and silence them. Praise God." While Mrs. Sanomi continued in this vein, Mother-in-Law grew as stiff as the taffeta on the table. "I have some men in mind. But, hmm, forty. I will call you." She smiled apologetically at Mother-in-Law. "To get the right match, that's the thing. Too many divorces these days. Every day I hear of another marriage crashing. The couples you would least expect. Nobody has shame today!"

Nicole wondered if Mrs. Sanomi was making a dig at her now, if she knew something about her and Tonye's rocky situation. She ignored Tamara's sly glance. Her smugness wouldn't last. When the euphoria of being married died away, Tamara would find new challenges in her in-laws' ever-shifting expectations of her: to get pregnant quickly; to have a boy; to have a girl; to have more; to breastfeed; to snap back; to manage her house; to raise healthy, well-behaved children; to be a submissive wife, keeping her husband and his family happy, always serving her wants and needs last like she served her plate at dinner, trying not look exhausted.

"Indeed," said Mother-in-Law brusquely. "Let's move faster, please. I don't want to be caught on the mainland late."

"Of course," said Mrs. Sanomi, collecting herself. She pointed across the room. "Have you considered a fabric in mustard?" She walked to the cabinet herself and opened it. With a dramatic flourish, she showed off a range of beige silks in organza, satin, and taffeta, as well as lace and velvet. "Mustard is the new pink. All the rage."

DUE TO the earlier rain, Nicole and Elias were the only diners eating lunch outside at the Grill by Ishtar, a newly opened high-end Lebanese restaurant popular during the cooler evening hours, when the bar was open as a place to smoke hookahs and listen to music and chat with friends over bites from the grill. At night, the place was always illuminated with colored lighting, pinks and blues. There was a private raised swimming pool area at the back of the courtyard, privacy maintained by curtains on a frame around the pool.

Since the April rains had begun in earnest, it was deserted. Theirs was the only table in the courtyard—at Elias's special insistence. A large umbrella shielded them from whatever might come. There were even roses on the table that he'd brought in a little glass vase. Nicole was impressed at his finding such a safe spot. Other restaurants at this hour were too popular; you wouldn't know who you might bump into. Here, the high fence on all sides protected them from prying eyes. There was no car park, so no danger Bilal might wander the grounds nosily and see them.

A couple of children's voices could be heard behind the curtains currently screening the swimming pool. No danger of being seen, but she wondered who might be beyond them. Even the thought of one person seeing them made her anxious after Tonye's outburst. She had never seen him so angry before. Who knew what he might do next? Throw her out of the house? Keep the boys? Carry out his joking threat to throw her into the lagoon?

"Relax," ordered Elias, following her eyes toward the pool. "You're not fun like this."

Nicole didn't feel very fun. Ominous clouds lurked above them threatening rain. How precarious it all was, this lunch, their affair, her life.

"I'm fine," said Nicole. "Just in my thoughts." She drank some wine and tucked into the food on the table.

He leaned over and stroked her arm. "Don't I always find the perfect spots for us?"

She couldn't deny it. Over the past couple of weeks, he'd been imaginative and adventurous with their dates, driving her to the mainland to find picturesque cafés and boutique hotels she didn't know existed. The nooks and crannies of the islands. He knew when popular spots like this would be deserted. Still, it increasingly felt like a game of Russian roulette, with her luck about to run out at any moment.

"Maybe we should go to Ghana together for a weekend," Nicole suggested, knowing there was no way she could, but liking the idea anyway. "Or Cotonou. We could drive all the way there. I speak some French."

"Your English ways. Your gray eyes. You understand the world so differently than me," said Elias, seeming delightfully amused by her idea. He traced a finger along her arm, looked right into her eyes then, and Nicole felt the tiny hairs on her nape frizzle up. He picked up her hand and kissed it. "Remember, when I'm with you, I feel like I've already traveled."

She felt his desire prickle through her veins. It felt so good she could almost forget Tonye's suspicion, his fury. Elias wouldn't understand. He thought they could continue hopping from restaurant to restaurant indefinitely.

"How are we going to resolve this situation?" she asked. "Tonye's been giving me hell."

"What about?"

"About this!"

Elias waved it away. "How can he know anything?"

"He's suspicious. He asked me why I was taking taxis." This news didn't seem to bother Elias the way she thought it might.

"Well, why are you? You have a driver."

"I can't trust Bilal. He might rat on me."

"He won't bite the hand that pays him."

"Tonye pays him."

"So pay him more. You have your gallery money now."

"He won't take it. He's so religious, always praying, everything is an abomination to him, he's too principled."

Elias rolled his eyes. "Principles are not bread. You can't chop them. Everyone needs something in Lagos. It's how this city is. I grew up in a church, and believe me, no one is too godly for needs and wants. If not for himself, for someone else. Doesn't he have a family member who needs a kidney transplant or a job?"

Nicole thought for a bit. "He has a brother looking for work. But I can't get him a job."

Elias clapped. "No problem, I'll get Yohanna to hire him. His father's got many businesses. No special job?"

"No, I don't think so. Bilal said any job would do. He's just come up from the village. Security or something like that."

"They are always hiring security at LAD to keep squatters away from Bar Beach. The Ishakus are major shareholders. I will enquire."

"Thank you."

"Did anything else happen?"

"He didn't outright accuse me, but we had a bad row. I said I might go back to the UK, and he blew up. Of course, I didn't say anything about you."

"Good to hear. If I'm going to have Chief Oruwari's men at my gate, I should know," he said with a smile. "Look, babe, I'm not worried about him."

"He said he doesn't care what I do, only if I tried to take the children . . ." She couldn't say it. She shivered again, even though it was in the seventies. She saw Elias looking over at her questioningly.

"So, okay, don't panic and don't run to the UK," Elias said. "We're not going anywhere."

"Then what? I'm not going to be able to continue doing this much longer."

"Stay with me," he said.

The thought had occurred to her in the early days, more as a fantasy—staying in Elias's apartment with the gorgeous artwork. He wasn't far from the compound. It was almost walking distance if the climate had been more temperate, with proper pavements and traffic lights and no risk of kidnapping. He was very clean and his apartment compound was secure, with power and clean water. But it was never a realistic possibility in her mind. She played in his house as if it were the Wendy house at infant school, where you role-play Mummy and Daddy for a couple of hours before changing into your real clothes. He said *stay with me* as if her life could be packed into a small suitcase to be slotted onto a shelf in his closet. She could see he had zero idea of what her life entailed—not just how dependent she was on Tonye, but how much went into her simply living in Nigeria. All her things, not just clothes but her books, her keepsakes, her documents, her medical costs, her driver. He complained about how expensive their lunches were. What would he think of how much she spent just on food generally? The 500-naira packets of foreign-branded crisps she bought for the children? Salmon at 5,000 naira, more than a day's salary for Bilal. His statement was disappointingly denialist, even if he was trying to be lighthearted.

"But what about my boys?"

There was a pause. Then Elias said, "Here, the children belong to the father's family. It's just how things are. Especially when they are male. But so long as they are educating and providing for them . . ." Even as he tried to be diplomatic, she could tell he hadn't factored them into the equation.

"They are *my* children," she said.

"So live somewhere else. He'll have to pay for it. Divorces happen all the time now." He said it as if it were already sorted. *Un fait accompli.* He was only a few years younger than her, just turned thirty. But she felt so much older. He'd never married or had children, evidently hadn't wanted that responsibility. He couldn't seem to understand how complicated her life was. His blasé attitude scared her, but perhaps there was a positive in it, if she thought outside the box. Perhaps she just needed to change her thinking.

"Talk to Yohanna," Elias said. "If he intervenes, they can't take your children."

She thought of Yohanna, drunk, laughing, an arm slung around Kemi's shoulders, sticking his tongue out at her.

"But why would he intervene?"

"Because of me. Yohanna relies on me, you know? He's been through a lot with his father. He tells me everything."

Nicole suspected Yohanna saw things very differently.

"If I tell you something," said Elias, "you must promise not to go running to Kemi about it." Nicole nodded, and Elias continued, "His father has arranged a marriage for him. He's given him an ultimatum."

"What? To who?"

Elias shrugged. "Some former president's daughter. She's young, just finishing her master's in London. Quite pretty," he added.

"But why can't he just marry Kemi?"

"What makes you think he wants to marry Kemi? Or marry at all? These are his father's orders. He has lost patience with him. He's in his eighties and wants his son to show responsibility to the family. If he doesn't marry, he'll be disinherited."

"But then Kemi needs to know." Nicole was already dreading the conversation. Kemi would be devastated, furious. After Wale, how would she take another knockback?

"Let him tell her," said Elias, as if reading her mind. "It's not your problem."

She nodded slowly, but knowing that it was very much her problem and that she would have to tell Kemi as soon as possible. She wondered why Elias had so much faith in Yohanna when it was obvious how self-centered he was

"Anyway, my point is that you shouldn't be stressed. You have a job now. I have other business ideas. Yohanna's already agreed to invest. We'll be okay." He launched into his pipe-dream business plans, when and where and how.

Two little girls peeped out from the curtained area by the pool, brown-skinned girls with pigtails. They looked very alike, identical twins. With a shock, Nicole realized they *were* identical twins—Imani's twins—and sure enough, Imani strode out from the curtains seconds later, shooing them down the steps in front of her across the patio toward the restaurant.

Nicole froze. If she stayed put, would Imani walk right past their table and not even see her? She seemed in a hurry. Cringing inside, Nicole slowly got to her feet. Perhaps Imani had already seen her and was trying to spare her blushes, in which case not saying hello would seem too suspicious. She couldn't take the risk.

"Imani, hi." It was their first time seeing each other since the trip to Mushin. Nicole hadn't attended any meetings since February.

"Nicole?" Imani stopped and said hello, while her daughters skipped around the patio, pulling at the climbing leaves on the wall and realizing they couldn't pull them off because they were artificial.

The women exchanged light conversation. Imani was full of praise for the swimming pool they'd had to themselves the whole morning.

"It was a spur-of-the-moment thing. We were sitting at home, then the sky cleared, and we jumped into the car. With rainy season under way, who knows when we'll get the chance to swim next?"

As Imani spoke, Nicole could see her registering everything: The lone table. Elias sitting with her. She imagined Imani taking note of his sandals, his tunic, his duck salad, the roses, and her half-eaten burger. It was all incriminating evidence she would keep in her Nigerwives files. To Nicole's relief, Imani didn't ask to be introduced to Elias, and she seemed to accept Nicole's claim to be on a work lunch and having a cold as an excuse for eating outside.

"Well, I'd better run. I have a salon appointment," said Imani at last, shepherding her girls inside. Nicole watched the door close and saw that Imani was moving through the restaurant, not hanging around to look back at them. Finally she turned back, to see Elias's face like thunder.

"Why didn't you introduce me to your friend?" he demanded as she sat back down.

"Introduce you, are you insane? Imani is one of the Nigerwives. She's not really a friend anyway."

Elias stabbed at his salad petulantly. "If she wasn't a friend, then why did it matter? You could have simply said I was your business partner or a friend."

"I suppose so."

"So then, why didn't you? Are you ashamed of me?"

"Please forgive me," said Nicole. "I'm just so worried."

"Yes, about Tonye." Elias's voice was hard. "We can't have him upset, can we?"

"He's still my husband."

Elias swept his hand across the table, knocking all their plates and glasses onto the floor. They smashed against the paving stones. Food upturned on the ground. The vase in pieces, roses and petals everywhere. The server came rushing out, exclaiming.

Elias stood up. "I'm sorry, very sorry," he kept saying, helping to pick up the broken pieces of glass and china. Another staff member came out with a broom and dustpan, followed by the Lebanese manager of the restaurant, a middle-aged woman, concerned to see what had happened. Nicole held her breath, watching for Imani's return, but it seemed she had already left.

"I'll settle it," Elias said. "It was an accident. Just give me the bill."

Nicole sat frozen to the chair, too shocked to be embarrassed. Elias's reaction had come out of the blue. What had she said? Tonye was her husband. It wasn't new information. Why had it set Elias off? She hadn't seen this side of him before. He didn't seem angry anymore. He sat down at the table next to her.

"Should we bring you anything else?" asked the manager, still looking worried.

"Just the bill," said Elias. He smiled sheepishly. "It's the heat," he said, making a big show of mopping his brow. "A mistake."

When the floor and table were cleared, they were left alone. Nicole didn't know what to say.

"I understand about Tonye," Elias said. "But he's irrelevant to me. I love you, and together there's nothing we can't do. So don't run. I love you."

I love you. He looked at her, seeming expectant to hear it back, but she was wary of using the term, especially as she hadn't known Elias for that long. She knew how easily even the strongest feelings could fade after a while. She had come to the lunch intending to warn him that she might have to leave, to prepare him for the fact that this relationship couldn't be serious for now. It wasn't him, it was her. She had to think about her life seriously, her future, and what to do next. As he clasped her hands in his, she wondered how she could tell him and what his reaction would be.

"And don't worry about your driver," Elias added, gazing at her intently. "We'll give him a reason not to talk."

Nicole nodded again. She didn't dare to do anything else.

CHAPTER NINETEEN

CLAUDINE
After

C LAUDINE WALKED through the glass doors into a white-walled gallery and asked for Kemi. As the receptionist called her, Claudine looked around at the sculptures and paintings on display, though she wasn't one for art and wouldn't have a clue what any of it meant. It was all slashes and pretty colors to her.

A sharply dressed woman with long braids and stilettos click-clacked toward her. "Hi, can I help you? Are you delivering something?"

"Claudine Roberts. I'm Nicole's aunt." Kemi looked at her blankly. Then she blinked hard. Claudine put a hand on Kemi's arm, worried she might keel over. "Sorry, I know you're not expecting me."

"Is this about Nicole?" Kemi asked.

Claudine nodded. "Yes. I've come from London to look for her. Can we talk?" She glanced at the receptionist, then back at Kemi. "In your office."

"Sure, sure, of course," said Kemi. "This way."

Claudine followed her through the gallery, another white-walled room of paintings, and into a glass-fronted office. There was a sleek white desk, and several of what she assumed to be framed paintings covered in bubble wrap leaning against the wall.

"Please sit down, auntie," said Kemi, pushing the various papers, string, and tape to one side of the desk. She herself seemed to drop limply into her chair. She opened her desk drawer and rummaged through it but closed it again without taking anything out.

She gave Claudine an anxious, wavering smile.

"Can I get you some water?" she asked in a hollow voice, as if going through the motions. "Tea, soft drink?"

"No, thank you," said Claudine, although her stomach begged for attention again.

Kemi picked up her mobile anyway. "Please," she said to whoever was on the other end, "bring water, soft drinks. Thank you." She stared at the phone in her hand, turning it over and over.

"Did Tonye send you?" she asked, still seeming to be in shock.

"Hadn't you heard?" Claudine was finding it hard to believe Kemi knew nothing at all about Nicole's disappearance.

"Heard what?" Kemi blinked up at her. Kemi seemed like a nice girl. When she was sitting, her long braids hung almost to the floor. Pretty and well put together. Her distress seemed genuine, but come on. *Shine your eyes*, Yohanna said.

"She's missing," said Claudine.

Kemi's eyes narrowed. "Truly missing?" she said doubtfully. "She hasn't traveled?" She repeated it almost to herself. "I heard she'd traveled."

"Heard from who?"

"I—" Kemi suddenly seemed flustered. "No one. I just assumed. I haven't heard from her in a while."

Claudine digested Kemi's reaction. On the one hand, she knew something was up with Nicole but didn't seem to believe it was serious. Was she trying to cover for Nicole, or did she have secrets of her own to hide?

"Nicole's been missing for almost two weeks now," said Claudine, watching Kemi closely. "I'm surprised you didn't know as her friend."

"Two weeks?" Kemi seemed very shocked. It was so difficult to tell. "Oh my God. So she hasn't traveled?"

"Nicole went on a boat trip with some friends and didn't come back."

Kemi shook her head vigorously, as if this was unbelievable.

"When was the last time you saw her?" Claudine asked, observing Kemi frown as if it was hard to recall.

"It was about a month ago now. At a café. She was talking about leaving Tonye. I honestly thought she'd traveled," Kemi reiterated.

"What made you think she'd traveled?"

"A few days after that, she stopped responding to my messages."

"And you didn't think to ask Tonye if she was okay?"

Kemi fell silent.

"I mean, you're her friend. Why wouldn't you ask?" All these people seemed to have gone on with their lives without missing a beat. It didn't really make sense.

"Well, I couldn't assume anything. I could have been wrong."

"Wrong about what?"

Kemi looked around the room as if for an escape hatch.

"I know about the affair," said Claudine.

Kemi's eyes flickered to hers. "What affair?" she asked faintly.

"Nicole and that guy, Yohanna's friend."

"Oh, that affair, yes," said Kemi. "I told her to break it off."

"Was there some other affair?" Claudine asked, fearing she was about to be hit with details of a second affair Nicole was having. She was trying to be open-minded but didn't know if she could bear hearing about another supposed affair.

Kemi opened her mouth, then closed it again like a fish. Everybody seemed to have something to hide in this town. Claudine wondered how long she would have to sit there before Kemi talked honestly. She couldn't be telling her everything. She wanted to reach out and shake this girl by her shoulders, but—*you catch more flies with honey.*

There was a knock at the door. They both looked up to see the receptionist with a tray of drinks and two men standing outside the glass.

"Miss Kemi," she said, putting her head through the door. "The men from Kuramo Waters Hotel are here for the artworks."

"Oh!" Kemi shot up from her chair. "Yes, I forgot."

"It's not a good time?"

"No, it's not," said Kemi, then changed her mind. "Actually, let them come. The paintings are ready to go." As the two men and the receptionist entered the office, she took a sheet of sticky labels from the pile on her desk. Then she crossed the room to show them the two paintings. Directing them how to handle the pieces, she dropped the sheet, which wafted to Claudine's feet.

Claudine picked up the sheet to be helpful. Couldn't help noticing who the stickers were addressed to—Mr. Yohanna Ishaku. As the men tested the weight of the paintings, Kemi started looking around for her sticky labels.

"These?" said Claudine, holding out the sheet to her. Kemi paused. *Mm-hmm*, thought Claudine. Kemi took it and peeled off a couple of stickers, pressed them on the bubble wrap.

The men struggled out of the room, with the receptionist anxiously warning them to be careful.

Kemi shut the door and sat down, putting the sheet on the desk.

"You can drop the act now," said Claudine, tapping the sheet. "Start talking. Don't make me come back with the police."

Kemi pressed a hand to her head for a few moments. Claudine made a big show of getting to her feet.

"Okay, okay. Just . . ." Claudine sat down. Kemi lapsed into silence again. When she looked up, Claudine could see tears in her eyes. Crocodile tears, no doubt. The truth rushed out like a burst pipe, about Kemi's relationship with Yohanna and Nicole's with Elias. Claudine was happy to finally have the name of Nicole's lover.

"I never understood Elias," Kemi concluded, as if still trying to make sense of it. "Why him? He had nothing. He was nobody. It made me angry. I didn't see the point to it."

"Where is this Elias now? Could they have traveled together?"

Kemi shook her head. "He's gone," she said. "Yohanna is protecting him."

"So when I came in, you knew all about the investigation. You lied to me."

Kemi looked apologetic. "I'm sorry. I still thought she might have run away." She picked up some tissues and cried into them, sobbing loudly. Claudine passed her a bottle of water from the tray. Kemi sucked it dry. Claudine watched her, her mind spinning. She felt caught in a game of chess with someone much smarter, but who?

"Since you know all about the affair, we should go public now," she urged. "We can go to the British High Commission together and tell them what we know. You're a witness! They need to do a proper investigation, arrest this Elias person. He might have—" She stopped abruptly. She didn't want to think it.

Kemi shook her head vigorously. "I can't," she said. "You don't know Yohanna, what he's capable of. I can't go around making accusations against people like him. His father's a general. Even Tonye. Please, please don't say I said anything." She was on her feet, pacing, crying, pleading.

"But she's your friend. Wouldn't she do the same for you?" asked Claudine, feeling just as desperate.

"Auntie, you don't know how hard it is being a single woman in Lagos. You are always under suspicion. You're always vulnerable. I can't afford to get involved. I'd have to leave the country. Promise me you won't say anything."

Reluctantly, seeing Kemi was in danger of getting hysterical, Claudine assured her she wouldn't involve her. Better to have the girl onside for now.

Kemi sat down again, dabbing her eyes with tissue. She combed through her braids, twisting them over one shoulder, and sighed. "I kept hoping she had just left and was going to work it out, then come back. It made no sense that she hadn't contacted me. I was too scared to speak to Tonye. I guess neither of us wanted to share information.

So I've just been getting on with things, not knowing what to make of it."

"But then what do you think has happened to her?"

Kemi began to cry again. "I don't know," she said in a small voice. "I don't see how . . ." She trailed off.

Claudine felt faint. "But how? Are you saying someone killed her? Or she killed herself?"

She didn't believe that.

"She was desperate the last time we spoke, wanting to leave Tonye but not knowing how," said Kemi.

"But why? What did Tonye do?"

Kemi looked uncomfortable. Then she broke and told Claudine about Tonye's controlling ways, how unhappy Nicole seemed, painting a picture of an uncaring husband who stayed out all night and didn't spend time with his children, all of which chimed with what Claudine had observed so far.

"But if everyone is just getting on with things, how will there ever be justice for Nicole?"

"Honestly, auntie, when the Oruwaris don't want to make a fuss and the Ishaku family are on the other team, you'll never get justice. I don't want you to get your hopes up. Perhaps you will find out. Perhaps we will never know what really happened. I don't want you to stay here in Lagos, thinking you'll get answers. You're a strong woman. But you should go home and be with your family."

It was true. No matter what she suspected, what could she do about it? Why would women put themselves in these situations, with no family, no help if anything happened? She suddenly felt angry. Angry with Nicole, Astrid, all the Nigerwives.

"I don't understand these Nigerwives," she said. "Why do they come?"

"For a life of privilege," said Kemi. "The big house with servants, the driver, the nanny. It's not rocket science. Isn't that what all women want? I'm sorry—they live better here than in their own countries. And they can leave if they want, visit their folks, go shopping, and then come back. They're not prisoners."

"Is that what Nicole wanted?" Claudine asked.

"Until it got boring." Kemi sniffed. It sounded strangely snarky.

"What do you mean?" asked Claudine. "You said things were bad with Tonye."

"Yes, that's more what I mean," said Kemi hastily. "Until it got bad."

There was an awkward silence.

"I hear the family is planning a huge wedding at the Landmark for Saturday," said Kemi eventually. "Isn't Tamara marrying that governor's son? Everyone is talking about it. They're saying kings and presidents are going to attend. It will be the wedding of the year."

"It doesn't seem right to me," said Claudine. "It's almost like they've moved on and no one speaks about Nicole anymore."

"Because of the affair?"

Claudine shrugged. "They even asked me to go to the wedding. Of course I said no, but I don't know how I'm gonna get through the day. The house is full of guests. Do you have any suggestion for where I could go?"

"There are places, but if you're staying on the islands, it's not a good idea to go out. Victoria Island will be completely blocked. Checkpoints everywhere. Whole roads closed."

"On the mainland then? I can't stay in that house."

Kemi nodded. "You could go to Badagry. Nicole visited a few times. The slave museum there. It's still in Lagos State but out of town, farther up the coast. It would be like a day trip."

"Why did she like it so much?"

"I don't know. Maybe she enjoyed finding out more about the history of slavery, transatlantic slavery. She could get a bit obsessive about all of that. Called it walking in her ancestors' footsteps. She went at least three times."

"Badagry?"

"Ask Tonye to organize it for you. You can't just go—in rainy season the museum might be closed. Ring ahead."

"Thank you, I'll check." Claudine hesitated, then asked, "Do you think Nicole was ever happy here?"

"Oh, auntie, yes. Nicole had a great life. Lagos isn't an easy city, but Nicole was happy here. She loved it. But when things went wrong with Tonye, she got very down. She was totally dependent on him. Never a good thing."

"No," agreed Claudine firmly. "Not for all the gold in Christendom."

Kemi talked more sympathetically about Nicole now, revealing experiences they had shared together: celebrating Ramadan at a friend's house, watching a ram killed, skinned, and cooked for a feast. Going to watch Bollywood movies at Silverbird Galleria's cinema. Getting Nicole working in the art gallery. Claudine felt much better knowing Nicole had a friend like Kemi. And to know it wasn't as awful a picture of her life as she feared.

Eventually it was time to go. Claudine rose.

Kemi got up also to hug her good-bye. It felt genuine. A tender moment.

Claudine walked toward the gallery doors with her head down. She hadn't expected Nicole to come walking in through the door at the compound, but she hadn't really thought about it all in such a final way. She'd kept a little hope. Especially hearing that Elias was missing too. She didn't know what she'd been hoping for, but at least that Nicole was alive somewhere. As long as there was life, there was hope. But there were no signs of life and no hope.

As their car pulled away from the gallery, another car pulled in. She was shocked to see Tonye step down from the car. He didn't see her. He walked into the gallery. It was definitely him.

It was too late for Bilal to backtrack; they were already in one-way traffic on Ozumba.

Claudine leaned back in her seat, shaking her head in disbelief. What was going on? Once again, nothing made sense.

BACK AT the compound, Claudine felt dizzy. She knew she needed to call Penny back, but right now she needed air. The temperature was warm, and it was still sunny. She walked around the side of the house to the garden, ending up by the railings, looking out across the lagoon. Today it was covered in rubbish and not smelling too great either. She gripped the railings, shook them, and screamed her frustrations out to sea.

"Hello, auntie," said a voice. "Are you all right?"

Claudine turned, startled. It was Abi, Tonye's sister, staring at her. God, she'd probably seen the whole episode. Well, Claudine didn't care. Who wouldn't scream after seeing what she'd just seen? Tonye at Kemi's office.

"No, I'm not," said Claudine. "I don't know what to think anymore." She didn't want to tell Abi anything. She didn't trust any of them now. Perhaps Abi would warn Tonye before she could confront him, giving him time to concoct a story. She was done with stories.

"It's a mystery, isn't it?" said Abi. Her eyes seemed to gleam. Claudine didn't like it. "People are starting to whisper about it. I had someone message me about it. Apparently the Nigerwives have been asking around."

"Well, that's good. At least some people care."

"Not like us, right?" She almost laughed. "Well, I care. I promise. Nicole was lovely. A little naïve for this family, but very nice. I pray that nothing has happened to her."

"But then where is she?"

"You never know," said Abi. "Lagos is a strange city, full of surprises. She could be hiding somewhere, not wanting to come home. It's possible."

"Tonye isn't doing much to help," Claudine said through gritted teeth.

"Why, do you think he killed her?" said Abi.

Claudine looked at her sharply. What a question to ask! Abi's expression was neutral, but there was an intensity in her eyes Claudine didn't quite trust. "Why? Do you?"

Abi shrugged, which shocked Claudine further.

"It's possible."

"Why would you say that?" asked Claudine, finding Abi strange and a little close for comfort. "He's your brother, isn't he?"

Abi looked out over the lagoon. "I don't have any proof, but it wouldn't surprise me. They argued all the time. He was out. Then she started going out. I thought, good for her. But of course, one rule for women, another for men in this house."

"He said he had nothing to do with it."

"He would say that. He's not going to admit to anything. He never does."

"What do you mean by that?"

"Did he tell you how our brother died?"

"No, he didn't. Chief told me."

"Oh yes, Dad would tell you the story. He is still heartbroken over it. Ebipade was always his favorite. The rest of us he didn't notice."

It was a sad story, but Claudine wondered what it had to do with Nicole and Tonye.

"He doesn't like to lose," pressed Abi, as if reading her mind.

"What do you mean, lose?"

"Tonye doesn't do second place." Abi turned to walk back to the house. "Especially to a woman. Have a good evening, auntie."

Claudine watched Abi leave. She'd thought Abi seemed the most sensible one in this house, but it seemed Abi had her own issues. She was jealous of Tonye, for a start. Not that Claudine trusted Tonye. He was a devil and a liar. And she would find out the truth. But clearly, Abi wasn't someone who liked to lose either. With siblings like these, who needed enemies? she wondered.

CHAPTER TWENTY

NICOLE
Before

A CRASH FROM somewhere outside Elias's apartment made Nicole jump. Although by now she was used to Nigeria's rainy season and June's raging storms, she was unnerved by the intensity of the rain tonight and the lunatic wind she could hear. It was perhaps day three of the seven-day rain period the meteorologists had promised. The storms had started with a beautiful sunny day. The boys had enjoyed a swimming playdate with friends, but by the end, the clouds were rolling in, dark and foreboding. And then, in the night, the sky imploded. She'd surfaced a few times to hear rain hammering on the corrugated iron roof, sheets of metal lifting and whumping in the strong wind. In the morning, there was water in the living room and the kitchen. Samuel and Blessing had run around with mops for almost an hour. Outside, it had been a thick gray with no sun, nothing visible on the water. Rain dripped from eaves and roofs and palm trees, running down windows. The street beyond the compound had flooded, she'd heard, all the way down to the shopping mall. "Knee-high," they said. "No way to pass." Some had tried, only to turn back. Chief got his foot stuck in a drain somehow, trying to get out of his stranded car and walk down Adeola Odeku, and had to be helped home. And the rain continued for days—sometimes a whisper, sometimes full operatic screaming with thunder and lightning. It hadn't stopped. Today the flooding had gone down somewhat, at least. Safe enough for Bilal to drive her to Elias's.

Shouting in the distance and a car driving into the apartment complex drew her toward the window, but she couldn't see anything in the roiling darkness except the odd, blurred yellow car lights. It couldn't be Elias—only minutes ago, he'd texted that he was stuck on Third Mainland Bridge on his way from the airport.

Returning to the kitchen counter, she unrolled the red runner she had brought from home—never used and wouldn't be missed—and shook the tea lights she'd bought from the Game out of their plastic packaging. Since his outburst at the Grill by Ishtar, Elias had been on his best behavior. She wanted them to move past it. To show him how much she appreciated him. Carefully she dotted them around the kitchen counter, a handspan apart. Then she laid out plates, glasses, cutlery. Bottles of white and red wine. Excited to see Elias again, she started on the white wine. It took the edge off. She'd ordered the takeout too early, and now he was running late. It was their favorite entrée from RSVP—Rabbit Lasagnette. It was a shame they couldn't enjoy the hot spot together, but this was the next best thing.

Funny how happy she was sitting alone in the open-plan apartment, pondering what he'd said about not worrying about things and taking life one day at a time. Was it possible for her to truly be with him? Live with him here in this little bubble, be his little woman fussing over him, them falling asleep in each other's arms, waking up together? *Love* was a tricky word. Some people found love once, or never. The rest of the time, wasn't it just what you said to make the other person feel cherished? Wasn't that pretty much how everyone felt about it? How could Elias love her after just a few months, when he hardly knew her? She was an idea for him. An idea of a woman. Not an actual flesh-and-blood person. He'd never even seen her in the morning, what kind of mother she was, knew nothing about her family, the person she was in London, someone who wore jeans and sneakers, not prim ankara dresses. Still, when he said he loved her, it made her feel good. Safe. Seen. Sometimes he was the only person to send her a message that day, asking how she was or wishing her a great day. Apart from her children, who else discussed their dreams with her, who missed her, remembered her? Asked how her night was? Only the staff. So, in a way, she supposed she did love him. But real love to her was a desperate, ragged emotion, something you would leap over a cliff for, and how would you know unless you were tested?

She lit a few of the candles to enjoy them herself. She hoped her efforts would cheer him up. Since finding out his father was sick, he'd been so worried he couldn't eat, he said, until he'd gone to Kaduna to see him.

There was the sound of scraping from outside the door, a flower-pot being moved and an exclamation, a man's voice, then a knock on the door. Elias was back quicker than she'd expected; she hastily smoothed her dress, clingy and shiny with a long split, paired with strappy sandals. She had made an effort because she was so rarely able to dress up for him. When they were out and about together, she had to appear even more conservative than usual, in case they were to run into someone she knew.

But when she opened the door, it was Yohanna, looking as surprised and displeased as she felt. He looked at her—the dress, her makeup—confused, and she clocked that his arms were full of snacks for a lads' night in.

"Hey," she said, trying to mask her annoyance at his rocking up like this. It had never occurred to her that Yohanna might show up at any time and expect to come in, even though Kemi had mentioned he owned the apartment.

"What are you doing here?" he asked, walking past her into the apartment, tracking mud across the tiles. "Where's E?"

She reluctantly closed the front door. "Stuck in traffic."

"This weather." He made a face. "Sick of it. Everywhere's flooded."

"Seven days' rain, they say." She tried not to grimace as he dumped a small mountain of wet nacho packets, dips, cookies, and candy on the counter and they began to landslide over her arrangement. He used his hand to shake the water off his hair. He picked up a tea light candle and twirled it in his hand.

"Oh, I get it. A romantic welcome home."

Was he sneering or smiling? Nicole couldn't tell.

"It's been a tough few days for him," she said. "I wanted to spoil him."

"Must be nice," he said. "So where is he now?"

"Still on Third Mainland."

Yohanna took out his phone, scrolled. "Hmm, he didn't message me. What is happening?"

Whether he was referring to the weather or the state of his friendship with Elias, Nicole wasn't sure as she tried vainly to stack his snacks together in a pile separate from her display.

Yohanna settled himself on one of the barstools and smiled at her. "Miss Jamaica—this dress on you." He made the hourglass shape with his hands. "Very sexy."

Nicole rolled her eyes and continued reorganizing the tea lights, regretting the effort she'd made.

"So we've both come to surprise him. But your surprise is much better." He laughed. *"Our wife,"* he said mockingly. Quite the opposite of the affectionate way Chief and Mother-in-Law always said it. And indeed, Nicole felt ridiculous now in front of Yohanna, as if she were playing a character in a melodrama. Performing. But already actually married. Either way, she was terrible at it.

Yohanna laughed at something on his phone. "Wow, this flooding. There's a video going around of a white man paddling a kayak on Ahmadu Bello by the Silverbird Galleria this morning. Did you see this?" He showed her the video of a postapocalyptic Victoria Island, cars hunched in the brown water like submarines, with only their windshields and roofs visible. The busy four-lane road that tankers thundered down was a lake, and the madman in the kayak the only thing moving, using his double-ended paddle to weave around the trees.

"Probably one of those expats from the Catamaran Club. They're pretty crazy," said Yohanna with a chuckle. "Tried to send it to Kemi, but I'm blocked, thanks to you."

"Sorry things didn't work out." Nicole checked the food in the oven. Still warm, not dried out yet.

"Smells nice. What is that?"

"Pasta dish from RSVP."

"Aww. Romantic. So this is why my boy doesn't have my time anymore," he said, picking up the open bottle of white and pouring what was left into a glass. "These days he won't come to the beach house with me because he has to drive you to the mainland to experience Fela's Shrine. Evenings depend on your husband's mood. Elias hardly ever walks my dogs these days. Of course, you are the only thing he wants to talk about. Pathetic."

"Are you staying?" Nicole asked. "I can order more food."

"Hmm, no food, thank you, but I'll wait. Enjoy my apartment for a bit. It all looks very nice. Well done."

Having finished his glass of white, he opened the bottle of red. After pouring some it into his glass, he made a big show of sniffing it, angling the glass this way and that, before taking a sip.

"Excellent, considering it's a screw-top," he said. "From the Oruwari wine collection?"

Nicole turned away.

"Relax. I'm joking." He took a proper draft. Put the glass down. "I'm curious, though—why you did that."

"Did what?" she said. "Tell Kemi the truth? That you're getting married?"

"None of it is your business. And it's strange coming from you. Isn't your own wahala enough, or were you jealous?"

Petulantly, he shifted the cutlery items on the runner until everything was out of place. Nicole knew that Kemi had blocked him immediately after a furious conversation where Yohanna had admitted his situation. She had needed to tell her. It wasn't the kind of secret you kept from a friend. As she'd predicted, Kemi hadn't taken the news well.

"Can you believe this guy? Lying bastard! Sick!" she'd screamed to Nicole. And, "He'll suffer, not me," she said with true Kemi confidence, rising already like a phoenix from the ashes. "Bored with some young girl he can't have an adult conversation with. What an idiot." To Kemi's credit, she hadn't shed any tears over him, and Nicole wasn't especially sorry for her either. Relieved, if anything, that it had ended before things had gotten more serious. Plus, Kemi had earned a tidy commission from two paintings Yohanna had bought. "So will you still see Elias?" Kemi had asked. "Because I think they're both playing the same game. Let's be serious now, Nicole. It was a cozy foursome, but where do you two go from here? Pretty sure there's a limit to what Tonye will put up with." Unsure of how to respond, Nicole had made an excuse to end the call abruptly.

"*You* lied," Nicole told Yohanna. "That's the difference between us. I haven't lied to anyone."

"You haven't lied to *anyone*?" asked Yohanna. "Are you delusional?"

Nicole said nothing. Had she really lied? Had Tonye really asked? Did Bilal count as someone who could be lied to? He was just a driver.

"I could give a fuck about Kemi," said Yohanna. "There's more fish in the sea. But of all the people to sit in judgment . . ." He stood and stretched, then walked around the apartment looking at his paintings. "What do you think of them?" he asked.

Nicole shrugged. "I like them."

"Better than keeping them on the floor in my house, I guess," he said. "No space. I have so many."

"Yes, they are very nice." Nicole checked her phone for any texts from Elias—nothing. She tried calling him, but it didn't connect.

"Which is your favorite?"

"Kemi's the expert on art. I just listen to whatever she says."

"Yes, we had that in common." He looked down at the table.

"Did you study art or art history?"

He snorted. "No Nigerian parent lets their child study art."

"Obviously some do, or all these paintings wouldn't exist."

"Yeah, perhaps if it's their third son or, preferably, their daughter.

I'm the only son of Adolphus Josiah Ishaku, the legendary general who saved Nigeria. What good would I be to him as an artist?"

"It's your life."

"When you're going to inherit a billion dollars, you don't get to have a life."

"Everyone has a life. It's your choice."

"What would you know about it?" he said, hunched over the counter morosely. "Because your family has some money, you assume you know me. If you have a few police on speed dial, a friendly judge here and there, a governor who owes you a favor, you're a big man. But my father isn't just a big man in Nigeria. He *is* Nigeria. It's impossible for you to imagine the pressures I'm under."

"The Joseph Eze is my favorite," said Nicole quickly.

Yohanna straightened up. "Do you know, I paid around a million naira for it. Now it's worth ten." He pointed to the next painting, an old man withered and blending into the brown sky behind him. "This one has also gone up. I should take them back, shouldn't I? Call Kemi to sell them. Tell Kemi to unblock me. No reason we can't have a professional relationship, right? It's money. Everyone wants money . . . except you."

He leaned over toward Nicole with a strange smile on his face. "Funny, that day at the beach, I thought *we* had the connection." He gestured between them. "Remember on the boat? You looked at me, I looked at you. Bit humiliating to find out you're more interested in my 'houseboy.'" He hooked his fingers for the inverted commas.

Nicole reared up, ready to hit back.

"Relax, I'm joking. Seriously, though, if you want out of your marriage, I can put you and your children somewhere your relatives can't find you." His greasy breath tickled her bare shoulders. She rubbed vigorously at the area. "There would be nothing they could do about it, unless they want to end up in the secret military prison." He laughed. She wished she could take the Pringles tube and ram it down his throat. "There are secret prisons, did you know? It only takes a phone call. Your father-in-law is not as bad as some, but I'm sure, if the right authorities look hard, they'll find some crime he has committed. Money laundering. Fraud. Tax evasion. No one's clean in this country. Even bread sellers have to bribe somebody. It's ironic, isn't it, that even though you didn't want me, you still need my help?"

"I've *never* needed your help."

Yohanna leaned away again, and Nicole relaxed a little.

"Do you love him?" he asked.

Nicole didn't answer.

"Wow. He's risking his life for you, and you don't even love him? What is it? Bored with your husband? A need for more attention?" The words fell like a judge's gavel. He shook his head. "Jesus, I will never understand women."

"I didn't say that."

"This"—he pointed to the arrangement—"should have never gone past fucking." He let out a mock sigh. "I told him not to get carried away, but he wouldn't listen. Something about you, I guess." His eyes traveled her body, and she turned away slightly. He rolled his eyes at this and laughed. "Please," he said, "my own wahala is enough."

Standing up, he grabbed a few of the snacks. "Since it's just me, my dogs, and Netflix," he said as he headed to the door. "Tell my guy I'm not happy."

Nicole stood by the window until she heard his car rev up and splash out of the complex, the gates clanging shut behind him. Even after that, she couldn't get comfortable again. She didn't know what to make of his backhanded offer of help, nor his self-pitying rant. She walked to the Joseph Eze and looked at the woman in the painting, who looked back at her.

Yes, Yohanna could help her out of her marriage. But then what?

HIS WORDS clanged in her head. *Our wife.* Chief and Mother-in-Law used it as an endearment. They were mostly very nice to her, buying her gifts when they traveled, taking her to the grandest weddings, paying upward of a hundred thousand naira for the aso ebi so she looked the part. They lavished attention on the boys. Mother-in-Law spoke more to Blessing than her, tracking the boys' movements throughout the day: what they ate, how they should bathe, double-checking Nicole's parenting at every step. Their favorite thing was for the boys to sleep over with her and Chief in their huge bed, somersaulting on their silk sheets, watching cartoons on the fifty-five-inch television. But "our wife" ceased to be a person after a while. Nicole's aso ebi were styled with the Bayelsa sleeves and wrapper, not her own designs. She was often the last to know about important family events, and was never involved with the planning. When she lost weight rapidly after giving birth to Tari, Chief warned her not to get too slim or people would think she wasn't "happy." He seemed more worried about how it would reflect on the family than whether she was actually happy or not. She wasn't. No one had asked what she would do in Nigeria. If she missed home. Until Abi's recent turnaround, the two sisters had barely spoken with her, or did so awkwardly, mostly avoiding direct conversation as if that too were taboo. Over the years, Mother-in-Law never asked her how she was, although she pestered Tonye and the boys for updates on their well-being. Nicole was frequently greeted with "How are my grandsons?" or "Where are my grandsons?" if she appeared alone on their side of the house. If Mother-in-Law sensed Nicole and Tonye were in a bad place, she prescribed unsolicited scripture. Her favorite was Ephesians 5:22–24, which Nicole now knew by heart. "We are the neck," she and her friends often said, "the head cannot turn except for—and of course, submit, submit, submit!" Everyone in the house had their place, though, under Chief. He often bullied Mother-in-Law at the dinner table—the dinner was too late. His glass was empty too long, staff lounged about the compound while the grass turned pale. Abi's unmarried status was unforgivable. Tamara was a silly child. Even Tonye was frequently at fault. The yield from the farm wasn't what Chief expected, the pesticides not strong enough. The compound staff were not sufficiently afraid of Tonye, siphoning diesel from the generator, smuggling their friends and families into the Boys' Quarters right under his nose. He was "too pampered" as a child to be an effective oga.

Mummy had been the bully of the family at Nedford Road. She didn't care anything about Ephesians 5 even if she'd read her Bible every night. She was the breadwinner, the head and the neck and the beating heart of the Roberts family. Loved and feared with, it seemed, equal passion.

Now Nicole belonged to Elias and Yohanna—or she *would*. That's how Yohanna perceived it. Subject to his expectations. Performing wifehood according to his standards, not Elias's. He already had his plan for how things would proceed. And as the breadwinner of the family, he would dictate the terms and conditions of her relationship with them. He would expect submission too, in some form. Could Elias see it? If he could, did it bother him? He seemed happy to be Yohanna's hype man. He had his place, and he was content. The dreams that he had, the plans he had made, were all dependent on his continued friendship with Yohanna. He also was a sort of wife-in-friendship, and when all of it—his apartment, the art, the boozy nights out, the boat trips, the proximity to wealth—was stripped away, who would he be? And would she even want to be with that person? She looked around the room, at the paintings, their pigments moldering in the dim light from the kitchen. The eyes of the Joseph Eze meeting hers in resigned solidarity.

The rain had a lulling rhythm when it fell continuously like this in sheets, its soft percussion taking on the notes of whatever it struck, tinny on aluminum, fingernails tapping on concrete, the muffled laughter of children as the bigger drops bounced off puddles.

She was almost asleep when Elias came through the door soaked, the rain dripping off his face. The taxi had gotten stuck in the road outside, he said, and he'd helped to lift it. The roads in VI were worse than on the mainland, he said. He looked exhausted. He peeled off his wet clothes down to his boxers, then and there, and threw them straight into the laundry cupboard. Water spread slowly from his shoes, and his bare feet left shiny footprints on the floor.

Nicole picked up her bag. She had tidied everything away. All the candles and rose petals. She'd changed back into her usual ankara. The wine was finished, the glasses washed and put back in the cabinets. She had texted Bilal that she was coming down. Elias had been right about Bilal. He'd eagerly accepted the position for his brother and since then had been much easier to deal with. She no longer worried about what he might say to others.

"I was about to leave," she said. "It got so late. I left your food in the microwave."

"I'm sorry. I know I came late. The rain was terrible. The flight was delayed—and then this thing with the taxi. But stay, at least an hour or two."

"It's after midnight now. I've been here since seven. I can't stay any longer."

"Wait, how can you leave? I've just arrived. I've been dreaming of seeing you every day I was away. I want to shower and then lie with you for a while."

"I'm glad you saw your parents."

"Why the rush? You've gone home later than this from the club." He took her bag and put it back on the counter.

"According to your friend, I shouldn't be here at all."

"Oh, he said something to you about us?"

"He came by." She gestured toward the snacks on the counter.

Elias smiled. "So how did you two get on?"

"Not well." Nicole filled him in on what Yohanna had said.

Elias laughed. "Babe, ignore him. He's just upset and jealous because I'm spending more time with you than him now. I will speak to him."

"You think it's funny?"

"I will speak to him. But you know you shouldn't have said anything to Kemi. That's what he's angry about—he told me. And seriously, we had a good thing going on with the four of us." He observed her stony expression and stopped smiling. "Just chill, babe. I've got this. I know how to handle him. Come into the bedroom. Let me shower and we can at least discuss it properly." He tried to lead her by the hand, but Nicole didn't budge. Even if she went into the bedroom, nothing less than the whole night would satisfy Elias. "I need you tonight," he said. And she believed it. His eyes were heavy. He had been emotional about going. His father had never really forgiven him for turning away from the pastorship, facing his parents with only dreams, not results. "I've been traveling all day. Use the rain as an excuse—that you got stranded. We don't have to have sex. I just want to hold you."

"Tonye isn't buying my excuses anymore."

Elias shrugged. "So tell him that you're with me. What can he really do?"

"Are you joking? You know his father."

Elias rolled his eyes. "Everyone thinks their father is a big man in Lagos. It's all hype."

"He can throw me out."

"Then you come here."

"What about my children?" she said, and when Elias sighed, she continued, "What if he kept them? What if he put me on a plane without them?"

"He won't do that. He won't keep you from your children. He's obliged to look after you. And you will soon be looking after yourself— the yogurts."

"How do you know he wouldn't do that?"

Elias shrugged again. "Take a chance," he said. "Show him you're not afraid. Trust me."

"I don't trust *him*."

"Then when?" His expression became suddenly searching. He squeezed her arm, pushing her to answer. She hadn't seen that expression before. As if he was trying to see into her heart—perhaps she was just like the others who had left him in the end because he wasn't rich enough. "When will you be able to stay? When will you tell him?"

She looked down, lashes shading her eyes from his interrogation. She was afraid of what he might see. "What should I tell him?"

"That it's over. He's a monster. Look how he's treated you. And I'm tired of skulking around Lagos. I want to be with you in public and not pretend I don't know you or always be eating takeout in this apartment."

Nicole didn't answer.

"Remember what we said? That we aren't going to let these big men win. We're going to create our own Lagos, on our own terms, outside of their rules?"

She nodded.

"So let me quickly shower. All this time in airports and taxis, I'm sure I stink. Five minutes. Then we can talk."

He reached up and stroked her face, his fingers damp on her skin. When he went into the shower, Nicole waited until she heard the rush of water, then she picked up her bag, opened the door, and left the apartment.

Heading back to the compound in the car, she texted Imani asking when they could meet. She didn't know what else to do.

CHAPTER TWENTY-ONE

CLAUDINE

After

"CLAUD, WHERE have you been?" cried Penny, breathless. "I've been calling you all day. Mummy took sick. She's at the hospital."

Claudine felt an icy hand clamp over her heart. She had lost track of Penny and things going on back at Nedford Road over the past few days. Now look. "What you mean, 'took sick'?"

"She's had a stroke, Claud." Penny sounded hysterical. "I don't know what to do with myself. They said she could've died. You better come home. Claud? Claud, you there?"

Claudine sat up in the dark, her headscarf slipping off. She swung her feet out of bed onto the AC-chilled tiles as if she were going somewhere.

"What do you mean?" she said again.

"She had a blood pressure spike. A stroke—not too bad," Penny rushed to add.

How could she say "stroke" and "not bad" in the same sentence? "She dying?" Claudine steeled herself.

"Oh, no, no, no." *Too many noes*, thought Claudine. "The doctor said she's stable. As long as there aren't any more strokes. She just needs observation, you know. Brain scans. Therapy. The hospital will monitor her for the next few days. But come back, just—just in case. I can't do this, Claud."

"Why would she have a stroke just like that?" asked Claudine. "Was she outside or upset about something? Was it too much salt? I told you about that."

There was the slightest pause, and then: "She forgot to take her medication."

Claudine nearly hurled her phone across the room. She struggled to keep her voice at a normal level, knowing everyone was asleep, but she was screaming on the inside.

"You mean *you* forgot her medication. I put it out in front of you. The blue one in the morning for the blood pressure. The green one at night for the angina. I said to do it every day, and you promised!"

"I had a few things to do. I couldn't babysit her morning, noon, and night. She said she'd take it."

"But that's what you agreed to do."

"I tried, I really did, but I couldn't stay in that house all day, every day. She's so mean. It was awful. I don't know how you've put up with it for so long. I thought she was better than the bad old days."

Then Claudine understood. They had argued. All hell had broken loose. Penny had stormed out, vowing never to come back. Had probably come back feeling guilty the next morning, only to find Mummy lying there, unable to move. So much for their cozy night in watching *Desmond's*.

"The doctor said she'll be okay." Penny started to cry.

WHAT HAPPENED *to the body lingers on in our mind*, thought Claudine. *We never really get over it. We carry it with us wherever we go.*

Mummy's name was Icylene. Claudine imagined Icylene as a girl sitting among the sorrel and the fruit trees, with tall hair and eyes colored like fog after rain, looking out at the hills that had more shades of green than people in the world, and felt the hurricane of fury coursing through her, an anger that ran barefoot through the bush, jumped gullies, a rage as livid as pawpaw juice, mouth boiling with curses for Miss Hortense—that lightning would strike her, that she would die in her sleep, fall in the pit latrine, trip and buck her head on a rock, and so on. Claudine could imagine it because that's how she'd felt herself about Mummy. Did Nicole hate her the same way? Probably. Wasn't that why she'd left for Nigeria? Walked away and didn't look back? Why did they all hold such anger toward each other?

Now Mummy was in the hospital, perhaps dying, and Claudine was here in Lagos looking for Nicole, who was perhaps already dead, and all she could wonder was how things had gotten to this point.

Mummy had said little about Miss Hortense, just like Miss Hortense hadn't talked about her. There was a distance between them wider than the miles of ocean. It had surprised Claudine back then. With Miss Hortense being so colorist and Mummy being so light, you would assume she would be the favorite. Mummy certainly acted like her light skin and long hair were something special. She loved to come home from work and talk about who'd thought she was Italian or Indian or Chinese that day. But Miss Hortense hadn't seemed to like her at all.

Claudine knew Mummy's upbringing had been harsh, even for a so-called light-skinned woman in a country that gave light-skinned people different opportunities and advantages. Miss Hortense was a rich red color, like the earth outside her house. Icylene had been the only one of her siblings offered a place at the junior school, and Miss Hortense had told her it was because she looked so white. All the family's hopes had been pinned on her, but she'd ended up messing around with a local boy and getting pregnant, crushing all those hopes and earning Miss Hortense's eternal wrath. A wrath that led her to give Icylene's baby away to the father's family.

There were times Mummy would have her moods. Sitting there lost in thought, she would, out of the blue, rock back and forth, wringing her hands and lamenting in strong patois how her mother was "wicked suh" and "gi wey mi firs born." Such moments came on like gusts of wind and blew themselves out just as suddenly. But she never cried. Claudine wondered if she'd ever seen Mummy shed real tears.

Now she looked at it, had Icylene gone with the boy willingly or not? Who could say, but Miss Hortense didn't care. What life had she had herself to find forgiveness within? Her own mother a sugar plantation worker all her life, one generation from slavery. It was a pattern of trauma that joined them all.

Claudine remembered the terrible things Mummy used to say to Papason when they would go at it, inflicting terrible wounds on each other, saying things you could never take back.

Sometimes she would even complain that her father, Fred, was almost white, and if she hadn't married such a dark man, her children would have been "white, white, white." And Papason would step in and say her white devil's blood was nothing to be proud of. That his mother was blacker than black and proud of it. It could get mean quickly.

"If looking white means sometin, why you here struggling with me?"

"Mi only marry you fi spite er."

The things they said to each other were awful but normal in that house.

"How you di whitest one but she hated you di worse?"

Seeing Mummy's love given to the children born in England, Yvonne and Jackie, while the rest of them got nothing, no hugs or kisses or encouragement, had hurt the worst. It didn't matter how hard Claudine scrubbed or tried at school. It was almost as if she wasn't really there. To get through it, she used to imagine she was still in Miss Hortense's garden. When snow fell, she pretended it was orange blossom. She *actually* believed it was orange blossom the first time those flakes gently floated past the window. The icy tap water was warm, tropical rain to her. She exchanged bitter apples for the imagined sweetness of mangoes. The stars in the night sky were faraway peenie wallies. She would sit on the front steps of 49 Nedford Road and try to remember the stories Miss Hortense had told her about family members long gone.

What makes a mother? Mummy's biology didn't mean much. Claudine never felt her motherly love. And she'd tried to give motherly love to Nicole, but it had gone for nothing.

But she still loved Mummy. Knowing she was sick and could die gave Claudine a pain like nothing else. She had made her own mistakes. She had allowed Len in.

SOME OF us aren't meant for happiness, Claudine reflected. Penny still believed in it, despite all of her disappointments. But not Claudine, not anymore, not since Len.

Len came into their lives at a time when Claudine wasn't even thinking about a relationship. She was looking after her late sister's child, Nicole, and that was all-encompassing—but if your heart is open, she thought with a sigh, it doesn't matter how smart you are, how cautious, whether you move slow or fast, if you're weak or strong, how good. If you leave the door open, someone's gonna find their way in.

We all need love after all. We may not seek it, like Penny in the food and veg aisles of Tesco, or in the mirror's unflinching stare, but we all have to feel something.

Len was the kind of guy who used to break into cars and take the radios. Of course he knew how to break into hearts. Looking back, he'd probably been watching them for days or weeks by the paddling pool, working out how to break the ice inside her.

She had never had a boyfriend. Strange to say she needed love, but she didn't know what love was supposed to look like. Mummy and Papason were constantly warring. That's when they were around. Hurtful blows were not a blueprint for any kind of long-lasting relationship.

"You don't take prisoners, Claud," Len would say with a laugh when her tongue tore through the air. She knew it was sharp. He just laughed about it.

She could still smell it sometimes, the brandy on his lips, the sour taste of cigarettes on his tongue.

Penny was never without a boyfriend growing up. She clung to love till it kicked her in the teeth, and when she was healed she ran straight back for more. Her life was a junkyard of failed relationships, but she didn't let that stop her. Even at their big ages, Penny looked for love under every flowerpot and basketball cap. Claudine could never understand what hole could be so deep it needed such a stream of men to fill.

Before Len, Claudine had wondered what love even was beyond the merciless taunting her parents did to each other.

But you're soft too, he would also say when they were together. *Softest person I ever met.* She believed it. She lapped up everything he said like a foolish dog.

Penny was skeptical.

"What's Len doing down there?" she asked one day. In the living room, looking out the window at Len shoveling dirt into a big pile in the garden.

"He's digging a patch for me so I can plant my fruit trees."

"What's he doing all that for?"

"I mentioned it. And before I could say boo, he ran round here to get on with it."

"You paying him?"

"No."

"Seems a bit too good to be true."

"Oh, don't start, Penny."

Penny didn't trust him. At the time, Claudine had thought it was jealousy. But even she didn't know what he had planned.

CHAPTER TWENTY-TWO

NICOLE
Before

THINGS COULDN'T continue as they were.

Elias wanted more, and how could she blame him? How long would anyone be satisfied with clandestine dates and a secretive relationship? Since the showdown with Yohanna, Elias had become more impatient. Nicole used to love his text messages. But increasingly now, she dreaded them. They were often hostile, accusing her of not caring, pressuring her to make a decision.

Bilal drove through the gates of Admiralty Way into Lekki Phase 1, passing Fun Factory, the new amusement playground for kids, empty today with the rain. Every time she visited Lekki, a new restaurant, supermarket, or entertainment venue had sprung up, a great place for Imani to live, with the after-school tutor club she ran from her compound. House prices had rocketed, and since the Lekki-Ikoyi Link Bridge opened, even old-Ikoyi snobs had quietly drifted over, to Phase 1 at least. Phases 2 and beyond were still considered controversial.

Nicole had tried to visualize herself living around here. A new neighborhood, a new life. But with what money? They were both dependent on other people. Divorcing Tonye wouldn't change that. All his income came from his family business in Nigeria, and Nigeria was a patriarchal country where his powerful family could easily influence the courts against her. His earlier threats couldn't be taken lightly. Losing her children was a terrifying possibility.

She could stay with Tonye, the easiest option, to live out her life on the Oruwari compound, hoping things would improve between them over time. But it would mean giving up on herself. What if Tonye divorced her later in life? He was too duty-bound for that—but what if he did? Could she end up abandoned and alone, like Ethel?

Or she could leave, like Christina had. But why *had* Christina left? What had led her to make such an impossible decision?

Bilal turned onto a quiet cul-de-sac, clearly a new street, half of it unpaved and underwater. Most of the houses were still under construction, bamboo skeletons shivering in the rain.

There was no way to drive into Imani's compound. Nicole had to hop from the car onto unsteady wooden planks covering the open gutters. Imani's gateman waited outside, ready with a large umbrella to escort her in.

Nicole had always liked how the Nigerwives personalized their homes, often infusing them with cultural influences. The Caribbean Nigerwives turned their compounds into flowery retreats and mini farms—growing food and herbs they sold or gave to friends. Some Chinese Nigerwives had pagodas in their compounds to celebrate New Year or other festivals. Inside, you might find the clean Scandinavian minimalism of a Norwegian Nigerwife, or sliding doors in a Japanese Nigerwife's home. Some liked Middle Eastern floor cushions; others built shrines. It was always interesting, revealing—what they saw as important. Entering Imani's home, Nicole appreciated the classic American décor. The marble tiled floors were softened with a warm rug. Drapes *and* blinds on the windows. Family photos were arranged symmetrically on the walls. A print of Martin Luther King Jr. took pride of place, and there was even a miniature American flag positioned on the console table.

Imani welcomed Nicole into the living room, asking after the boys and explaining that her girls had gone to a playdate with their nanny.

"This Oruwari wedding is really gearing up to be the wedding of the year," remarked Imani, passing Nicole a copy of *This Day Style* magazine, open to the engagement photos of Tamara and the Governor's Son. "That's your sister-in-law, isn't it?"

Nicole hadn't seen the magazine yet. They made a good-looking couple, but the Governor's Son sounded as dull in print as he was in person, talking up disingenuous philanthropic ambitions in the interview. She suspected he might bore bubbly Tamara over time—or anyone, really—but they both seemed genuinely in love, and who was she to judge?

She quickly filled Imani in on all the wedding arrangements so far, the endless meetings she'd had to attend, the scale of the planning, aso ebi distribution for hundreds of guests, and daily seamstress consultations. The invitations for the traditional ceremony had gone out to almost two thousand guests. Four presidents, twenty kings, governors, senators, foreign diplomats. Security was going to be a nightmare.

"Sounds incredible, though," said Imani. "I told Bola I didn't want any fuss on my wedding day. We had fifty guests and even that was too much!" She pointed to her framed wedding photos on a side table. In one, Imani and Bola were holding hands while jumping over a broom. Bola was obviously very on board with Imani's Americanness. Nicole wondered how he had changed in the years since they'd moved to Lagos. They all changed.

"Would you like some cheesecake? I got a big one from Crust and Cream for our Juneteenth party and turns out no one likes cheesecake except Bola and me."

Nicole wasn't a fan herself. Of all the things to order from Crust and Cream! It specialized in exquisite French pâtisseries—but she accepted. As Imani trotted off to the kitchen to instruct her cook, she looked around the room, liking how Imani's home felt like its owner, a simple bamboo basket on her coffee table and her dark-wood locally made furniture a welcome respite from the usual mirrors and gold. She wished she could say the same about hers. Chief's ostentatious tastes were suffocating. Even though her apartment was toned down, it still didn't feel like her place. It didn't belong to them. It was Chief's. They were grace-and-favor royals living at his majesty's pleasure.

"You have a lovely home," she said, when Imani returned.

"Thank you," said Imani. "We still want to change a few things, like build a swimming pool in the back, but after living with in-laws for the past ten years, it's just awesome to finally have our own house. You know what I mean?"

The maid entered the room with a tray of cheesecake slices and whipped cream and left again, shutting the door as Imani directed.

"I wanted to talk to you about leaving Nigeria," said Nicole.

Imani sat back in the sofa. She nodded.

"You don't have to tell me exactly what's happening, but are you all right? Like, right now? Do you need somewhere to stay?"

"No," said Nicole. She didn't know how much she should reveal, if Imani even wanted to know. "I just want to know what my options are. I know Tonye wouldn't easily let me leave with the children. He's already threatened me."

"This is very serious, Nicole," said Imani. "I can help you, but you have to be sure there's no other way, because if we do this, there's no coming back to Nigeria. You could be charged with child abduction or any number of crimes and thrown in jail. I'd have to deny all knowledge of helping you. There are two things that Nigerians consider sacrosanct. One is marriage, and the other is family."

Nicole wondered what Tonye might do to her if he even suspected she was having this conversation.

"My contact at the British High Commission has told me that in certain circumstances, they can help with the documents and the consular assistance to enable you to leave the country," Imani explained. "It would be treated as an emergency evacuation. You would have to fill out a statement saying that you were a victim of domestic abuse and that you feared for your safety in Nigeria and the safety of your children. No good-byes, though. Tonye couldn't suspect a thing. That means you couldn't take much with you, no suitcases, which might raise suspicion. You would leave in the course of your normal routine, as if you were taking the children to a playdate or school, but instead go straight to the airport, where you'd be met by a British diplomat and given emergency travel documents. Do you see?"

Nicole nodded, trying to take it all in.

"What about money?" asked Imani. "Do you have any?"

Nicole shook her head. "I thought the Nigerwives had a welfare fund?" she asked, feeling foolish.

"We could raise the money to get you out of the country while keeping your identity secret. But once you arrived at Heathrow and left Immigration, you'd be on your own. Can you take any money with you?"

"I don't know." Nicole thought about her joint bank account, which had a daily limit of just 50,000 naira; Tonye got an alert every time she withdrew cash from it. He would notice her emptying the account. Her engagement ring might get a few thousand pounds. There were a few other pieces, but not much. She wasn't into jewelry. She needed more cash.

"Before you do this, think about how that would work. Not just getting out of Nigeria, but how you'll survive back in the UK."

"How did Christina manage when she left?" asked Nicole. "Did she have family help?"

"You know I can't discuss her situation," Imani reminded her.

"Come on, Imani. Does it matter anymore? She's gone. Why did she leave? Was it her husband? He seemed controlling. Was he violent?"

"Did she tell you he was?"

"No, she didn't, but—"

"Why do you care so much?" said Imani. "What difference does it make?"

"We were friends. It must have been something terrible for her to want to run away and not say good-bye." *To me,* she added to herself, and burst into tears. She rummaged around in her bag fruitlessly for some tissues.

"Do you think leaving is only justified in the case of something really big? Violence, not just a slap but something life-threatening, a broken jaw, even rape? What about cheating? When does it count? I know, Nicole. I've been through it."

Nicole lifted her head, shocked. "Not Bola?"

"No," said Imani. "Never Bola. My mother. My stepfather beat her, even put her in the hospital a few times, but she kept going back to him. Domestic violence wasn't considered a good enough reason to leave your marriage back then. It wasn't until he hit me that she left. That's what finally pushed her to do it. And of course, then people said, why didn't she leave earlier?" Imani passed Nicole a box of tissues from the coffee table.

"I'm sorry to hear that."

"Yeah, my mom made me promise to never be totally dependent on Bola. I still have the house I bought before I met him, rented out, but it's mine. And he has to put money in my US account every month while I'm here. I'm raising my girls to be strong and independent. That's why I will not tie gele nor allow my girls to bow or call strangers auntie and uncle. You may not set out to end up disempowered, but perhaps one day you just wake up, and it's too late; you've got nothing."

How many Nigerwives were completely dependent on their husbands? Nicole wondered. You came for love and just assumed you'd be taken care of. You didn't think about "What if?" If they had thought about it that way, few would have moved, surely.

"I can't discuss Christina, but if it helps, I promise you, no one we ever helped regrets leaving, even if it's been hard. I know you might be thinking, *Who am I to complain? I can't be a victim when I have so much more than others do.* But you don't have to justify this to anyone, Nicole. You just have to believe it's the right thing for you."

Nicole thought about what Tonye had said that day in their shared dressing room, when they argued about the hog-ties. *There are no victims in this house.*

She checked the time. She had an idea.

TIMI AND Tari ran up to Nicole and hugged her as she reentered the apartment a few hours later. They were in their pajamas already, their hair a little damp.

"Mummy, Mummy," they cried. She put her arms around them and inhaled their vanilla honey scent. Blessing followed them out of the living room.

"Good evening, madam," she said.

"How are things?" Nicole asked.

"Fine, ma. They have just bathed." She shifted from foot to foot, obviously itching to close.

"Is Tonye here?"

"No, ma."

Nicole wondered where he might be. It was that weird time in the early evening when he could come back to change and then go out again, or he might just stay out all night. You never knew with him. "How long has he been out for?"

"Since the last several hours," said Blessing unhelpfully. What would she know anyway? It wasn't like Tonye would have the consideration to announce his departure to her. But it sounded like maybe he was gone for the evening.

"Give me a few minutes," said Nicole. Blessing's face fell. "I know you're due to close," she added quickly. "But I need to do something." With a long-suffering sigh, Blessing herded the boys back into the living room.

NICOLE TURNED on the dressing room lights and padded across the deep-pile rug. She hardly used the room anymore, preferring the privacy of her own space.

Tonye had left one of his closet doors open, and as she passed it, she smelled the woodsy cologne he wore. She buried her face in his row of jackets. It was a classic scent, one he'd worn since she met him in the G-Spot, that set him apart from the other boys and their trending colognes.

Stepping back, she caught sight of her reflection in the full-length mirror, her hair straight and long down her back. She was not quite the same person who had arrived in Lagos five years ago. She was becoming someone else, but she wouldn't know who until she had left this house, where she could only be Iyàwó. *Our wife.*

She went to the safe, knelt, and entered the combination. The thick steel door swung open. For all of Tonye's threats, he hadn't changed it, not believing she could walk away from everything they had.

Inside were his watches, some in boxes, others gleaming on the dark shelves, and numerous stacked bundles of cash neatly organized into different currencies along with important documents in protective plastic sleeves. She would need those too. Birth and wedding certificates. Green and burgundy passports. But first, the money. She counted the cash in the safe. Five thousand in pounds. Another five in dollars and five more in euros. Two million naira in thousand-naira notes. All in bundles secured with rubber bands. So perhaps twenty thousand pounds in total, their emergency fund, never used.

On the way home, she had asked Bilal to stop at the Kuramo Waters Hotel and visited the mallams, buying several bundles of crisp fifty-naira notes. Now she took them out of her tote bag and began swapping them for the bundles of higher denominations and other currencies, carefully covering each fifty-naira bundle with a pound, dollar, euro, or thousand-naira note before resecuring the rubber band and stacking them back in the safe. She took all the pounds, dollars, and euros, and a fair number of thousand-naira bundles—who knew who she might have to bribe at the airport. As long as Tonye didn't look too closely, he would never know.

"What are you doing?"

Tonye stood in the doorway of the dressing room. She felt weak. When had he come back? She hadn't heard the front door.

"What does it look like?" she said, trying to sound casual. Her heart thundered. "I wanted some money." She closed the safe and locked it, then stood and faced him. In her hand she had a bundle of naira notes.

Tonye frowned. He was dressed in traditional wear as if he'd just come from a formal event, the long shirt with gold fob chain, his black gambler hat, the cane still in his right hand.

"What for? Why are you suddenly grabbing money from the safe?"

"You weren't around and I need it for my seamstress in the morning."

"So stop at the ATM or ask me. That's our emergency fund." He put his hat on the shelf. Rested the cane against the wall.

"We're going to the market early to buy beads for my aso ebi for Tamara's wedding. I didn't like the ones she bought. I wanted something very specific. She keeps buying the wrong beads. The ATMs are always out of cash," she prattled on.

"Give it to me!" He held out his hand, and she mutely did as she was told.

He passed her and bent down, opened the safe, and put it back. Nicole held her breath as he looked into the safe, wondering if he would notice the rigged bundles. But he took off his watch and put it inside, then closed and locked the door. She exhaled.

He still gave her a sharp look when he turned around.

"You know that anytime in this country there could be protests, economic crisis, the banks could close. We have to be able to run. That's what the money is for, not your beads. How much do you need?"

"Eighty thousand," she lied. Who cared? As long as he didn't change the combination.

"For beads?" He raised his eyebrows. She shrugged. He reached into his trouser pocket and pulled out a money clip, removed half, and passed it to her. "Don't take again from here without permission."

"Okay," she said, accepting the notes. As she moved off, he caught her wrist and pulled her toward him. She almost dropped her bag on the floor. He forced her to face the mirror. Appraised their reflection. She felt his breath on the back of her neck.

"My pretty wife," he said, pressing himself into her back.

"Blessing is waiting to close," she protested, trying to jerk out of his embrace, but he held her tight.

"Put this down," he said, prying the bag out of her hand and throwing it aside. Sweat beaded along her spine. She didn't dare look at the bag, imagining the bundles spilling out of it. If he turned around, he would see it and know everything. She'd never be able to get away. So she allowed his hands to travel all over her body, keeping his eyes on her, the heat of them, allowed that desire she hadn't felt from him in such a long time to grow.

Tonye stripped her impatiently, tearing off her dress, her knickers, her bra until she was completely naked, then rolled her backward to the sofa. A thrill went through her as they crashed onto the cold leather. He parted her legs and thrust himself inside her with urgency, crushing her underneath him, the gold fob chain on his shirt digging painfully into her breastbone, his teeth on her earlobe. She had never seen him like this. And she responded, searching for him under his shirt, grabbing his buttocks, pushing him farther in. They cried out together and then he collapsed on top of her, both of them breathless. He muttered something like, "I'm sorry." She slithered out from underneath him before he could say or do anything else. He lay there, still heaving. He didn't look at her. She yanked her bag and clothes off the floor, fled without looking back, and kept going until she got to her bedroom. She locked the door and leaned against it, and, gasping, reeling, put her head in her hands.

CHAPTER TWENTY-THREE

CLAUDINE
After

TAMARA'S BIG day was tomorrow. Claudine's outfit for the wedding lay on the bed. Chief's Wife had sent a long underskirt of green silk onto which hundreds of peach-colored sequins had been sewn, giving the impression of wild hibiscus spreading out across a lush meadow. There was a second layer of green silk and sequins. Blessing had said it was a "wrapper" that tied over the skirt. Claudine imagined it would look something like a sari, although this material was not sheer and floaty like the saris she had seen in London. Small gold leather disks were sewn onto the wrapper, sitting above the sequins like floating lily pads. Some even had diamantés in the center. Claudine had done enough needlework in her life to recognize that it was all laboriously hand-sewn. There was a matching short-sleeved blouse. Simply made, obviously to estimated measurements, but it would fit. And then a stiffer, shiny piece of cloth like a shawl, what Blessing called the gele.

Blessing had been so excited, oohing and ahhing at how "very fine" the entire outfit was. Claudine, too, had never seen anything so luxurious, much less worn it. Under different circumstances,

Claudine would have loved to attend Tamara's wedding. She could only imagine how fancy Tamara's outfit was if this was merely the guest outfit and how lavishly decorated the wedding venue would be. She had heard from Samuel that over a thousand people would be attending. In addition, the interior of the house, the vast reception area, was swathed with peach-colored cloth to match the sequins. Last night from the balcony, Claudine had watched florists setting hundreds of flowers in place. The pavilion had been set up on the lawn, lights draped across it from a height. There were gold chairs set up under the canopy and tables decorated with elaborate floral arrangements.

If Claudine weren't so angry, she could have appreciated all of this. But seeing Tonye entering Kemi's gallery when he'd said nothing to her about knowing Kemi at all had emptied her of any goodwill she might have felt toward the family. She'd asked Blessing to text her when Tonye returned, which he did a few hours later. She took her bag and found him in his office, hunched over his desk, signing checks for another man who waited nearby with a large ledger in his arms. He would read from it and Tonye would nod, then quickly write and sign the check with a swoop and add it to a growing pile.

"Good afternoon, auntie," he said. "I'll only be a few more minutes."

Claudine stood to one side, watching as Tonye completed the task. On the wall hung a framed photo of Tonye and his father, Chief ensconced on some kind of gold chair as if on a throne, while Tonye stood respectfully behind him. It seemed the ordering around was mostly done by Chief. Tonye was just another skivvy.

"Tonye, I'm going to the High Commission on Monday."

The man picked up the pile of checks, put them in an envelope, bowed to his boss and then to Claudine before leaving the office, closing the door behind him.

"What is it now, auntie?" Tonye said wearily. He packed up the checkbooks and stacked them away in the filing cabinet by the desk. "It's not going to help."

"Your wedding will be over and I'm not putting up with your lies anymore."

"Lies? What lies?"

"I saw you entering Kemi's gallery. You never told me about her."

Tonye clanged the metal drawers of the filing cabinet closed and then locked it. He turned back to Claudine. "I went there to confirm some information."

"How long has it been going on?"

"I don't know what you're talking about," he said, eyes darting around, a clear sign of a nervous liar.

Claudine reached inside her bag. Tonye started when he saw the knife in her hand. She held it out as if ready to jab it home. "Are you mad?" he yelled, jerking back in his chair. "What are you doing?"

Claudine flashed the knife. "Nicole had this under her mattress. She slept in that room because you were having an affair, and she had this knife because she was afraid of you. I'm going to the commission on Monday and that's what I'll tell them. I have another Nigerwife who will confirm Nicole was trying to leave you." She put the knife back in her bag.

Tonye looked at her for a minute before his face suddenly crumpled.

"I didn't mean for it to happen," he said. "I didn't kill Nicole. I loved her."

He put his head in his hands and sobbed like a child.

"What do I do now? What am I supposed to do?" he kept saying over and over.

"You're going to come with me to the High Commission and bring your police chief and do things properly. My way." He nodded limply. "I don't believe you killed Nicole or I would have cut your throat already," Claudine said. "But you're not fobbing me off with any more lies. When did it start?"

"About a year ago was the first time. Nicole and I weren't getting on. She was withdrawn. I would see Kemi out and about. It just happened, and once we started . . ." His voice trailed off. It was enough to imagine.

"But Kemi was seeing Yohanna. The Nigerwives said so."

Tonye shrugged. "Yes, we had stopped seeing each other for a while. Nicole had found something out."

"That's why she moved into the spare room?"

"She didn't know who," he said, not looking at her.

"But then it didn't work out with the Yohanna guy, and Kemi came back. So you knew all about Nicole's affair."

Tonye was silent.

"So why didn't you raise the alarm properly?"

"I thought perhaps she'd run away. Left the country. I didn't think . . ."

"That she could have been killed."

He nodded.

"But why aren't you moving heaven and earth now?"

"My father said to wait."

"No, Tonye. This is your wife. Your father can't tell you to wait for anything." But she looked at him, cowering from himself in the chair, and she wondered if it was true. He was so under the thumb, he couldn't see his way out.

"I keep hoping this nightmare will end."

"It won't. Monday we go to the High Commission."

Tonye nodded. "I understand."

"In the meantime, you can go and play happy Oruwari families tomorrow. I don't care."

"I'm not in a celebratory mood either. It's family, you know." He glanced up at the framed photo of him and his father. "It's expected of me to attend. I'm the only son."

"You could be the son of God, but you've lost your wife and people should respect that."

It sounded to Claudine as if he'd been bullied into going. To make things look good. But she knew that trying to make your parents happy was like trying to fill a bucket with a hole in it. She was living proof that no matter what you did, they never loved you back if it wasn't in them. If you just weren't in their thoughts like that, there was nothing you could do about it. But she could tell Tonye wasn't ready to hear that. And probably never would be.

She sat down in the chair opposite him. He cracked his knuckles.

"Once I've informed the High Commission, I'm leaving," said Claudine eventually. "In a few days. Whenever you can make the arrangements for it."

She scoured his face for any sign of glee. But there was none.

"My mother is in the hospital," she continued. "And there's nothing more I can do here."

"Of course I will make all the arrangements," he said. If he was happy she was leaving, why wouldn't he be? He was certainly doing a good job of keeping a straight face. "I wish you—we could have gotten some answers."

They were quiet again for a while.

"Kemi mentioned Nicole liked to go to the Badagry Slave Museum," said Claudine finally.

Tonye looked surprised but said nothing.

"I think I'd like to go tomorrow if you can make the arrangements. I'd rather not be around here tomorrow. Get out of town. You'll all be busy with the wedding. I don't want to make things awkward."

Tonye looked at her questioningly, but only said, "Bilal can take you to Badagry. He knows the way. I will prepare him."

She thanked him and got up to leave. She exited the house and headed for the mango tree to catch up with Penny about Mummy's condition. Preparations were under way for the big day tomorrow. The poor cow was enjoying its last day on the lawn. Blessing had said they would kill it in the early hours of the morning and distribute the meat in celebration.

Keeping a watchful eye in case it broke free, Claudine took up her usual spot under the mango tree, from where she could see the whole back of the house and know that no one was listening.

"SOMETIMES SHE'S responsive, sometimes she's not," said Penny. "It's almost like she has dementia, but the doctor said she doesn't. Not yet, anyway." Claudine heard Penny sigh. "Last night she kept asking me where her child was. Saying her mother gave away her firstborn."

"We knew that—didn't we?" said Claudine. She didn't tell Penny about her conversation with Tonye. She just wanted to listen and feel at home.

"Oh, she talked a lot more about it. Everything that happened to her. Did you know she was only fourteen years old when she had Man-Man?"

"Well, it makes sense," said Claudine. "He would have been an old man now."

It certainly seemed like Mummy was having a moment. Claudine felt a little jealous at Penny getting all this extra information and not her. Apart from her hysterical episodes, Mummy had never been one to tell stories about her childhood.

"Also, she called me Pauletta," continued Penny.

"Come again?"

"Just now—today—she called me Pauletta. She was sleeping, and she said, 'Pauletta, get me some water.'"

"So what does that have to do with anything?"

"I've been telling you my name was Pauletta!" said Penny, sounding wounded that Claudine hadn't instantly remembered the thing Penny had been banging on about for years. "I told you she changed it to Penny because of my color. Remember?"

"You're sure that's what she said?" said Claudine.

"You still don't believe me, do you?"

"It's not that I don't believe you."

"Do you believe anyone, Claud? Do you believe yourself?"

"So that's what all this crying and carrying on was about?" Claudine retorted. "Feeling sorry for yourself over this Pauletta thing?" She kissed her teeth as if Penny were a child telling stories.

"I wasn't sorry for myself. I was sorry for you. For this family being so broken."

"Sorry for me?" Claudine didn't know what to say. Both knew the conversation better end soon.

"You've never been easy, Claud," Penny continued. "But when Len came on the scene, I saw a real difference in you. Everyone did. You softened. But after the—well, after he left, you just shut down. You became so hard and cold."

"Me, hard and cold?" said Claudine. She had to be hard because she was the one who had to look after everyone else. That's why she was here in Nigeria looking for Nicole when no one else could be bothered. Penny—Pauletta, whatever she wanted to be called—wouldn't understand that. She did what she wanted whenever she wanted and everyone else had to pick up the pieces. That's why Mummy was in the hospital, for God's sake. She just couldn't believe Penny putting that on her right now.

"She said something else, the night we fought." Penny sobbed. "She said—" Penny seemed unwilling to go on. "She said . . ."

What on earth could she have said that had been so bad? Claudine wondered.

"She said you let Len do it because it happened to you. She said Miss Hortense let it happen to you out of spite because she hated Mummy so much. I didn't know anything like that happened to you. It upset me. Is it true? What happened?"

Claudine sighed. "What did she say exactly?"

"I was talking about you—how you were getting on out there. And she just started sneering, saying you couldn't find out something if it was printed on your forehead and that you just feel guilty after Len . . ." Penny trailed off.

"If you say so," Claudine said quietly.

Claudine felt the *bang, bang* of her heart in her chest. There was a ringing in her ears. Between Penny's crying and the ringing, she couldn't hear herself think.

"Let me call you back," said Claudine, her voice quiet and thick like sludge. She hung up. She felt weird, like she couldn't really see. Like she was suddenly blind. In front of her, nothing made sense. She didn't know how she found her way into the house and to the bathroom. She threw up. Her whole world came up through her stomach and splatted into the sink. She sank to the floor, feeling like Penny had pushed her through a trapdoor, and now she was falling, falling with no end. There was no end to this.

CHAPTER TWENTY-FOUR

NICOLE
Before

W E SHOULD probably have another child," Tonye said, watching Timi and Tari trot around the paddock on their ponies with their trainers holding the reins. It was one of those days when clouds hovered, unsure of whether to laugh or cry. The polo club had a deserted air about it. Most of the horses had gone to tournaments abroad where it was sunny and dry. The stables were bolted shut or in the middle of being cleaned out by the skinny stable hands who chattered to each other in Hausa. The field where the matches took place had been partially stripped of its grass so reseeding could take place, and there were puddles of water here and there where the last rains had collected. It was just Tonye and Nicole sitting at the long oval bar's polished wood counter. Her stomach growled from the sharp, spicy nuttiness wafting over from the grill, which indicated that plenty of people were coming in to collect suya from beyond the white gates. Tonye nursed a brandy. Hair of the dog, he had said, after hitting the clubs for a friend's birthday. So he claimed, anyway. Maybe it was true, maybe not. Did it even matter anymore? She'd avoided him since that evening in the dressing room. Neither had referred to it again.

———

YESTERDAY, AT Delis Café, she had discussed a different problem with Kemi. Breaking up with Elias. "I'm sorry," said Kemi, in her way. "But I told you it would come to this, to just keep things fun."

"I feel bad."

"Bad for who? He knew what he was getting into, so fuck him."

The staid aunties at the next table had frowned at them over their eclairs and shaken their heads in disapproval.

Nicole had stirred her Chocolat Viennois and looked out of the window, down at the car park and the American women—they seemed American in their brightly colored yoga pants and trainers—heading into the expensive grocery below. She had felt disloyal but relieved at unburdening herself.

"Like, who is he? One Hausa boy with no finance. In this Lagos. What was he thinking?"

"How will I tell him, though? What do I say? I've been avoiding him for the past week, but he wants to see me soon." She didn't reveal her reason for avoiding him, but Kemi didn't seem too concerned.

"My dear," Kemi had begun in a patronizing tone that the older women often used, "Elias cannot support you or your children. He has no idea what you cost, so it doesn't matter what you say."

"He says we should live by our own rules and make our own way, regardless of what people say."

"Oh, well, take him to London with you, apply for his visa. Oh wait, you can't. You're married. Back to square one."

"He doesn't want to leave Lagos. He can't, anyway. He's starting a business."

"More like he doesn't want to go ten steps away from his meal ticket," Kemi had retorted. "I think I'll leave myself, actually. Lagos is full of shit, so fake and judgmental. I hate it here."

"You love it here. You won't leave."

Kemi shrugged.

"You *are* Lagos," Nicole insisted. "You're outgoing, a born hustler, love getting all dressed up for parties. Where would you go that could match this for you? London can't compare."

"I guess you're right. I do love it here. It's more than just parties, though. I'm Nigerian. This is home. For all its hardships, I love my country and my people," she said simply, then added, "I just can't find a husband. My eggs will be in cryo forever." She mock howled.

"You can have Tonye," Nicole joked.

"Don't joke, ooo. It's rough out there. Tonye probably has his second wife lined up already. The men here are so entitled. They can do whatever they want."

"Perhaps you should stop trying to date men from big families. Go for an entrepreneur living by his wits."

"My sister, it's all fun and games until one of your children gets sick and the hospital asks you for a four-million-naira deposit." Kemi was referring to their friend who had gone into premature labor and needed one of the few available fully equipped incubators in Lagos. Luckily for her, her family had paid.

"I don't know if I can leave," Nicole said. "Tonye says he will never let me take the children." She hadn't told Kemi about Imani's offer of help, or what had happened in the dressing room. Better if no one knew.

"It's not the big deal you think it is. One of my aunts left. Said it was for educational reasons. Better schools and whatnot. It's just how it is."

Nicole had thought of Christina. Somehow, wherever she was, Nicole hoped she was happy.

"So if you left without Tonye's blessing, how would you survive?" Kemi asked.

"I could stay at my grandmother's house. Work it out from there. But I haven't spoken to them in a while."

"Why not see what they say?"

"Since I moved here, I've drifted away from them. I don't know how they would feel."

"It's your family. Didn't they raise you?"

"My aunt Claudine did, mostly. But—I don't know. Things happened. It was a long time ago, but—"

"If it was a long time ago, as you say, then why not at least try?"

"Yes, you're right. I'll call her."

"Forget Elias. Get to London and get on Tinder. I'll show you the ropes." Kemi had stuck her tongue out. "There's a lot out there for you to explore. Women don't have to be shy anymore about saying what they like in bed."

Nicole grimaced, thinking about the sore spots she had from her rough sex with Tonye in the dressing room, and how every time she thought about it, it turned her on.

NOW SHE looked at her husband, the almost imperceptible prickle of grays along his jawline, as he downed the last of his cognac and waved his glass at the barman, who nodded and approached to top him up. There was the buzz of cicadas in the grass. Flies lazily circled the counter. Tonye checked his phone. "Time for one more before we meet Chiz and—what's his wife's name? Nnenna? Nana?"

"Nneka," said Nicole. Tonye nodded. He patted his forehead with a napkin. Even with the sun sheathed, it was still hot. "Why?" asked Nicole, returning to the conversation about having another child. "We were happy with two."

"Two is not enough. We should have at least one more. Don't you want a girl?"

"I did, but we kind of agreed—it seemed like two was enough."

"Yeah, but things change. The boys are older now and there's not much going on business-wise. It's a good time for the family, for us."

"A good time for the family? You mean for your father?"

"No. I mean, obviously he would like the idea, but you know three children is a proper family." He lifted his glass and sipped, then gestured to the boys on the field. "Look at them. They would love a sister or two."

"What about what *we* want? Forget the family. You would not be asking me this if it wasn't for *him*."

"It's not about what we want."

"So this isn't even your idea."

"Nicole, what do you want from me?" He held out his hands in exasperation. Nicole rolled her eyes. "And you—you've been spending too much time with friends doing God knows what. A baby will keep you closer to the home and occupied. You won't have to sit on the dumb balcony all day. You'll have too much to do."

"I have a job."

"Your *job*." His words were loaded with contempt. "What is my business with your job? It costs more to send you to work than you earn. And then there's no one around to manage Blessing and Samuel. They keep folding my shirts wrong. And the fridge isn't stocked well."

"Oh, come on."

"Well, I wear a shirt every day. I'm just saying. You are the madam."

"So you're jealous because I get to leave the house? Because you have to sit at home with your father? Do I have to as well?"

"It pays the bills."

"Well, *he* pays the bills, more accurately."

"Har-har-har."

There was a silence, but it felt easy. This was the most open they had been in a long time.

"Don't you ever get tired of it?" she pushed.

Tonye didn't answer.

"Come on, admit it. You're sick of working for him."

"You don't know what you're talking about."

"I know you're bored and frustrated because he doesn't give you any financial freedom to do your own thing."

"What do you know about it?"

"Don't you ever think of going back to the UK too?"

"What would I do there?"

"What you're doing now. You've got all these business ideas—you could start one. I could work there too."

"You?" he scoffed. Instead of waiting for her response, he got up from his seat and went to the edge of the field. He took some photos of

Timi and Tari, then sat back down. "So what do you think?" he said, showing her the photos he had just taken, smiling.

"What do I think about what?" replied Nicole.

Tonye mouthed counting to ten.

"Well, I'm not some sort of breeding machine," she said. "He has other children. Why should all the pressure be on us?"

"You knew I had responsibilities as an only son."

"Son, daughter—it shouldn't matter." The bartender looked over quickly before moving away to another part of the bar. Nicole lowered her voice slightly. "Tamara is getting married soon. Can't he wait?"

The edge came into Tonye's voice. "You know it makes a difference. You're acting like you don't understand anything."

"Because you don't tell me anything! You'd think I could learn things from you instead of from drivers, cooks, and nannies on the compound."

"I *protect* you from things you don't need to know. And idle gossip shouldn't be encouraged."

"Why is Abi allowed to swan around childless, then? Why does everything fall on you?" Her phone beeped. "Bilal is at the gate," she said. "He's asking if he should he come in?"

"What for? Is he going to play polo?" Tonye let out a short laugh.

"He could sit in the stands and watch the boys. He might like that."

"'He might like that.'" Tonye made the crazy sign. "Is he your child?"

"He's been so sad lately."

"Well, there was a death in his family. Let him grieve in peace." Nicole started. "He didn't say anything to me."

"Ah, because you would only have given him sympathy," said Tonye mockingly. "Please, leave the man alone."

Nicole didn't answer, and then there was just the sound of cicadas in competition with the Afrobeat music.

"So what's your excuse for being miserable?" said Nicole after a minute. "You have a wife you're not interested in, a father you hate, work that bores you. You live on the sea, but you can't even watch the ships go by with your children. You rarely go outside with the boys."

"They have you and the nanny for that. You know how I am with water."

"But what about your father? Isn't there something else you'd rather be doing than managing the farm and the hotel?"

Tonye said nothing.

"Talk to me, Tonye. Tell me something—anything—about your life."

"I know nothing about *your* life with your family," he said. "The day I met you seemed to be the day your life began—the one you like to talk about. What about your parents?"

"What is there to know? I told you my mother died young from a drug overdose and my father was never a part of my life."

"But you weren't raised by wolves. Since we're playing this game, why don't you ever like to talk about your aunt Claudine? Your grandmother? You grew up in a house full of people who no longer seem to exist for you."

"I used to speak to Claudine—now and then."

"I didn't say speak to, I said talk about."

"Well, there isn't that much to say," said Nicole. She sighed. "Why does it matter anyway?"

"Yes, exactly. You have your private thoughts and I have mine. And none of them matter."

He got up from the stool, downed the last of his brandy, and strode onto the field, shouting, "Stop holding the reins for them. They can manage the horses by themselves."

BY THE time they arrived at Cactus, the rain had started, so they opted to sit indoors and endure the shrieks of Timi, Tari, and their friends' two children zigzagging around the restaurant's tables. Nneka was pregnant, her tummy round and tight under her flowing bubu.

"So when will you go for number three?" asked Chiz playfully.

Tonye smiled at Nicole or, rather, *through* her. It didn't connect.

"Probably later this year. What do you say, babe?" Tonye turned back to Chiz without waiting for a response. "We'll aim for a summer baby, so there's no disruption for the boys."

"Very precise. Sharpshooter, eh? You won't miss," said Chiz. Tonye made an aim-and-shoot gesture with one eye closed, and the men laughed loudly.

"Will you take the children with you?" Nicole asked Nneka.

"Oh, no," Nneka said. "Chiz and my parents can deal with them. I'll go sit down in Dublin and rest until Chiz or my mother can come. It will be like a nice vacation for me." She didn't sound too sure.

"Dublin?" said Nicole, thinking of Ireland's constant drizzle.

"You know the UK doesn't give citizenship like that anymore. We go through Ireland. We had to do it for Chukwuemeka and Adaeze. They are EU citizens now. It's worth it."

"Why not America?"

"Too far, and I don't know it," she said. "America scares me. All that gun crime. I want to be able to go for walks."

"It'll be cold when you go. Ireland's so wet too."

"I won't mind the cold," Nneka said. "This constant heat makes me feel so uncomfortable. But what about you, Nicole? Are you done? Don't you want a girl?"

"I actually don't," said Nicole, and excused herself to go to the ladies' room.

In the bathroom, she splashed cold water on her face. She then went out to the back patio for air, ignoring Tonye's questioning glance as she passed.

At the back of Cactus was a paved outdoor area, its tables and chairs now packed away on the water's edge. The lagoon rolled past, indifferent to how pissed off she was by Tonye's performance just now. He really thought he'd laid down the law. That he'd won their argument. That they could just reset and carry on without any discussion about the hog-ties, or her affair—she was sure he knew. He didn't seem to care so long as the façade was kept up and they continued to present the picture of a happy family.

She thought about what Kemi had said at Delis about calling Claudine, seeing how they might receive her. She didn't really want to go back to that house, but they had the rooms, and she didn't know where else to go. Perhaps time healed all wounds, as Mother-in-Law liked to say, and she and Claudine could . . . not rebuild, but have *some* kind of relationship. Perhaps they could talk. They *should* talk.

She took out her phone and hesitated for a moment, staring at Claudine's phone number. *This might be a bad idea,* she thought. She debated whether to send her a message. But. What was the point? If Claudine wanted to call her back, she would. She put her phone back in her pocket, then laughed at herself. All this worry, and Claudine probably wouldn't even answer the phone. Would probably look at it and say, *What does she want now?*

Nicole knew moving to Nigeria would hurt Claudine. She knew that under her meek exterior there was a deep reservoir of rage. But was it really about Claudine? Was it really about Tonye? Where did it begin, and who should it be directed at? She wasn't sure. But it burned. Perhaps it was PTSD programmed into her from previous generations. She had read about it—epigenetic trauma. Generational curses passed down in your DNA. Her grandmother was so full of rage, she muttered curses under her breath as she cooked and cleaned. Penny was angry at the world for not giving her light skin. Claudine was angry with Granny. Safe bet that there was a long line of Jamaican women going back to the violence meted out under slavery.

Was she right to want to leave—or to be with Elias—or was she in some way destroying her family, the way her mother had done through self-destruction?

What do I do, what do I do, what do I do? Her thoughts flipped back and forth like oars on a boat stuck in a whirlpool.

"Nicole! Are you insane? You're out here getting soaked." She looked up. Tonye was in front of her, shielding himself from the rain with his hands. She hadn't noticed the rain. It was pouring down. Water dripped down her face. Her clothes were sodden. She could feel her breasts wet and cold underneath. Tonye looked afraid, embarrassed, and angry all at once.

"Can you just come and eat?" he said warily.

"Sorry, I needed a moment," said Nicole as he hurried her toward the restaurant.

"The food is getting cold, and everyone is wondering where you are."

Nicole stopped dead in her tracks.

"Do you love me, Tonye?"

"Oh God." He put a hand to his head. "Can we do this later?"

"Do you?"

"Of course I do—you're the mother of my children."

"Then what was it all about? The hog-ties, the staying out, being so closed off. Abi said—"

Tonye shook his head. "You haven't been listening to Abi, have you? She's nuts. What can she know about anything?"

"She said your family is broken."

"The only one who's broken is *you*," he shouted, anger now superseding his earlier concern. "A little broken fucking doll saying the same thing over and over. Don't come in for me. Come in for your boys."

He left her there on the steps. Nicole waited a moment. His venom still hung in the air. There was a clap of thunder. She looked back at the lagoon, which rushed along, fiercer now in the storm, like molten metal. She had the wild notion of walking into the water. Let the waves decide what to do with her. She rubbed her shaking shoulders. It was too late to save anything here.

CHAPTER TWENTY-FIVE

CLAUDINE
After

CLAUDINE SENSED they had reached Badagry when they arrived at a busy roundabout dominated by the bronze figure of a man beating a ceremonial drum taller than himself. As they orbited the statue, she took in the unkempt, patchy grass around it, the signs advertising various attractions: boat rides, hotels, crocodile viewing spots, eateries, and the umbrella stalls lining the roads with their bric-a-brac. Badagry had the humdrum feel of a seaside town as tired as she was.

What about this place drew Nicole time and time again? she wondered. It didn't seem worth the three-hour drive from Victoria Island. What kind of museum would they have in a rinky-dink place like this anyway? Mind you, anything was better than spending the day in the compound. Tamara's wedding party had started at dawn. Claudine had been woken by loud singing and drumming coming from the courtyard. A troupe of musicians in traditional clothes by the fountain. And when she went downstairs, she found the main house awash with flowers. Pink and purple roses lined the twin staircases, circled pillars, and sprouted from huge vases placed near the front door. She took it as a message that Nicole didn't really matter. They would carry on as normal. Appearances had to be maintained. It really made her want to piss all over the bougainvillea.

Bilal pulled into a petrol station diner, the only fast-food place in the area, he said. Claudine got down from the car and rubbed her arms. It was much cooler here, out of the city. But at least it wasn't raining, and yellow glimmers among the dingy clouds hinted at a possible big reveal later.

They ordered the usual chicken and rice. As soon as they sat down with their trays, Bilal fell upon the food. By the time Claudine had eaten a few mouthfuls, he'd cleared half his plate. He paused to wash it down with a swig of Sprite, then belched quietly and smiled.

It was the first time she had seen anything like a smile from him. Bilal usually moped about in his too-big clothes, clearly Tonye's hand-me-downs, a hangdog look on his face, but she noticed the farther they'd gotten from the compound, the more he'd perked up, becoming talkative at times. The traffic at Mile 2, he'd explained, was due to a huge open market that offered the cheapest fruits and vegetables in Lagos, and when beggars took advantage of it to rush their car, tapping on the window for money, he'd warned her some might actually be demons ready to whisk her off to the underworld if she touched them. "Ma, it happens," he'd insisted when she dismissed that as nonsense. She preferred it like this, without all the bowing and scraping.

"Ma, Mr. Tonye says you will soon leave. That you go back to the UK."

"Yes," said Claudine. "My mother is sick. She's in the hospital. She's getting on, so I should go."

"Oh, very sorry," said Bilal, tucking into his rice swiftly and with urgency. "I would pray for her good health."

Claudine could see why he would be happy to hear she was leaving. One less person to drive around.

"Do you know," he said after a few minutes, now really just nibbling at the remaining gristle on the chicken bones, "I will visit Obodo Oyinbo one day. Mr. Tonye promised to carry am abroad."

"When did he do that?" she asked.

"Ah, when we were younger," said Bilal. "Since boys. We played together. Football. Catching lizards. When he left for boarding school, he promised me, I would also see the white man's country."

"You grew up together?"

"Yes, ma. My father was head cook for Chief." Bilal gave a sad smile.

"So he must have been a great cook."

Bilal's eyes lit up proudly. "His food was very sweet. Chief would only eat my father's pepper soup. He would say it reminds him of happiness."

"So is he retired now?"

"No, ma, he passed many years ago. I was still in my teenage years."

"Oh dear, I'm sorry. What happened to him?"

"Heart troubles. He wouldn't rest."

Wouldn't or couldn't? Claudine wondered. She had noticed the long working hours of all the domestic staff. Blessing slept on a sponge mat in the children's room seven days a week. Claudine appreciated that it was a tough time for Tonye, but still. The poor girl was up early in the morning and had to tend to the children when they whined during the night. She noticed that Samuel prepared Tonye's breakfast before he went to the office, cleaned the apartment, and then stayed as late as was required until Tonye allowed him to close. At least he had his own room in the BQ, but he also didn't seem to take any days off. The staff seemed happy enough, and she hadn't witnessed any mistreatment during her stay, but this entitlement to their labor was disturbing. Her parents had worked Claudine like a dog; she hadn't been paid either and often caught a beating as a reward—but they were blood. She wasn't sure if that made it better or worse.

"You've been with the family a long time then," she said.

Bilal nodded. It explained why he had seemed so . . . flattened by life. She guessed he must be only about forty, from what he said about growing up with Tonye, but with his thin frame and permanently furrowed expression, he looked much older.

"And how long driving for the family?"

"Ten years," said Bilal, absently gnawing. "But Oga has promised I will be promoted. I will soon work in compound office."

Lord have mercy, another empty promise. At least they kept him going, she supposed. He didn't seem like he had many prospects. He wasn't the most dynamic person either. Much like her, he had stayed in the house so long he'd become furniture that wouldn't fit anywhere else.

"You didn't mind missing the celebrations today?" she asked. If he was practically family—and he seemed so devoted to the Oruwaris— wouldn't he be heartbroken to miss their special occasion?

"No, I received my meat this morning," he said. "I have delivered prayers to Allah for Miss Tamara to have a happy married life and many sons." His meat. She almost laughed. So much for devotion.

He stood up, having left a single polished bone on his plate and not one grain of rice. "We go sharp now to the museum, ma," he said. "Oga said we should not be on the road after dark. There can be bandits."

They got back into the car and, after a few minutes' driving, pulled into the parking lot of a muddy site. Pools of water had collected in places. The air smelled dank. As they got out, a man in a gray shirt waved at them from the veranda of a one-story building signposted as the Mobee Royal Family Original Slave Relics Museum. He introduced himself as their guide for the day and greeted Bilal in their patois, recognizing him from his previous visits with Nicole.

"Two thousand naira each person," said the guide matter-of-factly. Claudine looked around at the low buildings and muddy terrain. *Two thousand for what?* she wondered.

"It should be free for me. I'm from Jamaica. My people were probably sold through here."

The guide just smiled vacantly, as if he heard this a lot, and insisted on the full fee for each of them. Claudine reluctantly handed over the money. As they were ushered inside, Bilal seemed excited. Although he had driven Nicole to Badagry's museums before, it appeared she had never invited him to tour with her. Had she never considered he might want to go in too? This *Downton Abbey* way of dealing with people might be normal here but didn't sit well with Claudine at all.

There were no other visitors, unsurprising given how wet it had been lately. She didn't know what she expected. Perhaps she was just too exhausted to appreciate it, after dealing with Tonye and his family, trying to solve this puzzle pretty much by herself, but she didn't get what Nicole had kept coming back to this place for.

Inside the building was a room filled with photographs, pictures, and texts explaining transatlantic slavery. Many of the documents were copies of more famous works she had seen before. There were also artifacts on display: old-fashioned guns, chains, implements of torture from the days of slavery, and the like. She walked around, taking everything in. She didn't want to touch the iron chains that had shackled captives, even children, together. Bilal, on the other hand, eagerly lifted them onto his neck to see how heavy they were and tutted loudly at their weight. Horrible that anyone, especially someone in her history, must have survived this for her to be here. It made it feel so much closer. Miss Hortense used to tell her stories about their ancestors, what she knew, in her warbling, poetic way. Her mother had worked on a sugarcane plantation into old age. She'd been born in 1867, about thirty years after slavery ended in Jamaica. Before that wasn't known. Miss Hortense wasn't sure if her grandmother had been born free or not; it wasn't talked about. She remembered her nine night, a spiritual affair where the whole village came to pay respects. But nothing else. It was like Mummy said: "Only God knew they lived."

They crossed over to the neighboring Seriki Faremi Williams Abass Slave Museum and were taken into a dark room where some items people were sold for were displayed. Claudine recalled Mummy shouting, "Them sell we fi salt. Salt!" while watching *Roots*. There was no salt on display, but some ornate tableware, an old ceremonial umbrella, cloth. Also, the guide said, people were traded for furniture, bottles of alcohol, guns, mirrors. They were sold for so little, for items that were never even used. Their guide showed them actual barracoons where the prisoners were kept until traded, a courtyard of small cells, each holding forty. These were people who had been captured from hundreds of miles away either after battles or in raids. Most perished in the cells, which had a tiny opening for air and a pit latrine in the center.

The guide told a nice story about Seriki Faremi Williams Abass, the slave turned wealthy slave trader, whose descendants still owned the museum. Abass, he said, was transported to Brazil in the early 1800s as a child, educated there (which was illegal for slaves at that time), and eventually freed to oversee the slave transportation for his master, living happily ever after until his death in 1919. Abass was clearly still viewed as a great man around here, regardless of the cruelty he had inflicted on others. There were portraits and a photo of a statue of him that must still be standing somewhere. It was possible his grandchildren were still living off that money somewhere, like the British aristocracy with their great houses and wealth, but the fancy home he'd built here in Badagry had long since crumbled, only photos remaining, and his "museum" was falling apart.

It was a shock to learn that some of Abass's descendants were now living in the cells. Attempts had been made to convert them into "homes." Large windows had been cut into the walls. Clothes fluttered on a washing line that hung outside one dilapidated hut; a rusted satellite dish perched on the roof of another. Like putting lipstick on a pig, the results were almost comical. Who could live on a site of such horror? The dire circumstances of the descendants struck Claudine as a sort of karma, but she was sad to see their plight. They had nothing to do with slavery themselves and were barely surviving. But at least they were free. Bilal found it as bizarre as she did, shaking his head at everything, as he learned about transatlantic slavery for the first time.

AT THE end of that section of the tour, the guide led them to a scuffed blue canoe with a spluttering motor, which would take them across the strip of water to the so-called Point of No Return on the island of Gberefu, which lay between them and the Atlantic. The prisoners had been loaded onto ships from there and taken across the ocean to the Caribbean, South America, and the United States, where they would be sold off at auction like cattle. "Gberefu," he explained, "meant 'take them and go.'" *Take them and go.* He said the island had once been inhabited, but they'd all been carted off by the Portuguese too.

Bilal hesitated to get into the canoe. She heard him muttering prayers as they sat on the rough wooden slats and put on flimsy foam harnesses handed to them by the boatman. They set off. It wasn't far. Unlucky if the boat capsized right in the middle. Claudine tried not to think about the crocodile signs she had seen by the roundabout.

The island still had the remnants of a colonial jetty. Mildewed stone walls rose out of the water, recognizable English architecture, stone railings with curved posts. Many were now decrepit, fallen, crumbled. No attempt to repair them. They climbed the roughly hewn steps, arriving on flat scrubland. A trail of flattened earth led them through ankle-length grass with wiry bushes on either side and, in the distance, a forest of skyscraper palm trees. The guide said the walk was about a mile. At least Claudine had worn her running shoes.

They soon arrived at a simple brick well with a thatched roof over the top, surrounded by a white-painted stone wall. A sign read: ORIGINAL SPOT. SLAVES. SPIRIT. ATTENUATION. WELL.

"The Well of Forgetting," the guide said, "where the slaves would drink and forget everything before being loaded onto the ships." He kept calling them *slaves*, she noticed, as if they weren't people—his people. Africans. As if he had no connection. He pointed to an inscription. *Here you will forget your names, your people, your language, and become ghosts.* Claudine and Bilal peered down into the well's dark oblivion.

It sounded as if herbs had been put in the water. They'd drugged the prisoners—making them easier to move onto the ships. It also served as a ceremonial "last rites." From this point on, they were "dead." They ceased to exist, their identities erased. What happened next would no longer matter. And it worked, didn't it? Over the centuries, forbidden to speak their specific languages or practice their traditional spiritual beliefs, they forgot. What was left, fragments from different cultures and peoples, had been jumbled together along with the European and indigenous influences. A few words remained, some dishes, physical characteristics, cultural practices, echoes from unknown points of origin, like Papason's grandmother speaking the original "Swahili." He was adamant that was what it was, not that Papason knew any African language to know for sure. He couldn't remember any of the words his grandmother and mother had tried to teach him. But it was true that people still spoke West African languages in Cockpit Country, where his grandmother was born. They were Africans too, but Africa was an idea of who they might be, not a specific people they actually were or a village they could trace their ancestry to with certainty.

Claudine followed the guide onward, but looked back and noticed Bilal still staring into the well, overcome. It took her shouting to get his attention. And when he caught up to them, he wouldn't meet her eyes.

THE OCEAN sprang into view, suddenly and without warning, stopping Claudine midstep. After the dreary shrubs, its glittering surface seemed to light up the sky. Her ears were filled with the roar of the waves, and the ground rumbled beneath her feet. Surely the captives would have fallen to their knees in terror here, screaming, yanking desperately against their weighty shackles to see a great dark sea monster waiting in the water at the beach's edge to swallow them up and take them beyond the orange horizon to spit them out in another hell.

The beach was deserted. Its sands lay in crisp furrows like yellow frosting. Few people must come here. It was marked only by bits of driftwood, shells, and pebbles strewn across. Trees towered over it. She had never seen such tall trees. How long had it taken them to grow so high? She wondered how old they were. How far could they see, and what did they remember?

Bilal had walked ahead to where the ocean-froth laced the shore, his smart black shoes leaving dark imprints behind him. He seemed to walk directly into the surf, his shirt a fluttering white flag in the wind, becoming a silhouette against the sun.

Claudine was grateful to see a bench set back into the shade, because after that walk, her knees were going. She sat down, watching him and the guide, who kicked driftwood aimlessly along the sand.

The sea met the sky like the past meeting the future, with the present stuck on the beach, wondering where it fit in. Claudine recalled her coworker's remarks with a sad smile. The sky *was* bigger here. Had Nicole sat here too, thinking about her poor mother, Jackie? Her father? Did she have a garden in her dreams where her mother would be waiting for her, lying in the sorrel? Claudine wondered if they were now together. She couldn't see where Nicole could be on this earth or think of who she might be with. The mystery, it seemed, would never be solved.

"I'm sorry, Nicole," she said out loud. She gasped, or was it the tide that drew its breath before rushing forward again? And the tears she despised so much began forcing their way out relentlessly.

She was sorry about Len. She had brought him into the house and failed to protect Nicole. But worse, she had silenced her, punished her for speaking out, all the while masquerading as a mother-like creature. She had passed on the rage she felt at her own abuse. She could see that in Nicole as well. Too angry to come home, to pick up the phone, to talk to Tonye. Was there a chance she *had* killed herself out of rage?

Bilal returned. He sat beside her quietly on the bench, staring out across the sea, his face in shadow and unreadable.

"How are you doing?" Claudine asked.

"Am fine, ma," he said. It was the most mournful "fine" she had ever heard in her life. A dirge around an open grave as the coffin is lowered. *How great thou art. How great thou art.* She remembered him standing at the well, lost in his thoughts.

"You have anything you want to forget, Bilal?" she asked.

"Plenty things, ma," he said quietly. He shifted off among the trees to relieve himself. She might have to do the same soon. No finding toilets around here.

Her memories enveloped her once more. They'd been a family once, hadn't they? When they were all together at 49 Nedford Road, squeezed into the back room with the TV blaring. Someone doing her nails on the table, despite Mummy cussing about it from the sofa. Papason's jaw mashing through whatever was heaped on his plate. Jackie sprawled on the floor. Yvonne on the sofa next to Mummy. Michael sitting on a chair telling one of his tall tales. Was it just a picture in her mind she had painted, or one of those brief moments when it all came together and made sense? They were carrying too many mysterious scars, yet survived by keeping certain memories and letting the other ones drift out to sea, hoping that, out of sight, they would quietly disappear. But they lingered, lay in wait, surfaced unexpectedly, horribly. Never really gone. She didn't want to carry them anymore.

She was surprised to see Bilal rush out from the trees, breathing heavily, stuffing his shirt back into his trousers on his way.

"Ma, we should leave from here," he said when he reached the bench. "This place has curse."

"What's the matter?" she asked. He looked badly frightened. She looked back at the trees he'd just rushed from. They seemed normal enough. "Did something attack you?"

"Ma, this place has spirits that can never rest. In the well I saw them. And in the trees now also. We should go."

"Bilal," she said with a sigh, thinking, *Here we go again.* "There's no such thing as spirits."

He looked up and down the beach, agitated. "The dead slaves who died here. They are angry. They want vengeance."

"Don't be ridiculous."

Bilal pointed down the coast. "They entered water. Dragged Lamidi. The same cursed spirits that took my oga's brother and madam." He watched the trees warily as if these "spirits" might leap out at any moment.

"What do you mean, 'took madam'?" He wasn't making sense to her. "But you said you didn't know what happened to Nicole. You said you weren't there."

"Perhaps your ancestors seek revenge," he said, then muttered something to himself in his language. He sounded delirious. Claudine wondered if she should call the guide over.

"So are you saying Nicole has drowned?" She didn't know whether to take him seriously. She was starting to worry that the place *was* turning him mad, that there was something in the whispering trees. It was getting to her as well.

He dropped to his knees suddenly and groaned, holding both sides of his head like a watermelon about to burst. His eyes glimmered feverishly as he looked straight out to sea and the horizon was mirrored in them, his past, his future. "May Allah forgive me," he cried out.

Now he wanted forgiveness? For what?

She forced herself to speak calmly, to humor him even though she was shocked. "You don't have to keep these secrets any longer, Bilal," she said. "Whatever it is, it's killing you, I can tell. I know you're scared, but you can't carry this any longer." She held her breath, terrified of what he would say, but she also had to know. "What happened?"

After what seemed like ages, he finally spoke. "It was Kemi," he said.

CHAPTER TWENTY-SIX

NICOLE
Before

"A LITTLE RAIN can't ruin our day," Elias had insisted with a wink as Nicole stood doubtfully on the boat club jetty. The rocking waves made it difficult to get her footing. He steadied her awkward descent into the boat, laughing as her white dress lifted in a Marilyn Monroe moment.

It felt insane going to the beach house when heavy rain was forecast. Already the sky seemed set to burst, and the wind pounded them. But Elias pressed on unfazed, as if the sun shone on his face and the lagoon was calm. He liked to swim against the current. She had learned that about him. He did not pray for the serenity to accept the things he could not change, he grabbed what was his the way he had seized her. Everything in his world was by force, and here, he was in his element.

"Best weather for fishermen," he shouted enthusiastically, pointing to the canoes they passed along the creeks. "Fish like rain. They will be on the lagoon catching all night!"

But once they had arrived, Nicole appreciated the rare treat of having Yohanna's beach house to themselves. There was always tension around whether Yohanna was happy or annoyed, was getting enough attention or respect. His body language could change everyone's mood, and Elias was responsible for managing it, Yohanna's Soother-in-Chief. Now that it was just the two of them, she noticed how much more lighthearted Elias seemed, singing along to the Hausa ballads he loved. Men declaring their undying love for women in soft entreaties set to a skirt-swishing jingle, not the sex- and party-obsessed American stuff Yohanna favored. And she'd long had a secret urge to experience the drunken fury of a Lagos storm close up, to dance like a dervish in the hammering rain. Today she might get her wish.

Against the sky's apocalyptic backdrop, the sand looked lunar-pale and the molten ocean was an electric force field, vibrating in the distance. She stood on the edge of the pool, tingling with anxious static, for the weather, for her next steps, for an answer to her many questions, then slid into the water, half-swimming, using the bottom of the pool to launch her across its rippling surface. It wouldn't be long before the rain, she was sure. Already gusts of wind had blown sand and leaves into the pool, and the palm trees shivered. A mustard-colored mutt, one she'd seen on previous visits, got up from its snooze by the fence and moseyed off to find shelter.

But Elias seemed relaxed and oblivious, setting the wooden dining table with the food he had brought. He carefully laid out cloth place mats and silverware, unwrapped china plates, and positioned his vase of flowers, yellow roses this time, in the middle of the table.

She inhaled the briny sea air mingled with chlorine, wondering that he didn't seem to notice the turmoil within her. She had been feeling sick since waking up that morning, knowing she could never tell him what had happened with Tonye, that it would weigh on her forever. Even Timi had noticed. Climbing into bed with her as he sometimes did, warming his cold feet on hers, his furry head on the pillow, he'd stared at her, a hand on her face.

"You look sad, Mummy," he had said.

"I am a little sad," she admitted.

He'd snuggled her, just as she did him when he was sad. Full of empathy. But later, when he looked back and remembered that day—would he still feel sorry for her? Wouldn't he be angry with the one who walked away from the marriage and destroyed his family?

She had dressed slowly, deliberating on what to wear, really delaying as much as she could. She chose a white cotton summer dress Elias had never seen her in and her rubber Valentino jelly flip-flops. She took her hair down from its twists and fluffed it out. Her hair fell in soft waves now, but it would mushroom into a big curly fro with the sea breeze and the rain. She wanted to feel free today. Let her hair do what it wanted.

"Let's eat," Elias called. She exited the pool, wrapping herself in one of the large white beach towels he had laid out for her. Her wet hair sprang up in coily tendrils. She walked over to the table, where everything was set up for their romantic lunch. He passed her a glass of champagne.

"What are we celebrating?" she asked.

"Yohanna's agreed to partner with me on my graphic design company. I'm a business owner!" He whooped. They clinked glasses. "I'll soon be hiring staff and getting clients. With your posh accent, I'm sure you can bring me a lot of business. Those expats and Nigerwives you mix with."

Nicole smiled and congratulated him. This was great news, and he seemed so happy. She wished she could match his vibrant energy as he talked about the office space he'd already looked at on the twelfth floor of one of Yohanna's office blocks, looking out across Victoria Island. Just like their beach day, he had prepared for their relationship. The prospect of being with her had galvanized him into action. He was on his way to becoming the kind of man he wanted to be.

"What if you fall out with Yohanna?"

"Fall out? Why would we—hey, if you're still thinking about that other night, we discussed that. You have it mistaken. He was just being Yohanna. That's his humor. He even said he'll apologize to you when he sees you next."

"I'm just saying. Can't he pull the plug at any time?"

"Baby, he wouldn't do that." Elias seemed pained at her concerns. "Trust me, I know him. He wants this for me. And anyway, within six months, I'll have got things started—I won't need him." He again talked about a life they would have together. They would no longer be invisible in Lagos, relying on friends and family. People would have to take note of who *they* were. *They* would intimidate others. He laughed at the prospect. "We are the new Lagos."

It was everything she could have wanted to hear. But the more Elias spoke about his ambitions and how she would fit into them, the further away she felt. He was a man of this place, as much as he claimed to represent something different, and she was a woman of this place. A Nigerwife. They were both kidding themselves that there was any other way to exist in Lagos.

"I can't do this anymore."

He stopped midsentence. She hadn't meant to say that. It had fallen out of her, and she wanted to swallow it back. But she also felt oddly relieved. And from the way his face abruptly crumpled, she realized that all the talking was him trying to convince himself. He'd known all along this was a doomed affair. In spite of his insistences and solutions, of course he knew. Perhaps it was in him to pursue the women who would never stay. He couldn't help it, even though it broke him each time.

He shook his head. "No, baby, don't say that."

"I can't do this anymore," she repeated.

"What are you worried about? Is it Tonye? Did he threaten you again? Has he hurt you?" His eyes narrowed. She could tell he was already gauging how he would defend her. Who he would call. Whatever was in his power to arrange, buoyed up by the champagne and his new confidence. But his possessiveness just made her sadder. She didn't want to be passed from one man's protection to another's. He didn't seem to really hear her.

"No, he hasn't said anything."

"Then what can't you do anymore?" How easily his hostility seemed to switch from Tonye to her. "What have *you* done anyway?"

His hand hit the table, and the vase fell over. This one was plastic. It didn't break. "I've been the one doing everything. You just show up when you feel like it, leave when you want to. You've controlled the whole thing." She watched the vase roll off the table and bounce on the patio. The yellow roses scattered across the concrete. It wasn't easy to find yellow roses in Lagos—there were only a few places. He always wanted everything to be special for them, heightened, as romantic as the songs he sang. "Look at me!"

"I should have told you before we came here." She met his eyes. They were furious. Screaming. "I'm sorry."

"This isn't how you treat someone you love," he said.

Nicole didn't know what to say, and it seemed to enrage him further. He stood and stamped on the roses, crushing them into the ground. Petals freed from their moorings were tossed on the wind.

"Everyone said you weren't serious. That you would make a fool of me. That how could a rich woman like you ever be serious with me?"

Who was everyone? She didn't dare to ask. How many people had he told about their affair? Was Kemi playing both sides?

He lifted his chair and hurled it across the patio. She held her breath for what might come next. He wanted something from her, she knew. Tears, hysteria, something to match his intensity. To prove him wrong. But she didn't really know what she felt or what she could say that would change anything. She didn't even know if this love he spoke of was genuine. What was it Yohanna had said back in the gallery? Something about people not liking you for you? It wasn't really her Elias wanted—it was justice for the things he had suffered in life. Perhaps Yohanna's intentions had actually been purer. He could have any woman. He needed nothing from her. He wanted her for wanting's sake, nothing else. Elias stormed off down the beach, leaving her alone. She breathed again.

She picked up the bottle of champagne and tried to fill her glass, but her hand shook and the champagne splashed on the table, making a mess. She always made such a mess of things.

She downed her glass quickly. It didn't seem to matter what she said or did, everyone hated her in the end. Her family in the UK had been so quick to forget her. It was as if she'd never existed. And Tonye hated her like poison. So did his family. She could see it in their eyes, how disappointed they were. Even after two children, boys at that. She was the wrong sort. Not Nigerian. Not from money or a grand family like theirs. Abi had only reached out a hand of friendship lately to vent her own resentments over Tonye being the favored sibling. Elias was just the last in a long line of people who despised her. Even her children would soon hate her, when they got older and realized what she'd done.

She poured again and drank. She hadn't meant for any of this to happen. She hadn't meant to break his heart or ruin anyone's life. But she had.

Even her own mother had hated her. Something about being hated by your mother, it haunts you. It's a stain you can never shake off. Len had seen it, what a hateful creature she was. Someone thrown to the wolves. Someone not worth caring about.

It had been so hard, losing her mum at such a young age, no father around. She'd been totally dependent on Claudine. She'd trusted her. She'd trusted Len because of Claudine. He'd raped her, and Claudine had punished her for it. Len ran off, and Claudine froze Nicole out. Refused to even look at her after she told her what had happened.

Nicole drank again. What else was there to do except get drunk, pass out, and hope not to wake up? People just wanted what they wanted. Elias, Claudine, Tonye. She wouldn't be here right now if it wasn't for him. She wouldn't be trapped so far from anything she knew. She'd given up so much moving here, and he didn't care. She wasn't a person to him, but an appendage. And hadn't she tried to tell Elias many times that it wouldn't work? But he didn't want to hear it. He'd pushed her to this point. They'd all pushed her to her limits, and she couldn't take any more. She was done.

Sobbing now, Nicole smashed the champagne glass on the table. It broke into several sharp pieces. She picked up a sliver and pressed it to the soft underside of her forearm.

There it was. The red bulb. Seeing it bubble up from her skin was so satisfying. So alluring. She licked it. Salty, metallic.

She saw Elias striding back over the sand, and hurriedly tidied everything away, back into bags, throwing the glass pieces into the bin before he reached the patio.

He leaned over the table. His hands pressing down into it, his chest still heaving.

"She's not your friend," he declared.

"What?"

"This is all Kemi, I know it." He shooed away her protests. "Don't listen to her. She's not your friend."

"What does Kemi have to do with this? She doesn't even know I'm here."

"She's back seeing Yohanna. Did you know that?" Having delivered his "gotcha," he plumped down on a chair expecting a reaction.

Nicole blinked. Kemi hadn't said anything about that.

"She blocked him. Even Yohanna told me."

"But she unblocked later, begging, and they resumed. I didn't tell you because Yohanna told me not to—after the trouble you caused last time, which almost cost me his friendship, by the way, because I told you about his engagement."

It was weird that Kemi hadn't told her, but hadn't she also kept secrets from Kemi? What did it change?

"Okay, so she's seeing Yohanna. So what?"

"Wasn't she the one who said I wasn't worthy of you, that you should leave me? But even knowing my boy is getting married, she is still trying her best to secure him. What does that say about her?"

"I don't know. I don't want to talk about Kemi."

"I was nothing but nice to her and she tried to destroy my life."

"It wasn't about you."

"She thought she was too good for me. But, ha! This one. She is mad." He took out his phone, scrolled through his messages, and showed Nicole a photograph of Kemi, naked, contorted. Her hands tied together, her feet also tied, like a roasting pig. On her face, a smile.

"Your friend is a whore no man will ever marry. Yohanna sent this to me. He said she begged to be tied up. Like this." He laughed. "Kai! She is mad."

Nicole turned her face away from it.

Elias shrugged and put his phone away. "These Lagos babes. They would rather do all this for a guy who doesn't even care so long as he has money, or has a rich papa, or a big family name. But someone like me they disrespect. Even if I love. Even if I'm prepared to lay down my life. They won't even look twice at me."

He kept talking, but Nicole wasn't there. She was back in the compound, holding the package of hog-ties, staring at the woman on the cover, wondering who Tonye could have bought them for. And she remembered the little barbs Kemi had made, and Tonye's comments about Kemi. What a fool she had been.

"Don't do this," Elias was saying. "You're throwing everything away for a guy who never cared about you—who never even saw you."

Nicole felt like she was going to be sick. She needed to get away from this place.

"It'll be dark soon," she said, interrupting his rant. "I should go."

He stopped talking abruptly. Confused. Angry. Hot. But he grabbed his things without another word. He didn't notice the dried blood on her wrist. He didn't really see her at all in this moment. They locked up and left the house.

There were still men by the jetty to help them into the boat. Elias sliced the craft through the water in silence. There was just the rushing of the water and the churning of the motor. If Elias was concerned about the darkness that fell over them as they passed Tin Can Island, he didn't share it with her. He looked stonily ahead. Eyes boring into the night. She could feel the hatred coming off, a heat that kept her back. She texted Kemi to meet her.

> I really need to talk to you. Can you come to the Paradise Jetty?

That place?

> I'm headed there now.

Why? Why there?

Please. I just broke up with
Elias. I need to talk.

They passed a jetty bar, lively with multicolored string bulbs and Fela Kuti's songs. *Water no get enemy,* the people on the decking chanted. Laughter and the scent of grilled suya meat wafted over to them. It receded into the background, and the journey ahead looked even lonelier. A fisherman in a canoe, then nothing.

THERE WAS a rumble and then a loud crack overhead as Paradise Jetty came into view, and it began to rain insistently. The jetty was dark and desolate. The rain made it seem even more so. Nicole shivered as the drops hit her skin, sliding into her dress. From the boat's lights, she could see only the old wooden posts that disappeared into the indigo water. The narrow, planked walkway leading up onto the bank. Her heart shook. Why had she been doing this? Taking such risks. She was so happy she wouldn't have to do it anymore.

Elias pulled in, and his strong arms steadied her as she made to step up onto the wooden walkway. "Don't go," he begged, clasping her legs. She turned, and the lights from the boat made his eyes seem as if they were on fire. "Going back to him—it's crap. It's the end. Don't be like the others. These guys, they just take the parts of you they want and throw the rest away. You won't be happy with him. He doesn't love you."

All she had to do was change her mind. Sink down into his embrace. She would be forgiven. No one was perfect, but he was close, and in another life perhaps she could have loved him. She pulled free and climbed onto the jetty. Once her feet were firmly on the wooden boards, she looked back and watched him pulling away, his back receding, knowing they had become strangers again almost immediately and that they would never see each other again, and even if they did it would be painful and cold. She had joined the other women in his past who had broken him. She had become the thing about himself that he loathed. The boat gathered speed, an arrow of light that turned a bend in the lagoon and was gone. Cold and wet, she was impatient to get home, home to her children. She would sneak into their room. Listen to their breathing in the soft darkness. Just the thought warmed her somewhat.

A second crack and then a flash of lightning somewhere close by revealed Kemi hurrying along the jetty to meet her. "OMG, this rain! Nicole, why did you call me here? I thought you were stranded, but Bilal is waiting for you over there. What's going on?"

She looked fabulous as usual. Even though she had probably just gotten out of bed. Whose bed? She reached out a hand to touch Nicole, but Nicole backed away.

"I know about you and Tonye," said Nicole. "I know about the hog-ties."

Kemi had the grace to look surprised and concerned. "What are you saying?"

"Don't deny it," shouted Nicole. Then controlled her voice. "Don't. Deny. It."

"You bring me to this fucking place, to make accusations? You want us to get kidnapped for this nonsense?"

"Don't lie to me!"

"I'm sorry," said Kemi in that infuriating way. "But I really tried to help you be a little less stupid. To get you moving again. But you're so helpless, such a damsel. 'Woe is me, I have everything, I have nothing.'"

"My *husband*, Kemi!"

"Certain men want you because you're yellow. That's all. That's it. You're something to have, like a handbag or a watch. They quickly get bored of that when they see how dumb you are."

Nicole was speechless, and Kemi turned to go, but then turned back.

"Let me give you some advice. In this life, there is no man or woman you can trust completely. Even the one who loves you the most will hurt you in the end. That is why you can only depend on yourself. If you weren't such a parasite, maybe Tonye wouldn't hate you so much."

Nicole grabbed Kemi's arm furiously as she tried to walk off, but Kemi jerked it away. "Fucking leave me."

Nicole watched Kemi's receding form as she marched away. She considered running after her, but to do what? Hit her? They would fight, then what? She actually felt sorry for Kemi. She couldn't see Kemi and Tonye happy together. Both of them were too messed up, both hiding their true selves beneath glamorous exteriors. But even if they were, so what? She couldn't worry about them now. A car accelerated in the dark, tires screeching away.

Nicole stared at the frothing water, its hungry swells, thinking she would be better off dead, gone. But she wouldn't do that to Timi and Tari. This mess wasn't their fault, and Tonye didn't really hate her, even if he told Kemi he did. He just had his own problems, was fucked up by Ebipade's death and a dad who preferred his dead brother over him. Claudine had loved her. She'd been a mother to her. The best years of her life had been with Claudine until Len showed up.

"My Boy Lollipop." That was Claudine's favorite tune. *You make my heart go giddy-up!* She would sing it as she made curry goat or escovitch fish, whatever she was cooking, would dance with Nicole, spinning her around by her hand, as the promise of tomorrow spiced the air around them.

In the morning she would call Imani and say she wanted her to make the arrangements to get back to the UK, taking the boys with her help. She would start over, back at Nedford Road. Even if Tonye came to look for her there, the UK government would never let him take the boys back to Nigeria. It would be awful, but not forever. She didn't want to shy away from conversations anymore. To run. Claudine would have to listen. She would have to trust Claudine to listen. There didn't seem to be any other way now.

There was another flash of lightning, striking so close the whole jetty shook. She fell and cried out.

"Bilal! Help me!"

She tried to move forward, but the structure rocked, and as she took a step she almost slipped on the wet planks. She didn't trust herself in the soupy gloom. One misstep could land her in the water.

A flashlight approached—Bilal, in a familiar oversized shirt, carrying an umbrella. Thank God!

"Bilal!" she called out. "Please come over here. The jetty is rocking. I can't see anything."

He came walking toward her along the jetty. A silhouette, his face an inky pool of nothingness.

"Some of the rail is missing. It's so dark. Can you guide me?"

"Yes, madam," he said. He sounded as sick and tired of it all as she was. She got it. He needed to rest. He would rest after today. The affair was over.

He wordlessly took her hand, and they started heading back down the jetty.

Suddenly she felt a shove, and she was falling. She hit the water, flailing, as it sucked her under. So cold, so deep. She surfaced again, grasping at air. Screamed, but the lagoon's pull was relentless. She couldn't see anything now, not Bilal, not the bank, not the sky. She didn't even know which way was up. She thrashed about, trying to swim, feeling the water overwhelm her, her lungs bursting. Getting tired now. Desperate to breathe. She thought of her mother, and how much she missed her.

CHAPTER TWENTY-SEVEN

CLAUDINE
After

K EMI?" CLAUDINE squinted at Bilal, unable to fully take it in. She didn't know what she'd expected, but not this. She had only thought he would say something that he'd seen or heard. She felt dizzy and leaned forward with her head between her knees the way she'd taught Mummy to do.

"Kemi pushed my madam into the water. They fought on the jetty over Oga. Madam had anger. Very anger. I no sabi why. Madam was coming back from the boat."

"So you *were* there." All this time, he knew so much and said nothing. His still, silent waters ran very deep.

Bilal nodded. "She started seeing one man not far. One apartment block in VI. Mr. Tonye didn't know, but every day I drop her there. Sometimes stay late. Sometimes drop her to boat club. Sometimes, restaurant. To keep me quiet, she got my brother a job at LAD. I no gree. I no gree!" He fell to lamenting in his language, seeming so taken with anguish again. Beside himself. "But my brother he needed work. So I didn't tell Oga anything I saw, and they continued. That day, Sunday, I drove her to boat club. She said I must pick her up at Paradise Jetty."

"You'd been there before."

"Yes, ma. That's where she comes from the boat." He groaned. "When she finally came. Hai!" He put his hand to his head. "I don sabi wetin dey happen."

"What are you saying? Speak English!"

"Her friend came to meet her on the jetty. This Kemi woman."

"Kemi was there?"

"Yes, ma. I saw her arrive the same time as the boat came. She drove her own car. She went to meet madam on the jetty. I stay in the car until I hear one scream."

"Who screamed?"

"Kemi screamed. I ran. But when I got there, madam was gone. Kemi said she fell in the lagoon." Claudine's hands flew to her mouth in horror. "She said it was an accident and I shouldn't talk," Bilal continued. "That if I open mouth, she would blame me. To say I push madam." He let his head sink again. "Who would believe me?"

Claudine sat stunned. If she weren't already on the bench, she would have collapsed onto the sand. She couldn't feel her limbs. *No, no, no, no.* She kept saying it over and over, refusing to accept what he was saying. Nicole was not gone.

"I don't see anyting," Bilal said. "I come to assist, but no light. I can't see. I call her name. I call, 'Madam, madam.' No answer. No crash, no cry. So much rain. The water was boiling." His eyes took on a faraway quality as if he was no longer there on the beach with Claudine. "I wait on my knees, begging God for miracles. It be like say she vanish. Like juju."

"Juju?" she asked vacantly. He wasn't making much sense to her now. He looked up at the trees fearfully again.

"Be like say my fault because I took the job for my brother and didn't tell him about madam. But I never kill her." His voice climbed with anxiety. "Take am blood drop for drop if I lie!"

Blood. Drop. Fault. Kill. What did anything matter now, if Nicole was really dead? She felt the weight of it all, pressing down on her. Claudine lay down on the bench, hoping never to have to get up.

IT FELT like they had been at Badagry the whole day, but when they started walking back toward the mainland, it was still only 3 p.m.

Their trek passed largely in silence, the three on their own mental tracks. The guide kept a considerate distance from whatever was happening.

Replaying what he had said in her mind—Kemi and Nicole on the jetty arguing about Tonye, Kemi pushing Nicole in—Claudine decided there was still a chance that Nicole was alive. Bilal hadn't seen her die. There was no body. Not yet. He should come back to the compound and help them look for her, she said. She might be there somewhere. He looked at her like she was crazy. Perhaps she was. What choice did she have? If she really believed what he was saying, she would rather stay on this island and let the spirits take her too.

Bilal didn't even bother putting on his life jacket in the boat, just hugged it to his chest and looked into the bottom of the canoe as it rocked its way to the mainland. Back at the museum, Claudine called Tonye, and of course, he didn't answer. She texted him. Nothing. Blessing didn't answer either. She didn't have anyone else's number.

This wasn't a place Bilal seemed to want to linger either. Too many ghosts. They made the return journey into the city center, through the grinding traffic at Mile 2, the motorcycle taxis almost scraping the car as they wove through and onto the pavement, pedestrians jumping out of the way. The roadside stalls were still busy with Saturday shoppers. The beggars. All this passed without comment. Even when one beggar pounded on the car for attention, Bilal had no curse words for him.

Perhaps she slept. She didn't know. Questions swirled in her mind. Was Bilal telling the truth? Had he seen more he wasn't saying? Had Kemi even been there, or was he lying to get himself out of trouble? Could Kemi have killed Nicole—a crime of passion? Were Kemi and Tonye in on it together? Bilal too? Everyone had lied to her in some way. It made her angry.

She was glad of the stubborn traffic. She had tried to call Tonye repeatedly, but he wasn't picking up or answering her text messages. Probably having too much fun at the wedding. She wanted to see his face when she told him. To know if he was involved in any way—if he had put Bilal up to take the fall somehow. At least the cars hemming them in felt like a kind of safety. Although Bilal seemed to accept the wisdom of confessing, she wasn't sure his faith would stop him from driving off a bridge.

GRADUALLY THE skyscrapers of the island came into view.

"Let's go to the wedding venue," said Claudine, checking the time on her phone. It was 6 p.m. The wedding was definitely under way, and the whole family would be there.

Bilal said nothing, but she guessed they were approaching the wedding venue because the long road they were bouncing down had turned into an old-time shubeen crammed with black SUVs turning every which way, trying to squeeze past each other and all beeping at once. The venue was in the distance, like a house on a hill. But no way to get to it. Some of the vehicles were accompanied by trucks of armed police or soldiers who obviously had nothing better to do than escort rich people to weddings. As they got closer to the gates, she could see security in bulletproof helmets and vests, trying to marshal the traffic. Hustlers stood by the entrance waving bands of clean money at the arriving cars. Some stopped to buy. She thought that odd, but couldn't dwell on it as the security guard approached their car. "Where is your card?" he demanded impatiently.

"I don't have it," she said, remembering she'd left it on Tonye's desk with the clothes. "But I'm part of the family. I have an urgent message for Tonye Oruwari."

The man looked her up and down as if she had two heads. Then at Bilal, who just shrugged and looked away.

"No card, no entry," he said, waving them off.

"I have something important to tell the family."

"Go." The guard slapped the bonnet of the car. Bilal slowly inched forward. There was nothing Claudine could do. She'd called and called Tonye's line, but no one had answered. She could see that Bilal didn't want to risk angering the guards.

"Maybe I should get out and explain," said Claudine.

"Ma," said Bilal quietly. "Like this you cannot enter." He was referring to her clothes, she realized.

She guessed she looked a mess, T-shirt streaked with sand and dust. Hair, what there was, needing some gel. Running shoes brown from trekking around in the mud.

"Move along!" the guard shouted angrily. Bilal drove off slowly.

"Okay, let's just go back to the compound," she said. She didn't know what her game plan was anyway, even if they did get into the car park. If she got into the hall, then what? There were hundreds if not thousands of people. How would she even find Tonye? And what would Bilal do—wait in the car park while she went in, or just drive out and disappear? And then she could be stranded. No, it was better to head back to the house. Bilal stared ahead. His body language revealed nothing. Usually in the car he listened to the football reporting or a music channel, but the radio was silent. He was thinking, wondering what to do—she could tell. She also didn't know what to do, who to call. Certainly not the bought-and-paid-for Mr. Ogunsanya. She opened her bag. She still had the knife in the inner pocket. She felt its edge with her thumb. It was sharp enough to kill. What sort of justice could there be in a place like this unless a justice you made yourself?

THE COMPOUND was quiet. She could immediately tell the family wasn't there because of the amount of time the security took to open the gate. Bilal had to beep several times before one of the gatemen, his shirt off, in just a sleeveless vest and some tracksuit bottoms, opened the gate. And by their office, another slept on a bench. Children who must have belonged to the compound staff ran about the courtyard playing. A woman sat on a chair outside the Boys' Quarters having her hair combed and plaited by another woman. They laughed together in a way that gave Claudine a pang for home and for Penny. She wished Penny were with her. Penny would know what to do. She thought she'd always been the stronger one, but it was Penny who made her strong. The little sister looking up to her as a protector. She needed her now.

EMMANUEL WAS still at the house, as starched as ever. He opened the door and let her in, bowing, but had been fearful of her since their confrontation and scuttled away as soon as he could. The house seemed empty otherwise. Perhaps everyone had enjoyed their meat and was sleeping it off. The pavilion outside was empty, some of the chairs knocked over; any celebrants had come and gone.

She headed straight for her room to shower and change. Perhaps she would collect the card and go back to the wedding to look for Tonye. She didn't know. Bilal had said he would wait in the car—but would he?

She opened her bedroom door, and stopped short. Tonye was standing on the balcony, the doors wide open. He seemed to be looking out at the lagoon. He was dressed more like Chief, in a long-sleeved tunic that went to his knees, and wore a top hat like a lot of the other men she'd seen at the Door Knocking.

"Tonye?" she said, approaching him. Why was he here in her room instead of at the wedding?

"It doesn't feel so bad to look at," he said, not turning around. So why, she wondered, were his large hands gripping the rail so?

"Why aren't you at the wedding?"

"Haven't been yet." It made sense now why he hadn't answered the phone and was hiding out here. The whole world must be going crazy looking for him. "I wanted to be with her for a while. She always liked to sit here, watching the lagoon. I hated it, but it was her happy place. On Saturdays she would watch catamarans passing along the water."

Claudine looked out over the lagoon, which stared back at her hard-faced under a sky that looked ready to lash the world again.

"Tonye," she said, putting a hand on his arm. "Bilal told me what happened to Nicole. He said Kemi pushed Nicole into the water."

"Kemi? Bilal was there?" Tonye said, bewildered.

"He just told me at Badagry that there was an accident at Paradise Jetty after the boat trip," she said.

"A fucking accident? Where is he now?"

"He's downstairs, let him explain."

He ran out to the hallway and called the gate, speaking to the security rapid-fire.

"He's gone!" he exclaimed, hanging up. He started calling other numbers, shouting into the phone.

She waited expectantly in the doorway.

"He drove out some minutes after you left," Tonye said, seething. "Why did you leave him downstairs?"

"I didn't know you were here. I was going to take the card and go back to the wedding, and Bilal said he would drive me. I didn't think he would run. He said he would explain to you, the accident that happened with Kemi."

"He's not answering his phone. He's fled." She could see fury envelop him like a red mist. "But I spoke to Mr. Ogunsanya just now. The police are looking for him," he said. "Tell me exactly what he said."

"Bilal would drop her at the jetty or the boat club almost every night and wait for her, and in exchange for that and his silence, she got his brother a job at LAD. When he was waiting for her that night, he said, Kemi showed up, and there was a scream, but Bilal didn't see what happened. Kemi told him it was an accident and that if Bilal opened his mouth, she would blame him. He said he was scared to tell you in case you would say it was his fault for taking the bribe for his brother and keeping secrets from you."

Tonye smashed the wall with his fist, leaving dents in the plaster. "All this time—all this time! I will fucking kill him."

"What? It's Kemi we need to be going after!"

Tonye didn't look at her. "There are no accidents."

Realization crept over Claudine. Why would an innocent man feel the need to run? "What does that mean?"

Tonye flexed his hand. He seemed aware now of the blood on his knuckles where the skin had split.

"It's not for you to worry about, auntie."

"Tonye, tell me."

"Bilal's brother died on the LAD jobsite, during the flooding."

"What?"

"His brother, Lamidi, was working as a security guard at Lagos Atlantic Dream. There were heavy rains a few weeks ago, dragging squatters into the sea. Women and children. He took a boat to save them, but it sank. They were all lost." Tonye buried his head in his hands. "I had no idea Nicole was responsible for getting him that job. Bilal probably blamed her."

Bilal's words at Badagry rang in Claudine's ears: *They entered water. Dragged Lamidi. The same cursed spirits that took my oga's brother and madam.* Claudine thought she was going to be sick from the horror that overwhelmed her. "How will they find him?" she managed.

"Nicole used to track the car with GPS when Bilal was out with the children. But—" Tonye thought for a minute. "Perhaps I can get into her account from my phone. He doesn't know about it. That way we will find him."

"And suppose he abandons the car?"

"It doesn't matter. A crocodile comes up for air eventually. He must go to his village. My boys will be ready for him there."

Claudine wasn't so sure. Bilal didn't seem like he wanted to come up for air. He had looked like he wanted to drown.

"TONYE," SHE said, "let's go to Paradise Jetty. Kemi told me where to find it."

It wasn't far from the house. Easy to find, Kemi had said, off the busy expressway, next to a flashy flamingo-colored apartment block. They pulled into a small lane, barely visible from the road. It was tarmacked, not a dirt track. The lane became a disused car park, strewn with rubbish. How would Nicole even discover a place like that? Claudine wondered. It was such a lonely, creepy spot. But then that was the point, she supposed, somewhere private where no one would see her, the boat. Dangerous, but a risk she was willing to run. It's never the stranger anyway. It's always someone you know. The car park ended in a patch of wild bushes, and beyond that was a derelict wooden jetty leading into the water. Clearly not a place where you could board a boat anymore—the decking looked rotten, very unsafe. In one area, the jetty had almost split in two and was gaping in the middle. There was the faint smell of shit and the trash that was strewn across the bank. Something you would expect in the worst slums of Spanish Town, not among these expensive apartment blocks.

"Nicole would come here?" said Tonye, aghast. He walked to the jetty and looked out over the water. It was a no-man's-land. They were to the side of the neighboring apartment block, separated by a high wall. Nothing close by—no one who could have seen anything. It looked as though he couldn't believe it either. Clearly Bilal had kept Nicole's secrets. And what would possess Nicole to come here at night alone? Claudine imagined some strength of feeling for her lover if she could brave this place. Was it worth it? From her own experience, probably not.

They went kicking around the trash, checking for any sign of Nicole. Claudine had called Kemi and told her what had happened, that Bilal had tried to place the blame on Kemi. She'd denied everything with a lot of crocodile tears. But threatened with a visit from Ogunsanya, she'd come clean about what happened that night. She confessed to her affair with Tonye. Nicole had found out, and they'd argued on the jetty while Bilal waited in the car. She had left Nicole there. She regretted it. Sure. Claudine didn't buy it all, but hoped some of the details would be useful. The white sundress Kemi said Nicole was wearing the night she fell into the water. Her phone. The tote bag she was carrying. Her designer flip-flops. Claudine hoped to find something left behind—a shoe, a shred of white cloth, her wallet—but there was nothing. No clues. What a shame it had taken so long for people to be honest. Valuable time had been lost. They walked along the jetty to the spot where Nicole would have gotten out of the boat. They stared down into the murky water. It wasn't clear where, according to Bilal's story, she would have fallen into the lagoon. Perhaps when they eventually found him, they would know more.

"If someone drowns, what happens to the body?" Claudine asked Tonye.

After a moment, he said, "It will drift with the trash along the lagoon."

"So, if Nicole had drowned, someone would have seen her body and done something!" she said, feeling a flash of hope. Tonye didn't answer. He leaned over the wooden posts and vomited into the water.

BACK AT the house, Claudine followed Tonye into his living room, where he slumped on the sofa and started bawling. Big man-sized sobs came up from deep within his chest.

She considered leaving the room, but she didn't exactly trust him to be left alone, so she brought the tissue box from the coffee table next to him, then sat quietly until he calmed down in his own time. She understood better now why he had been so cagey and stiff initially. She didn't agree with it, but in a house like this—as big as it was, it made you small. You couldn't be yourself. No one could. It wasn't just the lowly staff like Emmanuel. Everyone had their master. And for all the pain she'd experienced growing up—she also had freedom. Even if she couldn't see it. She didn't *have* to look after Mummy. She could walk right out of that front door. Do whatever she wanted. Yes, they had blazing rows, but there was no hierarchy. She didn't have the sort of pressure this family existed within. What was the point of it when they all seemed like they'd rather be living different lives? As a woman, Claudine wasn't tongue-tied like Chief's Wife. She could tell Papason where to go if she liked, and then call him back next week. Even quiet Nicole was able to choose her path, marry who she wanted. She had even done that in Nigeria—put the middle finger to all of them and gone about her business.

"I still can't believe it," Tonye was saying. "He loved me. He would die for me. I know that."

"Like his father?" asked Claudine.

"What are you talking about?"

He pulled his shoulders up slightly, but said nothing else. Claudine got up to leave the room. She couldn't deal with his negativity. There was no body yet. She needed time alone to think. By herself. Next steps. This wasn't over.

"Strange, isn't it?" said Tonye, lifting his head to stare at the cluster of framed family photos on the sideboard. "The sea took his brother and mine? And now her. It should mean something. It should all mean something."

CHAPTER TWENTY-EIGHT

CLAUDINE LOOKED out at the lagoon from Nicole's balcony. Today it was a steely blue. Perhaps the color of the water depended on your mood, because she felt a steely resolve. Boats passed through the lagoon all day. Plus there were homes along the waterfront. Mr. Ogunsanya needed to get out there with his men asking people if they remembered seeing a body. You would remember something like that, a body passing in the water. Especially if it was a woman. There was still no sign of Nicole. And despite Tonye's insistence that Bilal would eventually surface, he hadn't either. The police had visited his village, and the various bus stations had been checked. Perhaps he never would. He could even be dead. Tonye seemed determined to find Bilal and bring him to justice—his version of it. Claudine didn't know what that was, but knew herself well enough to stay out of it.

Kemi also had flown the coop. Left the country, Tonye said. She blamed herself for leaving Nicole on the jetty that night. It was hard for Claudine not to blame her as well. But it wasn't her fault.

The children were on the swings in the garden. The creak of the metal frame reached up along with the faint chatter of Blessing on the phone in her language. Claudine went to the railing. Down on the lawn, the older boy, Timi, swung back and forth, his legs going like pistons. But from the way his head hung down, his heart wasn't in it. Poor thing. Perhaps he was even crying. Tonye had finally told them their mother was missing. The three-year-old was jumping around on the climbing frame. Playtime was playtime. It wouldn't make sense to him yet. But they would be all right, wouldn't they? Even if Nicole was gone. They had more than most, everything you needed to make it in a tough country like this. Unlike the Roberts family, fading like their old photographs, the Oruwaris had time.

"SO YOU'RE saying she's still alive?" Penny had asked.

"I don't know."

"But everyone else thinks she drowned. What do you mean *you* don't know?" In the background of the call, Claudine could hear very English sounds as Penny moved around her house. The tap of her shoes on hardwood floors instead of tiles. The high water pressure of the kitchen tap. A very London voice in the background—"Mum, Muuum, yoo seen mah cah keys?"

"I just have a feeling, sis. There's no body. Somehow I just know."

"Claudine."

"I can't explain it."

"You'll be out there forever."

"No, I won't. I just need a little more time. I'm not ready to call it quits. You guys will be all right without me."

"I guess you gotta do what you gotta do, but feeling she's still alive won't change anything."

"No," Claudine agreed. "And when I get home, Penny, I'm changing a lot of things. I want to live. Really live."

"Better late than never." Penny sounded doubtful. "You take your time then, Claud. Stay safe. You know, something you said to me when we were coming to the UK on the plane. I never forgot it."

"What was that?" Claudine was surprised Penny remembered anything about the plane journey. She had been so little, her feet unable to touch the ground.

"You said you would take care of me. Even though you was just a child yourself and we grew up in different places, you hardly knew me from Adam, but you held my hand and promised to always be there. Well, I'm here for you always, Claud, and if you need me I'll be on the first plane out."

And there they were again, Penny's tears, as sure as bills through the door and train delays. You could set your watch by them.

"Thank you," said Claudine. She wouldn't ever be able to explain to Penny how those words made her feel. "Talk soon." *Click.*

She'd felt like telling Penny too much just yet would alarm her further—Claudine's plans to sell Nedford Road. They didn't need that big place with all those stairs. That wasn't good for Mummy. Get a smaller place and say good-bye to all their secrets. Start again. One thing Nicole wasn't afraid to do was try something different. That was what living was really about.

It was time to leave behind her pear tree.

THE MORNING she was due to plant the tree, Len had kissed her before leaving for work and suggested they all go on holiday together somewhere. Him, her, and Nicole, like a real family, he said. She had gotten up happy. Made cornmeal porridge, fragrant and sweet, the vanilla scent of it filling the house. But Nicole had refused to eat it. Said her tummy hurt. She rested her head on the table and said she didn't want to go to school. Of course, Claudine sent her to school. She had to go to work herself. *Must be those sweets,* she thought. Just the other day, Penny had said she didn't know where the girl getting all those sweets from. It was true that recently Claudine had been seeing Nicole with all kinds of sugary things.

After Nicole had left, she'd gone into the girl's room and found a ton of sweets in a drawer. A shocking amount. More than she would have bought herself, and Nicole had never been one to cry for sweets like that. There were all kinds: sherbet bags, sugared cola bottles, jellied cola bottles, hard-boiled, the giant jellies, lollipops, pick 'n' mix bags from Woolworths. She didn't understand it, and she noticed other things while she was in there. Nicole's pajamas that she'd seen her go to bed in, scrunched up in a ball, stained and stinking. She couldn't go to work after that. She didn't know what to do with herself. She sat on the bed in Nicole's room trying to put it together, to make it make a different kind of sense.

It seemed she blinked and Nicole was coming in through the door again. She sat her down. Asked where all the sweets came from. "Len gives it to me," she'd said, with no emotion. But why? What for? "He touches me," she'd said, like she was so exhausted with carrying it, it just fell out of her.

Claudine didn't have the words and Nicole didn't have the energy. Mummy had been in her room all day and was none the wiser. Nicole and Claudine ate their dinner in silence and went to bed early. But Claudine didn't sleep. She lay in the bed until she heard the front door go, about 9 p.m.

She heard the tool bag clunk onto the floor as Len came in. His steps in the kitchen. He hadn't bothered to take off his shoes. The microwave ping, the fridge door opening, cupboards, plates. The television. Some comedy show; there was laughter. Then she heard him switch everything off. The first stair creaking under his foot. He stopped outside Nicole's door, the first one at the top of the stairs. Heard him try the lock. She'd locked it. Mummy had keys for every single room. Claudine had found that one and locked Nicole's door so he couldn't get in. She'd told Nicole not to open the door under any circumstances, just pretend to be asleep. She heard him rattle the handle again gently. Grunt softly.

She opened the bedroom door.

"Len, what you doing?" she asked him quietly.

His voice was light at first. "Oh, Claud," he said. "You know what, mi drunk. I thought"—he staggered as if he were indeed drunk, one foot back on the staircase, made a big show of swaying—"thought it was your room."

He didn't see the knife till she was close up to him. Took a step back. "Claud?"

He saw it fully now, the big one she used for carving up the roast chicken, triangular, long, and very sharp. She knew because she had sharpened it earlier. She plunged it into his chest. He could easily have stopped her if he weren't on the stair, but he'd put his foot back and wasn't balanced. His instinct was to grab for the banister, not the knife. It went in easily, and he tumbled down the stairs, the knife still in his chest. Broke his neck in the fall, because when she followed him down, he was dead with hardly any blood.

It wasn't easy, to pull him down into the basement. She could hardly take him around the front. Out the back door into the garden. The burying was the easy part. Len had already done all the work. The earth was soft and tilled. It was all of twenty minutes, to dig a slightly deeper hole, lay him in it, and cover him up with all the earth they'd bought for the tree.

NO ONE came looking for Len. No one left their room that night. In the morning, no one asked what had happened. Len was gone from their life as suddenly as he'd come into it. Almost as if he was never there. Penny asked after Len once. And Claudine just pursed her lips and said he left, she didn't know where to. The candy was cleared. Thrown away. And they moved on.

DEAD MEN tell no tales, but the tree knew. The pear tree she planted the next day, over Len's body, grew dark and tall. Like a sentinel, it kept watch, clinging to the house, seeming almost *sentient*, the way its leaves peered in through the Victorian sash window. Seeing. Listening. Tapping its fingernails on the glass, trying to draw attention to itself and the awful secret it yearned to share.

SHE LIKED the tree being there, in the winter shorn and sharp, in summer thirsty and full of its own self-importance. It was almost family.

It was a part of their story. Sometimes she even went outside and stroked the bark, rough under her palm, but she felt its heart beat inside of hers. The family complained about the tree's long shadows on the walls and the *tap tap* of its leaves, threatening to cut it down, but she knew they wouldn't. They would hem and haw and argue till kingdom come.

She hoped to tell this to Nicole one day. Reveal the secrets buried under the tree when she found her—and she would, because, as usual, she was the only one prepared to do what needed to be done.

EPILOGUE

After

SHE CAN'T understand their quiet chatter. Not Yoruba. Not Fulani. Not Hausa. Not Igbo. Not that she understands those languages, but at least she's familiar with those pitches and cadences. She sometimes thinks she hears French, which confuses her, but anyway, the running commentary is clearly about her. Her skin. Her hair. Her eyes. Who she might be and how she has come to be there. Questions, insistent speculations, and contrary opinions are recognizable in any language.

It is dark, but there's enough light to locate herself in a hut. It seems to be wooden because there are slivers of daylight where the planks don't meet. A sunbeam cuts across the earth floor. Sun! She feels herself on the ground but not in the dirt, resting instead on some sort of matting. Naked but under a layer of cloth. What a wild thing she is. Filthy and exposed. A creature. Not herself. But alive, breathing, and somewhere, just beyond the hut walls, there is sunlight!

She can barely make out the children, some of whom are very little, crouched around her expectantly, in various states of undress. Now and then, one presses a finger on her, perhaps to see if she's real, and the others chastise the bold one harshly, then slyly have a quick prod themselves.

One of the children offers her what looks like pap in a calabash bowl. She eats from the spoon the watchful girl holds out. It is slimy and cold. She manages a couple of spoonfuls, then shakes her head. It is enough. The girl eagerly polishes off the rest.

She hurts. Her whole body aches—her brain is receiving SOS messages from all over. Even her insides feel bruised. It hurts to think, and she dares not look under the blanket.

"Where am I?" she asks. Her mouth is so dry, her voice is a croak, barely audible. The children wawu at hearing her speak. One giggles uncontrollably. But they have no answer.

She tries to sit up, which alarms them. There is a great fuss about what this means. A swath of light cuts through the gloom as one of them darts out of the hut calling for help. The sounds from outside come in bright flashes: voices, the grind of a saw, radio music, chickens, pots clattering, an older woman's singing, a ship's foghorn, the everyday, the ordinary, before the door swings shut and her world goes dark again.

A WOMAN opens the door next, blocking most of the light with her fatness. She scolds the children in a deep voice, but then exclaims herself, seeing their invalid trying to sit up. Her expressions ring somewhere between disbelief and joy. She also calls to others.

AND THEN more come crowding in through the door with a glut of words and gestures in which she thinks she hears a few pidgin phrases—nothing concrete. Nothing sticks.

Someone hands her a repurposed water bottle cut in half, with a dark, fibrous potion inside. It looks like something she has seen before, a native brew for malaria perhaps. She sips gingerly. Very bitter. They urge her to drink more. She passes it back. They thrust it to her mouth again. She tries to swallow more but gives up. If she must die, then so be it, but she cannot drink that.

EVENTUALLY A man comes in. They've been waiting for him and hush, parting to let him through. He is old, but firm-bodied. Shirtless. Even without knowing him, she knows him, from somewhere. But where? Water. Lifting. Laying. Rocking. The creaking of a canoe. Before he speaks to her, she knows his breath will smell like palm wine.

"Mami Wata," he says encouragingly. The others laugh and echo his comment.

"She comot from sleep," the fat woman informs him.

"Do you remember?" he asks. She shakes her head. "I pull you from de wata. Bring you here by boat. Seven days you dey sleep. I tink say you die but God spared you." He makes the prayer sign.

Pulled from the water. No wonder she feels so battered.

"What is your name?" he asks.

She thinks about it for a while, trying to clear a path through the spinning galaxy of her mind.

Finally, she shakes her head.

"I don't know."

AUTHOR'S NOTE

The Lagos Wife is a novel about the mysterious disappearance of a British woman, Nicole Oruwari, in Lagos, Nigeria, and the psychological can of worms this opens up for her estranged aunt, who travels to Lagos to find answers.

Apart from the obvious question of what happened to Nicole, the novel also asks uncomfortable questions about marital strife, cultural isolation, and generational trauma.

Although the characters and events in this story are completely fictional, the inspiration comes from my own years as a Nigerwife. The term is well known in Nigeria and means the foreign wife of a Nigerian man. A support network of Nigerwives called Nigerwives Nigeria was established in the seventies to provide Nigerwives far from their homelands a surrogate family of their own.

Lagos was and still is an exciting, vibrant, diverse, and wealthy city. When I moved there in 2011, the oil price was rising and one US dollar was worth 155 Nigerian naira. Compare that to today's one dollar to 438 naira. Goodluck Jonathan was president, and Nigerians felt good luck had smiled on them too. During this period of optimism, a wave of Nigerians born abroad or who had left as children returned, excited to reclaim their country from its elderly patriarchs and rewrite the narratives about Africa. Nigeria was emerging from the shadows, with its literature, music, and film stars taking the world by storm.

But by 2014, the year in which *The Lagos Wife* takes place, mounting corruption and escalating terrorism led returnees to reflect that it was not so easy to change a country after all. It is more likely to change you first. In *The Lagos Wife*, all our returned characters have been changed in ways they could not have foreseen. Lagos is everyone's antagonist, intimidating, alluring, and inciting. Everyone has a story to tell.

This is Nicole's.

ACKNOWLEDGMENTS

This novel was many years in the writing, and I'm forever grateful to the following people for all their encouragement and support along the way.

My editor, Natalie Hallak, thank you for the commitment, rigor, and love you have shown *The Lagos Wife*. Working with you has been such a joy and it made me a better writer. Thank you, Laywan Kwan and James Iacobelli, for the mesmerizing cover, and to all at Atria Books for supporting this book so greatly.

Thank you, Ailah Ahmed, for choosing *The Lagos Wife* for the UK and Commonwealth. It's a dream come true.

Thank you, Amy Aniobi, for championing *The Lagos Wife* at HBO; also Aanch Khaneja, Cela Sutton, Kathleen McCaffrey, and Stacy Shirk.

Not sure where I would be today without the vision and expertise of my fairy godmother agent, Claire Friedman. Thank you for changing my life!

Thanks, Jemima Forrester, for all you've done in the UK, and Chris Lupo for your work and advice on the film side.

Thank you to the following organizations: Millay Arts and Tin House for their vital residencies that enabled me to take giant steps forward. Special thanks to editor Elizabeth DeMeo (Tin House) for her kind reading and advice; Gotham Writers' Workshop for their marvelous classes; Pen Parentis for all the support; the Center for Fiction Writers Studio; Martha's Vineyard Institute of Creative Writing and the Voices of Color community I met there; and GrubStreet Center for Creative Writing.

The fellowship of the following brilliant writers has been invaluable.

The Brooklyn Writers Project: Andrew Laing, Fiona Nichols, Patty Hamrick, Anton Prosser, Rachel Shapiro, and Diane Fener. Special thanks to Helene M. Epstein for beta reading the whole manuscript.

Heath's Ledgers: G. F. Ganz, Ziggy Rom, Aubrey LeClair, Samantha Palazzi, Catherine Keane, and Wendy Lu. Special thanks to Christopher James Llego for editing the manuscript.

Paragraph NY: Brian Schaefer, Pamela Holcomb, Donasia Sykes, Ryan Davenport, and Deanna Richards. It wasn't only the critique, but some months it was only the critique that kept me going.

Thanks also to the following readers for giving their time and energy to the developing manuscript: Professor Donna Raskin, Professor Tracey L. Walters, Ola Ibrahim, Signe Hammond, Christina Oshunniyi, Shobha Manaktala, Nakia Thomas, Nana Serwah Kankam, Monique James-Duncan, Clayon Huggins-Zephyrin, and Elaine Adu-Poku and her Let's Read book club.

Ever grateful to Alex Wheatle for not giving up on me as a writer. Bernardine Evaristo for reading and encouraging me. Mona Opubor for daring me to dream bigger. Afua Hirsch for reading, and for being such a champion of this book—I'm not over it. Gemma Weekes, my pen-sister, for helping me navigate the hidden country within.

A special thank-you to the Nigerwives Association and the Nigerian West Indian Association in Lagos, Nigeria, for the sisterhood. I still feel it. And thank you to the aunties who show so much love, especially Mrs. Doris Fafunwa for giving me permission to use some lyrics from her wonderful Nigerwife anthem in this novel. Thank you, Funke Bucknor-Obruthe, wedding planner extraordinaire, for the advice.

ACKNOWLEDGMENTS

To all my friends around the world who have cheered me on, no matter how far-fetched this must all have seemed sometimes, thank you.

Last but really first, to my family for loving me and keeping me going in ways that have nothing and everything to do with writing, thank you.

ABOUT THE AUTHOR

Vanessa Walters was born and raised in London. She has a background in international journalism and playwriting, and is a Tin House and Millay Arts resident. She is the author of two previous YA books and *The Lagos Wife*. She currently lives in Brooklyn.